The wonderful photograph on the cover of this edition was reproduced by kind permission granted by James Spada. If you would like to view more of Mr. Spada's award-winning photography and/or contact him, please feel free to visit his website at *www.spadaphoto.com*.

Many thanks to graphic artist, John Nail for his enthusiastic collaboration on the design of *View to a Thrill's* extraordinary cover. Mr. Nail may be reached at *tojonail@earthlink.net*.

Worldwide Praise for the Erotica
of STARbooks Press!

A View to a Thrill

The world of the voyeur and the men who like to be watched

A New Collection
of Erotic Tales
Edited By
PAUL J. WILLIS

STARbooks Press

SARASOTA, FL

Other Anthologies by STARbooks Press

First Edition Published in the U.S. in Summer, 2003
Library of Congress Card Catalogue No. Pending
ISBN No. 1-891855-37-9

Acknowledgements

This book is dedicated to two people: Brad for always making fantasies come true and for pushing me into his world of exhibitionism at times, and to Greg for being with me on our daily journey to create an interesting and fulfilling life together.

I would also like to thank the guys who have contributed their time and talent to this anthology. Without their experiences and stories there wouldn't be a book. During the process of bringing this project together, I was also given the occasion to get to know Michael Huxley and Paul Marquis at STARbooks Press—an enriching experience on both a professional and personal level.

I look forward to completing future projects with STARbooks, including the forthcoming anthology, *Kink*, which I am co-editing with Ron Jackson, and another anthology, tentatively titled *Dangerous Liaisons*, in 2004.

TABLE OF CONTENTS

Introduction: ALL THE WORLD'S A STAGE
by Paul J. Willis

Mardi Gras in New Orleans is one of the ultimate voyeuristic experiences. During the weekend preceding Fat Tuesday, my partner and I went out in the French Quarter and made a circle of the "fruit loop" stopping by several of the gay bars to check out the scene.

The energy at most places was festive. The dance floors were packed and crowds of men had spilled out into the streets. The balconies were three-to-four men deep. Beads were being tossed down as booty to men with big pecs, and to whoever would show their dick or ass. The herd ran the full gamut of gay men—all ages, body types and stereotypes were represented.

We moved up the street to one of our favorite hangouts. After making our way upstairs, we stood in the back of the bar and watched theater unfold in front of us. Fellow voyeurs were stationed around the perimeters of the bar, perfectly content to just stand back and enjoy the show. Some appeared to be shy types preferring to look and not touch, and others, like us, took pleasure in figuring out someone's "story" by watching them perform.

There were plenty of visuals to take in: men wearing harnesses and chaps, and boys with feather masks and glitter. Expert blowjobs were being executed around the pool table and in the restroom. An interaction that drew my attention involved two couples, obviously meeting for the first time. One duo consisted of locals that I recognized from around town and the other announced that they were from Dallas, dressed in cowboy boots and hats.

The four men engaged in small talk while eyeing each other up down. They took turns buying rounds of drinks, and within the hour, positions had shifted—Dallas top next to local bottom, local top rubbing on Dallas bottom. Shirts were removed and nipples tugged. By then several pairs of eyes were drawn to the performance unfolding at the bar.

Fondling progressed rapidly from playful to urgent. Dallas top turned the local bottom around so that he was facing the bar with his hands placed down on the countertop. The cowboy reached around the local's waist, unbuckling the boy's belt and unzipping his fly. The horny tourist then pulled the local's jeans down so that bare ass cheeks were presented. The man from Dallas knelt down and started to sniff and lick on his new buddy's hairy hole. Their respective partners looked amused by the stunt, each exhibiting a mischievous sneer. They, too, were getting to know each other a little more intimately.

The local top grasped the back of the visitor's head and brought it to his armpit. This action met with an enthusiastic response as each pit was licked clean before the Dallas boy moved down to suck some cock. The scene continued with the visitors' eating butt and sucking dick, stopping every once in awhile to swap a passionate kiss between them. The two local guys were standing up, enjoying getting serviced while making out with each other. The sexual tension in the room was building along with the erotic display—crotches were being adjusted and quick glances were becoming longing stares.

And as quickly as the scene began, it ended as the four men decided to pursue their pleasure elsewhere, most likely in a room at some hotel. Although there were a few looks of disappointment as the guys made their way down the stairs, there were more smirks, smiles, and lit up eyes from the satisfied audience. The couples' energy inspired others into action. Soon attention was diverted elsewhere and so the evening progressed, new actors taking center stage with different audience members eager to watch.

This Mardi Gras experience and others like it generated the interest in putting together this collection of stories that showcase the allure of voyeurism. These erotic glimpses, which include fictional as well as first hand experiences, explore various situations where a need for recognition or a desire for anonymity creates the necessary tension for the men involved to get together and get off.

View to a Thrill captures those moments where an unexpected or a planned gaze leads to a fantasy fulfilled, for isn't it true that fantasies built in the mind can oftentimes prove more powerful than even the reality of physical contact? There are many circumstances presented in this edition where co-viewing experiences lead to powerful release. For others, the risk of being caught spying is what triggers their arousal. Hustlers, strippers, strangers, couples, and straight men are all here—being watched.

These snapshots will take you to new heights—into the world of the voyeur and the men who like to be watched.

Which are you?

WINDOWS OF OPPORTUNITY
by William Holden

I've always been accused by ex-boyfriends; co-workers; family members, the list goes on and on; of being a bit strange when it comes to sex. Most people get their rocks off by having physical contact with someone else. But me, I get off in a different way. Sure the physical action between two hot, naked men is great, but my passions come from viewing. There is nothing better for me, than to watch men having sex. To see a businessman in a three-piece suit during the day, and thinking to yourself what he would be like in bed? What turns him on? Is he a top or a bottom? Then seeing someone slung up in the backroom of a club getting their cock sucked or their ass fucked, you gotta kinda wonder if that was the businessman you saw earlier in the day. The fantasies and possibilities are unlimited. The facial expressions of one man as he's being fucked by a 10 inch piece of meat; or the view you can get watching as that cock goes in and out of a tight, hairy ass. Watching as the skin and muscles of that hot ass are being spread wide open. The precome and lube leaking out as the fucking continues. The sweat soon breaks out on each of the men, in very specific places. You can count on seeing the first signs of sweat breaking out on their forehead; it then begins to appear on their chest. The hairs under the arms soon become damp and get matted to their skin. There's nothing better!

One of the most memorable sexual experiences I've had, happened a few years ago when I was living in an up and coming neighborhood near the downtown district of Atlanta. It was an older neighborhood, but rapidly becoming a hot spot for gay singles and couples. My next-door neighbors had lived in their home for several years and were excited about my moving in next to them.

David, the oldest of the couple was 41 years old. His hair was mostly gray, yet still showed some of the jet-black hair he had in his youth. He was a bit out of shape, with a slight beer belly. His face was perfectly rounded with small brown eyes. His partner, Steve was 34 and worked hard at maintaining his appearance. He ran every evening after work and visited the local gay gym on a regular basis. He always kept a day or two of stubble on his face which gave him that old time Miami Vice look.

For neighbors, I couldn't have asked for anyone better. They invited me over for dinners and introduced me to their friends and other gay couples on the block. They were comfortable with their lives as a gay couple, but maintained an outward appearance of a straight couple. I never saw them parading around in the yard with their shirts off, even in the hottest of weather. There was nothing in their home that would indicate their sexual preference, nor any resemblance of a gay life—which often bothered me in some deep part of myself.

I grew up as an openly gay man. I was always proud of who I was and wanted everyone to know it. When I went out for a night on the town, I clothed myself like any other club kid. The tight T-shirts to show off my muscular chest and abs, shorts to proudly display my toned, hairy legs and of course ankle boots with white socks. By the end of a heavy night of dancing my shirt was sticking out of the waistband of my shorts exposing my hairy; sweat damped chest and pierced nipples. So to be a part of a couple's lives that were so quiet about their sexuality somehow disturbed me.

One Friday evening I decided to sit out in my back yard to enjoy the cooling temperatures of fall. I was on my fourth margarita and feeling pretty good, when I happened to look over at David and Steve's house and saw the faint glow of candles coming from their bedroom window. I sat there for a moment wondering what might be happening behind those walls. Neither of them ever gave off any sort of sexual energy, so to think of how plain and boring their sex must be somehow intrigued me.

I stood up and walked over to the edge of their yard, the leaves that covered the ground crunched under my feet. I stood there quietly in the darkness as I watched for any shadows from their movement. Their bedroom was on the opposite side of the house from where I stood. Only one of the bedroom windows faced their back yard. It didn't allow for much viewing pleasure, so I decided to walk around the front of their house and over to the other side to get a better look.

As I made my way around to the side of their house, I broke out in a light sweat from the thrill of possibly getting a peak into my neighbors' private lives. The night air chilled my damp skin. My temples began to ache as the blood rushed through my body in anticipation of what I might see. The house to the left of where I stood was dark. Relieved at the thought of that neighbor being gone, I crept up to David and Steve's bedroom window. At first glance the room appeared empty. Only candles, from my view I counted nine, lighted the room. The burning flames cast an orange glow over the walls and furniture, dancing and bouncing as the air played with them.

The bedspread and sheets were pulled back, and neatly folded. I became aroused as I continued to peer through the window, knowing I shouldn't be there, but not being able to take my eyes off of their private things. I reached down to my crotch and adjusted myself, not moving my eyes from their bed. Suddenly a shadow appeared against the far wall of the room. By the smaller size of it, I assumed it was Steve. As I stood there waiting for someone to appear, Steve stumbled into my sight and fell against the bed.

He was dressed in tight fitting, faded jeans. A large rip in the seat revealed he wasn't wearing any underwear. His shirt was white and was unbuttoned down to his navel. His chest was covered in a mass of thick, black, curly hair. His nipples were erect and poked out of the opening in his shirt. He appeared to cower on the bed, as if terrified by something behind him.

My mind was confused with the sight in front of me. I couldn't get a hold of the situation, yet my cock was throbbing in my pants. Within a few moments David entered the room. My heart jumped into my throat at the sight of him. He walked in, dressed in full police uniform. The dark blue colors complimented his features. He walked over to the bed with a Billy club in one hand, tapping it against the palm of the other. David placed his foot up on the rail of the bed and quickly tapped it with his club. Steve looked up and immediately began licking his black boots.

I felt a jolt of precome shoot out of my cock as I looked into their secret lives. I could almost feel Steve's tongue on my own shoe as I watched him lick the smooth, polished surface. I slipped my hand inside my pants and rubbed the precome over the head of my cock wondering what they would think, if they knew they were being watched. I looked on with growing interest as Steve unlaced David's boots with his teeth. The laces were wet with Steve's spit as he slowly removed the boots. I could hear a dull thud in the room as they hit the floor. I closed my eyes for a brief moment, imagining the smell of the boots as they came off David's feet— the scent of warm leather, floating and caressing the air.

David grabbed a hold of Steve's legs and pulled his body around so Steve's ass was facing him. I could hear the faint whispers of voices through the glass, but couldn't make out what was being said. I stood motionless except for the slow back and forth movement of my hand stroking my cock as David began to undress. As he removed more and more of his clothing, I began to see that his entire body was void of hair, including his crotch. His cock remained flaccid as he finished removing his clothes, but he appeared to be well endowed despite his cock's current condition.

David walked closer to the bed and began squeezing Steve's ass. I could tell by Steve's expression that he was definitely the bottom boy in the family. I watched as he moved his hips up and down begging David without words to use him. I jumped in surprise as David grabbed the torn edges of Steve's jeans and ripped the hole wider to expose his entire ass. It was so sudden and forceful both Steve and I seemed to share the same emotion. I could almost hear Steve's heavy breathing as David lubed up his Billy club and began rubbing it over Steve's hairy cheeks.

Steve wiggled his butt as if he was showing off for me. He toyed with my vision as he tightened and relaxed the muscles in his ass, begging for me to enter him. My cock continued to lengthen in my pants as David slowly rolled the tip of his club around Steve's hole. I heard a muffled groan coming from Steve as the club made its initial entrance into his ass.

My heart seemed to stop beating as I briefly caught movement in the reflection of the window—movement that was coming from behind me. I was afraid to turn around and look. My hand remained on my cock, soaked with my own precome. My heart began again, this time more intense then before. Sweat broke out on my chest and armpits, making my shirt stick to my skin. I looked into the glass this time instead of through it, trying not to see David and Steve, but to see the movement again from behind. I moved slightly to the left to get a different angle and noticed the silhouette of a man looking at me from the large window of the house next door. There was movement from below and then I realized he was getting off on watching me watching them. At that moment nothing else mattered to me, but giving this guy something to remember.

I slowly tilted my head in the direction of the house. I wanted him to know that I knew he was there. He didn't move from sight, but instead stood there in full view, completely naked, stroking what appeared to be a seven-inch dick. His arm was resting on the top of the window ledge exposing the cleanliness of his shaven armpits. A small amount of dark stubble ran across his pecs, indicating that he shaved his chest hair as well. He smiled and nodded as if to tell me to continue on with what I was doing.

Without conscience thought I turned my attention back to the bedroom, just in time to see David pull the Billy club out of Steve's ass. Steve's cock bobbed up and down as the pressure escaped his tight hole. Precome dripped out of his cock, making a long, thin trail till it touched the bed and darkened the sheets. I wanted to concentrate more on the action going on in the bedroom, but my mind kept returning to the man standing behind me. I slowly unzipped my pants and let them drop to the ground. I purposely bent over to pull my feet through the legs to expose my nice firm ass to my admirer. I didn't dare look around, but I knew he was enjoying the view. I leaned against the house to give him a profile of my body. Out of the corner of my eye, I could see his appreciation. My cock stood out 9 inches in front of me, and I pulled and tugged on the foreskin—teasing myself and the stranger behind the window.

Steve rolled over on his back, throwing his legs up in the air. He shouted something to David. I read his lips as "Please sir. Fuck me!" Steve wiggled his ass inviting David to enter. David reached down and grabbed the lube and poured a stream of it over his rock hard cock, which was almost as big as the Billy club. The head was thick, and his cock appeared to be at least eleven inches. I watched in amazement as the head slipped into Steve's hairy hole. My own ass tightened voluntarily as David's cock popped into place. I reached behind me to finger my hole, filling it at first with one finger, than another. I wanted my ass stretched like Steve's, but even with four fingers digging their way inside of me, it was no match for what Steve was experiencing.

The lube and precome oozed out of Steve's butt as David began to fuck him. David's ass wiggled like gelatin as the force of his fucking picked up. Steve threw his hands up over his head and grabbed onto the headboard. His armpits were soaked with sweat. Even from my distance, I could see the droplets of perspiration running down his body.

I could feel the eyes of the stranger in the window burning into me. I wanted to please him. I wanted to be the cause of his orgasm. It was a strange feeling for me to have. Never before had I wanted to be watched with such intensity as I was feeling at that moment. I knew he was standing there, alone, watching me watch our neighbors. I wanted him to join me out here, yet at the same time I liked having the distance. The inability for anyone to touch anything but themselves. So I continued to stroke my cock, bringing my fingers up to my mouth to lick the large amounts of precome that clung to my palm and fingers.

My balls tightened between my legs as the come continued to build. I kept my eyes on the actions of David and Steve. Steve's ass was reddened from the force of David's thrusts, yet they continued to fuck. Steve opened his mouth to David's—they kissed passionately as their bodies seemed to blend into one. David leaned down and licked Steve's armpit dry. I licked my lips wanting to taste his sweat, to taste their bodies as they fucked.

I removed my shirt and threw it to the ground quickly so as not to miss anything. Every so often I would hear a slight knock on the window behind me as he jerked himself off, an exhilarating sound, letting me know I was still being watched. I reached down with one hand and grabbed my tight nuts, pulling on them playfully to make my building orgasm strengthen.

David moved his head downward and swallowed Steve's cock as they continued to fuck. As David plunged his cock deeper into Steve's ass, he lowered his head on Steve's cock; up and down, time after time, never missing a beat. I could hear Steve's voice rising to an uncontrollable pitch. He started gasping for breath, as he threw his hips up and down and unloaded his come into David's mouth. David continued to fuck him, as the come poured out of his mouth and onto Steve's hairy crotch.

My cock was throbbing as I watched the mixture of come and David's spit ooze out of his mouth. I leaned up against the house and shot the first of many loads over their aluminum siding just as David reached his breaking point. I continued to unload my cock as David pulled out and shot his come over Steve's chest.

As David and I both shot the last of our loads, I looked over my shoulder, the stranger had left, but not before unloading his own hot juice into the screens of his window.

I never mentioned that night to anyone before, nor did my neighbor and I ever acknowledge our shared experience. But even to this day, anytime I see candles burning in someone's home, I think back to that night, and wonder if they are having as much fun as the four of us did.

WHAT WOULD SCARLETT SAY?
by Randall Kent Ivey

My lover Jim and I had reached a point in our relationship where we no longer excited each other sexually. It was more my fault than Jim's, I will readily admit. Jim, nearly forty years old, still had the tireless libido of a teenager and would fuck anything that walks (and has, come to think of it), while I would be just as content to do other things—cook, garden, travel, etc.

Let me be clear and say that I had not completely lost my interest in sex but that my sexual drive had been re-directed. Truth is, participation in the sex act, no matter how potentially pleasurable it might be, had come to bore me. It became the same old heave-ho, the same old in-out, the same old huff-puff. Been there, done that, got the tee shirt, want to trade the tee shirt in for something else. I was at the point where I just lay back and let Jim have his way with me. Him slurping and slobbering and shoving his dick into whatever hole will have it, while I strained to watch Letterman or the late movie over his shoulder or around his hip or between his legs.

Watching! Now, of late, that's what turns me on. Watching two other men, preferably buff young men, entangling and knotting themselves up in all of love's wonderful physical complications. I'm afraid I have become quite the connoisseur of dirty magazines and even dirtier movies. Our bedroom closet is stuffed with boxes filled with back issues of *Blueboy* and *Torso* and *Men* and *Playgirl* and with those large, cumbersome cases videos come in. I never had much use for pornography up to recently. When I was younger I was too busy chasing actual sexual partners to watch a couple of strangers humping on T.V. Now the prospect of getting a new fuck tape makes me as excited as a fat man at a Chinese buffet.

I can't explain this predilection, this kink, if kink it is. Just call it good old honorable perversion and leave it at that. Why analyze? All I know is that at one point this new preference caused my lover to turn sad eyes upon me and say, "You get more excited with those books and movies than you do me."

Alas, all I could do was nod my head slowly and say, "You're right."

Actually the magic of porn had begun to wear off by that point. It was the same old heave-ho, in-out, huff-puff. The same old faces and bodies. The same old sequence of sex—kiss, suck, fuck, kiss, suck, fuck. What else is new? What I really became interested in was watching two men, not video transmission, fuck and suck to their hearts' delight. I mentioned this to Jim one night before we went to sleep. The notion seemed to spark his imagination (which, sexually anyway, is formidable). He thought that this might be a good way to solve our problem, that if I could have this great voyeuristic experience, I would undergo a kind of catharsis and get it out of my system and come back to him hot and horny. It was worth a try. Neither one of us wanted this little impasse to be the rock upon which our relationship crashed. We were still too much in love to let that happen.

So we sat and thought up possibilities. It was hard. We live in the very conservative upstate of very conservative South Carolina. Men are very discreet here and do not often advertise their proclivities far and wide. We could not just go out and order up a situation like this as we would a Big Mac or Chicken McNuggets. It would take time and planning.

"We could run an ad in a swingers magazine," Jim suggested.

I told him I was too impatient for that.

"Let's call one of those phone `dating' services then."

I shuddered visibly. "We'll probably end up with freaks who'll slit our throats and take our money."

Jim then suggested we go to the gay bars in Greenville and Spartanburg, the two largest cities in the area, and scout for "talent" there.

I laughed my head off then kissed Jim's cheek for his sincerity.

Jim sighed and rolled over to flip off the light. "*You* think of something."

I already had, and it could be summed up in one magic name: Atlanta.

Atlanta—where the dreams of any gay man in the southeast who doesn't want to buy a plane ticket to New York or San Francisco can be fulfilled almost as nicely. A location, and I already had the plan hatched. It came to me with Proustian clarity. I felt like I had just eaten a madeleine biscuit. I told Jim right away what I had in mind.

That following Saturday morning we packed Jim's Camry with our bags and set out for Atlanta. It was one of our favorite places, and we went there three or four times a year, if not more. It is only a three-hour drive, less if the traffic isn't too bad. This trip was multipurpose. We would go and enjoy all the amenities that great city had to offer—the dining, the shopping, the sights and sounds—but our main mission was to fulfill The Plan. We would be staying at the famed Georgian Terrace on Peachtree. A luxury hotel that had been renovated earlier that year, it was most famous as the place where Vivien Leigh and Clark Gable stayed during the premiere of *Gone with the Wind* back in 'thirty-nine. Jim had gone on the Internet and gotten us a good rate for a suite.

We were quiet on the ride down I-85 until we saw the "spaghetti arches", the high, crisscrossing overpasses through which the Atlanta traffic thronged, looming in the distance, as well as the skyscrapers reflecting sunlight and flashing it back off like lighthouses, and then we got excited. It was like a homecoming of sorts. We didn't check into our suite right away. We spent three hours at Lenox Square shopping then had a couple of excellent martinis and a stupendous prime rib supper at Houston's on Lenox Road. We cruised some of our favorite spots in the city by car—Ainsley Square, Chesire Bridge Road, etc.—astounded at all the beautiful young men wandering the streets. Most of them thickly muscled and model-handsome. There were hunks of every conceivable shape and size and color and age, strolling about as casually as could be. I literally purred at the sight of them, making Jim laugh.

"You're as bad as a teenage girl drooling over *Tiger Beat* magazine," he said, but I knew he was as overwhelmed as I was at this parade of Adonises.

Normally we would have begun our bar-hopping after this quick spring through town. We like New Order, in Ainsley Square, a bar catering to an especially "mature" clientele and their admirers. From there we would move on to Burckhardt's, Blake's, and The Heretic on Chesire, where virile bodies crush together with the promise of indiscriminate sex. And lastly, my favorite, Swinging Richards, on Northside Drive, a strip bar where the boys dance *au natural* and look like they have just stepped off a Colt Studios photo spread or a Falcon Studios video shoot. (If the damned place had a zip code, I would move there and live out my days in perfect bliss.)

But there would be no bar-hopping this trip, at least not until much later. We were in Atlanta for a particular purpose.

The Georgian Terrace suite was astounding. The most impressive place I have stayed since Jim and I attended a higher education conference in New York and we were put up at the Roosevelt Hotel on West 45th Street. The suite was tasteful but not showy and plenty roomy, with a large living room and a small adjacent study, a fully equipped kitchen and bathroom, and two bedrooms with, appropriately enough, queen-sized beds. One bedroom sat close to the den; the other was practically hidden away from the rest of the suite down a short, narrow hall, which was perfect for The Plan.

The Plan. Yes, The Plan. Before I forget....

One of the most charming things about Atlanta is that it is populated by handsome young men who are more than willing to shower you with their bountiful physical charms for the right price. "Escorts" they are tastefully and euphemistically called. Go to any Internet website devoted to male escorts, and the "Atlanta, Georgia" section will be chock full of these delightful creatures of every conceivable age and description. And there are in town at least two exclusively male "agencies." The last route, the agency route, was the one we chose to take. Jim, who has experienced just about all things sexual, has ventured into the world of "rentboys" now and then and made use of one of the agencies—Ambassador Escorts of Atlanta. The agency is run by an elderly, asthmatic gentleman named Chris, who describes all his boys with one recurring phrase: "Too beautiful to be alive! My God" and gets so excited he sometimes has to use his inhaler on the phone to recover from his epiphanies.

At first we planned to ask Chris to send over a couple of his best young men so that we could watch them frolic together. It would be like a porn movie come to life before our very eyes. It was one of the reasons we had requested a suite with two bedrooms—so that one of the bedrooms would be a kind of stage, a set, an arena for young sex gladiators. This would leave our own marriage bed "unstained" by others. It seemed like a simple enough plan and more than likely doable for the right amount of money. But I fell out of love with the idea almost at once. Jim saw me frown.

"What's the matter?"

I said, "The plan lacks something. Spontaneity. Naturalness. It's too…mechanical. I might as well watch one of my tapes."

Jim has the mind of a world class perv. He hit upon the perfect solution. His eyes sparkled and a malicious smile crept over his handsome mouth. "What if," he began, "we hire this escort for *me* to fuck, and you watch the two of us go at it, without our knowing it. We'll put you in the closet. We'll set you up somewhere secret so you can watch."

I laughed and clasped my chest in melodramatic display. "Oh, Jim, what sacrifices you are willing to make to save our marriage! You are truly a selfless hero."

So there we were, a few days later, in our double suite at the Georgian Terrace: Jim on the phone to Chris of Ambassador Escorts to procure our unsuspecting "boy." Jim recounted the conversation to me afterwards. Chris, he said, went effusive as soon as he heard Jim's voice. "Oh, yes!" he said, starting already to wheeze. "I have someone perfect for you. An absolute beauty"—wheeze—"Michael! Too beautiful to be alive! My God! He ought to be on a pedestal carved out of marble! Excuse me"—there came the sound of an inhaler being squeezed.

As we waited for the arrival of Michael, the living idol Chris had selected for us, Jim and I went round the suite, very nervous, trying to calm each other down. We wondered if this were the room where Clark had stuffed the daylights out of Vivien. Or, better yet, where Larry, Vivien's betrothed at the time, had rimmed one of the Terrace's bellhops as only the British truly can, with tongue in cheek, or maybe climbed the wuthering heights of some comely concierge. More importantly, we finalized The Plan. Jim would lead Michael to the rear bedroom and leave the door to the adjacent hall unlocked so I could at some point sneak down and station myself at an advantageous spot to watch.

Thirty minutes later Michael arrived at our door, holding a black shaving kit, filled, no doubt, with the various tricks of his particular trade. He stood looking at Jim and me, perplexed, smiling first then frowning then settling his mouth in an uncertain line. Then he spoke:

"Chris didn't tell me this was going to be a threesome. It will cost you all a little bit more money than we planned."

Jim stepped forward at once, all fatherly assurance, and slid his arm around Michael's shoulders. "No, no. It's just you and me. My friend here will stay in the den and eat his heart out at my good luck."

I laughed a fake laugh for the sake of show, but there was a little truth in what Jim said. Michael was very handsome and, yes, worthy of a pedestal. Chris had told Jim he was twenty-three. Twenty-seven or twenty-eight would have been more like it. There were the beginnings of lines around his pretty hazel eyes. But no matter. He still had that nice collegiate look, like a frat boy or college jock. A soccer player maybe or swimmer or tennis champ. He stood five feet eight in a black tee shirt and blue jeans and open toed sandals. The tee shirt, dark as it was, could not conceal his protuberant nipples, though. This was a boy who liked rough and heavy tit play. His short brown hair was slightly coifed, and he had a wide, white toothy smile. Right away I imagined him naked and helpless in my lover's grip and already felt the first stirrings of a hard on.

As though reading my mind, Jim pulled Michael against his ribs and smiled a smile full of humor and hunger, and nodded in my direction. "So, we'll see you in about an hour." He turned and led Michael down the hall to the back bedroom. For the sake of show he closed the hall doorway.

It is hard to express the excitement I felt at the prospect of finally getting to watch two men engaged in full body contact. I fidgeted about the suite, unable to calm down. I could hear Jim and Michael talking, getting acquainted, I suppose. I could not go down there until there was silence or the moans and groans of sex in progress. It wasn't long before their voices dropped and there came the hoarse, almost agonized refrain of "Yes, yes. Oh that's good." My erection stiffened. My heart galloped in my chest. My growing excitement nearly blinded me. Very carefully, so as not to be heard or detected—that would spoil everything—I opened the hall door and began the slow trek down the hall itself. Right away, of course, the gasps and moans and breathy words of encouragement became clearer: "Yes. There. Just like that. Oh. Please don't stop! Oh please!" Only voices. Nothing else. It was like ghosts copulating. I stopped a moment to listen to the sex play of men's voices. It was Michael calling to Jim. Jim has always been the active one in sex, the doer; he gets his pleasure from giving other men pleasure. Michael cried out again. Then came sucking sounds. Mouth on dick maybe or lips on nipples or two mouths meeting. The sounds stopped, replaced by Michael saying, "Oh, that's incredible" and Jim replying, "I could eat you all night long and never get enough." A shudder of vicarious pleasure swept over me. It made my own nipples tingle and my own cock throb. I massaged my dick through my pants and took it out. It was raging hot and hard and I gave it a couple of good, long strokes to appease it.

But it was time to *see* things, so I moved on down the hall a few more feet, close enough to see somewhat around the corner. Jim's back and ass and legs were visible. He was crouched down on his knees, bathed in bright, yellow light from the bedside lamp, no doubt sucking or licking the escort on some particularly juicy, ripe part of his young body. I stroked myself a couple more times at the sight of my lover naked. Jim is an incorrigible gym rat. He works out everyday, and, while no longer a teenager, he has maintained a youthful tightness and definition. And he's got a nice, thick seven inch pecker which, when I was still interested in such things (having sex myself, I mean), I loved to wrap my lips around.

"Oh my God! Can you suck dick or what! Please don't stop! Oh!" There came the sounds of rapid, relentless sucking. I moved closer, dangerously, dangerously closer. On the left side of the hall hung a pastel print picture of a pastoral scene in spring. The picture was positioned in such a way that Jim's and Michael's silhouettes were imprinted on the glass by the lamp light. I watched the picture and could see Jim's head, made transparent now and ghostly, between the boy's legs, bobbing away on his dick, while Jim reached up with both hands to screw and twist Michael's large, thick nipples. Michael had his head thrown back and his eyes shut tight, and he licked his lips in lascivious abandon. For a moment it was hard to tell who was the escort and who was the client. I took the opportunity to peek around the corner and see the actual lovers in the flesh. Michael had a good, solid, smooth build, as I suspected, and was brilliantly tanned, dark as a piece of mahogany, except for his hips and ass, which he had left chalk white for sexy contrast. Jim let the boy's dick out of his mouth and licked up Michael's belly, driving his tongue into the navel and twisting it, then moving on up to those luscious nipples, those jewels, those figs, those fat, fleshy points. He was biting them hard, I could tell from the slight shake of the back of his head and Michael's sudden, pleasure-filled grimace.

"Oh God!" Michael moaned and opened his eyes. I dodged back into the hall before he could see me.

"That feels so good! I love to be eaten like that! Please suck them hard!"

I watched them in the picture glass again. Jim had licked his way up to Michael's mouth, and they kissed each other deeply. I shot my first wad watching them kiss and had to restrain myself from crying out. For my money, there's nothing in the world hotter than the sight of two men in a tenacious lip lock. When they broke, Michael looked down at Jim and stroked his shoulders solicitously and said, "Please eat my asshole now! Would you do that for me? I want to feel your great lips and tongue down there."

"Oh yes," Jim answered in a low, throaty whisper. He flipped the boy over on his stomach. Right away Michael clambered to his knees and shoved his snowy ass in my lover's face. Jim spread the fleshy cheeks wide. First he blew soft breaths on the brown, puckered hole, teasing it. He flicked his tongue at it, making Michael jump with each touch, then buried his whole face in the mounds, squeezing the cheeks around his face. I peeked around the corner to watch again and work up another erection.

"Oh God! That's awesome!"

At some point Jim had the index and middle fingers of his right hand stuffed up the boy's bunghole, sinking them in deeply.

"I'm getting you ready," Jim told Michael in another forced whisper, "to have the hell fucked out of you."

Michael looked behind him. I stepped into the hall quickly to avoid detection. "Oh, I'm ready for it, man," he said in an already weary voice. "I want your fucking hard dick up there, tearing me up. You better fuck me hard too, man!"

"First you're going to suck me off."

Jim stood. Michael crawled on his hands and knees to the edge of the bed. Jim offered his stiff prick. Michael devoured it in a single gulp. I watched in the picture glass. At some point all I could see was Jim's back and ass shudder in response to the voraciousness of Michael's talented mouth and throat.

"Don't make me come, baby. Not till I've gotten in that hot little hole of yours."

From his shaving kit, Michael brought out a condom and a tube of KY. Jim slid the condom on himself and slicked it up good with the lube so that it shone in the light. Michael waited on him, once again on his hands and knees, his ass in the air, cloud-white except for the dark cheek seam. Jim went to the bed on his knees and smacked Michael's ass a couple of good times with his cock. He ran the dick up and down the crack, teasing Michael, getting him uncontrollably excited. He made a sound in his throat like buzzing. Michael reached around and took Jim's dick in his hand and pressed it against his butt and lunged backwards, as though trying to impale himself on it. Jim ended the boy's misery and sank the dick into Michael's hole and began his long, hard ride. I stroked myself watching, more impressed with my lover than I had been in years. He was absolutely fuck-masterful, changing his pace effortlessly, from hard thrust to gentle poke, reducing young Michael from wails to whimpers and leaving him begging for the rougher motion. I loved watching the muscles in Jim's arms and legs and ass appear and disappear as he fucked. I loved the chiaroscuro of Jim's paler flesh meshing with Michael's deep, rich tan. Jim's ass looked especially delicious, every bit as good as Michael's, and for a second I was tempted to throw off our charade of spontaneity and rush into the room and shove my face in between the cheeks. But I restrained myself.

Jim fucked Michael in various positions—on his back, on his side, and, for a brief spell, with the two of them standing, Michael braced against a wall. Finally Jim ended up on his back, and Michael crawled atop him, squatting till his hole caught hold of Jim's dick. Then he ground his ass into Jim's crotch, his head back again, his eyes closed again, his tongue doing its happy, horny little dance around his lips. Jim squeezed his nipples, pulling at the tips and jiggling them slightly, as he might a woman's.

"Oh yes! Yes! I love that!"

Michael couldn't get enough. He was wild. He knocked Jim's hands out of the way and pinched his own nipples and looked down at Jim with something like demonic fury, his eyes squeezed almost shut, his teeth bared. He jerked himself off at the same time and soon fired cum onto Jim's stomach and chest. When he'd recovered from his orgasm, he slid off Jim's hips, pulled the condom off his prick, and sucked him to climax. As soon as Jim announced he was coming, Michael pulled the cock from his mouth and jacked the juice from it. It covered Michael's tanned shoulders. Michael took the dick and wiped the remaining sperm on his swollen nipples.

I watched it all in the picture glass and in quick, discreet peeks, and when Jim shot his wad on Michael, I dispersed my own second load right there on the hall carpet then quickly disappeared. I went into the front bedroom to think about all I had just seen. I was horny and happy as a teenager. I heard Jim and Michael in post-coital conversation. They went down the hall. Suddenly there was the sound of something slipping and falling. "Oh dear God!" came an almost feminine squeal and then a bump. Someone had got caught on my careless sperm. Michael. The poor thing had taken a spill on my swill. I snickered. "You all right?" Jim asked. He's a gentleman. No doubt he helped the clumsy catamite to his feet.

"Hey, man," Michael said, all sexy tough guy again, as he and Jim continued to the bathroom. "It smells like cum right here. Was your friend watching? If so, I might have to charge double. I mean, he did get off and all." Jim's response was muffled by the closing of the bathroom door and the firing up of the shower. Ten minutes later Michael was dressed and Jim escorted him to the front door and thanked him for the evening's fun. As soon as the door closed, Jim called my name. I didn't answer. He hunted for me. I heard him in the den.

"In here," I said.

"I'm afraid we were found out," he said coming towards the bedroom. He opened the door. "That little bugger wanted to charge me extra." He saw me lying naked on the bed with my swollen prick in my hand. His eyes lit up and a smile rose on his lips.

"Hey!" he said. "It worked."

I smiled back with the trembling, uncertain smile of the dangerously horny, the unreasonably horny.

"God, you looked so good in there sticking it to that stud. Oh baby. Baby, I want to suck your dick so bad right now."

It was music to Jim's ears. "Of course." Right away, the satyr, he began unbuckling his pants.

I held up my hand to stop him. "But first…first tell me about Michael."

"What about Michael? You saw him." He smiled. "A beaut, wasn't he?"

"Tell me how he tasted—his mouth, his skin, his cock. Tell me how his flesh felt in your hands. Tell me about those exquisite nipples. Please, baby. Please. I got to know or I'll die right here!" I stroked myself and toyed with my own hardened nipples just as Michael had.

"You saw him," Jim replied with a smoldering, deep lidded look in his eyes. "*You* tell *me* how he tasted and felt." Then he slowly approached the bed, unbuttoning his shirt.

I thought about it a moment, closed my eyes to visualize, licked my lips to bring up imaginary tastes. "Well, he tasted smooth, of course, and warm, like heated copper. And his skin was scented with some mild body oil, something just slightly sweet to make you lick harder and harder. And he was hard all over to your touch, especially those nipples, pliant and fleshy in your fingers and wonderful to bite and suck."

"Oh yes," Jim concurred in a husky voice. "I couldn't stop myself from sucking them."

"The asshole musky, the seven inches of dick with the slight tang of piss."

"Yes, that's right. Go on."

Jim rubbed himself as I described the firmness of Michael's back and ass, the way his asshole gripped Jim's dick like a warm hand and would not let go, the sinuousness of his thighs and calves and slightly hairy legs. Jim had his dick out and was jerking it slowly. "Bring it here," I said. I took it from him and jerked it myself while he shed his pants. He straddled my chest and pressed his prick to my lips.

We sucked and fucked for nearly an hour, with all the anxiousness of new lovers discovering each other for the first time. Afterwards we lay together and talked and laughed and made plans for what was left of the Atlanta night.

Then, after second thought, I annulled all plans. The bars, even The Heretic and my beloved Swinging Richards, seemed flat prospects after what had just happened in our suite at the Terrace.

I had another of my bright ideas. I looked up at Jim and said, "Hey, you think maybe Chris could get Michael back over here tonight?"

Jim's eyebrows shot up. Then he smiled. "You're ready for a round with him yourself, aren't you? He was cute and hot."

"Hell, no," I said defensively. "I thought he could watch you and me go at it and learn a trick or two."

AFTER THE BEEP
by Simon Sheppard

The voice on the answering machine is deeply masculine and commanding: "I know who you are and I know what you're going to do for me. You're to follow these and all further instructions exactly. You'll strip down now, right now; stop the tape until you're completely naked."

He's just gotten home, is still in his suit, has a bag of groceries in one hand and the day's mail in the other. It's crazy. A joke. Even so, the hand with the mail reaches over and pushes the Stop button. What harm could it possibly do? No one can see him. He's had a hard day at work. He's come back to an empty apartment. He was thinking of beating off when he got home, anyway. What harm could it do? Might as well play it through.

Being a methodical sort of fellow, he carefully leaves his clothes in a neat, folded pile on the chair in the hallway. He's down to his Calvins before he realizes that his dick has gotten as hard as it gets. He steps out of his briefs. Hard-on wobbling ahead of him, he walks back to the telephone and pushes the Play button on the answering machine.

"Good. Now that you're naked, you're going to start playing with your cock. Very gently at first. Just take your forefinger and softly rub the little flap of skin under your dickhead. Feels good, doesn't it? OK, now run your forefinger down the underside of your cock."

His dick does a little spasmodic dance as he teases the tender manflesh.

"Thumb and forefinger now, in a circle around your dick. Still gently. Just tease it. Now rub a little faster."

A sticky pearl of precum forms at the piss slit.

"Good. Now I want you to spit in your hand and slowly rub the spit around your cockhead. Squeeze down. Harder. Now run that wet hand up and down the shaft."

He's leaning against the wall next to the front door, eyes closed, following every command of the unknown man's voice.

"OK, now I want you to really get to work on that boner. Yank it hard. Rub that cock of yours from the piss hole all the way to your blond bush."

So the man knows he's a blond! The man is able to picture him there, jacking off on command. The man is…

He groans loudly, tenses his stomach. His thigh muscles tremble. He shuts his eyes tighter and shoots a big load of cum all over the kilim on the hallway floor.

The message machine is still running. "...know you enjoyed that. To acknowledge your pleasure, you'll change the outgoing message, incorporating the phrase 'If this is Jack calling, please be sure to leave a detailed message." Now go wipe up. I'll be in touch." There's a beep, then the whir of the rewinding tape.

This is crazy, he thinks, while going to get a handful of paper towels to mop up his congealing cum. He pops a Lean Cuisine into the microwave, watches an animal show on PBS, and gets ready to put himself to bed. But before he turns in, he goes to the answering machine, pushes a couple of buttons, and speaks into the handset. "Sorry, I can't take your call right now. Please leave a message after the beep and I'll be in touch as soon as I can. And if this is Jack calling, please be sure to leave a detailed message."

***

The next day he has to restrain himself from picking up his phone messages while he's at work. When he gets home he's rewarded by the blink of the MESSAGES WAITING light on his answering machine. There are three messages, actually. The first is from his mother; he fast-forwards through that. The second is from his friend Anthony. Fast Forward button again. And then the voice, insistent, maybe gently mocking, sexy as hell.

"I see that you enjoyed last night as much as I did. If I know you, you're already getting undressed without waiting for my instructions. Well, I'll let it go this time. And I'll bet your cock is already hard."

Right on the money.

"Once you're naked, I want you to turn off whatever lights are on in the apartment. Then you're going to go into the living room, pull up the center Levolor, and turn on that little lamp on the writing desk."

My God, he thinks, *the guy's been in the apartment!*

"Do it now. Leave the machine running and keep it at top volume so you can hear my instructions."

He's reluctant to do what he's been told. He's shown off a few times in the steam room at the Y, been to a few sex clubs, but standing buck naked in the window of his own apartment...

"Do it. Do it now. What are you afraid of? Do it or you'll never hear from me again."

What is he afraid of? His apartment is several floors up. With only that little lamp on, on one who's looking for him is likely to see him.

He's switching on the lamp when the voice speaks again. The high volume has made the voice sound harsher. "Good. Now stand there facing out to the street. You don't have to press yourself up against the glass, but you must be within sight of someone standing across the way. That's right. Now play with your tits, gently at first. Just lick your fingertips and rub them over your nipples. Now press down harder. Grab 'em, pinch with your thumbs and forefingers. Go on, pinch harder."

He shudders with pleasure. He wonders if anyone can see him. No one on the sidewalk is looking his way, but the unlit windows in the buildings across the street stare back at him like rows of dark eyes.

"Now, keep your left hand on your chest and move your right hand slowly down over your belly."

His moist palm starts stroking his tautly muscled abdomen, ruffling the trail of very blond hair that gradually widens as it expands into a curly bush. The edge of his hand presses up against the base of his hot, achingly stiff erection.

"Now your balls. Use your right hand to hold your dick up against your belly while you squeeze your balls with your left. Yeah, stretch 'em out. And squeeze harder."

He watches his reflection in the window, watches his naked body as it obeys the voice. Outside that window, beyond his ghostly reflection, the city is going about its business. In a weird way, he thinks, he's having sex not just with himself, not even with just the unknown caller, but with everyone out there. He squeezes his nuts harder and with his other hand begins to stroke his shaft. His dickhead becomes slick with precum. He brings his left hand up, sticks his fingers in his mouth, and licks them clean.

"You're doin' good, real good. Now take your hand away from your balls and get the forefinger real wet with spit. Then reach on back and just slide that wet finger all the way up that slick asshole of yours. All the way up. Now turn around so your butt is facing the street. And take that finger and slide it in and out and in and out. And play with your dick while you're finger-fucking yourself. Now turn back around. Keep your finger up y our ass. No, why don't you take it out for a second, get some spit on your middle finger as well, and stick them both up your butt?"

He stares out at the city as his fingers penetrate his own wet heat. A light goes on in a window across the street. A middle-aged woman in a nightgown shuffles into view. She looks in his direction as she reaches up for her window shade and slowly pulls it closed. Has she seen him?

"Now get some spit on your right hand and start working that dick real good. Work that piece of meat until you come. Do it. Do it because I'm telling you to."

His hand works the wet shaft, faster and faster, until his asshole clamps down around his fingers. He gives a wordless shout, and arcs of cum shoot through the air, hitting the windowpane and running down the glass. He feels woozy, puts his wet hand against the window frame so he won't lose his balance. In a minute the voice speaks out again.

"Now that was fun, wasn't it? You can go clean up now. And after you do, change your outgoing message again. Make it 'Jack, my meat is yours.' Just that. Talk to you soon." And a beep.

***

The next day, he spends much of the afternoon thinking about getting home from work and checking his answering machine. The hours crawl by. He's so horny he has to go into the men's room and beat off. Within a half hour he's horny again.

When he finally gets home, the light on the machine is blinking. Two messages. His dick is getting hard. He pushes the Play button and reaches for his fly.

"Honey, this is your mother. I almost thought I had the wrong number until I realized it was your voice. Who is this Jack? Oh well, give me a call, please. You never returned my last call, and I'm starting to worry. Is anything wrong? You know I worry." *Beep.*

Second message. "So I guess our little arrangement is working out. But maybe it's time you had a rest. You've been working so...hard...to please me. Go out, treat yourself to a nice dinner. I'll be back in touch soon. Keep your hands off your dick until then. Don't shoot a load or you'll never hear from me again. Oh, and I really liked it when you licked your precum off your fingers. Very nice." *Beep.*

So he was being watched last night! The voice was there, could see him. The thought makes his dick swell even harder. If he could, if he was allowed, he'd reach down and...

The phone rings. He doesn't pick up. Outgoing message: "Jack, my meat is yours." *Beep.*

"Honey, it's your mother. When you get home—"

He picks up. "Yeah, hi Mom."

***

The rest of the workweek drags by. No message. By Friday he's so horny he's bouncing off the walls. Once, he catches himself humping his crotch against the underside of the desk. Luckily, his coworkers seem not to have noticed. He leaves work early and rushes home.

Yes! The light is blinking! He pushes the Play button. The tape rewinds itself and plays. He hears the familiar, commanding voice. "I'm sure you've obeyed me since our last encounter. Now I have some very specific instructions for you. You're to follow them to the letter. Got that?"

He finds himself nodding agreement.

"After dinner you're to change into a T-shirt and 501s. Wait until midnight. I don't care what you do until then, just as long as you keep your hands off your cock. Then you're to go to..."—he gives the name of a well known sex shop in the warehouse district—and buy yourself a cock ring and a buttplug. Go into the video arcade in back, enter one of the booths, drop your pants, and put the cock ring on and the buttplug in. Button up, leave the shop, turn right, and go down to the street a few blocks until you reach the playground. There's a pay phone at the northwest corner of the park. Wait there for further instructions. Got that?"

He finds himself nodding again, which is silly, since the caller can't see him. Or maybe he can.

Beep.

***

The place reeks of Lysol. The bored, pierced guy at the register rings up his purchases: a black leather cock ring with chromed studs, a shiny black buttplug, and a small bottle of lube. He buys a handful of tokens and heads back to the video booths, shopping bag in hand. A few guys are roaming the corridor between the booths. A cute fat guy in a business suit. A man in a T-shirt with a well-developed body and an attitude to match. A tall, skinny student type wearing glasses.

He ducks into a booth and latches the door. Dropping a token in the slot, he pulls out his prick and plays with it while two L.A. surfer types go through the motions on the blurry screen. When he's hard, he puts the leather band around the base of his dick and balls, cinches it tight, and snaps it shut. He's opening the lube when he hears the door rattle. Someone's trying to get in. He squirts a big gob of lube in his hand and reaches back to his butt. The door latch gives way. It's the skinny student. In the bluish light of the video screen he looks a little scared and awfully young.

The intrusion nearly makes him stop, but then he looks in the kid's eyes, and the kid sort of smiles and rubs the crotch of his jeans. So he turns around and, back to the young guy, he slowly and deliberately works the lube into his ass. With his dry hand he grasps the buttplug and starts working in the tip of the plug into his slippery hole. Feet spread, back arched, he grabs his ass with his free hand, pulls his ass cheeks apart and pushes the plug deeper and deeper until, with a little pop, it goes in all the way to its base. His dick is rock-hard as he turns back to the tall, skinny kid. The boy's prick is just fucking huge, and he's jacking it for all it's worth. Reflected in the kid's glasses, tiny little surfer boys are having sex.

"Sorry," he says to the boy, reaching for his pants, "I gotta save my load."

The boy's hand is moving at the speed of sound. "Just…one…minute…please." Pound pound pound pound. "Just…let…me…look." And the kid shoots, a little ocean of cum forming on the dirty floor between them. "Thanks, mister," the kid says, tucking his big, half-limp meat back into his jeans and walking toward the exit. The video screen's gone dark. The horny surfers have gone back to wherever good little surfers go.

***

At this hour, the streets around the playground are deserted—too late for basketball, too early for cruising. He's only there for 15 minutes or so when the pay phone on the corner rings.

He picks up the receiver.

"Very good. You follow directions well."

It's the first time he's actually had him on the line, the first time he can talk back. "Who are you?" he asks, but the voice on the other end just keeps talking, and he realizes he's listening to a tape.

"...reach down and play with your dick through your jeans. Stroke it until it gets hard."

It's already hard.

"Now unbuckle your belt and undo the top two buttons, and reach on down into your pants."

His hand slides over his hairy belly, down to the moist hardness of his dick.

"Start jacking off. Slowly. Go real slow."

He concentrates on playing with his swollen cockhead, stroking the sensitive flesh. A gooey drop of precum oozes from his piss slit.

"Now, keep one hand on your dick and use your other hand to unbutton your pants all the way down."

Awkwardly cradling the phone on his shoulder, he does as the voice commands. His pants sag to his thighs.

"Now peel down your briefs."

The streets are empty, but still...He looks around. There, across the street, just beyond a streetlight's glow, stands a man. A handsome, bearded black man, muscles bulging beneath a white T-shirt. Looking his way.

He pushes his briefs down to mid thigh.

"And now you'll jack off for me. Take your time. Do a real good job. I'll be watching."

He grabs his stiff dick. The cock ring has made it extra hard. Staring straight at the man across the street, he starts massaging his manflesh.

"Right. You have permissions to come. Eventually. In fact, you *will* come. That's an order. Hang up now. And stay there until after you're done. I'll be back in touch.

He hangs up, brings his hand to his mouth, spits in the palm. Lubes up his dick with the spit. He looks down; the pale white flesh of his wet cock is gleaming in the streetlamp's yellowish light. He looks across the

- 22 -

street. The black guy is playing with his fly, slowly pulling it down. He reaches inside and pulls out a big, dark piece of meat.

Every stroke makes his hole clamp down on the buttplug, sending rushes of sensation deep into his body. The other man is beating off now, too. He thinks he can see foreskin sliding over the man's swollen cockhead. The man takes a few steps back into the light and leans up against a building, thrusting his hips forward, never letting go of his big cock.

A car cruises by—a red Miata coming between them—but doesn't slow down. The black man is pumping faster now, a half smile on his broad, handsome face. Seeing the smile somehow gets him even hotter. He shifts his weight and his pants fall to his ankles. More spit. He rubs one hand all the way up and down the slick, vieny shaft and plays with his tightening balls with the other. Faster. The black man matches his pace. Beating off harder, faster. The black guy grunts, thrusts his hips forward, and shoots big gobs of cum onto the sidewalk.

He can't hold back any longer. He shoots too, buttplug deep in his hot ass, hard dick spasming again and again.

When he's caught his breath, he realizes his hand is dripping with cum. Looking straight into the black man's eyes, he brings his hand to his mouth and licks it clean. The bearded man smiles and brings his own hand to his mouth, licking his fingers one by one. Then the guy puts his still-hard cock back into his pants, nods once, and walks off.

The phone rings. He's standing there naked from the waist down, and the nighttime breeze is cool on his butt. He lets the phone ring while he reaches down and pulls up his jeans. Some of his load has landed in his briefs, and his crotch feels wet and sticky.

"Nice job. Wouldn't you say so?"

"Yeah, I tried my best."

"I'll bet you did." It's not a recording this time. The voice is actually talking to him!

"So was that—"

"The man across the street? No, it wasn't me. He was just a pleasant surprise. For both of us."

"I want to meet you."

"What?"

"Meet you. I want to meet you."

"Are you sure?"

"Yeah. Nobody's ever made me feel the way you make me feel. I want to meet you and repay you. Make you feel good. I'll do whatever you say. Anything."

"Say 'please.'"

"Please." He can't believe it; his dick is starting to get hard again. "Please, sir."

"Tomorrow night. Midnight. Your place."

"You know where it is?"

"I know where it is."

"Of course you do."

***

He spends all Saturday naked in his apartment, the buttplug firmly in his ass. Every time the phone rings his dick jumps. Pavlov's dick. At midday he finds himself stark naked talking to his mother on the phone while absentmindedly stroking his stiff cock.

"Is anything the matter, dear? You sound a little strange."

The afternoon drags by. By dinnertime he's played with himself so much his dick is getting sore. He wasn't given permission to jack off, but he wasn't forbidden to, either. So he pours a big glob of lube on his cock and goes at it again. But he's saving his cum. For midnight.

As he strokes his slick meat he tries to imagine who the voice belongs to. He flips through the men he knows. Men from the office. Guys at the gym. Old tricks who might have saved his number. Young guys. Old guys. Fat. Buff. Doesn't matter. The voice is pure, abstract. Whoever it belongs to will turn him on. Every man passing through his mind turns him on. He's vibrating with pure lust. His dick is a tuning fork.

He orders a pizza. Mushroom and sausage. When the delivery boy arrives, he opens the door naked, with a hard-on. The pizza man, a hunky Latino, doesn't blink; he's seen weirder than that in this city. He gets a big tip.

After dinner he's too distracted to watch TV. He flips through some old porn magazines. Pictures of Scott O'Hara sucking his own dick.

The phone rings. He rushes to answer it.

"Is Yolanda there?"

Wrong number.

Ten o'clock. He thinks about the messages. The faceless man who tells him what to do.

Eleven o'clock. The anticipation he's felt. The freedom of having sex with no one in particular, and so with everyone.

Eleven-thirty. The mystery. The pure distillation of desire and surrender.

Twelve o'clock, exactly. The doorbell rings. He snaps the cock ring on. His dick has never been so hard. This is it. He goes to the intercom.

"Who is it?"

"Who the fuck do you think it is?" The voice. Even through the tinny intercom, instantly identifiable.

Long silence.

"Well, buzz me in."

"Y'know, I've been thinking."

"Yeah?"

"Thinking that maybe it's not—"

"Not such a good idea to meet face-to-face, right?"

"It's just that it's been so good, so hot."

"So why ruin it, right?"

"You're angry. Are you angry?"

"I asked if you were sure you wanted to meet. Remember?"

"And I thought I did want to. Then. But your messages…your messages are so…powerful to me. I wouldn't want to take a chance on ruining that."

"You're jacking off, aren't you?"

"Yeah."

"You're gonna come. For me. And I want to hear you when you shoot your load. I want to hear you over the intercom."

It only takes a minute. He tries to hold back, make it last longer, but he's lost control. Moaning and cursing into the intercom, he has one of the most amazing orgasms of his life. When he recovers, he says, "Are you still there?"

Silence.

Cum drips down the wall.

***

He spends Sunday in a funk. Has he made a mistake, chased the voice away forever? He re-records the outgoing message, begging Jack to keep calling. He goes to the gym, the first time in weeks, doing an extra-hard workout to try and relieve his stress. It leaves him so exhausted he doesn't even pay attention to the hot middle-aged man jerking off in the sauna.

When he gets home, the phone is ringing. He fumbles with the key, lets himself in just as the machine is picking up the call. It's his friend Anthony. He never did return Anthony's call. He wants to talk about what's been happening, but he can't tell Anthony. Anthony wouldn't understand. No one would.

At the office the next day he throws himself into his work, tries not to think about the voice. He's still sore from his workout. He owes himself a hot bath when he gets home.

***

He opens the door.

The light on the answering machine is blinking. He presses Play.

"I'm gratified that you want to continue our relationship. Not that I expected anything else from you. I know how much you need to obey me." His dick is hard. "OK, go run a hot bath, strip down, and then I'll have further instructions."

Half an hour later, as his soapy hands work his dick, he hears it, and thick ropes of cum spurt into the lukewarm bathwater. The comforting sound, the sound that seals his devotion, his surrender.

Beep.

COMING OUT RIM
by Tom G. Tongue

I was driving my car like it was a weapon, tears rolling down my cheeks. Thank God I had gotten out of there without my Dad seeing me in that state. I swore he would *never* see weakness of any kind from me. I'd just left my parent's home for the last time; I was determined that I'd never go back.

My name is Tom Gallagher. I'm 20 years old, and in April, when this happened I was two months from college graduation. I'd gone home with one goal in mind—to come out to my parents. They had always been so supportive of me. Why wouldn't they be? I was the ultimate overachiever—captain of the football team, class valedictorian in high school; big man on campus, nationally-known star quarterback and Academic All-American. The NFL draft was the following Sunday, and I was predicted to be a low round one/high round two pick. I had it all going for me, except for the *secret*.

I'm gay and, even though I'd never had sex with anyone, female or male—yes, I'd had opportunities (the plumbing just didn't work with women)—I was just too scared to do anything about it. I lived a very public life, and I couldn't afford scandal. So, I dated like all my frat brothers, but didn't let anything get too serious. Jacking off to visions of my teammates was the extent of my sex life, and it didn't make me the happy-go-lucky-guy everyone thought I was.

Physically, I'm pretty lucky too. I have thick brown hair, sky blue eyes, and a strong jaw. I've had people tell me I'm "handsome," but I don't think about it. I'm just under 6 feet tall, weigh 190 pounds with a smooth, muscular body. The only hair on me (don't ask me why) is a bit under my arms, and a small patch just above my dick. Since I'm telling you everything here, I'll share that information too: My dick is nine fat inches when up and hard. And it seems to be that way quite a bit of the time.

So, this college jock, campus hero, soon-to-be a millionaire decided it was time to go home and come clean with his Mom and Dad (I'm an only child). Big mistake. When I told them, Dad turned a violent shade of purple, and Mom cried, hiding behind him as he screamed at me. Words like "no son of mine, you've blown your future, psychiatric care, faggot, cock-sucker" flew at me, left and right.

With my mother crying, and my father yelling, I loaded up a few cherished childhood items into my car, one that I paid for myself, thank you very much, and tore out of their driveway and their lives forever. The last thing Dad said to me was, "Don't come back here ever again, you fuckin' faggot!" That I will not forget.

So, there I was, crying like a baby, driving too fast down the interstate, heading back toward my off-campus apartment—still over 200 miles away. No, I didn't live in the frat house. The coach insisted upon it, and, for that, I was grateful. Those guys were just too wild for me. I liked to party, but I couldn't do it all the time with the pressures of school work and the team. So, my best bud, Bull, the team center, and I shared a two bedroom apartment. I liked him in so many ways, and was grateful that I was not attracted to him physically (his nickname is appropriately descriptive). We were a good team on and off the field.

After swerving my car for the second time, I knew that I had to get off the road. I pulled off at the next exit, saw a seedy hotel that didn't look busy at all, and thought I'd just check in for the night. Looking at my reflection in the rear-view mirror, I decided to rethink the checking in thing. I looked horrible. I pulled my car to the very back of the single story motel, which faced a wooded area, and parked my car in a space in front of a row of obviously empty rooms.

Sitting there alone in the silence, I thought about how I used to believe my Mom and Dad were the greatest, most supportive people in the world. Ugly small failures of my childhood crept into my mind. Dad was almost always disappointed, and Mom silently backed him, just as dismally disapproving of any imperfection. So, to please them, and to try my best to live up to their expectations, I became *perfect*. I was a nervous wreck most of the time, and I knew the only way to improve my demeanor was to be truthful to myself and to those I love—again, big mistake.

"Fuck them!" I thought as I sat there and continued to cry. I hardly noticed that someone was coming around the corner from the front of the building, walking down the sidewalk. Through my teary haze, I saw a guy staggering in my direction. I saw that he was a fine specimen of a man. He was backlit and his high-and-tight-buzz-cut hair was glowing around his head. He was wearing khaki shorts and a white tee-shirt which showed off a big, tall, hard muscular body. He was also carrying what appeared to be a brown liquor store bag, containing a bottle of something.

Just as he reached the door to the room directly in front of my car, he noticed me and smiled, his straight white teeth glowing in the pale light. As he stepped toward my side of the car, I used my sleeves to quickly wipe my eyes. I rolled down my window a bit just as he stopped. Before he bent to look at me, I couldn't help but notice the huge, and I do mean huge, lump in the front of his shorts.

He spoke, "Hey, man, you okay?"

"Uh, yeah…I've just had a bad night. I drove back here to clear my head a bit before getting back on the road. I'll leave now…" I reached for my keys, still in the ignition, to re-start the car.

"Naaaah, you don't hafta go nowhere. Ain't botherin' me none. What's got you so upset anyways?" I smelled smoke and alcohol on him, but it wasn't an unpleasant smell, not at all; it was actually sexy. And he seemed downright friendly.

"Oh, I had a fight with my parents. I told them something that they didn't wanna hear. It was pretty ugly, I'll tell ya."

"Well, dude, you just sit here as long as you like. Or knock on my door there if you wanna come in and share a little Scotch with me." He tilted his head to the door and waved the bagged bottle toward me, smiling again. I noticed how thick the muscles on his neck were as he stretched it. With this guy, all I could think about was sex—he was one hot fucker.

"Uh, not right now…but thanks, anyway."

He shrugged, turned and headed toward the room, digging in his pocket for his key, which pulled his already-tight shorts even tighter across his massive muscle-butt. I felt my dick tingle looking at it. Did I tell you that men's asses are my main fantasy? I had dreams of fucking one, of course, but I wanted to look, touch, smell and kiss one too.

I'd found a neat porno novel, summer before last on the beach when staying over at a frat bro's family's beach condo. Drunken revelry was had by all except me, it just wasn't my style. The book was about a high school jock who kept finding guys to have sex with him. Eating ass became one of his favorite pastimes. He started his voyage of discovery on a field trip, where he roomed with his baseball coach. Who seduced whom, I can't tell you, but asses were licked, sucked and fucked by all. His coach, his doctor, his mailman, his uncle, the pool boy, the twins down the street and finally, his best friend, all fell victim to his charms. I hid amongst the dunes that week while my fraternity brothers drank themselves into a stupor, reading it and jerking off. I buried it in the sand to retrieve it the last night we were there, only to discover that the tide had washed it away. I was sorely disappointed, but the fantasies it provided my horny mind were endless.

When the muscular stranger got the lights turned on, I saw that I was offered a birds-eye view of his entire room, shabby as it appeared—it was as though I was attending the theater with a front and center seat. The window through which I looked was surprisingly clean and big. He walked in and shut the door with a thud. I watched him walk to the desk, pick up a glass, fill it with ice from a cooler next to the dresser and pour a generous portion of golden liquid from the full bottle he had just brought in. In the back of my mind, I wished that I had taken him up on his offer of a drink, but I just leaned my head back against my headrest, remembering the horror of a few hours earlier.

I'd come closer to hitting my father than I ever had, and I did not like the feeling. I was bigger, faster and stronger than him, and Lord only knows what hell my fists might have wrought. I only restrained myself for my mother's sake.

After a few minutes of dark thoughts, I lifted my head again, and opened my eyes. There, ten feet from me, was the stranger I'd just met, on his bed, clad only in his tightie-whities, stretched out on his stomach, and talking on the bedside phone. He took a few sips of his drink and smiled as he spoke looking even more ruggedly handsome, if that was possible. His arms were huge, his back a v-shape example of hard work and his butt—high, hard, and round. The fabric bisecting his crack was stretched to the maximum. I noticed a small patch of golden hair at the base of his spine and I wondered what it smelled like.

I shifted uncomfortably in my seat, as my dick awoke and grew to almost complete hardness in my snug jeans, and it was painful. I had to unbutton my 501's as unobtrusively as possible and straighten my erection up my stomach to ease the irritation. I pushed my tee shirt down to hide my exposure as I looked around to see if anyone was in the vicinity. No one was. The place where we were was very secluded and he was apparently the only person staying in the back of the motel.

Looking back to the room, I saw him hang up the phone and push himself up and off the bed. He had massive pecs with tiny copper-colored nipples and a light dusting of blond hair, a rippled stomach with an innie bellybutton, and a pleasure trail of hair below it, leading to a basket that looked like it held a kielbasa sausage and two ripe tomatoes.

He seemed to be totally unconcerned with my presence, although I knew he knew I was there. He moved to the back of the room—the view of his backside full on was breathtaking, even in the snug jockey shorts. He reached down to scratch his right butt-cheek as he walked, almost like he *wanted* me to check out his ass. He turned on the light by the vanity and disappeared into what I guess was the bathroom, and seconds later, I saw a white object come flying out. It was his underwear.

While I imagined what he was doing in the bathroom, my hard-on grew to its full height and began to ooze pre-cum. I reached down, unconsciously, and, pushing my tee-shirt out of the way, began rubbing my right thumb across the smear sending a pleasure chill down my spine that I actually felt in my asshole. With my left hand I reached under my shirt as well, and began tweaking my already erect right nipple, sending more jolts throughout my sexually charged body.

Why was I thinking this way? The guy in the room didn't do or say anything to make me think that he was coming on to me, but he was so damn sexy and nonchalant about it…like he knew but didn't care. He didn't care that some dude he had just met, sitting crying in his car, could see him almost naked…Shit!

Just as that thought crossed my brain, he stepped back into view, with a towel held around his waist, his body dripping wet and shining. I say "held" because there was no way a small towel like the one he held was going to go around him; almost his entire right hip was exposed. He turned to the vanity that was on the wall opposite me, and in it I could see him from the waist up in the front and a full view of his back. And then it happened, he dropped the towel.

He didn't seem to care one bit. He crouched down, with his right hand on the counter for support, and leisurely picked it up with his left hand, pausing for a moment in that position, holding it as he stood again, only to set it on the counter. While he was squatting, I got a perfect view of his asshole, his low hanging balls and the head of his prick. He went so low, his dickhead and balls settled on the floor.

He stood again, his bare ass open for the world, and me, to see, and leaned forward across the sink, looking closely at his face. For a moment, it seemed his eyes glanced back at me, but it was so quick I couldn't be sure. My focus was his ass—two big loaves of protruding muscle. Below it, his thighs and calves were thick and corded. Either this guy did some serious gym work, or he'd done some major physical labor of some sort. There was not a portion of his body that did not seem muscular. Even his face seemed toned and firm.

After looking for a few moments for some invisible facial flaw, he picked the towel back up and began vigorously drying the still-wet areas of his body. I still hadn't seen his dick, but I knew he'd be turning around soon, and that I'd see it. I wasn't complaining; the back view was just fine by me. Finally, he turned around and I was disappointed to see that he was holding the towel loosely in front of his crotch. When I lifted my eyes, I saw that he was watching me, and smiling.

Still holding the wet towel, he walked to the door, opened it completely, and spoke; I'd never rolled my window back up and heard him perfectly, "Hey, dude, come on. Have a drink with me. I think you need it." He left the door open, turned his back to me and went to freshen his drink.

I quickly fastened my jeans, with my dick sticking above the waistband, and made sure my tee-shirt was coving me. Thank God it was an oversized one. I rolled up my window, sucked in a deep breath and climbed out into the crisp spring air.

I walked into the room and saw him on the bed with his back against four pillows on the headboard and his towel primly covering his lap. He was smiling at me as I entered, and my knees felt weak. He nodded toward the cooler and said, "Help yourself."

I closed the door and quickly fixed myself a drink. I looked in the mirror to see him staring at me, not me exactly—my butt! My prick lurched again.

I took a sip, almost choking on the strong mixture, and said, "Thanks, uh…"

"Rick." He reached out his hand, and I stepped around the bed to shake it. His grip was firm.

"I'm Tom. Pleased to meet ya, Rick." He held onto my hand for an extra second or two, looking deep into my eyes, and, again, my dick pulsed.

"If you don't mind my saying it, you look like shit, Tom." I had to laugh. There was no maliciousness in the statement. He laughed too, and it was the best I had felt in hours, no make that days. I was so nervous about the visit to my folks that I hadn't slept well. The true event was way worse than I had anticipated, so it felt great to laugh again.

He spoke, this time more serious, "Tom, why don't you jest jump in the shower. It'll make ya feel better, I'm sure." I paused for a moment, not sure what to do. "Go on, Tom. You can trust me."

"Uh…okay, just let me get a change of clothes out of the car"

"Naah, I ain't gettin' dressed. Why should you?" Again he smiled, and I just went with it. I did go into the bathroom, with the door closed, to disrobe. My hard-on had gone down a bit, but I didn't want him to see it. I'd taken the drink in with me, and gulped it down before stepping into the hot running water. Rick was right; the shower did make me feel better. As I dried myself off, I realized I faced a dilemma; should I redress? He'd made no effort to close the drapes, and I wasn't sure. "Fuck it" I thought, and I stepped out of the bathroom, carrying the towel in front of my crotch, as he had.

"Now, don't that feel better?" I froze in my spot. He hadn't moved from his position on the bed, but the towel had moved. He had the majority of it on the bed between his widespread legs, with just one corner pulled up above his navel—he was bare otherwise. The other thing was that he had a hard-on—no doubt about it.

He patted the bed next to him, and shifted a couple of the pillows against the headboard, without the covering around his crotch coming undone. He spoke again, "Now, why don't you tell me more about what's got you so upset." I noticed that he was looking me over pretty closely too, but nothing sexual had been suggested. I was in a motel room, with a total stranger who was sporting a massive hard-on, and my own was rapidly expanding. It was very sexual, but not enough to freak me out…I guess because I was so nervous.

"Do you mind if I close the curtains, Rick? I feel funny being so undressed and so open like this."

"Leave 'em open. There's nobody gonna be out there. I've been here three nights and haven't closed them yet. I like 'em open. If somebody is gonna look, let 'em look. I ain't got nuthin' I'm ashamed of. And, man, look at that bod on you! You ain't got nuthin' to be 'shamed of neither."

So, it was a *fuck it* night, and I said it to myself again, and plopped myself down next to him, being very careful to keep my crotch covered. "Rick, I'm not really in the mood to talk about my problems…"

"Hey, where's your drink? Did you leave it in the bathroom? I need a refill." He jumped up, holding the towel, bounced to the bathroom and came back to the desk. Both of his hands were full with our glasses, but the towel was still on his crotch; his big ole hard-on was holding it there like a hook. Offering me another closer view of his lightly fuzzed butt, he filled our drinks once again. I had drunk my last one so quickly, and without dinner, my head was buzzing just a bit. He was so damn nonchalant.

"Here you go, Tom." He plopped down next to me, and I noticed that I could see both our reflections in the mirror above the desk. I also noticed that I had a clear view of his lemon-sized balls that rested loosely on the bedspread, and just the base of his huge organ. The damned towel covered the rest.

Turning to face him, and taking my eyes away from his beautiful low-hangers, I spoke "Thanks, Rick. Why don't we talk about you? What are you doing here in the middle of nowhere—and for three days, did you say?"

"Well, I just got out of the Marines two weeks ago. My Dad has a job waiting for me when I get home, one that I don't wanna take, but I convinced him that I needed to travel around a little before I settled down. So, I've been hitchhikin' and hangin' out. I've been here for three days cuz I'm doin' some work for the owner of this here motel, and he's letting me stay here free."

The Marines. That explained the haircut and his body. "Oh, how long were you in for?"

"Four years. It was great, really. I miss it. I was a corporal in a basic training unit, and I really miss my sergeant. I called him Sarge."

"Oh, why do you miss him so much?" He got a spacey look on his face for a moment.

He leaned over to the bedside table and pulled out a large joint. "Why don't we get high, and I'll tell you all about him? It'll take your mind off your problems, too." He plopped an ashtray between us on the bed, and lit the joint, holding it up for me after he'd filled his lungs.

Like I said, it was a *fuck it* night, so I took it. We were silent for the few minutes it took to smoke the weed, and without realizing it, my hard-on had reached its full height and my towel tented obscenely between my legs.

Looking into the mirror again, I saw that Rick was looking at that tent, and he was smirking. But it was a friendly smirk. He reached down to give his balls a scratch, and, in the process, revealed another few inches of the base of his thick, upstanding cock. Our eyes met in the mirror, and for some reason, I just knew I could trust this guy. We just smiled at each other, goofy drunk/high smiles, and I felt extremely comfortable.

"So, Rick, tell me about the Sarge." I pulled on my towel, until my balls and a few inches of my dick were exposed too. He watched me in the mirror, and gave me that goofy grin again. Putting the ashtray back on the bedside table he slid a little closer to me, until our knees were touching. I swear I felt electricity.

"Well, when I joined up, I was jest uh 18-year-old scrawny kid from East Bumblefuck, Tennessee. Sarge took a likin' to me, I guess, and he rode me harder than anyone durin' boot camp. Did I tell you that he was my DI?" I shook my head. "He transformed me, body and soul. I put on over twenty-five pounds of muscle, and for the first time in my whole life I felt good about me. After I'd finished training, he helped me get my PFC stripe, and after six months overseas, and my promotion to corporal, he requested my transfer back to his unit, to work with him and his platoon. I wuz honored and pleased to be back with him; he's really a great guy.

"I mean he can cuss and chew out a guy three ways to Sunday, but once I got to know him better, I knew his fussin' was for our own good. He made men out of us."

I spoke, "Well, if your torso is any indication of his work, I'd have to agree. You are a well built fellow, Rick."

"Ya think so?"

I nodded. He flexed his coconut-sized right bicep and stroked a hand across his hard pecs. "Thanks, Tom. I've worked hard to get this body, and I plan on keeping it this way. Sarge is proud of it and his own muscles too. He and I would sit around naked together all the time. I love bein' naked." With that he grabbed the towel and pulled it off, tossing it across the room and into the corner.

My eyes nearly popped out of my head. His dick had to be close to mine in length, but his was so fat. It was as thick as my wrist I'd bet. I looked at it directly: I didn't want to see it through the mirror. He saw me looking and thrust his hips a bit making it bounce against his stomach for me. Reaching out with his left hand, he grabbed my towel, and yanked it free, sending it flying with the other one. I made no effort to stop him. He took a good hard look at me too, and I did the bounce thing for him. Unlike him, my dick was leaking steadily, and as it bobbed my pre-cum created a puddle just above my bellybutton.

I had to ask, "So what did you two do while you were naked together, Rick?" No mention was made of our arousal; it was the most natural thing in the world to be there exposed to the world, hard as hell, and on his bed.

"Well, we stripped off our clothes in the barracks as soon as the lights on base went out. Sarge is bigger than me, everywhere!" He looked down at his dick as he spoke, and we both laughed again. "He's been a Marine for over ten years, and he's got muscles on his muscles. But when we got naked, we just talked and did all kinds of fun stuff...wrestlin', jerkin' off together, talkin' dirty, givin' each other back rubs...all kinds a fun stuff." He looked at my dick again, watching the pre-cum leaking, and asked, "Hey, Tom, I know! I'll give you a backrub. That'd make you feel better. You'll forget all about that fight you had with your folks."

He turned a bit and used his left hand to squeeze the base of my neck. I groaned at the sensation. His touch made my dick throb and sent another squirt of pre-cum on my belly. I turned my head and looked into his bright green eyes. "I'd like that...if it's no bother."

"No bother 't'all. Just roll over on your belly here, and let me at it."

- 34 -

I did as instructed, putting my face into the pillow he'd been leaning on—liking its smell. I felt him climb on top of my back, his big balls resting on my spine. They were red hot, and I liked the way they felt there. His hands started by rubbing my shoulders and neck, they weren't exactly smooth, but they weren't rough either. They felt good. He knew just what to do, and soon all the kinks in my upper torso were just gone. He scooted down until I felt his balls fall in between my spread legs and actually hit mine. As he leaned forward to reach my shoulders again, his huge cock, hard as a rock, wedged itself into my ass-crack. He'd begun to leak, and as he rubbed me, he rocked back and forth a bit, spilling his lube into my valley, and I liked it.

He backed up yet again and I expected to feel his hands on my butt next, but I was disappointed to feel him pick up my left foot and begin massaging it. He worked on nerve endings on my sole that I did not know existed. He spent time working up my calves and my thighs, stopping just short of my ass-cheeks. He was straddling my leg and I felt the contact with his balls, but nothing else was sexual, just very sensual. When his hands grasped my upper thigh, his fingers brushed lightly against my ball sac, and I seeped some more lube onto the bedspread.

He repeated the process with my right leg, just as slowly and masterfully. My body felt totally relaxed and open. On this trip upward, he grazed his still-erect cock against my upper thigh a few times, leaving a wet smear, but, again, I liked the feeling. Moving off my leg, he pushed my calves apart and knelt between them. He turned his hand over and lightly dragged his fingernails upward on my legs, across my butt and up my back. I felt his breath against my ass-crack.

Turning his hands again, he lightly traced his fingertips down my flesh in the same pattern causing major goose bumps. This time, however, he stopped at my butt, slowly spreading his fingers until his palms were resting on each cheek. "You know what, Tom," he asked breathily "you have a mighty fine lookin' butt here? It's so smooth, but so muscular too." His fingers began to knead my flesh, sending more waves of pleasure up and down my spine. My cock dripped some more.

"Uuuuuuhm, that feels sooo good. Rub my butt, man!"

"You like that huh?" I groaned in response, feeling him pulling my cheeks apart. His thumbs were inside my moist crack, tracing up and back, lightly grazing my virgin pucker hole. I began writhing, pushing my ass back to meet his exploring hands. He backed up off the bed, grabbing my ankles and pulling me down until my lower body was dangling from the edge of the bed. He grabbed my dick, almost causing me to cum, holding onto it as he used his other hand to push me forward just enough for my cock to be pressed against the mattress, pointing down.

He grabbed a butt cheek in each hand again and spoke, "Tom, spread your legs wide open for me." I complied gladly. "Now there's the source of your tension, buddy." I felt him blow a warm stream of air on my vulnerable hole. "My hands are busy right now, or I'd use them to rub it...you understand don't ya?"

"What ya gonna use instead, Rick?" I was pretty sure, but wanted to hear him say it.

He didn't seem to hear me. "So smooth, so tight..." He did that thing I'd been dreaming about. I felt his hot wet tongue drag from the base of my balls directly to my exposed hole. Within seconds his pointed licker was digging into my aperture, sending spasms of delight throughout my body.

"Oh shit, Rick! Lick my hole, man. I can't fucking believe how good that feels. Rim me. Eat my asshole. Oh God, yeah. Never stop, never ever stop!" I was pushing my ass back onto his face. He stopped tongue-fucking me for a second to lean lower and lick from the head of my drippy dick past my balls and back to my spit-wet hole. "Oh, Rick, don't stop, I'm gonna c..."

But he stopped, and started blowing cool air across my ass, making my hole twitch. He whispered into my ass, "No, Tom, don't cum yet. The fun is jest startin'! This here chute tastes better than Sarge's and that's saying sumthin'. I wanna eat on it for a bit more. Can I do it without you blastin' off?" He gave me another quick lick.

"Yeah, Rick. You can eat my ass all night if you want to; just gimme a sec to cool off again."

He leaned in and started licking and biting my cheeks, pulling clumps of flesh up with his teeth. It hurt, but it felt good at the same time, and within seconds, I was back to normal, and my balls dropped back to their normal position. He noticed and dove right in again, licking, lapping and lashing my hole with his nasty tongue. Speaking of nasty, words came out of my mouth that surprised even me.

After ten or fifteen minutes of divine pleasure, I realized how one-sided things had been. I didn't want him to stop; his long tongue was deep inside me...but I had to see what it was like to eat an ass. Surprising myself, I rolled over and stuck my taster out, wagging it out at him. "Rick, can I...uhm...massage you too? I've never done it, but I want to really bad."

His handsome face was wet with spit and my ass juices. He smiled as he stood, leaning forward against the desk, "Well, give it your best shot, Tom. I'm sure you're gonna do jest fine."

Sitting on the edge of the bed, I could see his smiling face in the mirror as I reached up and grabbed his butt. Putting his chest flat on the desk, he brought his hands back, placing them over mine. Together, we pulled his big hard ass-cheeks apart, revealing a blond-fur-lined valley with a pink, hairless rosebud in its center. I leaned forward, about to start licking, but I wanted to smell it first. So, I put my nose right against his hole, and inhaled through it. It smelled so good that I nearly came just taking in his scent. I pulled back a few inches, and spoke in a gravelly voice, "You smell good, Rick. Bet you're gonna taste even better."

And my tongue was on an asshole, a delicious moist, sweaty sweet asshole, and I loved it. I drove my face into his crack, but couldn't get deep enough. I was frustrated, trying to pull his muscle butt more open so I could stick my tongue up his silky smooth tunnel. Rick realized I was getting frantic, and solved my problem by straightening enough to lift his left leg and put his foot flat on the desk. His trench was wide open. I quickly turned around and sat on the floor, and, grabbing his hips, I pulled down until his pucker hole landed directly on my extended licker. We both groaned in pleasure.

As I slurped and licked his delicious hole, Rick bounced up and down on my tongue. He wasn't short on words either.

"Tom, you've never don't that before? Coulda fooled me! You're takin' to it like a two-dollar whore. Lick my shit hole. Clean me up. Deeper man. Stick your tongue so deep I'll feel it in my fuckin' stomach. Yeeeeaaah. Eat me. Get it nice and sloppy wet man. I've got a surprise for you!"

After a few more minutes of mindless ass-rim pleasure, he spun his leg off the desk, and in one quick move, pulled me to my feet. He grabbed the desk chair, pulled it out till its back was against the bed, and pushed me into it. I was shocked, but my astonishment was short lived as he straddled me, facing the mirror. He reached between his legs, grabbed my pulsing prick at the base, and lowered his ass until my leaking head was touching his dripping hole. He sat down, and my dick sunk into his blazing hole like a hot knife into butter. We both moaned in pleasure.

I almost came just from the incredible heat and tightness. By leaning to my right a bit, I could watch him in the mirror. His eyes were rolled back in his head, his tiny nipples were pinpoint nubs, and his dick was even bigger (if possible) dripping and throbbing against his stomach. He bounced on me three times, and pulled himself off my prick, much to my disappointment. He grabbed his own ass-cheeks, pulling them wide apart and jammed his hole back onto my face.

"Lick it again, buddy, get that tongue really deep in there and wiggle it around."

He was slamming his hole on my face and I loved the new tastes, as I got deeper, and the skin was so smooth. I was turning my head from side to side, trying my best to jam as much of my taster into him as I could. I could hear myself grunting and groaning in the effort. Spit was dripping out of me and landing all over my lap. His wide-open hole was filled with my juices. He was just grunting. Words that sounded like *lick* and *rim me* we're coming toward me, but I wasn't hearing anything.

He straightened up again, and turned himself around, straddling my legs, hands on my shoulders. His massive penis was inches from my hungry mouth. Just as I was about to lean forward with my mouth open he sat down again, and, amazingly, my cock found its mark with neither of us aiming. I looked deep into his hypnotic eyes as his face came level with mine. His prick was jammed between our chests, dripping profusely. His arms wrapped around my upper back as he settled down, and he pulled us closer together.

I pulled my head back and looked at his face. I noticed how thick his lower lip was, and realized that, "I want to kiss you, Rick. Can I?"

He replied by bringing his lips to mine in a chaste kiss. Then there was another longer one, and finally his tongue slid out and into my hungry mouth. Throughout all this kissing, he was moving up and down on my cock lightly. As our kiss grew in passion, so did his bouncing. I reached around his back and grabbed an ass cheek in each hand, pulling him more wide open to my cock. He groaned into my mouth, and his ass muscles started clamping down on my boner, sending me over the edge, and I was soon humming too.

Still in the throes of our tongue-tangled moan and groan fest, we came! In unison, our orgasms began, mine deep into his molten cavern, his on our chins, necks, chests, pretty much everywhere. I'd *never* cum like that before. I felt like my balls were gonna be lodged inside me for life, they were so drained. I wanted to do it again.

He pulled back from my mouth long enough to scoop up a dollop of his thick cream from my shoulder, and with his tongue sticking out, and his spooge resting on it, came back to kiss some more. I loved it. I pulled back to lick up some from his neck and repeated the process. With my still-hard prick buried inside him we ate every drop of cum we could reach, and kissed a lot more.

"I just wish I could taste yours. Wait, I can!"

He stood up again, backed up two steps, and swallowed my prick to the root. Humming deep in his throat, he milked my joint for the last few dregs of cum. I looked into the mirror and saw his gaping open hole, with my jism leaking out, and my hard-on was pulsing, ready for action again. Rick stood, moved forward and sat right down on me again.

This time when we kissed, I got the great taste of his ass, and my cum. I wanted to latch my mouth to his hole again, but it was otherwise "occupied." Suddenly he pulled back from the kiss, his eyes wide. "Oh shit, Tom. I've got somethin' to tell you, and I hope you don't mind…"

I thrust upward into him, causing him to grunt in surprised pleasure. "What is it, Rick. You've made me feel so good. I'm sure it'll be okay." I thrust again, and we both grunted this time.

He leaned forward and gave me another tongue-swiping kiss, and began rocking on my cock, slowly. My first load of cum made his creamy smooth ass walls even slicker, and my dick, still being somewhat sensitive from the massive orgasm I'd just had, loved the feeling.

"Do you remember me telling you that I was doing some work for the owner of this place?" I nodded and reached between us, and began stroking his big dick as he bounced. "Well, his name is Pete, and he's an old lecher. When I first checked in here, he offered me the room for sex, and I said 'No Way!' So he told me that he'd let me stay free if I'd let him see me naked."

He was still bouncing, and I was still feeling great, but a nagging sensation hit the back of my head. "Go on," I said. He was picking up the tempo, and my balls outweighed my brain and I began lifting my hips to meet him.

"Well, I told him that I'd never be alone with him in the altogether. But I love to be naked and I did hint that I'd probably leave the curtains open."

"Oh my God, he's watching us *now?*" His bouncing was at a fevered pitch by then and I just said out loud "Fuck it!" I stood up, showing strength I didn't realize I had. As I picked him up, he wrapped his legs around my waist, still impaled on my prick. I walked us over to the window. The vibrations of walking were wonderful.

There was a table there. I laid him back on it, and asked "You ready to get fucked for real now, stud?" He nodded and smiled. It was better than the first time. We acted like a couple of porn stars. When I pulled my deflated prick from his hole, and sucked my two loads out of his deliciously stretched ass, I could have sworn I heard a moan from outside the window.

As I pulled myself free of him, and crawled over to the bed, Rick closed the curtains on our little show. All I could think was that I'd really come out in a *big way* that night.

***

As we left the next morning, we saw splotches on the outside of the window, and we knew where they had come (cum?) from. After the football draft and my agent worked out the signing bonus, I moved Rick to our new hometown. I hired him as my live-in strength and conditioning coach. He's gonna put 25 more pounds of muscle on me. What we do naked behind closed doors is our own business. We've talked about going back to that motel and visiting Pete again, but…

WATCHING
by Kyle Stone

It looks warm and dark and inviting in the alley behind his apartment house. I am walking back from the parking lot, cutting through from the street along the lane that services the building where Partners Bar is. I can still hear the croon of the guitars and the wail of a man singing. I jump down from the cement divider, into the shadow. There is no wind here. My boots make only a dull thud, the sound cushioned by layers of damp leaves and someone's old mattress. I pause a moment to get my bearings.

It is the secret hidden world behind those golden windows that draws me. I have always been fascinated by the lives of strangers, how people change when they shed their outer skins at their own front door and slip into something more comfortable, more themselves. I do it myself. But even if you go with them, follow them home though the night, follow them into that small stale apartment with the old socks in the corner and the bed unmade since this morning, you never catch them, never see the change first hand. At best you have efficient, hurried sex, after a desultory conversation. At worst, the stranger seen against his intimate background is no longer anonymous enough to satisfy. But glimpsed through the window, moving uninhibited through his own clear space, he becomes unattainable, an object of infinite conjecture. Desire twists inside me and the barrier of glass turns the scene into magic.

I hunch forward into my denim jacket, hands in pockets, and glance over my shoulder. Separated pools of light etch deeper shadows against the chain link fence and the corners around the loading dock. Nothing stirs. The soft night air touches my face, my neck, riffling against the exposed skin of my throat like a careless hand and leading me on. Head down, I move along the wall, sure of my way even though the night presses close here, hiding all detail. I keep to the edge of the alley, instinctively treading where the leaves cushion my footsteps.

At the gap between the buildings, I turn and plunge without hesitation into the narrow space. Above me, the buildings lean towards each other in conspiring darkness. With a soft grunt of exertion, I swing up to the grill that covers the deep well of the heating system. I t is warm, here, the dampness of the decaying leaves strong on the air. I put one foot against the wall behind me, and lean back prepared to wait. However long it takes this time. Like always. My head is at just the right angle. For a moment, I feel a stab of panic, a quick falling away in the pit of my stomach. Perhaps I am too early. Perhaps he has decided to spend the evening with friends. Above me, I can hear the sound of a radio, the heavy beat of the bass line throbbing. The window lights up. I see him.

I take a deep, careful breath. It's like inhaling the essence of what is outside, and what I see in that room behind the glass. I draw it down into my lungs and from there it moves into my blood and the man I watch becomes a part of me. His straight fall of black hair. His intense dark eyes. The small cleft in his chin. The long mouth that crooks up slightly at one corner. He throws his leather jacket over the back of a chair, drops a magazine on the coffee table. He moves through the room, loose-limbed inside his clothes. I lick my lips, tasting the night and the sharp edge of my own longing.

A scrabbling in the dry leaves startles me, as a cat runs by the alley. For a moment, I lose the thread, my mind shying away from the man safe in the room in front of me, snagged by a moving shape in the shadows. Then it is gone. My eyes refocus, as the man stretches his arms above his head, pulling off his t-shirt. The light from the lamp by the tape deck highlights his cheekbones and the curve and dip of the muscles of his shoulders as they emerge from the shirt. Soundless in the circle of golden light, he stands and looks at his reflection in the mirror, a reflection I can just see if I tilt my head to the left. It is an image twice removed from me, a fainter likeness, a picture that is closer to memory than reality. If I lean across the damp air and touch the glass of his window, I cannot touch the man, or his image, and the gap between us widens in my mind, even as my longing for this touch jolts through me with despair. In the darkness, I fumble with the snap at the front of my jeans.

On the other side of the glass, my icon begins to study his reflection, moving his hand slowly over the expanse of his broad chest as if discovering himself. His fingers rake through the swirl of black hair between his dark nipples, move lower, pausing over his ribs. He breaths in. His ribs stand out, each bone curving sharp and precise under the skin. His belly sucked in, leaves a slight space between the silver buckle of his jeans and his concave stomach. He bends his head and the black hair falls over his eyes. I hold my breath, waiting, watching as he glances up again at his reflection, as if trying to catch himself off guard. It almost makes me laugh, except that for an instant, I see his eyes and they are deep with fear. My own hand falters, and I shrink against the wall, feeling like a child caught spying and about to be punished. But the moment passes, and when I look again, his eyes are flat and self-absorbed, his hands against his back, holding his body like a chalice, studying the effect.

My own body relaxes and the warmth grows inside me as I watch. He moves away from the mirror, his arms swinging, now, shoulders lifting to untie the knotted tension between his shoulder-blades. As my hand moves deeper, my fingers curling around my own hardening flesh, my eyes drink in the lean figure above me, every detail sharp as he loosens his jeans and they drop without sound to the floor. He stands unmoving, the jeans, shapeless pools around his ankles, the lean flanks dark, bronzed by the yellow light. I can feel the air against my naked skin as my own jeans hang open and am touched by the darkness and the cold hand of night. I shiver, but the sensation of vulnerability brings with it the heightened thrill of possible discovery, sharpening my senses, arousing me at last, as the connection between me and the almost naked young man inside tightens, twists, builds to a crescendo within me. I brace myself against the brick wall. My hand moves faster. He turns towards the window. I close my eyes, almost as if I think by not seeing him he can not see me, but when I open them again, he has turned away and is walking, slim-hipped and now completely naked, towards the door. He pauses, bends over, picks up his jeans. I smother my cry as I see the soft insides of his thighs, the secret darkness between his cheeks, open for a few seconds to my hot gaze. My knees are weak and my head arches back against the unfeeling brick. My breath is fast, coming in ragged gasps.

It is over.

Inside, the young man has turned off one of the lights. In partial shadow, he walks away from me, armed again in impenetrable mystery.

Outside, in the darkness, I bend my head and do up my jeans. The air is cool Damp. There is moisture on my cheek. I walk out of the alley, narrowly missing the garbage cans set out by the corner of the building. I walk the streets, aimless, watchful. Seeing everything and nothing. At last I go home.

"How are things at the bar?" Evan asks, as he always does. He's wearing his dressing gown, old and barely decent, but it comforts him. I know this and try not to comment.

"Same as usual," I say. I pick up his leather jacket from where he always leaves it over the back of the chair and hang it up with mine.

"If it's always the same, why do you bother?" he asks.

"Perhaps because it *is* always the same," I say, more to annoy him than anything else.

He surprised me. He smiles, his long generous mouth crooking up on one side, his dark eyes laughing at me. "Touching," he says.

I flush. My jaw tightens. I can feel the anger, but I refuse to give in to it. "Sure," I say. "I'm going to bed."

"Want a smoke first?" Those black eyes hold me, skewered, squirming.

I hesitate, wondering what he knows, what he feels, if he still wants anything from me. I shake my head. "I gave it up, remember?"

He shrugs and picks up his book. His black hair is damp from the shower. Long tendrils curl against the soft vulnerability of his neck.

I watch him for a moment in the mirror. I can see him there as the boy he used to be, the young man he is now, and the spectre of what he will become, and my chest tightens painfully. I lay my hand against the glass, against the reflection of his bowed head, waiting till the hard surface absorbs my heat.

"You'll leave a smudge," he says.

I feel words, like knives, in my mouth. I don't let them out. Instead, I pick up the belt with the silver buckle and take it into the bedroom.

WELCOME TO CHUCK CHAT
by Jim Buck

Welcome to Chuck Chat, the Official Chat Channel for the ChuckCam! Watch Chuck live on the ChuckCam every evening from 6PM to Midnight, CST. There are currently 5 users signed on to Chuck Chat: Big1, BlkDaddy, Hung9, Spunky, and Sticky.

Sticky> Where's Chuck? It's 10:00. He should be naked by now.

Big1> He was on at 7:00. It's Friday—maybe he's out with the guys. We should maybe give him a break.

Sticky> Not me. I've got the house to myself tonight and I've got a family size bottle of baby oil on my desk and I'm not leaving 'till I see some action. <grin>

Big1> That's your prerogative....

BlkDaddy> Somebody sounds like he isn't getting any at home.

Hung9> Where are you, Sticky?

Sticky> Atlanta. You 9?

Sticky> I get plenty, Blk.

Sticky> BTW, What refresh rate are you guys getting?

Big 1> About every 15 seconds, Sticky.

Hung 9> NYC, Sticky. Every 20 seconds or so.

Spunky> Same rate here—20 secs or so.

Spunky> Atlanta here, too, Sticky. Which part?

BlkDaddy> Seems like you'd have better things to do if you did. Why cruise a cam if you've got dick in your bed?

Big1> Alright boys, cool it. No reason to fight—there's nothing to fight over. Chuck's not even here.

Sticky> Who says I keep dick in my bed?

Sticky> Griffin, GA Spunky.

Spunky> No fucking way! I'm 10 minutes from you. Wanna hook up?

BlkDaddy> What else are you gonna keep in your bed?

Hung9> You bi, Sticky?

Sticky> That's for me to know, ho.

Sticky> Yeah, I could go for that, Spunky. E-me a pic & your phone.

Spunky> k

Sticky> Well my page is refreshing about every 2 minutes or so.

<Coco has entered Chuck Chat>

Coco> Hi, all.

Big1> Hi, Co.

Hung9> Hey, Coco. S'up?

Coco> Nothing here, girls. Where's Chuck? Why are we looking at his cat?

Big1> We guess he stepped out for a while.

Hung9> Close all your other windows, Sticky. It'll run faster if you haven't got 4 javacams running at once.

BlkDaddy> Meanwhile, some people here like looking at pussy.

BlkDaddy> Ain't that right, Sticky?

Coco> When's he going to be back?

Sticky> Eat me, Blk.

Big1> No telling. Maybe he won't show up.

Coco> How could he do that? His homepage says 6 to 12.

Coco> Where could he be?

BlkDaddy> I think I'd rather have you eat me, Sticky. You like dark meat?

Hung9> Don't get all worked up, Co.

Spunky> Yeah, your mascara'll run.

Sticky> When there's lots of it, Blk. Tonight, it's about quantity.

Sticky> Nice pic, Spunky. I'll call.

Spunky> Kewl.

BlkDaddy> I've got quantity AND quality.

Hung9> Hey, guys, true love's blossoming at Chuck Chat.

Big1> Spunky must have it going on in the meat department.

Big1> Hey, Spunk, how big?

<NJmuscle has entered Chuck Chat>

Coco> Well, I'm not going to hang around all night and watch some freakin' cat.

NJmuscle> No sign of the Chuckster?

NJmuscle> The Chuckmeister?

NJmuscle> Chuck-o-rama?

Hung9> WE GET IT.

Big1> No sign, NJ.

Coco> I want to see Chuck! Where is he?

BlkDaddy> This ain't Dionne and the Psychic Friends, Coco.

BlkDaddy> If we knew where he was, we'd have told you five minutes ago when you blew in.

NJmuscle> If you're that horned up, go see Chad—he's raging right now.

Coco> What's that address?

Spunky> All right guys, next time you hear from me, I'll be going down on Sticky.

NJmuscle> www.seechadlive.com

Big1> Give us the play by play, Spunk.

Big1> Or the blow by blow.

Big1> };>)

Coco> I'm out of here.

Hung9> LOL, Big1.
Hung9> I'm with you Co. I'm gonna see who's at the Spike.
Hung9> Later.
Sticky> Thanks, Hung. It's refreshing a lot faster now. C ya.

<Coco has left Chuck Chat>
<Hung9 has left Chuck Chat>

Big1> Thanx, NJ. She was starting to get on my nerves.
NJmuscle> No problem. She's kinda messy that way.
NJmuscle> How long's Chuck been away?
Big1> At least 20 minutes.
BlkDaddy> More like 30.
Sticky> I've been here for 45 minutes and no show, but there was a blur on the first pic that came up. It could have been him leaving.
BlkDaddy> Since then, Sticky's been jacking off watching Chuck's cat.
Big1> You guys be nice.
Sticky> Hey! Speak of the devil!
Big1> Heeeeere's Chuck!
NJmuscle> Nice pic, Chuck.
BlkDaddy> He's not on chat, NJ.
NJmuscle> Well, nice pic anyway.
BlkDaddy> Nice dick is more like it.
Sticky> Worth the wait!
Sticky> I like the beer bottle. Good prop.
Big1> Someone DID go out with the boys tonight! ;-)
Sticky> Very nice.
Sticky> I love a good fat fire helmet cockhead. I could suck juice out of that all night.
BlkDaddy> If your g-friend isn't around, you mean.
BlkDaddy> Right, Sticky?
Big1> Nice nuts, too.
Big1> I don't ordinarily like it when guys shave their balls, but this guy looks good.
Sticky> She doesn't like the way cum tastes. She prefers to lick my nipples and my nuts.
Big 1> They're tight—it's either really cold or he's gonna cum any second.
NJmuscle> I'd spread my furry little cheeks for that dick any day, man. Ride it like a fucking pogo stick.
NJmuscle> He wouldn't even have to do any of the work. I'd ride it 'till he came.
NJmuscle> Milk it all out.
BlkDaddy> You like to ride cock, NJ?
BlkDaddy> 'Cause I got a big ol' horsecock for you.
BlkDaddy> You want some fat black dick?

NJmuscle> Love it, man. Send me a pic.

BlkDaddy> K.

Big1> Is he gonna sit on that bottle or what?

Sticky> I hope so.

Sticky> I like the way he takes a sip & lets it dribble down his chest.

Sticky> His pubes probably smell like Budweiser.

BlkDaddy> Mmm. Nothing like beer on a man's dick to get me hard.

NJmuscle> You up, Blk?

Big1> Jackin' off, Blk?

Big1> You should have your own webcam.

BlkDaddy> Up & strokin'.

BlkDaddy> I sent you a pic, NJ.

NJmuscle> Thx.

Big1> Let us know how it is, NJ!

Big1> Shit! Chuck's got a sweet ass!

Sticky> I'd fall off the bed if I got my legs up that high.

BlkDaddy> I'd hold you in place, Sticky. With my dick.

NJmuscle> Nice pic, Blk. Got any movies?

BlkDaddy> Maybe for you...

Sticky> Thanks, Blk, but I'm a top. Nothing I like more than an ass like Chuck's wrapped around my dick.

Big1> You guys all beatin' off?

NJmuscle> Up & running, Big1.

BlkDaddy> You know it.

Sticky> Yup. Up & waiting for Spunky to get here.

Big1> Tell me what you're doin', NJ.

NJmuscle> I got my ass on the edge of the chair, and I'm rubbing back and forth.

NJmuscle> Feels like a guy brushing his cock against my ass before he fucks me.

Big1> Hot! I'd like to spank your hole with my cock, man.

Big1> Hold you up like Chuck & slide it in, lubed up.

Sticky> Hey, you guys are missing a good show.

Sticky> Looks like Chuck's gonna fuck himself with that bottle.

BlkDaddy> He doesn't need to waste a good fuck on a bottle.

BlkDaddy> I'll take care of him myself.

Sticky> Finally—Spunky's here. Maybe I'll be back.

Sticky> I'll probably need both hands.

NJmuscle> Well, someone's gonna get lucky.

Big1> We've still got Chuck.

Big1> Man, I want inside that ass of his.

NJmuscle> You could fuck me instead, Big.

Big1> Love to, but BlkDaddy's first in line, right?

BlkDaddy> We can share.

NJmuscle> I can take both of you on.

Big1> We could recruit Chuck & make it an even 4-way.

Big1> Fuck, I'm so close to cumming.

Big1> The thought of fucking you NJ while you're sucking on BlkDaddy's dick.

BlkDaddy> Mmm. I'd fuck his mouth with my fat dick.

BlkDaddy> Pull out & spank his face with it, getting spit on his cheeks.

BlkDaddy> Force him down on my balls.

NJmuscle> No forcing needed, Blk. I'd lick your nuts 'till they were all wet.

NJmuscle> And I wouldn't miss a stroke, Big. You'd fuck me all along.

Big1> Damn right I would.

Big1> And I bet you'd like it more than Chuck likes that beer bottle.

NJmuscle> I dunno—he looks like he enjoys it a lot.

NJmuscle> He's almost got the whole thing in his ass.

Big1> I'd throw a fuck into him like Babe-fucking-Ruth drivin' it home.

BlkDaddy> Hey, who's that?

NJmuscle> Chuck's friend? Boyfriend?

Big1> Chuck looks surprised.

Big1> I don't think Chuck has a boyfriend.

BlkDaddy> Whoa! Chuck sure sat up fast. Mr. Stranger looks underwhelmed.

NJmuscle> Could be his brother.

Big1> His FAQ says he's an only child.

NJmuscle> Neighbor, then. Doesn't matter.

Big1> Where's the bottle?

BlkDaddy> In his hand.

BlkDaddy> The left one.

Big1> oic

Big1> Well, that's an odd position.

NJmuscle> Is it just me or is he bending over?

BlkDaddy> All I see is ass.

NJmuscle> Is he showing off the goods?

NJmuscle> Looks like he wants the guy to fuck him.

Big1> Yup, that's what it looks like to me.

BlkDaddy> Well, stranger's getting a good view.

Big1> Hey! Stranger's hung, too.

NJmuscle> I'll say. Nice meat!

NJmuscle> Looks like there's gonna be a whole lotta fuckin' going on.

BlkDaddy> Slide it in! Fuck the shit out of him!

Big1> I'd do the same.

NJmuscle> My ass is twitching at the thought of it.

BlkDaddy> You save that ass for me & Big, NJ.

NJmuscle> There's plenty to go around.

NJmuscle> I can fuck for days.

NJmuscle> I'd suck your nuts dry, Blk.

BlkDaddy> Not before I fucked the shit out of that ass, doggy-style NJ. I'd get right up to it and put just the head in.

Big1> I'd get below you Blk. NJ'd be suckin' on my dick while I licked your studly balls, man.

Big1> I'd suck 'em while you fucked him 'till my face was covered in lube & spit.

Big1> It'd be dripping on me, I'd smell like dick & ass.

BlkDaddy> And I'd be fucking NJ like this guy's giving it to Chuck.

NJmuscle> Chuck seems like he's having a good time.

Big1> Wouldn't you with that piece of meat?

NJmuscle> I'd do more than just lay there like Chuck's doing.

NJMuscle> I'd lay him down and sit on it.

BlkDaddy> You mean lay ME down, right?

NJmuscle> You got it, Blk. I'd lay you down and swallow every inch of that dick with my ass.

Big1> I'd be standing next to ya', NJ.

Big1> You'd be getting my cock down your throat and his up your hole.

Big1> I'd hold your ears & fuck your face.

NJmuscle> And I'd be bouncing up & down on Blk's dick.

NJmuscle> Rubbing his nuts, pulling on 'em.

NJmuscle> Trying to get more of him inside me.

BlkDaddy> I'd be fucking you so deep, you wouldn't need anymore, boy.

Big1> That's tellin' him, Blk. Fuck the little dumbass.

BlkDaddy> You want more dick, NJ? Sit on this, motherfucker.

NJmuscle> Shit, I can feel it in my stomach, man. Fuck me hard.

BlkDaddy> I'm throwing you off my dick, boy.

NJmuscle> No, I want more!

BlkDaddy> Shut the fuck up, boy! You're gonna get more than you can take. On your stomach!

NJmuscle> Yessir!

BlkDaddy> Spread those legs, son!

Big1> Give it to him.

NJmuscle> They're spread, sir!

BlkDaddy> Sit in front of him, Big.

BlkDaddy> Hold his arms.

BlkDaddy> Force him down on your cock.

Big1> Suck it, man.

Big1> Eat my dick.

BlkDaddy> Don't let him touch his horny little prick.

BlkDaddy> He's not cumming 'till we're through.

NJmuscle> You're in charge, sirs. I'll do whatever you want.

Big1> I want you to shut up & finish spit-shining my dick, dumbass.

NJmuscle> Yessir!

BlkDaddy> Alright, my cock's at your hole. I don't want to see you flinch when I put it in.

NJmuscle> No sir!

BlkDaddy> Alright, there's the head.

NJmuscle> Mmm. Feels good sir.

BlkDaddy> Shut up, boy. I'm not finished, yet. Here's another inch.

NJmuscle> Yessir. Thank you sir.

BlkDaddy> You want another?

NJmuscle> Please!

BlkDaddy> What's that, son?!

NJmuscle> Yessir, I would love another inch of your beautiful cock up my ass.

BlkDaddy> That's what I want to hear.

BlkDaddy> Shut him up, Big. Choke him on your dick.

Big1> Eat it, boy. Take it all the way down to my nuts!

NJmuscle> Mmm.

BlkDaddy> That's all I wanna hear from you boy.

BlkDaddy> You want more of this dick? Grunt for me if you want it.

NJmuscle> Unh!

Big1> Slip it to him, Blk.

BlkDaddy> Good. I'm gonna give it all to you. Here goes-

BlkDaddy> Aaaaah! What a fucking sweet ass!

Big1> Man, I love to watch you fuck some ass.

Big1> Big black cock sliding in and out of his whiteboy ass.

Big1> Show him how to fuck.

BlkDaddy> You got my balls to churning, boy. You want a load up your hole? Grunt for me.

NJmuscle> Unh!

BlkDaddy> Alright, boy, hold on. I want you to fuck his face while I cum, Big.

Big1> I'm ramming my dick down his throat, man. He's a cock-hungry little fuck. He's gagging on my meat, but I'm holding him down.

BlkDaddy> Fuck, man. Watching him lick that pretty dick of yours is gonna make me shoot. Here I go, boys.

Big1> Shoot him full of cum, man.

BlkDaddy> Oh, fuck man, fuck!

BlkDaddy> I'm gonna blow like a geyser! Shit!

Big1> You want some on your tongue, too, boy?

Big1> I'm gonna hose you down!

Big1> Eat my dick, man! Eat that cum! Fuck!

BlkDaddy> Load those tonsils up with jizz, Big. Make him choke on that shit! Don't you lose a drop, NJ!

NJmuscle> Nnnh-nnhh!

BlkDaddy> Damn, that's some sweet motherfuckin' ass. You liked that didn't you, boy?

NJmuscle> Yessir. I loved it.

BlkDaddy> Well, now it's time for us to service you. Roll over.

BlkDaddy> Kiss him Big1. Clean that jizz out of his mouth.

BlkDaddy> Spread your legs, boy. I'm gonna clean up that ass of yours.

Big1> Nothing like the taste of my own spunk...

NJmuscle> Oh, shit! Lick my ass, man. Just your tongue on my hole is going to send me over. Shit!

BlkDaddy> Shoot it in my mouth while I finger your ass. Give it to me!

NJmuscle> Yessir. Here you are, sir. Drink my cum, sir! Oh, sir, suck the head of my dick, please! Fuck, sir! I'm cumming!

BlkDaddy> Give it all to me, boy. Don't spill it!

NJmuscle> Oh, sir, eat me!

BlkDaddy> Mmmm. Your cum tastes sweet, boy. Good work.

Big1> I'll say.

NJmuscle> And clean, too. My sheets aren't stained at all.

BlkDaddy> Alright, hombres. I'm gonna go clean up this lake of spunk that's drying on my belly. Catch y'all later—maybe Thursday.

Big1> C ya, Blk.

NJmuscle> See ya, and thanks for the load.

BlkDaddy> My pleasure...

<BlkDaddy has left Chuck Chat>

Big1> Hey, perfect timing. That new guy's just getting off.

NJmuscle> Man, Chuck's ass is red from the fucking he's gotten.

Big1> Well, look at that dick! I mean, it took some effort to take that for as long as he has.

NJmuscle> You're right. Way to go, Chuck! You've got chutzpah!

Big1> I think he just knows a good dick when he sees one.

NJmuscle> Well, the stranger's thirsty.

Big1> I hope he knows where that beer bottle's been!

NJmuscle> When he walked in, it was halfway up Chuck's butt. I think he's got a pretty good idea.

Big1> Maybe. Thanks for the fuck, by the way.

NJmuscle> You're welcome. Anytime.

Big1> Which part of Jersey are you in anyway?

NJmuscle> Jersey City. Where are you?

Big1> Not far—Brooklyn.

NJmuscle> We should get together for some real fucking.

Big1> Sounds good to me.

Big1> Shit!

NJmuscle> Am I seeing what you're seeing?

Big1> I think so.

NJmuscle> Is this real?

Big1> Well, unless he works for a theatre company that stocks breakaway glass, that's a very real beer bottle being shattered on his very real head.

NJmuscle> Fuck, man! We're total witnesses.

Big1> Uh, yeah.

NJmuscle> I think this is a put on.

Big1> Doesn't look like it to me.

Big1> I mean, if it were fake, they'd have staged it better—not off to the side like it is now.

NJmuscle> Well...

Big1> And to top it off, that stranger's going through Chuck's drawers.

NJmuscle> OK, I'll buy that.

Big1> We've just witnessed assault, battery, and now robbery.

NJmuscle> And if this guy really broke in, we might have been watching a rape, too.

Big1> You're right.

NJmuscle> You think it's a break-in?

Big1> Either that or a trick gone very wrong. Could be someone he hooked up with online.

NJmuscle> Yikes. So what do we do?

Big1> I dunno. We're sort of accessories if we don't report it.

NJmuscle> Yeah, but we don't have pics of the guy or anything. How could we be expected to know him in a lineup?

NJmuscle> "Pull out your dicks, guys." I can see it now.

Big1> We could pull up the last 10 pics. One would have a face pic.

NJmuscle> We could...

Big1> Let's see if Chuck moves...

NJmuscle> K...

Big1>...

NJmuscle>...

Big1> Well, the stranger's gone.

NJmuscle> Is that his hand moving?

Big1> I think it's probably the wind.

Big1> I take that back. It's his cat. See the tail by the curtain.

NJmuscle> Yeah.

NJmuscle> Well, at least he's got company.

NJmuscle> He'll probably be okay.

Big1> Maybe...

NJmuscle> Yeah, I'm sure he'll be fine.

Big1> Well...

NJmuscle> So when do you wanna meet?

Big1> Mmmm...how about Wednesday? Wanna meet in the city?

NJmuscle> Sure. How about the Big Cup. 7:00?

Big1> K. I'm kinda tan with short brown hair and a little goatee. I'll be wearing a wifebeater and baggy jeans.

NJmuscle> I'm blonde, muscular, with a tattoo of barbed wire around my left bicep. I'll wear a wifebeater, too, and some Adidas shorts.

Big1> K. See you Wednesday @ 7:00.

NJmuscle> Cool. I'll be lubed & ready.

Big1> Bye.
NJmuscle> C ya.

\<NJmuscle has left Chuck Chat\>
\<Big1 has left Chuck Chat\>

THE GERMANS DON'T FOOL AROUND
by Jay Starre

I had found exactly what I was looking for. To both my horror and my delight, I discovered that the Germans don't fool around. They take their sex seriously. Chaps, boots and black aviator caps, all in black leather, are their uniform, sadism and masochism second nature to some of them. The three I met on a rainy spring afternoon proved this to me without a doubt.

On a visit to San Francisco, I struck up a conversation with the lean, goateed Willi on the street. When I told him I was a porn writer, his reaction was common. He wanted to tell me all about his experiences so I could write about them. I had heard a lot of hot and weird shit that way. But as we found a quiet spot and he began to spill his guts, I conjured up a wild idea of my own.

"Do you think I could watch you? You know, while you're getting into an s/m scene?" I asked.

"You want to see some real hard core action? Come on over to my place. I have two German tops arriving at three o'clock. They're the best," Willi had grinned, his bright teeth flashing.

He was a good-looking dude, dressed up in leather jacket and tight jeans, black leather cap and vest to match. He was definitely hot, with wispy blond hair, a pale blond mustache and sparkling blue eyes, to my mind typically German. I sprang a hard-on just imagining Willi under the power of a pair of leather tops.

We had gone to Willi's place and I had hidden in the closet.

Willi warned me beforehand. "These guys are German like me. They're from Berlin and they are serious with their play. Don't let on you're here. No telling what they will do if they catch you. And I'll suffer the consequences as well. They don't like surprises. Everything has to be under their control."

Before I knew it, I was ensconced in a closet watching the hottest s/m scene unfold I had ever personally witnessed.

Willi was strapped to a bondage table, a low padded bench with restraints that cuffed both wrists. Willi's thighs were splayed wide apart at one end leaving his bare ass exposed. That ass was receiving a furious paddling at the hands of one of the two brutes who stood behind him. The blond studs were taking turns either laughing or taunting their victim.

"Little Willi wants his ass beat? Little Willi gets his ass beat! How is Little Willi's ass doing? Is it hot enough yet for a good butthole workout? Is Little Willi's hot hole quivering and hungry for a dick, or a dildo, or a big fist?"

I was breathing so heavily behind the closet doors, I feared they would hear me and find me out. I tried as best I could to stifle my excited gasps as I gawked at the incredible scene. And I had an excellent view. Earlier Willi had removed a slat from one of the doors while I had crouched behind it all eyes and ears. I heard every guttural growl and lewd suggestion the two Germans spewed out over their bound captive.

I also heard the resounding smack of leather against Willi's widespread buttcheeks. Willi had a very sweet ivory pale ass. Although he himself was lean and muscular, his ass was round and full. At that moment it was flushed pink from the pounding it was taking.

I held my breath and squeezed my hard cock as I tried to remain as quiet as possible while I watched Willi getting his ass worked over. I had stripped off my pants and underwear while waiting for the tops to arrive, and at that point I knelt on the carpet mostly naked. Clothing hung around my shoulders while I peered out into the brightly lit bedroom at the hot scene unfolding

The two men had arrived in their leather gear earlier, discarding all but chaps, vests and caps immediately. Tall and blond, both looked to be in their early forties. With stubbled beards and tight mouths, their ice blue eyes sent shivers up and down my spine. They had growled at Willi to get on the bench the minute they arrived. Guttural German added to the harsh thrill of the scene as they barked their orders viciously in both languages, and somewhat arbitrarily it seemed to me. But it was their scene, and I was just a sneaky spy in the closet, so I couldn't complain. They slapped Willi harshly on the side of the head when he failed to move swiftly enough.

"*Achtung!*" one of them shouted in Willi's ear as he dragged him to the bench by the hair. That one had then strapped Willi to the bench and then shoved a bandana in his mouth and tied it around his head, effectively gagging him. The other had removed a leather paddle from a big duffel bag they had brought.

This dude, thicker and more muscular than the other, with a tattoo snaking across one large biceps, employed the paddle with real relish. The other rummaged around in the bag until he found what he was searching for. He produced an enema bag and bottle.

"We'll clean out the slut's hole before we stuff it full," he said in his brutally accented English.

"Excellent idea, Karl," the paddle-wielding one laughed evilly.

I was all eyes as they shoved the lubed end of the enema tube up between Willi's parted asscheeks. I had a perfect view of that ass as the tube began to fill with water from the bag. Willi bucked on the bondage table, lifting his ass and groaning even more loudly than he had when he was getting paddled.

Willi's buttcrack was pristine clean, and shaved smooth like some kind of satin ivory. Contrasting that pale flesh, he wore a pair of gleaming black leather chaps like the other Germans, exposing his sweet available ass. He wore a pair of heavy black boots and he had donned a studded black harness across his chest before the tops had arrived. Surrounded by and encased in black leather, he writhed moaning on the bench as his ass filled with warm water.

"Willi likes that, don't you think Hans? He loves his ass filled to the limit. He's got quite the hungry hole!"

They both laughed and slapped Willi's naked butt, the big mounds jiggling and quivering with tension. They shouted "*Achtung!*" several times and laughed as they slapped Willi's ass with gloved hands. Meanwhile Willi raised his hips in the air in an attempt to alleviate the pressure on his stomach from the water filling his asshole. I inhaled sharply in empathy, conjuring up sensations of my own stomach distending and aching along with Willi's.

The two hot Germans hooted as they continued to fill Willi's guts with another bag of water. Some of it squished out of Willi's lubed hole as he tried to contain the copious amount of fluid within his distended insides. The men laughed some more as they poked and pinched Willi's writhing buttcheeks. Then they finally removed the enema tube and stood back to survey their handiwork.

Willi was straining in his bonds, sweat beaded on his forehead. His back was arched, his ass up in the air, his small asshole palpitating furiously, a dribble of liquid leaking out of it. It was obvious he was having trouble restraining himself from letting go and spraying his own carpet with a load of liquid ass juices.

The two leather studs relented eventually and released Willi. He ran to the bathroom and squatted over the seat, emptying his belly with a groan. I could see it all through the open bathroom door. The two Germans had followed and were gripping Willi's short wispy hair with their gloved fingers. Their taunts continued.

"Is the slut cleaned out? Is your hole ready for some more action?" they said, then barked out some German garble that sounded rough, brutal and sexy before continuing in English. "Get on the table again boy, on your back this time and spread your legs. Your butthole is getting drilled," Hans ordered, dragging Willi off the toilet and into the bedroom by his hair.

Willi stumbled to the bondage table, his cock bobbing in front of him, hard and drooling. I could tell he was appreciating the rough treatment. I wondered if I would feel the same. My cock was certainly stiff just from watching.

Hans shoved Willi on his back over the table. He then quickly and efficiently tied Willi's hands together over his head with leather strips to a ring in the head of the bondage table. Then he sat down on Willi's chest, his big naked ass settling down to pin Willi to the bench. He gripped both of Willi's chap-clad thighs in his arms and pulled them wide apart and back toward his chest. That exposed the young German's red-striped asscheeks to full view.

Hans then snarled something to Karl in German.

Karl was quick to obey the apparent command, rummaging in the duffel bag and producing a huge floppy dildo, flesh-colored and monstrous. My asshole twitched at the sight of that giant piece of rubber. It was a two-headed thing, over two feet long. Poor Willi I thought.

Karl knelt between Willi's thighs and held the dildo there while offering Hans a can of grease he had also produced from that duffel bag full of toys. Hans had both arms down between Willi's legs, his biceps bulging, as he scooped out a generous amount of pale grease and then immediately began to rub it all over Willi's hairless crack. He took his time, his leather gloved fingers spreading the grease all around Willi's pouting asshole, teasing it apart with two fingers of the other hand. Then he began to pack the hole with grease, shoving those two fingers into it, scooping out more from the can and then packing more into the hot, gaping orifice. I couldn't see Willi's face, but from the contortions of his ass, writing beneath the bulk of Hans' weight, I could tell he was feeling that.

"*Ja*, now is the time to fill the little slut with rubber dick. Shove it up his ass! Hans growled to Karl.

Karl lifted the flopping dildo and pointed the head at Willi's dripping butthole. Hans spread the buttlips apart with his fingers and grinned wickedly as Karl took aim and then abruptly shoved with all his might. A good six inches rammed up Willi's greased anus.

A muffled shriek, "*Nein!*" could be heard beneath Hans' big ass, which had gone back to settle over Willi's chin. That huge dildo must have battered Willi's poor prostrate something fierce. My own hole twitched with sympathy again and I shuddered where I hid on my knees behind the closet doors.

"Fuck him with it. Let him feel that big thing up his hungry asshole," Hans ordered, his eyes focussed on the sight of Willi's straining anus as it palpitated around the shaft of the dildo.

Karl's muscular arms tensed as he began to fuck their captive's ass with the rubber cock. Squishy slurps filled the room as the dildo slid in and out rapidly, each time a bit deeper as Willi's booted feet kicked and shook in the air. Grease oozed out of the violated hole, dripping down to pool on the leather bondage bench.

They continued their lewd play to the muffled caterwauling of their captive, Hans urging on his partner Karl as he pumped the dildo in and out of Willi's ass. His legs finally collapsed to relax in Han's powerful grip. It was then that Hans decided it was time to move on.

"We will fuck him before we fist him," Hans grinned at his partner, his blue eyes cold and piercing.

Where I hid in the closet I felt as if Hans had stared right at me and I shuddered with dread. I had wanted to see what s/m was all about, but now that I was witnessing the brutal manner in which the two tops dealt with poor Willi, I was a bit frightened. It was then that something fell on me from a hanger above. It fell on my lap and I picked it up, in the darkness barely able to figure out what it was. It was a studded leather collar, one that would fit around Willi's neck, or mine. I lifted it to my nose and inhaled the scent of leather, and the reek of sweat that lingered there.

Just at that moment the closet door flew open. Shouts in German accompanied strong hands that dragged me out into the light of the bedroom. I momentarily freaked out with fear, staring up at the two brutal, blond tops that hovered over me, their fists clenched, their eyes burrowing into mine.

"Put the collar on, slave. Do it, now!"

I finally realized what they were shouting at me. I still had the collar in my hands. Amazingly enough I hadn't dropped it in my embarrassment at being caught spying on the leather scene. With trembling hands I obeyed, not entirely believing this was happening to me. As the collar snapped around my neck, I shuddered involuntarily, my cock leaping up of its own accord.

"Look at the little pup. He's got a hard cock! We will see what he is made of," Hans was growling above me.

I felt my shirt being torn from my body, literally. The material ripped in shreds as the two Germans pulled me forward until I was crouched just before the sprawled Willi. The victimized German was still lying on the bondage bench, his thighs apart, the big dildo hanging lewdly from his butthole. His hands were tied above his head to the back of the bench and he could not rise up, but his head was craned upwards and his eyes were wide open as he stared helplessly at me.

I didn't say a word, too shocked to offer any resistance. I was all too aware of my own hard cock as Hans held me by the shoulders and Karl moved in front of me. I looked up at him. He was leering at me, and appraising my muscular build. In his hands he held two painful looking tit clamps. It was at that moment I consciously decided to go along with the bizarre scene. I knew this wasn't going to continue with me there, unless I participated. I could have gotten up and walked out. But I didn't. It was just too hot. Those German were studs, and I wanted sex with them, s/m or not.

Karl's eyes were on me. Small and ice blue. It almost seemed as if he was reading my mind. Then he reached down and fastened the tit clamps to the end of both my nipples.

I cried out, in fact I practically screamed as the electric sensations bombarded my tender nipples. The clamps were viciously biting into my flesh, and Karl yanked on the two attached chains. Almost immediately I was shoved forward and my legs kicked apart so I was on my knees and leaning into Willi's greased buttcheeks.

A loud smack resounded in the bedroom and I blurted out another scream. I had been struck from behind by the same paddle they had been using on Willi. As another blow landed on my bare buttcheeks, Karl yanked on the chains attached to my nipples. The twin sensations were dizzying in their intensity and I groaned as I collapsed on top of Willi's crotch.

But that was not to last. "Suck that dildo. Get it between your sweet little lips, boy," Hans barked behind me as he laid another resounding smack on my shivering buttocks.

I obeyed without thinking. It had all happened so swiftly my head was spinning and I could think of nothing but the fact that my body was in agony, yet my cock was hard and burning with a fierce lust. I spread my own thighs and lifted my ass to take the blows more easily, then dropped my head down and searched for the dangling end of the dildo protruding from Willi's hole.

The head of it filled my mouth as I opened wide and swallowed it. It tasted like rubber and grease. It stunk like sweat and ass. I gagged on it as my nipples were torn forward and my butt was pounded from behind. I stared at Willi's ass, flaming with red stripes. His asshole quivered right in front of me with the dildo impaling it a good ten inches or more.

"*Ja*, that's it. That's a good boy. Swallow that big dildo," Hans growled into my ear. The big German had taken the tit clamps from Karl and was tugging mercilessly on the chains that tore at my tender tits. His breath was hot and he smelled like a man, the stench of ripe armpits and a dripping cock invading my nostrils. I snorted and nearly choked as the dildo slid into my throat.

I had forgotten about my own hands until they were gripped from behind and clamped in leather cuffs and then clamped together tightly against the small of my back. I was now helpless. I groaned, nearly sobbing with the power of my emotion. My cock seemed so hard I thought it would burst. I had never been so excited or horny in my life.

"Get up, slave!" Hans shouted at me.

I realized the paddling had ceased. My ass was on fire, but thankfully not being pounded any more by the leather weapon. The flesh on my buttcheeks felt as if they were in flames, and my asshole throbbed in time to the tugging Hans continued with on my battered chest. But I managed to stumble to my feet as ordered, spitting the dildo out of my mouth and gasping for breath.

"Turn around. Bend over. Your turn to take that dildo up your ass. Let's see if you are as much of a pussy as Willi here." Hans was staring into my face, then he laughed and spit directly in my mouth before whipping me around and forcing me to bend over.

I felt fingers prying into my parted ass from behind. I groaned as a leather-clad hand began to force grease into my asshole. I was packed with it, just as Will had been earlier. Two blunt fingers crammed the grease beyond my gripping ass rim and then added more until I felt like I was swimming in the stuff.

But I appreciated all that lube as I felt the thick head of the dildo begin to penetrate my butthole. I gritted my teeth and willed my ass to open up, shuddering with the effort. Two harsh yanks on the nipple chains were enough to have me lunge backwards and impale myself fully on the fat rubber cock. I heard my own shriek.

My wail of desperate denial rang out as my ass was shoved backwards. The formerly tight hole expanded and throbbed over fat rubber. It stretched me painfully but seemed to make my cock even harder at the same time. Karl had taken the tit clamps and was in front of me. He ripped at the chains attached to my nipples and I shook between the two seats of agony and ecstasy. My chest strained forward, my body held up by Hans' arms around my waist, forcing my ass backwards onto the fake cock that invaded me without mercy.

In the fog of my own shouts, I heard Willi's muffled protests from behind me. The gag over his mouth prevented him from speaking, but I knew what he was feeling. All the shoving of my hips backwards was forcing more of that dildo up Willi's guts. There wasn't much I could do about that, and to tell the truth, I did not care at that moment. My only concern was my own agony as that giant dildo stretched me wide open. It had begun to rub the tender flesh of my asslips as Hans shoved me back and forth over the length of it with his arms wrapped around my waist. The giant Hun was powerful, his sweaty arms like pythons around my torso and waist.

My hands were bound behind my back, my body held by the giant German, and I inhaled the reek of sex all around me. At that moment the laughing Karl rammed his own hard cock between my moaning lips. The taste was heady, leaking pre-cum and salty sweat mixed together. I licked avidly, gurgling over the meat in an effort to take my mind off my burning nipples, flaming buttcheeks, and aching asshole.

All those conflicting emotions and sensations suddenly became too powerful. I felt my ass sliding up against the greasy buttocks of my fellow victim and realized the dildo was entirely buried between our shared assholes. The thought drove me over the edge. With a mouth full of cock, I whimpered out my surrender as my body suddenly exploded in a fiery orgasm. It was not just my cock. My prostate throbbed, my asshole clenched and pulsed, my balls tightened and my guts churned as a load of jizz rocketed up the shaft of my cock and sprayed outward, all over Karl's chaps in front of me.

"*Ja' wohl!*" Karl shouted out gleefully. "The big slut is shooting his load with a cock in his mouth and a dildo up his butt."

My head was swimming as my body contorted in the throes of orgasm. The pain was there, surrounding me, but it was so intense I could not distinguish it from the pleasure of my ejaculation. But then I was being moved. I felt the leather gloves on my skin as Hans' powerful hands pulled me upright. The cock slipped from my mouth, and the dildo from my sloppy ass.

I felt fingers probing along my crack and into my stretched hole.

"Nice ass, hard and muscular. We will have some fun with this." Hans was laughing as he fingered my trembling ass.

They weren't through with me! Oh course not, just because I had cum. They wouldn't give a shit about that. I shuddered as I inhaled Hans' particular odor. It was different than Karl's, more rank yet bittersweet too. His scent was some kind of powerful cologne that wafted into my nostrils as I was bodily lifted and then draped over Willi's bound body. Our eyes met. Willi had beautiful eyes, now wet with tears as he winced with painful pleasure. The cruel pressure of the dildo rammed far up Willi's ass and the tit clamps on my nipples pressed into his own tender chest. My entire body weight crushed him from above. My sticky jizz-dripping cock flopped between Willi's hard meat as our thighs were entwined.

"Now we will see what their sweet little assholes are capable of," Hans remarked from behind. "Pull the dildo out, Karl," he ordered.

I was still staring into Willi's eyes as that dildo was unceremoniously ripped from his guts. They grew wide and startled.

"*Ja*, look at that hole drip grease. Both slots are hot, gaping wet and hungry!" Karl laughed from behind us.

We were spread-eagled over the bondage bench, my naked body over the chaps-clad Willi. Our asses were exposed and vulnerable. We were both bound and helpless. We both realized that and knew that whatever the big Germans planned to do, we would have to accept. The thought had my stomach churning. What would they do to my too accessible butthole? Would they beat me again, or would they fuck me, or would they shove some other large instrument up my poor asshole?

I was able just to see Karl and Hans from the corner of my eyes. Karl got on his knees behind us. Hans stood over him and placed his hands on Karl's big shoulders. They were both grinning. "First you, Karl," Hans said.

I didn't know what they were talking about, until I felt gloved fingers beginning to ply at my violated butthole again. Two blunt fingers slid inside me. At the same time I was sure two others were sliding up Willi's asshole.

"That's it, finger them both. Get them wide open for my fist," Hans ordered.

I stared into Willi's wide eyes as we both felt fingers probing our assholes. Two were three, then four. I slumped on top of Willi, my entire being focussed on the fingers opening me up from behind. My cock had gone limp from the powerful orgasm I had experienced. My body was on fire, but the pain was only a throbbing second thought as I concentrated on willing my asshole to accept the four fingers rubbing and prodding into my guts. My assrim stretched and ached, but also felt strangely stimulated. Every time the four fingers went a little deeper I actually started raising my ass to let them in. That was the first time I'd had four fingers all the way up my butt, and I was amazed. Karl was good, pushing with just enough force to stretch me and maintain a steady aching pleasure. I was mewling. I was loving it!

"Perfect. We've got the hole now! He's ripe for my fist. Get out of there," Hans ordered. I felt the fingers slide from my throbbing butthole. I shuddered, the sensation of emptiness almost ore painful than the presence of that big hand stretching me apart. But that only lasted a moment as Hans replaced Karl on his knees between our spread asscheeks. Fingers once more began to invade my hole.

"Add some more grease. We want these little pigs nice and slippery as we fist them," Hans growled.

I was really going to get fisted. For one second I almost freaked out and shouted for them to stop. But then I felt more grease being stuffed up my ass. The pleasure of that slippery lube and those big fingers sliding in and out of my asshole robbed me of my will to resist. Willi's slippery body beneath me writhed and bucked as he too was fingered full of grease. Hans worked a big hand into both our assholes. Lube coated his gloved fingers as he inserted four then began to add a thumb.

I shuddered and groaned as that thumb began to penetrate my already tautly stretched asshole. My body was on fire from the intense stimulus. But strangely, as the thumb slid into me and then the wide part of the hand, I succumbed to a totally different emotion. The thought of that powerful fist on the verge of impaling me from behind was overwhelming. The Germans laughing taunts, and Willi's squirming all combined to rock me into an altered state. My asshole gaped open. Hans fist slid inside.

"They're both opening up. My fists are going in. What a pair of pigs!" Hans groaned.

I floated around the fist stuffed in my guts. It slid deeper. It plunged into me. My asshole throbbed around the beefy wrist that worked in and out in a pumping motion. I stared into Willi's wild eyes and then I dropped my mouth down and kissed him right through the slobber-soaked handkerchief gagging him. I began to hump backwards over the fist up my ass as I tongued and drooled over Willi's gag. I was in another world. But it only intensified.

"Punch them, Hans! The pigs can take it," Karl laughed wildly.

I gasped with the power of the sensation. A huge fist pulled out of my ass abruptly, then slammed back inside me. I cringed but then threw my thighs wide and sat back on the second punch, taking it fully inside and loving it.

"They're taking it. The pigs are getting punch-fucked and loving it," both men crowed together.

From behind, Hans was removing his gloved hand, grease splattering out of our two violated holes, then he was ramming it back in entirely, more grease squishing and oozing out of our gaping slots. It was unbelievable. I was totally open, and apparently so was Willi.

I pulled my mouth off Willi's. I turned my head to see what was going on behind me. Karl had knelt down beside Hans and reached into his crotch to take his thick hard-on in one gloved hand. He took his own in the other and began to whip them back and forth, grease coating both of them. As Hans howled and continued punch-fucking us, Karl whacked them both off furiously.

I suddenly felt Willi cumming beneath me, sticky cream leaking all over my stomach. My own cock was limp, unimportant now that my entire being was focussed on the giant fist pummeling my poor hungry butthole. I was reveling in it like a true pig, my asshole gaping wide open to take the ramming fist. I heard the others shouting out as they came, and my body seemed to experience an asshole orgasm, my will dissolving as my butthole became nothing more than a wide-open pit for Hans and Karl's gratification.

The fists were withdrawn. We were left bound and sweating, grease dribbling from our gaping holes, our bodies shaking with the aftermath or our orgasms.

I felt hands releasing my wrists.

Hans and Karl were laughing and moving around, packing up their bag.

"Thanks for the fun Willi. And you too Jay. We're glad you liked it," Hans growled out as the door shut behind them.

I rose and stared down at Willi. He was grinning through the handkerchief. I was an idiot! They had planned it all. They had conveniently "discovered" me in the closet. Hah.

But what the hell, it was an experience never to be forgotten. And hasn't been repeated so far. I had found out one thing for certain. The Germans don't fool around.

BONFIRE
by Max Reynolds

The screen spread before Drew, wide and white. From his seat in the second row he could see a large seam down the center where it had been repaired. He had made a similar repair himself on campus one night at a screening in the student lounge when an over-eager freshman had snapped the screen so hard it had torn almost in half. He remembered that freshman—not his name, but the way his face had colored at Drew's upperclassman displeasure and the way, when he had bent over to pick up the torn piece, his khaki's had outlined his ass with the linear perfection of paint-on-glass animation. Drew had turned away then as he wanted to do now, half-rising from his seat, then sitting again, almost defeated by the screen brightening to color.

Why was he here? It was three in the afternoon on a rainy Saturday in early November and the chill outside had crept into the theatre like a malevolent patron. He remembered a movie he had seen in his "Feminism on Film" class—*Variety*, about life at a porno theatre in Manhattan. He felt like a cheap stereotype, slunk in his seat in the last remaining men-on-men porn house in town.

All over campus signs met his gaze on an almost daily basis. When not advertising some queer event, they were lauding coming out dances and gay or lesbian or transgendered or bi-curious get-togethers. He should be at one of those, not in some sleazy theatre with cum-stained seats that smelled a little too strongly of disinfectant and not enough of popcorn. But Drew had what were commonly called "issues" and one of them was his place on campus. There were no queers in his fraternity, of that he was certain, and there had doubtless been none in that same fraternity when his older brother Scott had been there three years earlier or when his father had been there in the early 80s. Family tradition hadn't gotten him into Penn; that Ivy League benefit had come from hard work and an award-winning documentary in his senior year of high school that had been shown on PBS in his home town in upstate New York. But the fraternity pledge had come with strings and a price; that, he knew.

Tall, lean and just buff enough to have been used as a model at the local art school before he left home for college, Drew was no jock and never would be. He liked swimming, but team sports had failed him as bitterly as he had failed them. His nearly black hair, blue-green eyes and sleek hairlessness looked good in the water, but it didn't lure the girls like the hulking footballers or the sinewy soccer men. But then Drew hadn't cared; his only girlfriend had been the quirkily intellectual Lisa Loeb-alike, Diana, and she, like he, had been, he now knew, a closet case from that first freshman dance where they had met. She had come out to him right before their senior prom, sweetly teary-eyed and deeply apologetic. She was crazy about Alana, an inaccessible fellow senior she didn't have a prayer of wooing, because Alana, as Drew knew only too well, was nyphomaniacally attached to any dick she could get her hands on and those had been plenty. He came out to Diana that night, but couldn't bring himself to tell her about how Alana had felt him up outside the cafeteria after the last meeting of the Greek club she chaired and he attended.

Diana, good sport and great friend that she was, had dutifully visited Drew on campus at Penn. Her artfully slinky presence had led to knowing looks and jousting among his fraternity friends and deflected any attention that might have accrued from what Drew knew to be a hotly dangerous attachment to Jake, the frat's second-in-command and the would-be-lover that had led him to this ridiculous moment at the Bobcat Sinema.

Bobcat Sinema. Drew nearly laughed out loud. Not quite 21 and already a caricature. What would happen when he was 50, he suddenly wondered as he discreetly swiveled his head to see who else had entered the plush little room since the trailers had started.

On screen the action was beginning. *What was he seeing?* Right, *Soccer Boys.* Not much imagination in that title but then when it came to soccer, and Jake, the Fast Forward as he was called by the team, Drew's imagination was all that was needed on the topic of the sport.

The men on the screen were young, buff and sinewy as Jake. And like Jake their hard-ons strained against their shorts with the same ferocity as they strained to kick the ball around the grassy, mud-flaked field. British accents with barely intelligible slang peppered the room as the men—boys really—kicked and scrambled their way into each other, building the tension that Drew knew would soon be released in the obligatory locker-room scene.

He knew about those scenes. He had gotten into sports in high school solely to witness them. Hard young jocks prancing naked in front of him, soaping up and wetting down, fondling their own dicks and balls and rock-hard six-pack abs and occasionally, as he had caught one afternoon when he was late for swim practice, each others' in exaggerated *faux* circle-jerks meant to dismiss any notion that the sex was as real as the stiff and spurting cocks might imply. No moaning like he soon expected and, if he were honest with himself, hoped for on screen. Moaning implied consent; he knew this. Moaning implied it wasn't just a whack with a wet towel or a quick shove into a locker. Moaning implied desire and desire meant queer and queer meant he would be kicked out on his fairy ass from the fraternity his father still talked about and his brother had been president of. Moaning was what he ached to do beneath Jake's slightly less than six-pack abs and taut thighs. Moaning was what barely escaped his lips now as he found his hands had gone from resting on his thighs to massaging his balls and working up the shaft of his now intensely hard dick.

Why was he here? This time the question came not from inside his own head where he still hoped to find some way to reconcile his queerness with but from the guy who had lowered himself so quietly into the red seat next to him that he hadn't even noticed.

Drew dropped his hands from his crotch guiltily, as if the nuns had caught him as they had so many other boys at school. "No, don't stop," said the man, taking Drew's hand and putting it back on the bulge in his 501's.

The moaning had begun on screen but Drew was staring at the face next to his. Clean-shaven, sandy-haired, 30ish, taller than is own 5'10", if the legs that stretched out in front of him were any indicator. A brown leather bomber jacket covered a khaki shirt that tapered into jeans much like his own. The legs ended into richly textured cowboy boots. The guy had bucks. What was *he* doing here?

"I'm a film student," Drew quipped as if he'd been caught by one of his frat men. "Research," he added, knowing just how true both statements were. "You?"

Drew's eyes drifted to the guy's package. They were, after all, in a porn house. Wasn't he obligated to look? Stiff as his own cock pulsed the man's dick against the harsh fabric of the jeans. *What had he gotten himself into?*

"I'm Bob." *Had he really just held out his hand as if they had just met for coffee?* "I own this place and you seem like you might be under age to be here."

Drew didn't know whether to be offended or flattered. The veritable Bobcat himself carding his patrons? Drew knew there would come a time when he'd be happy to be thought younger than he was; he wasn't there yet, however.

"Well over 18 and ready to play ball." The words came so unbidden from him that he felt his color rise the way that freshman's had in the student lounge a few weeks back. *What* had *he gotten himself into, indeed.*

"You look like you might play soccer—or swim," nodded Bob whose gaze had more than drifted—fixated—on Drew's crotch.

"We should watch the film," Drew said, searching for a tone somewhere between demure and off-hand. "I hate it when people talk in the movies." The heat had spread up his thighs, through his groin and into his abdomen. Bob the Cat was no longer just looking. His hand squeezed Drew's thigh so hard it almost hurt. His dick ached and he instinctively unzipped his pants.

This is how he had wanted it to be at the bonfire last week with Jake, Drew thought as Bob the Cat, owner of the Sinema, became the first man other than himself to touch his cock, as Bob the Cat slunk low in the seat and caressed his dick out of his now too-tight Speedos and ran his hand deep under his balls gripping them strong, but not hard, not the way he had grabbed Drew's thigh.

The screen was alive with fucking now. One soccer player was stark naked, another dressed only in a jockstrap. Three others stood, open-shirted but shortless, massaging their own dicks as the jock-strapped player edged the naked one onto the locker-room bench. Beneath the bench, next to a towel, some socks and a cleated shoe, was a convenient can of lube and as the jock-strapped player pushed the naked one forward in a sportsmanly act of one-up-man-ship, the naked player let out the moan Drew was holding behind his own clenched teeth.

His own shirt had become unbuttoned to the waist. *How and when had he done that?* wondered Drew as he searched his naked chest and belly for answers. "No hair," murmured the Cat as he ran attractively rough hands over Drew's sleek abdomen and plunged them into his Speedos.

His dick was, as they say in the movies, throbbing. He ached to come but didn't want to—not yet. This was new, this was a little scary, this was so intense and exciting that he was surprised he hadn't come already, just from the sheer tension of it all.

He slid down a bit in his seat, spreading his legs wide. *Were there others in the theatre? Did it matter?* He'd become part of the screen now. It was one of those time-split screens, like in that dreadful Mike Leigh movie he's had to dissertate on last semester. Three separate sequences played before him. The soccer movie, with Mr. Jock Strap pulling his admirably sized cock out of the white elastic and brown leather contraption and slicking it up with lube. The moans from the naked player whose beautiful Latino ass quivered suggestively as Mr. Jock Strap played with his asshole, smearing it with lube and slowly pushing one, then two fingers in, spreading the cheeks wide, had grown just a little more intense, a little more urgent. Mr. Jock Strap whacked at his cock, jerking it off a little and then pushing it against that smooth, dark ass. The head of his dick disappeared into the hole ringed with soft black hair and the naked player reached desperately for his own cock, but Mr. Jock Strap had that too, fucking and jerking at the same time.

Bob the Cat had seen this movie before, certainly. He was squeezing Drew's balls and stroking his cock with a lightness that was so tantalizing Drew thought he might explode. Not come, just burst into bits all over the small plush room. "Touch me," Drew murmured, his voice suddenly deeper than any 20-year-old's should be. "Put your mouth on me, jerk me off, touch me." His voice held all the urgency his cock felt.

Bob reached into his pocket and pulled out a condom in a mint-green wrapper. Drew took his own dick in his hands and held it as Bob ran the silky pale-green rubber over his steamy cock. Then he put Bob's hand back on the shaft, leaned back and closed his eyes.

Bonfire night had been two weeks ago. The game had been a big event for the frat house. Partying and drinking would be a two-day long ritual, but the game was the intro and Jake had asked that everyone be in attendance. Drew would have gone regardless. He never missed an opportunity to catch Jake in action—skirting the field his legs nothing but sinew, his thick, brown hair sweaty on his forehead, his arms tensed as his feet traversed the field. Jake was a god, there was no denying it. Girls paraded in and out of his room at the house like he was interviewing for jobs. There was no one special girl, Drew knew. Jake claimed practice made perfect—on the field and off—and he was going to get as much practice in as he could before he was forced to settle down back in Michigan at the family law firm.

Drew wasn't sure how he and Jake had ended up at the bonfire together later that night. It had been a blur of a night. The game had been fantastic: fast-paced and tense, a 5 to 4 score with seconds to spare and Jake, of course, making that final, fabulous goal, the muddied ball a white streak into the net.

They had ended up lying on the grass as the bonfire was lit by underclassmen. Jake was lit himself, two beers chugged in rapid succession and another half gone in his hand. "What a night," he'd exclaimed with all the reverential sadness of a 20-year-old knowing nothing would ever again be this sweet. "What a fabulous, fucking fantastic night, huh Drew?" Jake had fake-slugged Drew then, pushing him down on the grass under the tree and pinning him by the shoulders. Drew had felt himself go hard, harder than he thought he had ever been and the urge to kiss Jake had been overwhelming. The jet-black eyes had searched his own for a second, maybe longer. Had Jake seen the desire streak across his face the way that final goal had streaked into the net?

"Fucking fantastic is right, you asshole!" Drew had arched his body and swung Jake off onto his back and laughed. It was a cover laugh, he knew it but perhaps Jake was too drunk to know for sure. The most dangerous moment of his life, the moment when everything might have changed forever had passed. Or had it?

Jake wanted to wrestle then. "You pussy," he yelled, tossing his beer across the field as sparks flew around them from the bonfire and groups of students cheered and grabbed each other, girls jumping up and down together and guys shoving each other in the way guys do when they want to touch but can't.

They rolled around on the grass for too long. Drew had felt it, when Jake pushed down on him—the hard cock against his thigh. He felt it when Jake continued to rub against him, harder and harder until he knew Jake was going to come, going to come against him, but not on him, not in him, not with him.

"What a fucking night," Jake breathed again as he rolled back onto the grass, leaves crunching under the weight of him. He pulled his shirt out lazily, matter-of-factly, from his pants, covering the stain spreading over the crotch where seconds before he'd come hard against Drew's thigh, Drew's own dick pulsing in his pants, aching to be touched, aching for Jake to come against it, on it, make it slick with cum.

Drew was coming now. He could feel it rising from his balls to his shaft and begin to spurt through the head of his dick. The moan he'd held back that night with Jake and earlier as he watched the men fuck on screen and when Bob the Cat had first touched his cock, the first man ever, he was truly queer now, he thought, that moan sizzled past his lips and he grabbed Bob's hair in his hand and felt him suck, suck, suck on his pulsing cock until there was nothing left but the sighs of the men on screen and the limp, pale green rubber on his slowly softening dick.

The computer shone blue in the half-light of his room as Drew tried to organize his storyboard for tomorrow's film crit. Images of naked men super-imposed themselves over the smooth digital icons he was drafting. Bob the Cat's card lay to the right of the mouse. Discreet as their encounter had been it read simply, Bob Catt, *films*, with number and email address.

Bob *had* taken him for coffee yesterday after the movie ended. They had walked eight blocks to Cosi and had lattes and omelets and talked about film for two hours before Drew took the bus back to campus. Diana had emailed him several times. Did he need her to visit next weekend? Otherwise she was going to a women's festival with some classmates.

Did he need her to visit? Nothing had happened to make Drew think Jake even remembered bonfire night. Jake had come back to the house and drunk himself into a stupor with two of the other frats and some frat groupies. Drew had picked his way over the bodies on his way out to run the next morning. He and Jake had taken two classes together since then and swum a few laps and had a beer one night at Smoky Joe's. Nothing. Drew was safe because Jake wanted to be safe.

Drew stood, stretched himself out and walked to the bed, flopping down, his legs wide apart. He closed his eyes and thought of how it felt to come in a man's mouth in a darkened theatre, how it felt to have the boy he wanted more than anything rub and rub and rub against his thigh until he could feel the stickiness seeping onto him. His cock hardened at the memories, the flashes of sex between the soccer players, Bob and Jake.

He stood and walked back to the computer. One more semester and he would be out of this school, out of this fraternity and out of the closet that was tighter and more suffocating than his pants had been yesterday when Bob had made him truly, truly queer.

He squeezed his legs together, his balls touching his thighs in the loose sweat pants, his cock throbbing against his stomach and he hunched forward and tried to think about his work. It was after midnight and the class was at 8:30. If he were going to show, this was going to be a long night.

The knock on his door rattled his concentration. Jake's voice, slightly slurred, announced his entrance. Jake tipped into the room, his hand around two Sam Adams, one of which he proffered to Drew.

"Can't," Drew waved the beer away, "gotta finish this storyboard for tomorrow's crit." Drew kept his eyes on the screen as Jake ambled to his bed and fluffed the pillows under his head.

"All work and no play, my man," he sneered and pushed at Drew's chair with his outstretched leg.

"Really, man, let me get this done." Drew felt Jake's presence, smelled him—salty and grassy like he had been that night, as if he had just come from the field. He swiveled around in his chair, took the beer, drank a long draught.

"I don't have the old man's firm to go to, remember, Jakester. I got to work for a living," the joke barely broke the tension between them. Drew felt his breath catch in his throat with the taste of the ale. He could drop to his knees right now and take Jake's thick cock in his hand, his mouth, even up his ass, he was that ready.

Jake leaned over, clinked his bottle against Drew's and toasted to "the old men."

"Come on, Drew, come over and tell me a story. I screwed up on the field tonight and I'm damned depressed. Play me a little movie for my head in which the goal always hits the net and *I* am *always* the star."

His black eyes sparkled with ale and the half-light and his hair fell low over his broad forehead and Drew thought, not for the first time, that Jake was indeed a god, a god whose light would fade in the years past school. He would be like Paul Newman in *Cat on a Hot Tin Roof*, replaying the scenes of his youth again and again because they were so acutely perfect and because he would never again be this beautiful, this sexy, this deeply, fabulously, intensely sweet.

Drew stood and walked to the bed. He shoved Jake's leg back with the playfulness of the field. He sat down and turned, looking over the sprawled, beautiful boy who lay before him ready for a story, ready to be taken, perhaps aching to be taken. And then he began to talk about a split-screen montage of a bonfire, a soccer game and a trip to the movies on a wet, cold November afternoon.

INVISIBLE
by Mark Wildyr

I've been Baron Jeffers's best friend since we were seven years old; I've been in love with him since we jerked off together when we were thirteen although I didn't fully understand my feelings until recently. We'd been so close that it got all mixed up with 'best buddy' stuff in my mind. I never figured this was different from what all the guys go through at one time or the other until I started noticing weird things. For example, every time I walked behind him, I'd look at his butt, trying to figure out why it was different from everyone else's. Had to be different or else I would've looked at theirs, too, wouldn't I? I did, of course, but only to compare them with Bar's high, tight buns. His weren't flat like a lot of guys...mine, for instance. They were nicely rounded so that his pants hugged his butt. Don't get me wrong, it wasn't anything like a girl's ass, but just…well, different. And his chest. Baron works out and swims a lot…we both do…and it's given him this big, broad chest that looks great. That should have clued me, but I wrote it off as something like penis envy.

The thing that made me put another spin on things happened on a double date our high school graduation night. We drove out to the lake after the dance, and one thing led to another. Bar and Willa Moss had been going together off and on for almost a year, but I knew for a fact that he hadn't gotten in her pants; he'd complained about it too often. He'd done everything short of it, but not the dirty deed, itself. I took a quirky satisfaction from that. Here I'd fucked my girl, Mary, a couple of times, but handsome, sexy, popular Bar Jeffers hadn't done it yet!

Well, he did that night, and I watched him do it. I mean, I just stood and gawked. They had walked down the beach at the pond-sized lake where we'd parked. Mary was willing, but feeling a pressing need to take a leak before the main event, I meandered over a hill and lopped it out. While waiting for it to deflate so it would pass piss, I started wondering how old Bar was doing. Finishing my business, I sneaked around the hill and found them. I wish I hadn't because the sight squeezed my heart so much that it almost quit.

He was doing it to her, fucking like he'd done it a thousand times. I watched that butt I admired so much flash in the bright moonlight, his knees digging into the blanket every time his strong, swimmer's thighs threw it to her. The muscles in his back bunched and played like ripples in quicksilver. His black hair fell into his eyes as he labored. Shit, even the soles of his size-ten feet were sexy.

Bar climaxed with a groan while I stood there like some wide-eyed kid. Suddenly, he pulled out and rolled on his back, his rod still halfway stiff, the big dickhead wet with his cum and her juices. It was bigger than when we jacked off that one time five years ago...lots bigger. I wondered what it felt like to Willa, you know, stroking her insides. Must have felt okay, because she reached over and grabbed it, sighing with pleasure. It was all I could do to keep from rushing down and slapping her hand away.

Realizing that I was standing out in the open, I eased back over the hill and went to mollify Mary who pouted that I'd abandoned her. I not only convinced her she was wrong, I proved it. I fucked her so hard she almost complained...almost.

"Mario Richards!" she breathed when I pulled out of her. "What got into you? You never did it like that before."

"Never graduated high school before," I grumbled, stuffing everything back where it belonged just as Bar opened the car door. Had he seen us? For some reason, I hoped that he had.

That was the night that I became invisible. Not literally, of course. A six-foot, hundred-seventy-five pound male isn't undetectable walking around in plain sight, but sometimes I felt like it with Bar. It wasn't that we weren't friends anymore or didn't run around together, we did. But I wasn't in his *mind* anymore, not like I had been. For five years I'd nursed the idea that one day we'd do what we had again, and this time I'd take his cock in my hand and make him cum. I'd make it better for him than simply masturbating himself. He'd groan and thrash and shoot up a flood of cum and tell me that was the most wonderful thing ever! Well, it wasn't going to happen now. What did I have to offer that Willa Moss didn't have lots more of? Damn her and her pussy, anyway. I was totally invisible as a potential sex partner now. Invisible, immaterial, and irrelevant.

We drove around after taking the girls home while he confessed that he'd scored, punching me on the arm and getting all excited as he told me how 'Wow!' it was. Sharing made it some better, I guess, but I was still jealous as all get out. After he climbed out of the car and tripped up the stairs to the house, I sat a minute coming to grips with the new reality. Baron Jeffers would remain my friend, he'd always be that, but he'd never be my lover. *Lover?* That was stupid! I didn't wanta be lovers, I just wanted to be the one to take care of his needs. I know. I know. Crazy, loopy reasoning, but that's the way it played out in my head.

The dreams started that night; the first wet dreams of my entire teenage life. I never had an erotic dream during the long, dry years, and now that I was finally fucking my girl, I woke up just in time to catch my spurting, sticky cum in my shorts. Scrambling to save the covers from a soaking and trying to get through an orgasm at the same time isn't an easy thing, you know. Didn't accomplish either one very successfully. Afterward, I lay back down, heart pounding, and tried to recall the dream. The only part I could remember was me standing in front of Baron Jeffers beating my meat while he ignored me. I was invisible.

That summer Bar and I took a couple of classes at the junior college to get some of the hard stuff like freshman English and Physics out of the way. Several of our classmates enrolled, including Willa. Bar and I sat together in English, but he chose Willa as his physics lab partner, and that about tore me up. To make matters worse, I got saddled with Jerzy Podowski as *my* partner. Jerz is smart and does his share of the lab work and is decent-looking, but he's queer. Well, that's the rumor, at any rate. I'd never paid him any mind except to note that he's kinda sissified…not always, just sometimes when he lets his guard down.

I guess he confirmed the rumor when he kept finding ways to touch me in the lab. Now I've always known I was a good-looking guy; after all, I spend as much time before the mirror as any other adolescent, but Bar and I had been so tight that queers never bothered me. Truth to tell, there probably wasn't another one in our small southern New Mexico town besides Jerzy. Once when I went up to Albuquerque to look over the University of New Mexico, I bumped into a couple in the men's room at Zimmerman Library, and I couldn't get out of there fast enough! I looked on them with the horror typical of any church-raised, small-town kid. But no way did I consider what I felt for Baron Jeffers in the same light as what those guys were hunting. What I wanted from him was what good buddies sometimes did, and that was different from faggots who simply like cock.

Midway through the six-week course, Jerz and I were in the lab after hours working over a particularly exacting experiment when he stunned me.

"You and Baron ever do it together?" he asked out of the blue, his hazel eyes searching my face innocently.

"What?" I almost screeched. "Why kinda question is that?" I managed to summon up some righteous outrage at the suggestion.

"Two best-looking studs in the school. Tighter'n two sweethearts. Living in one another's back pocket for as long as I can remember. It's a natural conclusion. Ninety percent of best friends get it off with one another at least once," he acted like he was quoting a known statistic.

"Well, that means ten percent don't!" I snapped, avoiding an answer.

He noticed. "I guess that means you have. Boy, I'd like to have seen that. What'd you do, jerk off? I could do more for you," he added, lowering his voice to a barely audible whisper. "You ever had a blowjob?"

"Fuck no," I yelped, not quite understanding why I didn't get up and smash his face, or at least stomp off indignantly.

"I figure since Willa's moved in on Bar, you're feeling some frustration. I can ease it some. Hell, I can ease it a lot. Make it go away."

"I've got a girl for that," I said calmly.

"She suck you? Go down on your dick?"

"None of your business."

"You really never had a blow? There's nothing like it. Look, I'm meeting this guy tonight. He always takes me out to Blue Mesa Park. If you'll get there early, you can watch me do it to him. See how much he likes it."

"Keep your dirty perversions to yourself," I said harshly to cover a pinprick of interest.

Jerz shrugged. "Okay. But we'll be at the south end of the park. There's a little grove of trees there. Won't get there until about nine."

"Shut up about that sick, faggot stuff," I snarled, lifting my butt from the lab stool and stalking off all stiff-legged.

I could hardly wait to find Bar and tell him the outrageous stuff Jerzy Podowski had been saying. Out in the hallway, I stopped short. Why did I want to tell him that shit? So he'd share my outrage? So he'd get turned on? So we could allude to the time we'd stroked our cocks until they spit up kid-cum? So he'd get so turned on we'd do something? What? Go find Jerzy and get our cocks sucked together? Or he'd look at me through those big brown eyes and say, "How come we never did it again?" Then he'd take my hand and put it on that big cock of his. Jeez, I was as sick as Jerzy Podowski!

Maybe so, but at that moment I knew for a fact that if Baron Jeffers ever let on that he wanted me, I'd take him in my mouth and suck him until he came down my throat. I'd drink his cum, lick his cock, nuzzle his balls. Anything. Anything at all. Suddenly aware of an erection, I sneaked into the men's room and locked myself in a stall to stroke my cock to an orgasm while picturing Bar's handsome, athletic body feeding his big cock to Willa Moss's pussy.

I fought against it, but at eight-thirty that night I silently harangued myself as a sick son-of-a-bitch even as I settled back against a tree in the bushes at Blue Mesa Park. While I waited, my dick got so hard that I took it out and squinted at it through the darkness. I didn't need to see it clearly. I knew exactly what it looked like. So thick at the root that my thumb and forefinger would hardly go around it. Flat on top, round on the bottom with a long foreskin that I now rolled back from the spade-shaped tip. It was a little under seven inches with a slight leftward bend because I jerked off with my right hand.

A car door slammed, spooking me, but it was too late to bolt or even do up my fly. A couple pushed their way into the small, well-protected clearing. One was Jerzy Podowski and the other was an older, bulked up, Hispanic boy who'd played football in high school and was now on the New Mexico State varsity team. Macho son of a gun.

Maybe so, but he stood in a small pool of moonlight and allowed Jerz to fall to his knees and rub his denim crotch. They mumbled something I couldn't hear, and then Perry Michoa spread out a blanket and lay on his back, letting Jerzy strip him naked. I slowly stroked my erection as Jerz knelt between Perry's knees and put his tongue to the broad chest, slurping noisily at the nipples and working his way down the long torso. With a groan, Perry spread his legs so Jerz could have access to his balls. The fairy sucked at them before starting to work on the big, hard prong.

It took Jerzy a few tries, but that bone eventually disappeared down his gullet. Perry was obviously enjoying the hell out of the blowjob. Before long, he held Jerzy's head in his hands and fucked the open mouth. He was a noisy fucker, groaning and gasping and muttering things like 'take it, cocksucker,' 'swallow my load.' He cut loose in Spanish when his nuts blew, roaring so loud that he disturbed the birds nesting in the trees over us and covered my soft 'uhhh' as I came.

Perry rolled over on top of Jerz and fucked the kid's mouth so hard he must have been ripping out the tonsils. Jerz didn't seem to object; his hands were all over the bigger boy's butt, fingering the crack, poking in it. With a mighty "Ahhh!" Perry finished his orgasm and fell off Jerzy like a man struck dead. He wasn't though because his brown chest heaved like crazy as he fought for air.

"Fuck, Jerz," he growled in his man's voice. "You're getting better at that."

"I try, Perry," Jerz said, his eyes darting here and there like he was searching for an unseen watcher. "But I try harder for you," Jerz added. "You're such a man. I like blowing you."

Perry sat up and started pulling on his shirt. "Tell the truth, cocksucker. You like cock…any cock."

Jerz didn't seem offended. "Yeah, guess I do. Not *any*, but lots. There's this stud I partner with in Physics lab. He wants it, and I'd sure like to give it to him, but he's playing hard to get."

My ears flamed as he talked about me like that while I tried to deal with cum puddling in my lap without giving myself away.

"I don't wanta hear about your boyfriends," Perry snapped, standing to pull on his trousers. He had trouble stuffing all his equipment behind the zipper. I got more than a little pissed at hearing myself characterized like that by a guy who'd just had his cock sucked.

"You're not gonna fuck me?" Jerz asked plaintively, driving thoughts of character assassination right out of my mind and almost shocking me into revealing my presence.

"Naw. Haven't got the time. Supposed to hook up with some of the guys. But I'll throw it to you before I go back to school," the bigger boy said, gathering up the blanket and heading for his car. "Wait here till I see if the coast is clear."

"How'd you like it?" Jerz asked in a stage whisper. "Get your rocks off?"

With a start, I realized he was talking to me. Since he wasn't looking my direction, I figured he was hoping I'd give away my presence. I kept my mouth shut. A moment later, he slipped out of the glade. I waited until their car moved off before I pulled out my handkerchief and mopped up my congealing semen.

I didn't let on to Jerz that I'd spied on him when I saw him at lab the next day. He gave me a couple of looks, but when I didn't respond, he apparently decided that I hadn't showed. He casually mentioned that he'd had a good time on his 'date.' I tried to ignore him.

Mid-week, Bar pried his handsome nose from Willa's pitiful little bosom long enough to ask if I wanted to grab a sandwich somewhere. Of course, I did. I'd drop everything to be with him for an hour. Pitiful, isn't it?

Baron Jeffers is a smart guy, but he's not as book smart as I am. A couple of things about the physics class were getting to him, and he shamelessly picked my brain as we ate a greasy hamburger with oily fries and sucked down fatty milkshakes. I happily contributed what I could to his general education, grateful that he needed me for *something*. Willa was as smart as either of us, but it didn't fit his self-image to get help from her. After all, he was the dominant force in that twosome. While we ate, he told me exactly how dominant. I concealed a hard-on for the next half-hour.

After allowing our food to digest and my erection to subside, we hit the pool for some exercise. I sneaked a peak at his groin as we changed into our trunks. I'd seen his cock a thousand times over the years, but it was never enough; I always wanted one more look. Frankly, I felt a proprietary interest in the handsome thing, no matter how unjustified.

We wore ourselves out competing, as usual. Sometimes it was distance; sometimes it was speed. Today it was distance. We called it a draw at sixty laps. While I was trying to get some oxygen into my system as we hung over the edge of the pool, Jerzy strolled through the place. The guy didn't have a bad body...for a queer. I noticed him catch the eye of a boy on a lounger and inspect the guy's groin. So help me, the kid, somebody from the college I didn't know, gave a little nod. After Jerz walked on, I scoped out the hunk on the lounger so hard that I missed what Bar was saying.

"Earth to Mario. What the hell you looking at?"

It was an opportunity, so I took it. "Jerzy."

"Jerzy? Jerzy Podowski?" he asked incredulously. "Why you looking at that faggot? You turning queer?"

I felt my face go red. "No, you idiot! I saw him make contact with a guy."

"What guy?" he wanted to know.

"The one on the lounger. The guy in the blue trunks."

"Shit," Bar laughed. "He's stepping up in this world. That guy looks decent. Probably trying to put the make on him, and got rejected."

"No. I saw the guy nod."

"No shit? Wonder why. Looks okay. Oughta be getting his ashes hauled by some skirt."

"Maybe he just needs relief," I ventured.

"Relief? Fucking a girl, that's relief. When I'm with Willa—"

"Yeah, yeah," I said sourly. "We know all about you and Willa."

"Well, fuck, Richards, it's not like you aren't sticking it to Mary."

"Maybe he just wants a change," I blurted.

Bar looked at the guy again. "You think?" He sank under the water, surfaced, and turned to me. "What about you?" he asked, swiping away a face full of water with a broad hand. "You ever go for a change?"

"No, but I've thought about it a couple of times," I admitted.

He brayed. "Get serious, Mario. You thinking about going queer?"

"Keep your voice down," I hissed. "Didn't say that. Just said I thought about a change." I paused a beat. "Not everybody who does it is queer, you know."

He looked at me strangely. "Maybe not when you were a kid, but now?" With that, he swam back toward the shallow end.

Son-of-a-bitch! What had I done now? I swam after him and trailed his buffed body into the locker room. By the time we were dressed for the street again, he had moved on to other things. Just like that the opportunity was gone. Message sent and not received. Overture rejected…well, not rejected. Missed entirely is more like it.

The remainder of the week passed with Jerz making sure I knew he was going back to Blue Mesa Park on Friday night. I ignored him, but there wasn't a doubt in my mind that I'd be there ahead of him. My near-outing with Bar had left me feeling so edgy that no amount of masturbation relieved the tension. Old Bar walked around with his head up his ass…or rather Willa's ass…with no clue to my agony.

I managed to fake a stomach ache Friday night early enough to dump Mary and beat Jerz to the grove on the south side of the park. He was late, and I was wishing I'd got it on with Mary instead of hiding out here in the bushes when they arrived. The guy who followed Jerzy Podowski into the clearing was the college kid I'd seen give him the nod at the pool. Shouldn't have surprised me, but it did. Brad, as Jerz called him, was as handsome and hunky as anybody in town…except maybe Baron Jeffers. And when he walked, he walked like a man.

From all the comments I caught sitting in the bushes not ten feet from the two of them, this was Brad's first time with Jerz. In short order, the faggot had him stripped and lying on a blanket ready for action. Brad had a truly awesome body, but only a so-so cock. It was fat, but a little stubby, I noted smugly. A good inch, inch and a half shorter than mine. But Jerz didn't seem to mind. He gobbled that cock without much foreplay at all.

Then I understood Jerz's strategy. Get him hot and committed, and then play around. He came up off that cock and licked and sucked and tasted old Brad from head to toe. And Brad dug every bit of it.

I think we were both shocked when Jerz lifted Brad's legs and rolled his butt up in the air. Then the queer buried his nose between the hunk's buns, shook his head and went, "brrrrrr!" Brad almost came up off the blanket before he settled back and let old Jerzy's tongue go to work on his ass. I was so stunned that I forgot to keep jerking my cock.

That wasn't anything to what Jerz had planned next. Right in the middle of turning the guy to putty, he got up and stripped off his clothes. Then he straddled the hot hunk's groin and squatted. It took a moment to realize that he'd sat down on that fat, stubby pole and took it up his ass!

It looked like Brad was about to protest until Jerz lifted himself up and down a couple of times, and then the guy started fucking the ass that encircled his pole. And I mean, he fucked. He screwed so hard that he about bucked Jerz off of him. He fucked with such abandon it even took the faggot by surprise. Then he rolled over so he was on top, and they squirmed and wiggled damned near right on my boots. But neither one of them had a clue that I was within a mile of the place; they were too wrapped up in themselves.

Brad's handsome face was on a level with mine and not more than three feet away. I watched the intensity of his features while he pounded the boy underneath him. Ecstasy claimed his countenance as orgasm approached. It struck hard, rolling his eyes back in his head. Then he really turned loose and tore Jerzy a new asshole. Brad went wild. He drilled his way through the ejaculation like a jackhammer breaking concrete. For one brief instant, I wondered what it felt like to be on the receiving end all of that energy.

In the sudden silence after the fury, Podowski's hand held his own cum-slick cock. He'd gotten his rocks off while his ass was being fucked by a tornado! How in the hell would *that* feel?

"You're a hell of a man," Jerz said, still puffing hard from his exertions.

"Shut up!" Brad snarled. Anger replaced the look of pure joy of an instant before. "Why the hell did you do that?"

"Seemed like the thing to do," Jerz said innocently, giving the sturdy body a good once-over as the boy rose and batted Podowski's hands away from his legs.

"I said you could suck me, you fucking queer. I didn't say anything about fucking your shitty ass!"

"Seemed like you came pretty good," Jerz flirted with disaster.

"Shut your fucking mouth. You better not ever tell anybody about this, you hear? I'll break your fucking balls if I hear any talk."

"Sure you will," Jerz said dismissively. "But don't go trying to tell me you didn't like it."

"Shit, I'm all dirty! I oughta make you lick it clean."

"That would be different," Jerz said, rising lazily from the blanket. "But I brought a washrag for that." He fumbled around in his clothing and came up with a baggie. "Still warm. Oughta feel good. Here, let me do it."

"Keep your faggot hands off me," Brad warned, but he didn't stop Jerz from lovingly washing his cock. The queer took his time, so much so that to Brad's obvious discomfort, it began to grow. By the time the faggot was finished, it was fully erect. Jerz let it beat in the air a few seconds before he took it in his mouth. Brad forgot to protest, and just stood there until another orgasm rocked him back on his heels.

The two left the glade a few minutes later, Brad acting like a jerk, and Jerz cheerfully taking his guff. It was like the stud needed to assuage his own guilt by laying it all on Jerzy Podowski. It also crossed my mind that old Jerz accepted this as the price for getting a pole to suck. Me, I just sat there, legs splayed, and jerked myself to a very satisfying climax. As I closed my eyes at the last moment, Brad's face was replaced in my mind's eye by Baron Jeffers's beautiful, manly features.

Dark, shadowy figures moved at the edge of my dream that night. I was walking in the woods...no, it was the park. Somebody was fucking somebody else in the glade. Naked and fearful of what I would find, I walked to the side of the struggling figures. I exhaled with relief when the broad back and driving hips did not belong to Baron Jeffers. I don't know who was fucking Jerzy Powdowski, but it wasn't Bar. Jerz gave me a broad, knowing grin and rose up to take me in his mouth. I wanted to stop him, to move away, but I was helpless. I stood there while he sucked greedily. I woke too late to prevent the flood, and spent fifteen minutes scrubbing my gooey cum off the bed linens. I threw my shorts in the sink and left them to soak while I returned to a sodden, uncomfortable bed.

I'm not certain when I started plotting to spy on Bar, but I desperately wanted to see him screw Willa again. My initiation into voyeurism left me thirsting for more...more Baron Jeffers. The opportunity came the next weekend when I met them coming out of the movie house as I was going in. Mary was tied up in some family thing, so I was alone for a change. As we stood in the lobby talking for a minute, I got the distinct impression that old Bar was going to actively pursue a piece of ass that night. As soon as they were out of sight, I left the theater, movie as yet unseen, and rushed out to the lake.

I found Bar and Willa tucked away in the sand at a fold of rock providing protection from all but the most depraved of spies. That was me, I guess, because I lay atop a rock almost directly above them and watched shamelessly. Willa was a pretty little thing, but she couldn't hold a candle to Baron Jeffers when it came to physical beauty. Where her face was small and delicate; his was broad and strong and manly. His breast, padded with flat pecs and large aureoles, was far more interesting than her small tits. She had a smooth, round belly where his was flat and ridged with muscle. And below the groin, she had nothing except gash in a scraggly bush of pubic hair; his ended in a big display of manhood that rose and throbbed at the touch of her tiny hand. She shocked me by taking the end in her mouth, but that was about all she could handle. Hell, Jerz would have gobbled the whole thing down.

Why, I bet I could take most of it myself. I tried to imagine his big, hard prick in my mouth. It didn't seem all that revolting. Not at all. At that moment I knew that's exactly what I wanted to do. And when my friend mounted Willa, I accepted without qualm that it was *my* ass I wanted him to fuck. A little tingle ran from my pucker string right up into my guts. Trying to put aside the acute jealousy that wracked me, I concentrated on watching him make love. Old Bar had no technique. He just climbed aboard and stabbed her repeatedly until he shuddered to a halt. Of course, she squealed her way through a couple of orgasms in the meantime, but that didn't matter to me. Then he rolled off her onto the blanket and stared right at me.

It took all the fortitude I had to keep from moving. I knew from his lack of reaction that he hadn't seen me. When Willa nestled contentedly in his arms, he turned his head, and I slipped away, making it all the way to my car before I tore open my britches and pumped the seed from my body moaning his name over and over as I came.

My life went from bearable to downright miserable. So long as I didn't *consciously* admit that I wanted to fuck my best friend, I could hold things at bay with vague dreams of masturbating him. Now that I realized things were more serious, I became not only invisible, but *miserably* invisible.

And in my misery, I began to look at Jerzy Podowski in a different light. I sure as hell wasn't invisible to him. I even got about half-hard a couple of times in the lab, and old hawk-eye didn't miss it.

"What's the matter?" he finally asked with an amused smile. "Trouble in Heteroland? Mary cut you off?"

I almost dropped a beaker. "Shit, don't say things like that when I'm holding sulfuric acid," I snapped.

"I know," he smirked, ignoring me. "You'n old Bar did a double date and double fucked your girls. Only problem is, you wanted to be under him instead of on top of her."

I had the presence of mind to put down the acid before I caught him right on the chin and sent him sprawling over on his ass. The entire class froze in the middle of pouring liquids, lighting Bunsen burners, measuring chemicals, or whatever the hell they'd been doing. I stood over Jerz, my ears flaming from embarrassment and rage. Poor Jerz looked like he was going to cry. Just before the Physics teacher's bulky form got in the way, I looked straight into Bar's surprised eyes and saw him whisper something to Willa.

Jerz and I ended up evicted from the lab for the rest of the afternoon, earning a big, fat zero on one of the most important experiments of the term. I tried to apologize to Jerzy, but he scooted down the hall like he thought I was going to pick up where I left off. He stumbled a lot, and I think it was because he was crying so much he couldn't see. I felt like a fucking asshole, realizing I flew off the handle because he had been absolutely right. I *did* want to be beneath Baron Jeffers.

Bar looked me up in the swimming pool after Physics and jumped into the water beside me.

"What'd he do, proposition you?" were his first words.

I kept stroking the water. "Yeah. Something like that." At the end of the lap I swam up out of the water and planted my butt on the edge of the pool. Bar pulled up beside me. I wondered if I looked as graceful and sexy as he did with the maneuver.

He laughed, and I knew he'd be merciless, drive it right into the ground. "You must be awful touchy about it to lose your cool like that. Right in Physics!"

"We'll see how you like it when he tries to grab your ass," I snapped sourly.

"Aw, shit, Mario. He's tried a hundred times. You just gotta put the little creep in his place, that's all. But not so spectacularly—not in front of the whole damned class. He eyed me speculatively. "Don't tell me that's the first time he's put the move on you."

I saw red. I saw green. I saw black. Rage and jealousy shook me to the soles of my dripping feet. That fucker had tried to get Baron. My Baron! He didn't have any right to—

Mortified, my flesh turned a bright pink from my chest to the top of my head. My scalp prickled. Without a word, I leaned forward and fell into the pool. Baron caught up with me in the locker room.

"What the fuck's going on, Mario?" he demanded, looking so handsome and sexy that I was afraid I'd get an erection with my trunks pealed down to my knees.

"Don't let him get to you," Bar continued with a laugh. "Hell, look at it as a compliment. He only goes after the good-looking guys."

"*You* may consider it a compliment, but I don't."

Bar turned serious. "Hey, man. What's the matter? You're overreacting, okay?"

I turned on him, outraged and out of control. "The motherfucker wasn't just trying to get into my pants. He was claiming that I wanted to get it on with you."

That outburst left both of us with our mouths open. Agape is a better word. Bar was astounded; I was mortified. What the fuck did I say that for?

I was prepared for anything but what happened next. He suddenly burst out laughing. "Maybe we oughta put on a show for him," Bar said in falsetto, reaching out a long finger to tickle my balls."

Surprised, I swatted his hand away. A nanosecond later, I was sorry. "Yeah! Maybe we should," I said, squeezing the cock hidden in his tight trunks.

"Hey!" he yelped, dancing away. Immediately, he turned serious. "But didn't you ever think about it?"

"Are you saying you did?" I snapped back.

"Well, sure, a couple of times. You didn't?"

I drilled him with my eyes. "Every fucking day," I growled, turning away and heading for the shower. We always showered after leaving the pool, so I expected him to follow. He didn't. After a few minutes, I realized that he'd dressed and left. What the hell had I done?

I had become even more invisible, that's what I'd done. When I saw him in English class the next day, Bar tried to act like nothing had happened, but after a couple of attempts at small talk, he turned away and talked to the girl on the other side of him. Willa was waiting for him to go to Physics as soon as the period was over. Instead of joining them as I usually did, I trailed along behind, wondering what he was telling her about my slugging Jerzy yesterday. Would he blurt out everything? I was one miserable shit when I dragged my ass into the lab and saw Jerzy sitting at our table.

"Sorry, man," I mumbled as I put my things on a spare stool. He already had our gear laid out for the period.

"Forget it," he mumbled back. Then he couldn't let it alone, of course. "Hit too close to home, I guess."

"Fuck you, too," I snarled.

"Any time, peckerwood. It would be better than Mary's beaver box." he shot back. I'll give him credit. He had gall for a faggot.

We spent a very uncomfortable hour and a half working like robots, speaking as little as possible, staying as far away from one another as we could and still work on the same experiment. The instructor hovered nearby the entire time.

My grades for that summer session did not match my usual standards. I lost interest, thereby losing my edge. I passed, but with a 'B-' and a 'C', the first one I'd ever gotten. As soon as the term was over, my folks whisked me off to Denver for a week to visit an aunt and uncle and a couple of cousins. Their older son, Derek, was about my age, but was a world apart in his interests. He lived on the computer, and all his social intercourse seemed to be conducted on that blessed machine. He had good chat buddies, but not many flesh and blood ones. I went into the bathroom at night and played with myself while Derek played with his computer.

I felt strangely at a loss in my own hometown after we got back from vacation. Normally, I'd have made a beeline for Bar's house, but that didn't feel right this time. I half-heartedly looked up Mary, but we had started the teenage ritual of breaking up. Not that we were mad at one another, we were just drifting apart. Right that minute, I wanted to take her somewhere and fuck her cross-eyed, but I don't think she was interested. Didn't act like it, anyway. Sorta cool.

I ran into Bar, of course. Bound to in a little town like Mesa Azul. He seemed a little distant, like it was an effort to be friendly. Neither of us mentioned the exchange in the locker room, but it was on both of our minds, and it showed. Miserable, I invented a chore at home and cut it off. When I was about to leave, he acted like he wanted to talk, but I was committed to my lie and went on home.

I was so mopey over the next few days that my mom ordered me out of the house. I hit the pool and summoned the energy to play some soccer, but my heart wasn't in it, and I made bad mistakes on the field. Shit, even Jerzy Podowski got around me for a goal, the only one he made ever in his whole life so far as I know. Baron Jeffers seemed to have disappeared off the ends of the earth.

The nightmare happened a week before I was to leave for Albuquerque to enroll at UNM. Restless, I had trouble going to sleep that night, so I did something I never do, took one of those Tylenol PMs. I would have made a cheap druggie because one pill zonks me every time. Restlessly asleep, I followed a naked Baron Jeffers through swirling mists as thick as any London fog. I don't know how I knew it, but he was on the prowl for a sexual partner. I kept yelling at him, trying to get his attention. "I'll do it. I'll do it for you, Bar. Anything you want. Please!"

He didn't hear me, just kept going in that man's gait that was so sexy. He was walking while I was running, but I still couldn't catch him. To my horror, I saw where he was headed. The glade at the end of Blue Mesa Park. No, Jerzy would be there. Screaming at the top of my lungs, I lunged for his broad back. He disappeared into the trees. Slowly, I made my way through the brush, knowing what I'd find. Jerzy was on his back, nude, with his legs raised obscenely. Bar fell to his knees and thrust his hot, hungry erection into Jerzy's exposed ass. Crying aloud, I ran around in front of my friend and screamed at him, offering my own hard cock, my ass, my mouth. Beautiful Bar ignored me. Why not? I was invisible, wasn't I?

Baron Jeffers's features turned beatific as his orgasm took hold. I could not help myself, I came, soiling my bedclothes and pulling myself out of that horrible nightmare. I sobbed quietly as I lay soaking in my own juices. Why is it that you can't remember most dreams, but every hateful minute of this depraved vision was painfully clear?

The next day, I heard the gossip. Everyone at the drive-in was talking about it. Bar and Willa had broken up. Ruptured. Bad. For sure. Permanently!

Immediately, I forgot my troubles and imagined how Bar must be feeling. I swung by the pool, his house, the tennis courts, the soccer field. Nothing. No Baron. I even went home and checked to see if he'd called, but he hadn't. He must be hurting something terrible. Where would I go if I was in pain? To him, of course, but that was before I made an ass of myself at the pool. I checked the one roadhouse that let underage drinkers sneak in, but his car wasn't there.

Finally, I found his coupe parked at the south end of the lake. The weather was overcast; he wouldn't be swimming, so I started walking the shoreline. I found him in the same nook where I'd watched him screw Willa. He hadn't spotted me yet, so I stood quietly and watched him for a few minutes. He sat on a rock and stared vacantly out over the lake, his broad, strong shoulders hunched against the world. Once or twice, he angrily swiped at his eyes when they'd leak a tear.

I backed off a few steps and made a noise as I approached. He swung toward me aggressively, but softened when he saw who it was.

"Mar," he said quietly.

"Bar," I responded, recalling when the term 'Mar's Bar' referred to us collectively without any sort of smutty connotation.

I sat beside him. "Heard about it. You need company?" He gave a silent shrug. "Wanta talk about it?"

He was quiet for so long that I had decided he didn't when he cleared his throat. "Didn't know it was so hard to grow up," he finally said.

"Yeah, they shoulda warned us," I responded.

"Guess they did, we just didn't listen."

"You okay?"

"I'll survive." His strong arm fell over my shoulders. "As long as I've got a buddy, I'll make it."

I awkwardly patted his hand. "You got one, pal. We've always been there for one another. No reason to change now."

"No. No reason." He removed his arm. "Shit, Mario," he said in such a low voice I could hardly hear. "I don't even know what happened. Things were going so good. I loved her, man! I really did. And she loved me. I *know* she did. But things changed. When we started doing it, you know, making love, things got rad. Sometimes she acted like that's all I wanted from her, but that wasn't true. Then things would get all right again. Making love drew me closer to her, but it did something different for her."

"She wasn't ready for it, bro," I said, dragging up a scrap of wisdom from somewhere. "She couldn't handle it."

"When she got back from vacation this summer, she was all changed. Didn't want to do it any more. That was okay, I guess. But I felt like I was losing her. So I pushed her for it, and she lost it. We had a fight. Said she didn't want to go out with me." His voice choked.

"Aw, she'll get over it," I said.

"No!" he shook his head sadly. "It's over." Turning to me, he suddenly clasped me in his arms, burying his head in my shoulder and sobbing heavily. He was grieving like he'd lost her to a car accident or a terminal disease. In my newfound role of sage, I realized he was letting go of Willa totally, completely. I was glad that I was the shoulder he decided to cry on. I felt myself take on substance, become visible again. Holding his firm, muscled torso tightly, I shamelessly took comfort from his misery.

"Look, if it is over, then it's meant to be. Lots of fish in—"

His arms tightened, warning me to shut up with the platitudes. Being a sage is 'iffy' some times when you're not very good at it. The deep, wracking sobs subsided, but he still held on tightly.

My hand found his head and stroked it gently. "It'll be all right, Bar. I promise. The sun will come up tomorrow morning and go down tomorrow night. You'll be—"

"Will you shut the fuck up!" he growled, catching me by surprise. His grip loosened. His head moved. His cheek slid along mine, the faint stubble of whiskers scratching my skin. His lips were damp from his tears. Overjoyed, I went weak-kneed when he kissed me like a child, mouth firmly closed. Then I damned near swooned like the proverbial maiden as he kissed me like the man he was with soft, parted lips, tongue hesitantly exploring. Suddenly it was inside my mouth thrusting, twisting, generating sparks, igniting my nipples, heating my cock, burning my testicles. He groaned. I moaned. We broke apart with a rush of air.

"S…sorry," he stuttered.

"I'm not," I said breathlessly.

"Me, neither," he admitted, pulling my lips to his again.

Oblivious of everything, we rocked back and forth in a tight clasp as we did a tongue duel, breaking apart only when we fell off the rock onto the soft sand. On top, I immediately moved my head to his torso, sucking at his aureoles through his shirt. He thrust his chest up at me as I ripped his buttons apart to get at him. Unable to believe what we were doing I sucked his nipples until he squirmed in protest. Afraid to stop and think, I tore open his jeans and yanked them down around his knees, exposing his manhood, full and hard and throbbing in a splendid erection. And it was all for me. For *me!*

I bent to him, but he caught my head in his hands. "Not so fast, man. Take it easy."

"You…you might change your mind," I panted, expressing my worst fear aloud.

"No. I won't change my mind. But I want to be comfortable. Right now I've got sand up my ass," he laughed.

Reluctantly, fearfully, I rose, watching as he got to his feet, wiped sand from his butt, and pulled his pants into place."

"I thought—"

"Don't worry. I won't chicken out." He grew serious. "But I want it to be right for us, Mario. We've waited long enough. We can wait a while longer."

"Why?"

"Will you go to the movies with me this evening?"

"Sure."

"Afterward, we can take a drive somewhere. Maybe go up in the hills where nobody goes. Remember that old cabin up where we go deer hunting? Maybe we could spend the night."

"Oh, God, Bar! If only we could!"

"Why not? Please, Mario. That's the way I want it to be for us."

"I'll be scared every minute until then."

"No need. I'll be there. I promise," he said with a slow smile.

I don't even remember getting back to town from the lake. I kept living and reliving the feel of him against me as he sobbed out his sorrow. The slow movement of his head from cheek to lips. The halting kiss. The hot kiss. His tongue. His cock. His *everything*. I was in love, and it felt great that I was there for him when he needed me.

I used all of the hot water on my shower and shaved my thin beard until the skin was sore. I probably smelled like a French whore from all the aftershave I slathered on. My favorite purple shirt looked great on me; it went well with my skin coloring and dark blond hair. I preferred my 501's, but didn't want to fumble with buttons, so selected a pair of black jeans instead. Glossy black loafers finished my ensemble. Examining myself critically in the mirror, I decided that I looked as ready for the most important date of my life as I was able. I tried out a confident, cool smile for the mirror while my guts danced and jiggled and gurgled from nervousness.

If I looked like a million dollars when I met Baron Jeffers at the movies that night, he looked like a zillion, When he flashed his killer smile just for me I felt like everyone in the place knew what we were up to. And you know what? I didn't give a shit. I wanted to shout it out loud for the dunces who missed it. I didn't, of course. That would have sent my Adonis, my Apollo running for the hills…without me.

The film we went to was forgettable; the dimly-lit movie theater wasn't. Feeling giddy and daring, I kept my knee pressed against his. He pressed back. The armrest we shared became a playground. His elbow rubbed my side; my hand draped over the end and touched his thigh lightly. Once, he leaned over to offer me some popcorn, and his hidden hand groped my groin. It took a boy…a man…to make me understand every teenager's enthusiasm for the back rows of a darkened theater. Damned if I didn't go all giggly.

The drive up into the hills where we went deer hunting every autumn was surreal. The moon was huge and luminous, painting the countryside silver with deep, contrasting shadows. It was beautiful. We kept away from one another until Bar reached out and clasped my hand as he maneuvered the narrow, two-lane track up what passed for a mountain in this country.

When we arrived at the cabin, we both went nervous, and I was terrified that we'd lose our nerve. But once our bedrolls were untied and spread, Bar turned to me. By the light of a small fire laid in the old fireplace, his eyes searched mine. They were big, beautiful brown eyes. I liked brown eyes better than any others, probably because his were brown. But they seemed to express the soul more clearly than cold green or hazel eyes like mine. Blue eyes demanded to be regarded as, well, *blue* eyes. Brown ones were portals. Gateways. Sensual. Bar's.

Without a word, he drew me to him for a long, shattering kiss. I knew he felt it because his strong frame shook from emotion and excitement. The groin pressed against mine hardened. He *wanted* me. I sobbed into his mouth and pulled him close. My hands roved his broad back, clasped his firm buns, and pulled him even closer.

"Jeez, Mario," he gasped "I fucking want you. Do you want me?"

Blubbering like a baby...or like a *sissy*...I slid down his long frame, bruising my lips on his buttons and belt. I didn't care. My mouth at his groin, my arms clasped around his butt, I sucked at his fly, trying to pull the heat, the essence of what I wanted right through the denim. His hands caressed my head while his manhood grew beneath my touch.

"I guess you want me," he laughed gently, lifting my chin up to face him. "I was worried about this," Bar continued. "I was afraid we'd just jack off like we did that one time. And that wasn't going to do it for me. But it's going to be okay, isn't it? You're going to make it good for me, aren't you?"

"As good as I can," I gulped. "Bar, I'm still scared. I don't have any experience. What if I can't do it good for you?"

"You can," he whispered, stepping away and slipping out of his clothes. "It'll be good just because it's you."

I froze on my knees as he revealed himself to me. It was as if I were looking at that carved, perfect body for the first time. I saw things in the half dark of that little cabin I'd never noticed before. The depth of his navel. A dark patch of skin on his hip. The *fullness* of his balls. The big slit in his penis peeking out of the half-retracted foreskin. The life...the throbbing, eager, excited, powerful life in that beautiful cock,

I shuffled to him on my knees and felt the marble of his flesh, the sinew of his muscles, the magnificence that was Baron Jeffers. He undressed me and carefully spread my 'stud duds' over an old chair. I loved him for that, in addition to everything else that earned my devotion.

I discovered a thousand new things that night. I learned that each part of him had its own particular taste. I learned that everything about him was beautiful, not handsome, not good-looking...but beautiful. That he was ticklish right below his belly button. That his nipples stood up like tiny pricks when excited. That his skin goosefleshed just before an orgasm. That I loved him deeply, unreservedly, selfishly.

Taking him in my mouth seemed as natural as anything I had ever done. He was clean and eager to give me his seed. And I worked without choking or gagging to make it happen. I sucked him gently, washed him with my tongue, took as much as I could down my throat, experimented with this and tried that, until finally, he told me what felt best. I came out to the end of that big cock and worked it with my tongue until his flesh puckered and he moaned as if in pain. And then he erupted. He filled my mouth with sweet, sweet cum, his seed, his semen, his jism, that essential part of him that he shared so generously.

Not once did I feel revulsion, the need to retch, the necessity to reject his gift. I swallowed it, gloried in it, and desperately sought more. I felt like a virgin giving her all to the one she loved at the right time in the right place. He had to pull me off him, begging me to stop.

We lay in one another's arms after that, and I passed from loving to contented to frightened. Why didn't he say something? What did he think about what I'd done for him? Was I just a queer to him now? A faggot? A fairy? And then he spoke.

"I've wondered for years what that would feel like."

"What? A blowjob? Jerzy could give you a better—"

"Hush your fucking mouth!" he said, laying a finger across my lips. "I'm not talking about a blowjob. I'm talking about being with you. Doing things with you. Having you touch me."

"Really?" I asked, afraid of probing, but feeling the need. "And how was it?"

"About the greatest thing ever," he said quietly.

I rose on my elbow. "You're not just saying that? You mean it?"

"I mean it, Mario. I've wanted to…you know, be intimate with you ever since we jacked off together, but you're so fucking macho I didn't know how to go about it."

Amazed, I sat up straight. He pulled me down again. I lay on his arm. "Shit, Bar, I wanted it, too. For a long time. But…but why'd you cut me out when I admitted I'd been thinking about you…like that?"

Bar took a long time answering, and I knew it was because he was seriously considering the question. "I was starting to have trouble with Willa, and I knew that if I turned to you, it would be over with her. I'd give myself to you completely. And…and I guess I wasn't ready to do that yet. The only way I could do that was to freeze you out." He pulled my cheek to his. "God, Mario, I never even dared to dream you'd do what you did for me. Well, I did, too. Had more than one wet dream about it!" he laughed. "I figured that at the most we'd jerk each other off."

Surprised, I sat up. "Oh, Jeez, I had dreams, too!"

"Shut up," he repeated, pulling me down once again. "But I never dreamed I'd do this," he added, rising above me.

The kiss was deeper, more nerve wracking, more meaningful than before because he was kissing the mouth that had held his erection and taken his semen a few minutes before. But he didn't stop there, he worked his way down my torso, doing as I had done. Tasting. Sampling. Teasing. Experimenting. And then the love of my life, the man of my dreams, the century's greatest hunk took my hard, leaking cock in his mouth and gave me the clumsiest, most inexpert, most dynamic, most *awesome* blowjob in the history of mankind. Skyrockets went off when I blasted my balls. I was hardly finished with my orgasm before I pulled him up and kissed him greedily.

He went quiet; I babbled. "Greatest, most awesome thing ever—in my life! In recorded history! I never knew your nerve ends could let go like that without electrocuting you."

Bar laughed and clasped me to his naked chest. "Man, you're making it hard to do an encore."

"But we are, aren't we?" I bobbed up again. Patiently, he pulled me down a final time and covered us with a sleeping bag.

"Yeah. We are."

He fell asleep long before I did, and I'm surprised that he didn't awaken as I toyed with his flesh. Hardly believing that I had the freedom to roam his buff body, I touched it all while he slept the sleep of the innocent and dreamed the dreams of the licentious...I hoped. Eventually, I nodded off.

Something disturbed my wonderful dreams, and I rose slowly to consciousness to find Baron Jeffers spooned against my naked backside. His huge erection was between my legs, poking at my balls as he hunched gently.

"Can I, Mar?" he grunted.

Only half understanding, I consented. Immediately, he placed the tip of his cock between my crack. Shivers ran through my body.

"I'll be gentle," he whispered before assaulting my ass with a red hot poker. I cried out, and he froze. After a moment of silence, he pushed again. I tried to swallow the pain, but was unsuccessful. He halted again. Then he slid the rest of the way in so easily that the discomfort was manageable. When his groin flattened my buttocks and his thick black bush was ticking my flesh, he nibbled my ear.

"This feels great, Mario. Does it hurt too much?"

"No. Not too much. The pain's going away. But I sure do feel full."

"I love your fucking ass, Mario Richards. I love *fucking* your ass."

"A little more than that, I hope." It came out as a gasp when he began moving his hips.

"Every bit of you. Every pound. Every inch. You're my Man, Mar. You're my...lover!"

I noticed the hesitation and understood that he wasn't certain how I would react to the word. I let him know right away. "Yeah. My lover and my beloved. I love you, Bar. Have for five years. Didn't know I wanted your cock up my ass, your balls slapping my butt, your chest hugging my back, but man, oh, man, I do. Fuck me!"

"Naw," he said between thrusts. "I'll make love to you."

He did that magnificently, probing where no man had ever explored. Before it was over, he abandoned the love-making and started plain old fucking. After he coated my insides with his cum, while his chest was heaving against my back, as his testicles retracted to begin filling with semen again, I knew without a doubt that it had been great for him. Better than with Willa. Better than anything. Probably better than it would ever be again. In a sense, we'd busted our cherries all over again. His first time fucking me…another male…and my first time being fucked in the ass by the most *male* male I knew.

I sensed the words and their sincerity before they ever came. "I love you, man. I love you, Mario Richards. I don't know what's gonna happen in the future, but I can tell you one thing for sure. I love you more than I'll *ever* love anyone else."

Then he made the night absolutely perfect. He lay on his back, lifted his long, swimmer's legs, and absolutely insisted that I fuck his beautiful, virgin butt.

OUT
by M. Christian

I'm not gay. Getting my cock sucked had quite an effect, but not that. And this is not one of those overly-enthusiastic denials that convicts more than it convinces. I mean it simply, logically, coolly: I had some realizations that night, but being queer just ain't one of them.

It was one of those parties, the kind we only seem to have here in San Francisco. If your zip code begins with '94' then you might know what I mean. Down in the carpeted basement of a nondescript Victorian house, on piles of pillows and mattresses, were a dozen queer boys (but in this crowd a slippery definition), a dozen queer girls (but in this crowd also a slippery definition), some punk, some hippie, some young, some old, some fat, some lithe. All fucking, sucking, licking, stroking, whipping, or getting beaten. Exceptional for some places, but for '94 San Francisco, just another frisky Saturday night.

I'd been to many parties like this one. I knew most of the people. I'd fucked and licked and beat and gotten beaten at lots of parties such as this—I'd just never gotten my cock sucked standing in the middle of a crowded room before.

Gay? Me? No venomous denial there, I'm just unabashedly straight. Sometimes, I wish I was gay, but the fact is boys just don't get me hard. Tits do, cunts do, cocks don't, beards don't. I've tried a couple of times, but without the female accessories it just doesn't work.

Well ... until that party, that one night in San Francisco.

There I was, naked except for a pair of bike shorts. I was smiling at all my friends, thinking about this pair of tits, that lovely slope of thigh, that pretty pussy over there ... maybe she'd want to do something, or maybe her—when I felt a rather strong hand reach up from below and grab my crotch.

"Hey, Chris," my friend 'Paul' (name changed to protect ... well, anyway, this isn't his real name) said from where he lay, sprawled out on a gigantic gym mat. Paul was a good friend, tall and lean, with a tan that made him look almost wood-stained. He had a curly beard, long kinky hair, and a ring in his left nipple. We'd sit in the hot tub out on the deck sometimes and talk science fiction movies and comic books. Now he wanted to suck my cock.

"Come on. Chris," he said, flashing a brilliant smile up at me through the tangle of his beard. "Just a little."

I'm not gay; right, I said that. But did I mention that I'm also really, really shy? So there I was, my queer friend asking so politely to suck my cock; and suddenly I'm aware that my other friends are lying around in various states of arousal, covertly watching me.

I felt myself flame with embarrassment. What choice did I have? Turn my pal down, shame myself in front of my friends (who had never, ever given me a hard time about my—sigh—heterosexuality), or try something that, who knew, might even be pleasurable?

"I'd be honored," I said gallantly. Okay, what I actually did was giggle like a schoolgirl and hide behind my hands. But I didn't say no, so give me that much credit at least.

Bike shorts are easy to lose. A finger hooked in the top, a quick tug down, and my ass was bare, my cock free—semi-rigid and starting to swell. There, in the middle of a crowded room, my cock started to swell. Paul reached up and put his soft hand around my cock and gave it a long, practiced stroke.

He didn't suck it at first. First he stroked it again, looking up into my amazed eyes, smiling slowly as it went from that soft, fat finger of tissue into a near-full hard-on. I watched him do this, my focus blurring from my churning emotions. My eyes darted from his pleased smile to the baby-dykes sprawled in each others' arms a short distance away. I looked to the fat, hairy man leaning against a distant wall like a Neanderthal Buddha; then to a pair of muscled boys, one earnestly feeding the other his fist, Crisco frothing around an asshole; and to the chubby girl standing—just standing—in a corner, watching. I looked at their faces, then into their eyes. With a sudden shock like a 220 jolt, I saw the colors of all of those eyes (green, blue, brown, jade, mahogany, and green), and I realized I was painfully hard.

There was a wet socket around my hard dick. Paul's mouth on the fat head of my dick, exploring with tongue and lips what he'd just seen, savoring my meat—a connoisseur making appreciative noises. His strong fingers started caressing my swollen balls, gently squeezing, firmly pulling, and skillfully twisting.

He was watching me. Staring at me. Lost in what was happening to me. Distantly, I looked at the others again: the chubby girl, the fat man, the two dykes, the two fag boys, and they looked back at me—watching Paul suck my dick.

It felt so good. He had a big mouth so I wasn't afraid of teeth scraping my shaft or cockhead. Strong tongue, so it didn't feel like a flaccid, wet sock puppet jerking me off. And firm lips, like thick, plush fingers ringing my straining shaft. Good, oh yes, damned good.

But there was something missing ... something missing when I looked down at this guy sucking my cock. Something that seemed to drain the concrete out of my shaft, and lower my heartbeat.

Then I looked back up at the room. The two dykes were still wrapped around each other, one of them caressing the tits of the other, both sets of eyes on me. The fat guy was pulling at his sad little dick, staring intently at me. The two boys were stroking their own cocks, looking, looking at me.

I was hard, I was screaming, motherfucking hard. The come came before I was aware of it, before I recognized the cramping in my balls and the heavy propulsion of a tight, quivering orgasm. Right out there in public, right there down Paul's hungry throat.

The looks were enough, really, the looks in their eyes. But the applause was dessert. The clapping, loose and sporadic at first, became an intimate little crescendo.

It was then I knew what had happened. I knew I'd crossed over; I wasn't the same Chris who'd walked in the door. The "me" who walked out that night had seen the new face of his cock.

I wasn't gay. Paul was still a good friend and he'd done a wonderful job sucking my cock, but he was just the catalyst in my powerful moment of truth. What really got me off, and what I really needed, were all those eyes.

Today I am an exhibitionist.

And now you may applaud. Please?

MR. WORLD BUNS (A Story Without a Moral)
by Felice Picano

DENVER, COLORADO: 1981

It all began on a Sunday. Larry Damrosch remembered that quite clearly because Howard found the huge ad announcing the contest in the large, multi-sectioned edition of the *Denver Post*. They were in bed, following a late night out. It was now almost three in the afternoon. Howard, as usual, was going through the entire paper before he settled on something to catch his interest. Larry was in the bookpages, deeply involved in reading a review of a controversial new biography of Sigmund Freud he'd heard mentioned at the clinic.

"Look here, Larry. Mr. World Buns Contest. All may enter."

"Terrif," Larry said. His lover's words barely made an impression. Larry turned over on the edge of the bed, searching on the carpeted floor for a ballpoint he'd dropped. He wanted to mark the review, to remind himself to pick up the book tomorrow.

"Cash prize for first place, five thousand dollars. And a two week trip to Rio de Janeiro for two, all expenses paid."

Where was that pen?

"This is just what we've been looking for, Larry. This is it!"

There it was. Larry could just make out the nub end of the pen. He stretched his fingers for it, still couldn't reach, so he stretched his entire body. He almost had it, when he felt the slap on his ass. He lost his balance and fell off the bed.

"Hey! What's that all about."

"You weren't listening," Howard said, holding up the ad. "Look! This is where you and I are going over the holidays. Without this we'll never get away, we're broke."

"Okay. Enter."

"The regional preliminary is being held right here in Denver. At The Broadway, next Friday night. All you have to do to enter is call and appear that night."

"Great! I won't stop you," Larry said. He crawled under the bed, found the pen, then got back on top of the covers again. "Shouldn't we be getting up and having breakfast soon?"

"Think of it, Larry. Christmas in Rio. All expenses paid. We're in debt to plastic so deep we'd never be able to afford it. Not with what you earn."

"You don't earn that much yourself," Larry said. Which wasn't exactly true. As a psychiatric social worker, at least he had a future.

Howard—a bartender at the Triangle—took home more, true, but he worked more sporadically too.

"Five thousand dollars," Howard mused. "We could rent a place in Breckenridge for the winter. Be right near the Bunkhouse. Ski, sled, build fires, have friends up."

"Sounds terrific," Larry said. Having marked the bookpage, he moved onto the film section.

"How about it?" Howard said, straddling Larry and taking the newspaper from him.

"Sure."

"Then you'll do it?"

"Me!? I thought you were going to enter."

"You're the one with the beautiful ass," Howard cooed. "The best in Denver. And I ought to know."

"I couldn't. I'm a psychiatrist."

"So What? You have the buns. That's all that counts."

"I can't, Howard," Larry said, and began a half dozen explanations why not. Howard seemed not to listen. Instead, he began kissing Larry's face, his shoulders, his nipples, his navel. He only looked up when Larry said it was chap and exploitative to enter a beauty contest.

"Sexist too," Larry added. "Treating bodies like objects."

"It was all right, when *I* was going to enter," Howard said.

"That's different. You're already a sort of public figure, working at the bar and all."

Howard arched an eyebrow, then dropped his head into Howard's crotch. "Please. Pretty please."

"Stop, Howard. It's still sore from last night."

Howard got up, but rolled Larry over, and began kissing his buttocks, murmuring all the while, "This is our gold mine."

"What would Dr. Royce say if he found out," Larry protested. "And my parents, what if they…?"

His protests diminished with every rotation of his lover's hot and probing tongue.

"I can't, Howard. I just can't."

***

Friday night Larry was standing in a fairly dark corner behind the raised platform that served as a stage at the Broadway. The place was jammed. Every square foot of the place was taken. People were three deep at the back bar, and against the walls. Not all gays either. There were students from Boulder in quilted coats and skirts, shaggy dressed straight couples up from Colorado Springs, elegant Jet set types who'd driven or flown private planes from Aspen and Vail. They all looked relatively young and hip, however, which was a relief. Not much chance of anyone from the clinic where Larry worked showing up. And, they all seemed to be having a great time. Better than Larry who was panic stricken.

"You're next," someone said to Larry.

"I can't do it, Howard."

Howard dipped a hand to pat his ass through the loose fitting gray sweat pants.

"Gene Frazer," the emcee on stage announced, "Gene is a student of archaeology at the University of Colorado. His specialty is Amerindian digs."

Gene was a six-foot-two inch blond hewn god, wearing a tiny golden bikini over his lean muscled body. He stepped up and forward, and turned slowly around in the spotlights as comfortable as though he were in front of his bedroom mirror. The crowd cheered and whistled. In one corner of the room, Larry could make out the judges—two local bar owners, both gay, a pretty woman whom he knew edited a local alternative newspaper, and another older woman, who worked in fashion, Howard had told him.

"I'm backing out. I can't do it."

Gene crossed the stage, and stepped down in front of them.

"Break a leg," Howard said, pushing Larry forward. "And remember. Do exactly what I told you."

Larry stumbled on the step, but caught himself just as a house light came over to meet him.

"I'll get you for this, Howard," he hissed, then, rebalanced with his anger, he stepped onto the stage.

"Larry Damrosch," the announcer began. "Larry is a local boy from Denver. Twenty-four years old. Larry is a psychiatric social worker at the downtown clinic attached to…"

His words were drowned out by calls from the audience.

"Where's his ass? Buns! We want buns! We can't see them!"

Larry walked across the stage, past the emcee whose recitation was completely lost amid the continued boos and calls from men and women alike. Someone began clapping in rhythm and others took it up, chanting "Buns, Buns, Buns!"

Larry wore a close fitted black T-shirt over what he knew to be a small, but well-muscled torso. That and the gray sweat pants. And under those a small black jock strap. Nothing else. Not even shoes. He faced the audience, deafened by their noise, bowed a bit, turned to face the judges all of whom seemed a bit perplexed, then looked back at the announcer, who'd given up and just stood there, shrugging.

"We want buns," the audience chanted. "We want buns."

So Larry turned to face the emcee, then undid the ties of the sweat pants, opened the front, and dropped them to the floor.

Behind him, the audience's shouts died down to nothing.

Larry bent forward, mooning them, drew the pants off his ankles and feet, then turned to moon the judges. Behind him was a breathless, silent pause. He could feel eight hundred eyes on his back, eight hundred hands itching to reach out to him.

"Now that's what I call an ass," a woman said in a whiskey charred voice.

Some cowboy in the back of the room let out a yippee that echoed around the room. It was taken up by a few others, then by shouts and applause and whistles that rose and crested, rose, crested and rose again.

When he felt hands on him, Larry took off, running off stage to much cheering, past Howard and the others standing on the side, into the bathroom, where he locked the door and looked at himself in the mirror.

His face wasn't flushed as he's thought, but glowing. He'd liked it.

"You idiot!" He said to his reflection. "How did a smart guy like you get talked into a performance like that?"

He changed into his denims, waited a bit, then finally slipped out. Howard grabbed him and ignoring his protests, steered Larry to the side of the stage again.

"I'm getting out of here," Larry said.

"They haven't announced the winner yet."

They had announced the second runner up; he was standing on the stage. Now the emcee called out the name of the first runner up; Gene Frazer, the archaeology student."

"Come on, Howard. I've had enough of this."

"Not yet," Howard insisted.

"And the winner, and Rocky Mountain Regional Winner for the Mr. World Buns contest"—the emcee began—"The man who will represent our area in the final contest in New York City next month, and already the winner of our special five hundred dollar prize and a weekend with all expenses paid at the Aspen Lodge…and by the way, folks, it was unanimous. Our own…

Larry never heard his name. He felt Howard and someone else propel him onto the stage. The music played a fanfare, lights crisscrossed in front of him. The emcee and male judges shook his hand, the woman kissed him demurely, someone put a check in his hand, the audience jumped up and down, raising toasts with beer bottles and wineglasses.

"Now folks," the emcee said. "Let's take another look at those prize winning Rocky Mountain globes."

Still amazed, Larry had to be turned around, his denims unbuckled, and dropped. He managed to catch them just below his buttocks.

The audience cheered until it seemed bedlam was about to break loose.

"I can't believe this," Larry mouthed to Howard on the sidelines.

His lover smiled back, like a man who just heard he's discovered a mother lode.

NEW YORK CITY: SIX WEEKS LATER

Larry had just gotten the key into his hotel room door when the phone began to ring.

"Where've you been? I've been calling all day."

It was Howard—more than a little pissed off.

"At a luncheon," Larry said, dropping onto the bed and kicking off his shoes. Outside the window, he could see blocks and blocks of the Manhattan midtown skyline, building lights just going on.

"A luncheon? It's five-twenty!"

"Don't blame me. You didn't tell me I was going to have to be Miss Congeniality, Howard. It's been one meeting after another from the minute I got here and checked in. First all twenty-five finalists had a briefing with the representatives of the company backing the contest. And guess what, Howard? It's a swimsuit manufacturer. We all have to wear bathing suits in the contest. No bare buns like in Denver."

"Don't worry about that."

"I am worried. Then there was a gathering of finalists. You ought to see them. I'm certain my being here is a fluke."

"Cute? Howard asked, although he seemed inattentive.

"Cute!? Man some of these guys ought to enter Mr. Universe competitions. And others have been posing for skin magazines all year. Half of them are professionals, I'm sure of it. They've been in a dozen contests like this one."

"Oh yes?" Howard said, seeming more far away than before.

"They're gorgeous. I don't have a snowman's chance in a furnace."

"It's all about *buns*! Howard said. "What's the difference if they have great bodies. It's the *buns* that count."

"Well, it's a good thing I found out from someone at the desk that there's a gym in the hotel. I'm going to be there every spare minute I have."

When Howard said nothing in response, Larry went on to tell him about their other activities—meeting with photographers and the photo-sessions—alone and with groups of the other finalists. Then the luncheon at Joanna's. They'd had to wear ties, although luckily not jackets. He supposed the others at the big table were company executives and their wives. It was excruciating. And tonight there was to be a cocktail party where they would meet New York celebrities, underground stars like Divine, writers like Andrew Holleran, fashion designers, reporters from *Interview* and *Wet*. Tomorrow, more photos, another meeting with some other group. Then the contest—at a brand new discotheque downtown. Larry was already worn out, and he hadn't even begun.

"And the other guys," he added, "they're all right, pleasant and all. But half of them are straight."

"Oh?"

"And none of them are very bright. When they saw me reading *Freud, Biologist of the Mind*, they did everything but kick me out of the hotel. I swear, Howard, I saw one of them move his lips when he was watching TV."

"Stick it out, you'll win," Howard said. He sounded awfully unconcerned. Maybe it was the long distance?

Larry went on talking. At one point, he thought he heard his lover speak to someone else, and asked who was there.

"No one," then louder. "I don't think you know him."

They had an "open relationship," true. But Larry was both hurt and annoyed that Howard was tricking on him after only a day or so away.

He quickly admitted that he was being irrational, and dropped the subject fast. Allowing Howard to get in some pep talk before they disconnected.

The phone rang again immediately. It was Jake, one of the "chaperones" assigned to the finalists, asking about the cocktail party at ten that evening. Would Larry like to have dinner with Jake and a few other contestants before hand, he asked.

Jake was large and oily looking. Larry had already made it very clear to Jake that he had a lover back in Denver. That didn't seem to make any difference. Before hanging up, Jake unctuously told Larry he had a real chance for being this year's Mr. World Buns. "I can spot a winner."

***

The gym on the top floor was attached to a shower and sauna room, and next to an olympic-sized pool. It was out of his way, hard to find, through a long, unused looking hallway. But the minute Larry opened the door, it was clear he wasn't the only one who'd asked at the desk. The place was filled with finalists for Mr. World Buns. Every Nautilus machine was in use, every weight bench occupied by groaning workouts.

"I should have known!"

A few minutes later, he found a spot in the gym not in use. One wall held calisthenic equipment: hanging rings, mats, a horse, even parallel bars.

He warmed up with push ups, sit ups and a few other light exercises. All the while, overhearing conversations around him.

"I'll never get these lats in shape by Sunday."

"Forget the lats, honey. What about your lower back. Those dimples look a little deep to me."

"Are you saying he's fat?"

"That was the year I was Mr. Data Boy."

"I know an exercise for your lower gluteus. From ballet."

"I don't go in for ballet, I'm straight."

"Could have fooled me."

"Plenty of straight guys here. Joe there. That German guy."

"Someone was chewing on my ass last night. Think it shows?"

"I use Oil of Olay."

"Ever try Estee Lauder?"

"I don't wear makeup on my ass. I'm straight."

"You told us. You told us."

"That black guy Dwayne has the best ass of all. But he won't win. Blacks never do. He'll come in second, or third."

"It's called Callipygian."

"Cally-what?"

Larry looked up from his half minute of doing the Boat, his hip bones alone touching the mat, his hands and chest lifted up, his thighs and feet up too, feet and hands clasped in back.

"Who said callipygian?" he demanded to know, falling out of his boat position.

"I did. Why?"

The man who stepped forward looked about his own age. But tall, surfer slender, yet with huge shoulders and arms, a thick curling helmet of golden hair, and a tan that was obviously natural and could only be described as brandy-laced pumpkin pie whipped through with heavy cream. Set beneath perfectly straight, thick, sunbleached eyebrows were ice-blue eyes. His nose was slightly aquiline. His outlaw-style moustache was red and gold. He had a mouth designed for kissing, a perfect jaw with two dimples and a cleft.

"Why?" he asked again.

"Nothing," Larry said, stepping forward. "I just wanted to take a look at the intellectual of the group."

"Hal Sykes," he said, stepping forward. "That's yoga you're doing, right?"

The others went back to their workouts and talk.

"Right," Larry said, "No room at the weights."

"You're Larry Damrosch," Hal said, not asking. "How come you're always wearing loose pants, like those sweat pants? Is that supposed to mean you've got something special back there?"

"Sure does. I don't want people to take a look and lose heart, maybe even drop out of the contest," Larry said, taking up the challenge.

"Oh, yeah?" Hal stepped back. "Well, I've got my eye on you," he said, half joking, half serious, before walking away.

"Keep looking," Larry said, watching him walk away. Hal Syke's buns, like all the rest of him, were scrumptious.

***

The champagne bottles were empty, the bartenders bored, most of the party balloons deflated by now, and the big room almost empty. Larry leaned against a wall out of sight, glad to have the celebrity encounter over. He felt like an aging debutante. He was tired of smiling, tired of being nice, tired of meeting people and immediately forgetting who they were, tired of parading himself around. All he wanted was to get up to his hotel room, get into bed, and read the Sullaway book on Freud, before blissfully falling to sleep.

"Hi!" a small cute blonde number said to him. "I'm Burt, from the upper Midwest. Me and a few other guys are going down to the Village to play around. You care to join us?"

"Well, I don't know."

"C'mon. We'll have fun. We might even go to the Mineshaft. This is Buddy. Rory. Chuck."

"Not me," Chuck said. "The last time I went to the Mineshaft, I was crawling around on my hands and knees by morning. My ass was all scarred up, and no accounting for it."

"C'mon," Burt said. "We'll have fun."

"I don't think so," Larry said, and managed to escape past them.

"Don't run away so fast," someone said, grabbing him by the belt. It was Jake. Out of the frying pan and into the fire. "My, you were looking good tonight," Jake said, circling his shoulder with a fat arm. Larry tried not to flinch. "You've already made a big impression on several of the judges, you know."

"Were there judges here tonight?"

How could he get away from this creep?

"Well...great," Larry stammered "Thanks. See you later. I've got to go."

"You're not going out tonight, are you?"

"No. Straight to bed. My beauty sleep."

"Would you like to be tucked in?"

"I'm expecting a call from my lover tonight," Larry lied, and got away.

Hal Sykes was standing at the elevator bank.

"Where's your friend?" he asked.

"Not my friend!"

"He come on to you?"

"You too?" Larry asked.

"Once. I told him I was straight and I would deck him if he touched me again."

The elevator arrived and they got in. Larry had seen Hal a few times across the room at the cocktail party, "mixing." It had seemed as though he'd always been near or with a woman. And at yesterday's luncheon too. He might have known it. The best looking guy here, the only one who even vaguely interested Larry, and he turned out straight. No luck at all on this trip.

"How come you didn't go out with the others?" Hal asked.

"Guess I wasn't in the mood."

"So what now? Beddy-bye? It's only midnight."

"I thought I'd read a little."

"You play cards? Hal asked.

"Sure."

"Poker?"

"If you remind me which is higher, a flush or a straight."

"Oh, one of *those*."

"I have a lot of beginner's luck," Larry said. "Every time."

"All right. My room or yours?"

An hour later, Larry had lost nineteen dollars and seventy five cents to Hal.

Despite the loss, he'd enjoyed the time. Hal had dynamite grass, they got beer from room service. Hal had talked a lot about himself. Larry now knew that he was as bright and personable as he was handsome. Hal was married and divorced. He worked for his father—as a partner in their Oldsmobile franchise in Laguna Beach. He could be funny, ironic, satirical. He was better looking and sexier with every passing moment.

He shuffled the deck and said, "New variation. Aces low."

"That's my mad money for the night. Count me out."

"You can still play. Don't go yet."

Larry sat down on the bed and finished the beer.

"I have an idea. Let's play for something else. Let's play for clothing," Hal said.

"Boy, you really want to see the competition bad, don't you?"

"You bet! I want to win. And—aside from you—and Dwayne who won't win anyway—I'm it. But I've got to be sure."

"All right," Larry said. He didn't care anymore.

Almost an hour and a half later, after a hard game in which both of them were reduced to their underwear, Larry put out four queens with a smile on his face. He'd been getting more and more excited by their stripping down. He wanted to see what Hal was hiding in those jockey shorts that puffed out so enticingly.

"Flush!" Hal said, laying out the royalty with a flourish.

Larry couldn't believe it. But he wasn't about to be a sore loser. So he stood up, turned around, and took off his underwear.

"There. Satisfied?" he asked.

"Come into the light. I can't see from there."

Larry stepped back, and stumbled. He was caught in Hal's hands.

"Well? How do we stack up?"

When Hal didn't answer, but kept holding onto his hips, Larry looked over his shoulder. Hal was sporting a thunderbolt erection that was trying to burst through the cloth of his jockeys. His tongue was unconsciously licking his moustache.

"Well?" Larry insisted.

"Not bad. Not bad at all. But I think they need a little loosening up," Hal said. "And I know exactly how to do it."

His last words were mumbled, as he was face deep between Larry's buttocks.

"But I thought you were straight," Larry remembered to ask him, later on, as Hal was preparing to fuck him again.

"You don't think I'm stupid enough to let a little thing like that get in the way, do you?"

***

Backstage at the Saint consisted of a large storage room filled with sound and video equipment, adjoining the runway each contestant would walk on—one third of the length of the lower level lounge—before pausing on the central section, then going off along the other ramp. Under ordinary circumstances, the room couldn't have been too orderly. Tonight, with twenty-five nervous potential Mr. World Buns, not to mention a half-dozen chaperones, newly made friends, recent tricks, girl friends and wives, it was the absolute pits.

"You touch that phone and I'll bite a chunk out of your rear end this big," Larry said to the contestant from New England. The big, red-haired tow-headed guy looked as though he tore men Larry's size for the exercise. But he was scared off by the threat anyway.

Larry dialed again, let it ring, waited to ten, decided to try twenty rings this time, no maybe fifteen. What was that? Twelve? Or thirteen?

"Hello!" Howard. Breathless.

"Where have you been all day? I go on in ten minutes. Where's all the moral support you promised me back in Denver?"

"You'll win. Don't worry."

All said so breezily, that Larry had to ask: "Who's in the apartment with you?"

"Oh, just Andy."

"Andy?" Larry replied. "That sounds like he's pretty much of a fixture there."

"What are you wearing?" Howard said. Subtlety was never one of Howard's fortes.

"A bathing suit."

"What color?"

"Oh, sort of pale blue and sea green and pink. A little yellow too. It's sort of a seascape."

"On a bikini!"

"It's not a bikini. It's trunks. I tried on all the briefs. They didn't show me off well. These are short, square, nice fitting. You know I always wear trunks at the pool."

Howard was audibly moaning. "No one ever wins in trunks! We just blew it. Trunks always look dowdy."

"Not with this design, they don't. And they're sort of silk. They fit perfectly. You'll see in Rio. We get to keep the suit."

"We'll never *get* to Rio," Howard said. "Not with you wearing trunks."

So they argued. From bathing suits, the argument led to Andy, then to how terrible a time Larry claimed to be having in New York, and finally worked itself back to a month before, then three months before, then a year ago. Finally, Larry had enough and hung up, fuming.

"You look sort of uptight, kid," Jake the chaperone said. "You want a valium or something."

"I just broke up with my lover because of this rotten contest," Larry said.

"I've got to find Mr. Caribbean," the chaperone said, and beat it.

"Creep!"

Southern California was called, and Hal Sykes came by the phone.

"May the best buns win," Larry said; at least he'd be sporting.

"They won't," Hal said.

"They won't?"

"No. You've got the best buns. But I'm going to win."

***

Hal did win. Dwayne, the black, was second runner up. Larry, to his surprise, was first runner up.

"Honey," one contestant cooed after Larry had stalked onto the runway a minute after Hal had come down. "I've never seen anyone look so butch in a bathing suit in my life. You looked as though you could kill. And in those silly trunks too!"

While standing by their trophies in the center of the huge crowd, Larry happened to look down into the mass of men. He'd never seen so many drop-dead numbers in one place at the same time. To hell with Howard. True, they were mostly dark haired and he preferred surfer blondes (like Hal Sykes, now beaming, now on top of the world!). But Larry was sure their obvious adoration of him would carry through into action later on. He might even take off the whole two weeks he had coming to him as vacation time, hang around and investigate New York's fabled after hours night life.

He was interrupted briefly by the emcee, who announced that the judges had been so impressed by all three finalists that they had arranged for a second prize of a thousand dollars and a third for five hundred.

This was getting even better. Now Larry would even have spending money for his two weeks in the city.

How about that guy there, the one with the long sweaty torso, clothed only in denims and a leather thong around his neck. Or those two guys together there, both of them with close cut hair and perfume-garden eyes, cruising him rather obviously, as they felt each other up.

Ah, freedom. He forgot what it felt like. He would take that vacation.

But a half hour later, after he'd gotten out of the trunks and into a pair of jeans, he found none of the three men he'd considered while onstage: all were lost in the dancewhirl crowd he walked into upstairs. The lights were low in the big domed room, the music funky, the dancers into it. He was about to be very annoyed, when someone slid up behind him and put his hands on Larry's hips.

"How about a rumba."—Hal Sykes.

"I thought you'd be with your fan club?"

"I did that already. How about a dance?"

"I don't know."

"Then how about a fuck?"

"With your pick of the crowd here, tonight. You're crazy."

Hal turned Larry around to face him. He was leaning against a section of the wall. He tucked Larry right into his legs and held him.

"No dance. No fuck. What can the man want?"

"I don't want…"

"I've got it. How about two weeks in Rio, all expenses paid."

"You're kidding."

"Who else am I going to take? My ex wife?"

On the flight down to Brazil the next morning, Hal confessed that the reason he'd taken Larry away from the Saint so fast the night before, was so that no one would come to their senses and reconsider the prize.

"No more public exhibition for those buns," Hal said. "Not while I'm around." Then he leaned back into the seat and looked out at the clouds.

Larry found his place in the Freud biography. "That's all right by me."

WROUGHT IRON LACE
by Greg Herren

The guy who just moved in across the courtyard is gorgeous.
I would guess that he's still in his early thirties, maybe still the late twenties. Since I turned forty it's really hard for me to judge age. Twenty year olds look like babies, fifty year olds look forty, and that group in between I just have no fucking clue. I watched him move in the day after I came home from the hospital. I have three pins in my leg from the car accident, and I have to keep it elevated as much as possible. I can't stand on it yet, even with crutches, so I have a nice loaner wheelchair from the hospital. Friends are running errands for me when they can, and checking in on me to make sure I'm not lying on the floor in the bathroom helpless. I don't think I've ever spent so much time at home by myself ever before. It's amazing how little there is to watch on television, even with eighty cable channels. Is there anyone left on the planet who has not seen the movie *Sixteen Candles*? Why do they have to keep airing it?

It was a Saturday, and if ever there was a day of television hell, it's Saturday. There's nothing on, at any time of the day. I don't really care that much about billiards, snowboarding, or timbersports, thank you very much. I knew that the vacant apartment on the other side of the courtyard had been rented, the lower one, but I'd forgotten someone was moving in. My apartment is the second floor of a converted slave quarter, and my balcony has a view straight into the living room and bedroom windows of the lower in the back of the main house. I had seen the young lesbian couple who had lived there naked in the bedroom entirely too many times, and had trained myself not to notice those windows.

What can I say? I was bored, bored, bored. It was eleven o'clock in the morning, I'd been up for three hours, and I wasn't expecting anyone to come by again until two o'clock. I put a Jewel CD on, and pushed myself out onto the balcony. It was a beautiful October morning, the sky blue, the sun shining and warm, but none of the humidity that made New Orleans almost unlivable in the summer. There was a stack of books on the balcony table, and I figured this enforced captivity was a pretty good time to catch up on my reading. On top of the stack was a hardcover with two incredibly pretty young men giving each other the eye on the jacket. They were fully dressed, so I knew it was a romance rather than some porn. The sex would be soft-core, the characters fairly two-dimensional, and the problems they faced would be most likely vapid, but it would while away some time without requiring a vast degree of thought.

The door in the gate opened, and this guy came in. Wow, was my instant reaction. I put the book down on the table. He was wearing a black tank tee, tight black jean shorts that reached almost to his knees, with the bottom inch or so rolled up, and calfskin ankle boots with heavy socks pushed down on top of them. He was wearing a black baseball cap with the fleur-de-lis emblem of the Saints on the front. He had a key ring in his hand, and he walked right over to the door of the vacant apartment and unlocked it. When his back turned to me, my jaw dropped. He had without a doubt the most beautiful ass I have ever seen in my entire life. It was hard, it was round, perfectly curved. It was an ass to make men weep, an ass that belonged on an underwear box, an ass that could launch a thousand hard-ons.

I lit a cigarette.

A couple of other guys, muscular, attractive enough but nothing like the first, came back carrying boxes. Any other time, I would have probably been attracted to either or both of them, but the incredible beauty of the first boy (I found myself thinking of him as a "boy" strangely) made them seem like the girls who don't make the Top Ten at Miss America. I'm sure they were used to it—it probably happened to them in bars all the time. I sat there for several hours, watching them move boxes and furniture, occasionally breaking to have a beer or a smoke at one of the iron tables in the courtyard. The also-rans eventually removed their shirts, displaying fairly nice torsos, one with some hair, the other completely smooth. Again, under ordinary circumstances I would have been fantasizing a pretty damned vivid three-way scene. If I could walk I'd be down there helping, flirting a little, feeling them out about trysting. I would watch the sweat glistening on their bare skin in the sun and wonder how it might taste, if their armpits were becoming a little smelly perhaps from the sweat, if their underwear was sticking to their asses. But my mind was solely on my new neighbor, hoping that he too would take his shirt off, give me a glimpse of his chest and back, maybe the waistband of his underwear showing above his shorts. It never occurred to me that they might be aware of me, the aging man in the wheelchair up on the balcony watching them hungrily without even saying hello. I never saw them look up or give any indication they were being watched. For all I knew, when they were out of sight on the street taking stuff out of the truck they could be laughing their asses off at the perv on the balcony, thinking he's hidden behind the wrought iron lacework. But if that were the case, it wouldn't have mattered to me at all. I could not tear myself away from watching the boy in the black tank tee.

They did talk loud enough for me to finally figure out their names: my neighbor was Mike, the tall redhead was appropriately enough Sandy, the shorter Italian looking guy's name was Axel. They were easy with each other, joking and teasing in that way people who have been friends for a long time have. Every once in a while one of them would say something as incomprehensible to me as Sanksrit, and they would all burst into hysterical laughter. They each knew the secret language of their friendship, which had been learned over too many drinks at the bar on Saturday night, from brunch on Sundays, from long involved phone conversations. The rest of us were excluded from it.

I found myself wondering if Mike was dating either one of them, if there was more than friendship between them.

I also wondered if Mike slept with his curtains closed.

I watched until they apparently were finished, Mike's shirt remaining on the entire time, as though he were teasing me, knowing how desperate I was to see his bare torso. His shirt was wet with sweat, and it clung to him tantalizingly, just enough for me to see the outline of his round pecs, his flat stomach, to see the play of the muscles in his back. It was around four when Sandy and Axel took off, left Mike to deal with the boxes and the bags and the assorted debris of his life. I sat there on my balcony, watching the bedroom window, and sure enough, after a few moments Mike walked in carrying a can of Diet Pepsi. He stood in front of the dresser, reached down, and started pulling the shirt over his head. His skin was tanned, firm, supple and smooth as silk. He wiped his face with the shirt before tossing it into a laundry basket, and took a big drink from the can. The muscles in his arms moved under his skin, the afternoon sun glinting on the sweat. He then moved out of sight. I sat there for another few minutes, hoping that he would come back, remove the shorts and underwear, but the seconds ticked away maddeningly.

Reluctantly, I pushed myself back into the apartment.

I spent the rest of the day avoiding the balcony. Some friends came by to bring me dinner and cigarettes, I must have flipped through the channels about a thousand times per hour, and finally around ten I gave up and went to bed.

I woke up at three in the morning. Wide awake, staring at the ceiling, unable to go back to sleep. I lifted myself into the annoying wheelchair and pushed myself out into the living room. I lit a cigarette, but resisted turning on the lights. I wheeled myself out onto the balcony. The night was quiet, even though the insanity of Bourbon Street was just a block away. I sat there, staring at the clouds reflecting the neon of the Quarter back down at us, and was about to light another cigarette when I heard the gate to the courtyard slam shut. I heard laughter.

Sure enough, it was Mike and some guy. Mike's shirt was tucked into the back of his jeans, his torso glistening with sweat in the moonlight as he tried to put his key in the lock. I couldn't get a look at the guy he was with's face, but it wasn't either Axel or Sandy. The moon just then came out from behind a cloud, and as the silvery light bathed the courtyard in an eerie almost otherworldly glow, I got a good look at Mike's companion.

I knew the guy—his name was Blake something or another. I'd seen him around in the bars for years, dancing with his shirt off. He was very big. He towered over Mike as he stood back waiting for Mike to get the door open. He was about six three, and weighed about two hundred and thirty pounds of thick muscle. His pecs were as big as cantaloupes. His biceps were bigger than my head. His ass was big and thick and meaty. I had many times watched him moving on the dance floor with his shirt off, hoping against hope to catch his eye. It never happened. Well, I never really expected it to, you know? Great big muscle boys never noticed guys like me. No, they only noticed other muscle boys or hot little numbers like Mike.

The door finally opened and they went inside. The living room light shone through the blinds. I went ahead and lit the cigarette.

The bedroom light came on.

The two of them entered, and I caught my breath. Blake was carrying him. Mike had his legs wrapped around Blake's waist, his arms wrapped around his head, and they were kissing. Blake's hands were firmly planted on Mike's ass. He turned and set Mike down on the dresser and stepped back. Mike's hands went to Blake's belt buckle, unfastening it and tearing the buttons open on the fly of Blake's jeans. The jeans slipped down a bit, and I could see the top of Blake's ass. It was white against his dark tan, wiry black hairs running in a patch just above the whiteness where the deep crevice between the thick cheeks began.

Mike grinned at him, and yanked Blake's pants down.

Oh, man.

Mike slid down off the dresser to his knees, slightly pressuring Blake to turn a bit to the side. By doing so, I could see Blake's long thick cock, his low hanging purplish balls, the thatch of black hair. Mike's tongue flicked out, licking the head of it, and Blake brought both of his hands down on top of Mike's head. Blake tilted his own head back, his eyes closed, as Mike started working on his cock, slicking it with his spit, his mouth moving back and forth, his hands moving up to tweak Blake's big round nipples, then squeezing those massive pecs, pinching and pulling on the nipples again.

I dropped my hand to my own dick, which was erect.

Blake reached down and put his hands underneath Mike's armpits, and the muscles in his upper body flexed as he lifted Mike bodily into the air. He set Mike down on the dresser again, opening Mike's shorts and yanking them off. His tongue snaked out and he began licking Mike's neck, then moving down the center of his chest. Mike's head went back, his eyes closed, and Blake pulled Mike's white boxer briefs down. Mike's dick was smaller than Blake's, but thick, nestled in perfectly trimmed hair. Blake's head went down and I knew he was suckling on Mike.

This was better than any porn tape I owned.

Blake raised his head from Mike's dick, which glistened with spit. He reached under Mike's arms again and picked him up, turning him so that he was standing on the dresser with that beautiful ass right in front of Blake's face. He pushed Mike's thighs apart, reached up and spread the firm white cheeks apart, and then his face went in. Mike's back arched, rounding his ass even more as Blake feasted upon his asshole. Mike's arms and back flexed as he shifted slightly, writhing from the pleasure of Blake's tongue licking and probing him. Blake's hands smacked the white roundness, leaving reddish prints, over and over again.

I could almost hear the sound of hand striking flesh.

Blake stood back for a moment, and Mike turned to face him, squatting down until he was sitting on the dresser. His eyes were half-closed, his hair slick with sweat. Blake grabbed hold of his ankles and pushed them up in the air, until Mike was lying on his back, his ass hanging off the end, his legs up in the air.

Blake shoved his cock into Mike's ass.

Mike's back arched up, his abdominal muscles springing out, his mouth open, his head going back.

I could almost hear the moan coming from between Mike's lips, the moan of pleasure, as Blake slowly slid back. Mike's body trembled as Blake paused, then flexed his meaty ass and shoved all the way back in. Again, Mike's body convulsed.

My cock started to leak a little.

The strokes I made on my own dick were slow and steady, matching Blake's inside Mike's ass.

Blake brought his big hands down on Mike's chest, squeezing, kneading, pinching. Mike's face was lost in the joy of getting so thoroughly fucked, fucked by a beautiful big muscle stud who knew how to fuck a pretty boy.

Mike's calves were resting on Blake's big shoulders.

The rhythm of the fucking began to pick up.

Blake must be getting close, I realized, increasing the stroke speed of my own hand.

Mike's entire body tensed up as Blake sped up, the strokes still long and deep, just faster and faster.

Cum began spraying out of Mike's cock, shooting up and splashing on his stomach, chest. One shot flew over his head.

Blake pulled his cock out and shot his big load all over Mike's torso.

They stood still for a moment, frozen in a moment of time.

Blake leaned down and they kissed.

And I came, my load shooting up into the air, all over my hand and arm.

They moved out of my line of sight.

I lit another cigarette, my breath coming in gasps.

I wiped my arm and hand off with a towel.

I sat there, smoking, for a moment, replaying the scene in my head. My dick began to stir again.

Mike's front door opened, and they walked out. Blake had his jeans on, his shirt tucked into the back. Mike was wearing his white boxer briefs. They glowed a bit in the moonlight. They walked together to the gate, around the corner of the main house, out of my sight. I heard the gate open and close.

Mike walked back into the courtyard and over to his front door. He paused for a moment on the sill, then turned and looked right up at me.

He raised his right hand and waved, a smile on his face.

The door shut behind him.

And I wondered, in the darkness behind my wrought iron lace, when the next show would be.

SENSITIVE NEW AGE GUYS
by Bart Magma

Listen to me: I am not a homosexual poster boy. I am a *fag*. A big, fat, anonymous-sex-in-the-park, queer, buttfucking fag. Get used to *that*.

A fag, when confronted with something soft that should be hard, responds by saying, "Catch you later!" An uncooperative dick is not an *issue*. It is just some shit that happens—mostly to other people, of course. A fag simply moves along to the next stinky flower. No voices are raised. No tears are shed.

This is how it always was. I liked it.

This was my happy life, that is, before my guy infected me with his narcotic pollen. Now no other flower stinks quite the same as Karl does, and I need it. My stigma quivers for that pollen. I quiver for his stigma. Love, I guess you call it.

Which should not be a problem, ordinarily. Even for fags like us. That's what you'd think. But that word, the "L" word can have strange effects.

Such as: Once we were *in love*, Karl insisted we must have tender loving. Karl swooned—he said—for my tender loving. Karl's dick, however, had different ideas.

Karl diagnosed fear of commitment. Mine.

Which is how I came to be sitting on this mauve leather couch while the guy sitting next to me—my guy—talks about his feelings. The worst part? I'm next.

The professionally attentive homosexual (not a fag, no, categorically *not* a fag, and gods help the man who utters the "Q" word in this room) sitting across from us will wait until my guy finishes and then he will turn to me. He will say, "Now, Dean, how do you feel about what Karl just said?" And I will tell him. Sort of.

Karl and I and The Homosexual have been doing this every Wednesday for a few months. Voices have been raised. Tears have been shed. The Homosexual gives us homework, as he calls it, and we do it. Then we report back to him. You'd think we were trying for a damn badge.

Why? How did this happen?

I am a fag! Not a scout of any kind, but a fag.

Now Karl is looking at me. The Homosexual is looking at me. Obviously it is my turn and, to be quite honest, I haven't been paying attention. How can I? How can they? Don't they smell it? Karl's scent is so thick in here that I can't believe we're not talking about it, if we're being so goddamn honest.

I rub my chin (stubbly) and then the mauve leather (smooth). I want to look like I'm thinking. I am thinking—about that sweaty, hairy, slightly shitty odor we're awash in, the thick chunky Karl soup garnished by a rosette of Ivory soap.

Damn you, Karl. Damn you and your intoxicating pollen.

I don't say that.

I say, "Karl, I don't think I heard you clearly. Will you please restate what you said?"

Lame, but The Homosexual does not roll his eyes. The Homosexual smiles encouragingly.

That's what I hate about homosexuals. They let you get away with shit like this and they call it "honesty."

Karl says, "I want more kissing, and I want to look into your eyes when we're making love. Is that clearer?"

Oh yeah. Totally fucking clear, along with the fact that Karl's ass smell just intensified about 10 times, which I would not have thought possible.

My dick wants your ass, fag, so bend over and grab your ankles. If you want to look into my eyes while I'm fucking you, glue a picture of my face to your kneecap.

I don't say that.

Instead I say, "I hear that you want more kissing and you want to look into my eyes when we're making love."

Karl is staring fixedly at the top button on my shirt. If he moves his eyes, they will roll. He will sigh. He might say something sarcastic and, in this room, sarcasm is even worse than the "Q" word.

The Homosexual asks Karl, "Did Dean get that right, Karl?"

"Yes," Karl says. His eyes dare to rise as far as my nostrils.

It's my turn now. The Homosexual is going to say, "Dean, what do you think about Karl's desire?"

He says it. This time I am ready with my answer.

"Karl," I say, gazing meaningfully into my guy's right eyebrow, "I will be happy to kiss you more and to look into your eyes while we're making love. I want you to be happy. I want us to be happy. Is it also all right with you if I still fuck your brains out from behind? And may I still ream your stinky rose with my fat, wet tongue, tickling your balls with my deep, manly grunts as I press my face into your ass?"

Karl's lips part. His head tilts back and his chin juts out. He exposes his neck to me. He blushes.

I don't need to move my eyes away from his to know that Karl's nipples are hard rivets inside his light-starched, machine-pressed, blinding white shirt. His more-than-respectable dick, restless in his boxer briefs, will be bent now in a way that is no longer comfortable. Karl's anus will be fluttering slightly, wondering whether to fart or itch, greedy for my fingers and my cock.

The Homosexual, who gasped audibly despite himself when I said what I said about Karl's stinky rose, recovers finally. He says, "Karl?"

I think, *Leave us alone, fool.*

Karl will be thinking, *Shut up, fool.*

We don't say that.

And I don't grab the front of Karl's blinding white shirt. I don't pull him toward me roughly, his perfect pearl-white buttons bursting off as I twist the fabric and crush him against my chest, my fist bunched between our two racing hearts.

I don't say, *You want kissing? I'll kiss you, boy.*

I'll press my rough, stubbly face into your smoother, darker-skinned face. I'll bite your lips hard enough so it hurts and you don't want to pull away, until you go numb and your jaw relaxes. And then I'll push in my impatient tongue and slide it along the skanky, coated insides of your teeth.

Yes. I'll kiss you.

Karl, who wanted me to look into his eyes while we were making love, is looking into my eyes now. He wants to shut his eyes. He sees me and he sees my thoughts. He fears he will succumb right here, right now. His arms twitch to slide around my neck. His fingers are greedy to bury themselves in my unfashionably long hair, to smash my face into his for a bout of tonsil tango. He aches in his boxer briefs. For once, he wishes he were soft when he is hard.

My stinkflower struggles. He has almost forgotten about The Homosexual.

I have not forgotten. I can feel the pulse of anxiety and arousal washing over us from The Homosexual's direction. I like The Homosexual's discomfort. I am belligerently sexy.

Some things I have forgotten: Why are we here?

Is it our turn to talk?

Whom did The Homosexual address?

What did he ask?

What does he want?

The Homosexual clears his throat. "Our time is almost up," he mumbles.

Karl and I are engaged, immobile. If I move, I'll leap on top of my guy, who is frozen in flight like a doomed gazelle.

"Dean," The Homosexual interrupts. "Karl? We need to end now."

Karl clears his throat and looks at The Homosexual. He half-smiles.

"I want you to do homework for next week," The Homosexual says. He's more confident now that he has Karl's attention. "I want each of you to set up something purely for your partner's pleasure. Surprise him or let him know what's coming; just make sure you focus on his pleasure."

This week, it's my turn to write the check. I scribble it quickly and place it on The Homosexual's credenza, avoiding The Hug. By the time I walk down the hall, Karl is standing in the waiting room, looking tall and lean and hard-edged. He gives me a crooked, boyish grin.

As we walk out to the car, he says, "Be ready for anything on Tuesday night." I open my mouth to ask him questions, but something in his face—mischief, with malice seething not far beneath it—stops me. OK then, I can do this. I can wait.

But guessing games aside, Tuesday is too far off. I decide to surprise Karl on Sunday.

He gets no warning. When he walks in with the groceries, I take the bags from him and tell him to get naked. I've got the perishables in the refrigerator by the time he strips and tidies himself up. (Help me. I am drowning in stinkflower pollen.)

I blindfold Karl and lead him into the bedroom, which is heated by dozens of candles in custard dishes. After I tie Karl face up, spread eagle, to the bedposts, he gets to suck my dick while I sit on his chest. I am nice. I take off the blindfold so he can see me. (Do I get an "A" on my assignment, Homosexual?) I even prop up Karl's head with pillows.

I look down my hairy chest and belly at my slurping guy. He can't get me all the way down his throat in this position, but I press myself into him until his eyes bulge, until there are tears oozing out of his eyes and broad streams of saliva running out of both sides of his mouth.

I don't let Karl drop contact with my eyes, even when I can no longer make sense out of the pattern of light and shadow that comprises the face I'm fucking. It could be Karl. It could be a Halloween pumpkin after the candle inside has burned out.

Just before it's too late, I yank my slick, slimy dick out of Karl's mouth. He has been sucking hard, absorbed in his task, not expecting my premature evacuation, so I come out of his mouth with a loud, soggy pop. My balls hum angrily as my dick bounces, seeking warm wetness.

But I am not ready to be done.

I crawl backwards and off the bed. I untie Karl's feet, grab the ropes and pull his ankles toward his head, lifting his ass. His right ankle gets tied to the headboard above his right wrist, and then his left ankle above his left wrist.

Now I've got me a curled-up Karl taco with his ass invitingly tilted up toward me. My dick, restless, strains toward its favorite hole.

I pull Karl's hips even higher and slide a towel under his ass. Then I scoop out thick lube and slather it on his hole. I kneel up between his spread legs and bend forward over him as I begin to work the lube into his ass with my hand. Karl lunges at me with his mouth. I nip at Karl's lips and tease him with my tongue. Eventually I let him connect and I push my face into his, grinding my stubble into his chin and cheeks.

My guy has the angular grace and wispy facial hair of his grandma's Nez Perce heritage. I have the burly body and broad furry cheeks of my Celtic granddaddy. The surface differences turn me on, yes, but it is

Karl's dark fag heart—just like mine—that I root for with these kisses. I want to snake my dick up his ass and shove it into his soul. I want to shake him up. I want to jolt Karl out of his earnest, misled head, which mistakes my greed on a cellular level for his unique stinkflower and only his; which looks at lust and sees some sitcom-gay, psychologized inability to distinguish his scent from any other.

You fool, I'm thinking as I shove the tip of my dick against his greasy anus.

Think like the Big! Fat! Queer! you are, my dick says to Karl as I jam myself into him in three hard thrusts.

You piss me off, Karl, I purr as my dick parks inside him, just feeling the heat and tightness of him as his muscles clutch me. I look into Karl's face, which is turned away from me, mouth open, veins protruding in his neck and forehead. *Look at me, fag. Isn't this what you said you wanted?*

I pull out and slam into him.

Again.

Again.

Slowly, but brutally hard, each thrust pounding his feet and hands against the headboard where he has braced them.

Don't? You? Feel? This? I thrust at him, speeding up now. I jab myself, my whole self, into him, fast now, bending his backbone toward his shoulders.

I do not give him a chance to breathe.

I just fuck him. I look at his face as he grits his teeth and grunts. I'm going to shoot in his ass, inside him, face to face like a girl. *I'm fucking you like a girl, is that what you wanted?* I slam-ask him.

His dick is hard between us. His hands are tied and he cannot touch it and I'm busy lifting myself and coming down hard into him.

I'm glad Karl is not the kind of guy whose dick shrivels up when his ass is getting attention. I'm glad he's the kind of guy who gets hard and squirts on me from the pressure of my weight on his ass, the pressure of my dick relentlessly assaulting his asshole.

He squirts before I do, as a matter of fact, wildly flopping around and spattering my belly, his thigh, his chest and my chest. The hot jizz landing on me makes my own dick let go inside him, inside my buttfucking boyfriend, my Karl, my stinkflower.

My arms turn to rubber then and I belly flop onto Karl. I lie and pant on his heaving chest, glued together with our sweat and Karl's jism.

When I'm strong again, I sit up and crawl off him. I slide to the headboard to untie his arms and legs. Freed, we lie side by side, breathing together.

I am making up my mind already, minute by minute, deciding to like whatever Karl has planned for Tuesday. Because there will be times like this, and that's enough to look forward to, and someday he'll get it that *this is it*, this is what my buttfucking heart looks like—and his too.

We fall asleep together like that Sunday night and we wake up together Monday morning. But Monday night I want for myself. Monday night is mine.

I still have my own apartment. I spend Monday night there because I want to wank and savor our Sunday, and all the days and nights with Karl, and all the times with everybody before Karl, and the guys I look at and who look back at me, and myself. My own greedy flesh.

Whatever we were supposed to learn according to The Homosexual, what I have learned is to show Karl who I am, the real man, the real faggot. I can show him the faggot he is too, the *queer goddamn buttfucker*.

I want to know, for at least one more day, that this is good enough. Tuesday will come and I will learn what I learn—not according to The Homosexual, but according to what makes a bead of precum form on the end of my dick.

But first, my dick. Me. Mine. Me touching me.

I get into a rhythm, a trance like I can get into when I know I won't be disturbed. I slide into almost-cum after almost-cum until I am about to fall asleep and then I speed up and I get off hard. I fall asleep before the jism cools on my belly.

And I wake up too early, sticky and resigned to the night of homosexual romance Karl must have planned.

Karl phones me at work. "Looking forward to tonight?" he asks, sounding pleased with himself.

"Of course!" I reply, trusting bad cell phone reception to make me sound convincing.

Karl wants me at his place by 7 p.m. on the dot. I am there on the dot, carrying a bottle of pinot noir because my guy likes red meat and he knows I do too.

But when the door opens, there are no cooking smells. The table is not set. There is not a package wrapped in corrugated gray paper and raffia and a tastefully suggestive anthurium sitting on the table near my plate. Karl takes the bottle and says, "Thanks honey. We won't be needing that tonight."

Karl is more python than puppy tonight. My Karl, my sticky-pollen stinkflower, a python?

I suddenly lose 10,000 feet in altitude and land on a rusty iron spike of anxiety. I was ready to be disappointed. I wasn't ready to be actually surprised. What has my stinkflower concocted?

"Are you ready?" he asks. "Do you need some water to drink? Do you need to pee? Because we're ready for you."

We? That one word sweeps me into full apprehension.

It feels damn good.

"No, I am ready," I say. "Take me now, big guy." I reach for Karl's ass, but he slithers away from my hand.

"You might want to save your energy," Karl says over his shoulder. He is already walking away. "Follow me."

He is so sure I'll follow him that he doesn't look back. He's right.

We're heading for the bedroom. OK, so maybe it's no surprise after all.

Karl holds the door open halfway, standing behind it. The small opening forces me to slide through sideways.

It's bright in here, so bright that my eyes are overwhelmed.

But it's not just the light.

Karl sits calmly at the foot of the bed, legs crossed, leaning back on his hands. His dark skin, the brown silk shirt and linen pants, the stubble of black hair on his shaved head are perfect against the copper bedspread.

I am not the only one present to appreciate it.

Lining the walls on both sides of the bed are the dining room chairs, three chairs on one side of the bed and four chairs on the other. Each chair holds a gentleman sitting just as calmly and elegantly as Karl sits on the foot of the bed.

I recognize a few of them: a former professor who introduced Karl to the pleasures of Ecstasy; a guy Karl shared a house with for years; a boy Karl took care of for months last summer after the boy's first Daddy dumped him. The others are strangers to me. They are all looking at me with polite expectation.

"We're going to have a gallery tonight, Dean," Karl says in a normal tone of voice, as if he's asking me whether I need A-1 for the steak.

I'm sweating now. My dick is already half hard.

"Kiss me," Karl says, as he pulls his own softy out of his unzipped pants and waggles it at me.

My blood is all in my neck and cheeks. I can feel my heart pounding in my sinuses.

I don't know how I get across the room to the bed, but I find myself crouched over Karl, who is lying back on the copper bedspread, his mouth open, his jaws working. I have my fingers wrapped around his neck. My hands are not tight enough to strangle him, but they are tight enough to make it difficult for him to breathe, to block the blood flow through his carotid.

"You want me to kiss you?" I growl. "Fuck you and your romantic crap."

Karl squirms between my thighs, which tightly squeeze his hips.

"Dean?" he gasps. "Dean. Dean..."

I hear some chairs moving. I see some turned over in my peripheral vision, but I don't care.

When I let go Karl's throat, he gulps breath. I snatch and pull the front of his shirt. Buttons slice through silk. Fabric tears, revealing Karl's flesh. Red meat! I can feel the living heat of Karl's heart through his smooth chest. I want to rip it out and taste it.

I fasten my mouth on his right nipple. He likes the hot saliva and intensity at first, but then I bite hard. I gnaw on the copper-brown nugget of his nipple, which tastes coppery too as I draw blood.

Karl makes a sound that isn't crying or laughing; it is both at the same time. His hands clutch at my biceps. His fingers dig in. They pinch me. It hurts. The pain goes right to my dick.

I leave Karl's nipples and grab his wrists. I pin his hands above his head and drop my whole weight onto his body. My dick is so hard by this time that, even inside my pants, the loose edges of zipper on Karl's pants chafe me.

I want flesh. I must have flesh.

I let go of Karl completely and stand up. Nothing except me and Karl exists; the eyes I feel on us make that even clearer. Their attention creates a grid, a cell in which we are the animals, the only live animals in this room.

I undress slowly—for Karl and to tease the watchers. Karl methodically removes his shoes and socks and pants and briefs, never taking his eyes off me.

I shrug off my undershirt, the last clothing to go, while I rub my crotch open-palmed, rolling my dick back and forth like a potter getting ready to throw a vase. I look at Karl, the coiled snake, through the eyes of prey turned predator.

Naked, I know I look pale and huge in this light-washed room. Looming over Karl's dark, lean shape, I move toward him slowly. He does not stir. He half-smiles, the corners of his mouth quivering slightly.

Karl's dick is half-hard, puffy. It arches to one side of his flat belly, where it greases his hip with precum, pulsing a little. His hands are on his belly, nearly but not quite touching his dick.

I grab his puffy johnson in one hand and drag it toward me. I stroke it a few times, pulling and stretching. Then I cradle it in one hand while I slap the base of it near his belly. He *oofs* and his knees start to come up, but then he immediately flattens his thighs on the bed. I press my thumb into the underside of his dick below the head and I rub hard in circles. I feel him transform under my hand, rubber turning steel, brown turning brick red, warmth turning fever hot.

I hear a soft, involuntary moan to my right. Karl hears it too. He inhales slowly and holds his breath, lifting his hips toward me, offering his genitals to me.

Red meat, red-brown and reeking.

Precum shiny on his dick head.

Succumbing to his smell, I bend and bring my broad face close to his flesh.

I part my lips and slide him into me a millimeter at a time. I don't know who suffers more from this slow gobble, Karl or me. When I hear grunts and moans on both sides of me, I realize neither Karl nor I is suffering the most. Together, we are torturing these men, the watchers. I smile around the shaft in my mouth.

I drop my head and let Karl's dick violate my throat. I gag and bring up thick mucus, which lubricates us both—his dick and balls, my lips and face and chin and neck.

I open to him. I take my hands away from the base of his cock and slide them down under his buttocks, forcing him toward me. Karl's ass doesn't need to be asked twice. It rises into me, fucking my face slowly while I growl around him, swallow him and gag-flutter his dick head. I drool on him until his crotch hair is drenched and my saliva coats his balls.

I feel Karl's dick setting into pre-explosive concrete. My throat wants that. It wants his load, the sweet-salty pudding of him coming where I can taste it...

But no. My dick wants its stinkflower even more. And I can't have both—not yet, not this way.

Someone to my left grunts rhythmically, "OOOooooooo fuck O god O fuck O jesus fucking christ." A wad of cum splats on my ribcage.

I slide Karl's dick head out of my throat and along the cupped valley of my tongue, through the lip-cushioned portal of my teeth. Then I grab his slimy column in my hand.

Karl's lips are pulled back from his teeth. He looks feral and ready to rip out my throat. His eyes are slitted and pleading, vicious and needy.

I stand up and slap the outside of his thigh.

He whimpers. My dick jumps and blurts out a spoonful of precum.

"Turn over and give me your ass, boy," I say. Politely. *Please pass the stinkflower, you piss-ant. I need seasoning on my red meat.*

He knew I would do this. He knows what I want.

He rolls slowly—shoulders first, the rest of his body following, sleek, snaky. Long sighs and wheezing come from either side of us. I smell buttcrack-sweat and precum in five different flavors around us. It intoxicates me.

I look around. The lube pots that Karl thoughtfully supplied are all in use now. Karl was so thoughtful that he hid one tub of lube for us under the bed. He reaches for it and discreetly places it next to his butt, which is facing me now, upturned inquisitively.

I dip my fingers in. I daub his buttcrack with lube and leave it to his heat to melt it. Karl is waving his ass at me. Insolent stinkflower. He has both hands under his pelvis, working his dick.

I grease my hands and jerk my own dick, smearing myself with plenty of lube. I know my dick looks big and juicy when it is this hard, when I am this ready. Groans around us affirm it. I enjoy the show. I enjoy being the show. My juicy dick preens like a jock for a cheerleader.

I grab Karl's hips and pull him toward me on the bed. I yank until his feet are on the floor and his hips on the edge of the bed, then I pull his pelvis up and back toward me. He is jackknifed over the edge of the bed now. He leans on the bed with one fist and manhandles his cock with the other one. He has not availed himself of any lube; he prefers tough love when he's wanking.

I cradle my penis and offer it to Karl's spread ass cheeks. It investigates his cleft, up and down, pausing longer and longer at the bud of the stinkflower. Finally, I press there. I lean into it. Karl knows it is his job to fuck me into him, to thrust until his ass swallows my dick.

"O god," somebody says.

Karl waves his hips from side to side, bending and straining my dick, making my balls swing.

"Sweet jesus," somebody else says.

Karl moves his ass in a circle, a ripply circle because he is jerking so hard on his dick now. *Don't you dare come before I do, prick!*

Karl is enjoying this. Karl is showing off, the little shit. Retiring homosexual? My ass.

I take a handful of Karl-ass in each fist then and put an end to his display. I thrust hard at the same time I tug him back toward me, and my dick barges into Karl's ass. It takes a few strokes for the lube to work in around his defensively tight sphincter, but I keep tugging and thrusting, fucking him hard. His spasms—painful to him, no doubt, and hard on me— squeeze my engorged dick. My belly slaps against his ass. The room around us grunts in rhythm with our slap-slap-slap.

He's been teasing me for too goddamn long. I come fast and hard, burning into Karl. I hear a roar; I realize that's me. I hear a high-pitched yelp; that's Karl. Jism is flying around us and landing all over—on my legs and the bed and on Karl's balancing arm. It's all hot, all mine; I own it. It's as hot as my own jism pumping invisibly into Karl and the feeling of his prostate jumping inside as he shoots spooge.

I keep pumping the boy beyond my pleasure and his. Still hard but too sensitive, I'm not willing to waste a minute of dick, no matter how much it hurts.

I do want to hurt Karl, my impertinent stinkflower, the master of ceremonies, my fucktoy and performance artist, my crash test dummy. I want him to feel the ache in his ass for days. I want him to remember what a fag he is and get over the politically correct crap. I want my guy back, my man.

I don't stop until I have to, until I lose the power to stand up. Then I crash forward, taking Karl down with me onto the soggy bedspread. The copper fabric is slimy with lumps of cum—our own, and cum from all of these strangers.

I'm not looking into your eyes, stinkflower. Get that. I'm not kissing you either, just drooling and panting into your sweaty neck and stroking your sweaty baldstubble head. Do you get it now? Do you get that we're buttfucking freaks of nature? Do you?

"Karl," I breathe into his sweat-slick neck. "Karl, you faggot, I love you."

Karl's chest jumps. He's laughing. The stinkflower's laughing! At last. He laughs at his stinkflower queer stinky faggot self, all covered in unromantic jism and who cares whose it is?

I put my greasy hands around Karl's sweaty skull. I cradle his queer hypothalamus and squeeze out the pus of his stinky thoughts. *Get this, faggot. It's good. Just bend over and love it. Love me.*

He gets it. The sweaty sticky queer faggot gallery gets it.

And the stinkflower stamen, as several witnesses can attest, is no longer a problem.

Karl will make the call tomorrow.

The Homosexual will have to find someone else to fix on Wednesdays from 5 to 5:50 p.m. We've got laundry to dirty, holes to fill. We're queer and we cannot come to the phone right now.

OVEREXPOSED
by Ian Philips

W. 42ⁿᵈ & 8ᵗʰ Ave.

Words aren't my thing. You'll get that as we go along. It's not like
I'm illiterate or won't read. (Translations of classical Japanese haiku or
graphic novels when I feel in the mood.) It's just I'd rather see the words of
others pass by—like the blur of houses and parking lots and trees seen from
a commuter train—than spit them out all by my lonesome. The reason is
one of the few uncomplicated things about me: I'm all about the eye. Not
just what we can see but how we see what we need to see. Like in framing a
shot. With a camera. Not a gun. That's traditional weird. I'm not traditional.

I'm into guys too. Okay, that's more traditional than you'd think. I
like to watch guys. Not all guys. Just the hot ones. What makes a guy hot?
It's in the eyes. His some. Mine mostly. I get hard for the ones who make
my eyes widen a bit as they walk towards me. Dart quickly to the side
before they pass. Force my whole head to turn to check out the curve of the
back of their heads, the slope of the necks, the breadth of their shoulders,
the heft of their asses. Again, very traditional. But that's not what I really
wish, really want to see. It's the look of their faces in those singular seconds
before they come and that sole magical one when they actually do. That's
what I walk the city searching for. That's why I take the pictures through
my fingers.

Not so traditional.

W. 22ⁿᵈ & 8ᵗʰ Ave.

Take six months ago. I'm walking to hook up with a friend for
coffee. I spot this guy. I don't really *see* him until I look at the pictures later.
And I'll look at them a lot. But I'll get to that. Now, looking back (see how
words fail me), I remember him as a tall slight Black man. As for his face, I
don't need a memory. I have hard proof of why he makes me hard. He's got
a kind of wild 'fro that must've waved with each step, skin the color of
coffee (two creams), a thin nose that flares a bit as it points down to his lips
that are so beautifully swollen they barely touch. His eyes are closed so I
can't tell, can't remember either, what color his eyes are, but I've imagined
them from every shade of brown to a piercing green.

Anyway, the first moment his face washes out of the crowd, when
he doesn't catch my eye but seizes it, I shove my hand in my pocket and
squeeze. Not my dick. That always comes later. No, I grab for my digital
camera and hold it as tight as I can. I press my fingers into the warming

metal and rub my middle finger over the lens. Again and again. Then I head home. I know I'm blowing off my friend. But I'm no good for coffee. I'm too distracted. I have to go home and download. I can't wait. If I do, the image fades. Or doesn't even show up. I've "taken" hundreds of photos before this one and done a few controlled "experiments" that've left me convinced of this. And as blue as my aching balls.

I get inside my walk-up walk-in closet that only in New York can be called a studio and still get the rent they're asking for it. I turn and slam the locks shut. All the while I'm kicking off my shoes, fishing the camera out of my pocket before my pants fall to the floor, tossing it from hand to hand as I shuck my jacket and sweater and T-shirt, stepping on the end of my sock with my other foot and wriggling free. I hear my feet slapping against the floor as I walk the few feet over my futon to my desk—my boner pointing through the fly of my boxers, pointing the way. As I plug in the camera, I slip off my shorts and put them over the cold plastic of my chair. Mouse in one hand and dick in the other, I download.

A couple of clicks and there he is. In some of the most intimate seconds of his life, a whole string of them which I double-click to enlarge until I find the one. Each is a head shot. Of the man who has seized my eye today. The lighting and framing just right. Illuminating, if you want to get arty or religious about it. As if done in a studio, not the street where I've just seen him. I don't know how I am able to do this—to capture the face of a man at his most private—or why this happens to me. Maybe where there's a will there's a way. I don't know. I just make the most of my good fortune and watch. Stroke my dick and watch his face. Stroke and imagine what has gotten him to the point that he has to make this totally pure expression: a beautiful frown that makes the hairs on my balls stand on end.

I find the one. It's him at the second he comes. The perfect moment. The perfect face. I mirror him and I become aware my hand is sticky and a shudder is fanning out over my back. I sit back, close my eyes, and run a finger over the tip of my wet dick.

God, he's hot.

For the rest of the day and into the night, I imagine him. The color of his eyes which, like I said, I can never know because they are always closed—almost—always rolling back. The slow jumping of the muscles in his chest and his forearms as he pumps or jerks or fondles or strokes, underhand or overhand or on the side or with both hands, his dick, which is sometimes fat and cut or long and veiny or curved and uncut, the skin so black it's nearly purple or a swirl of earth tones giving way to the pink or the hard red of the head of his dick. Until each and every one of these different, beautiful dicks shoots, cum splattering his ribbed or soft, small gut and his muscular or narrow, lean thighs with the heavy sound of paint hitting a drop cloth.

God, he's hot.

8th Street–NYU (subway entrance)

A month (and forty or fifty men) later, I run into The One. He's coming out of the subway as I'm at the top of the stairs about to go down. He's not super hot. What's super hot? A guy who knows he's foxy. Humpy. Well, that's what the old farts who were my age in the last century used to say. You know, like the guys in a really good porno that you rewind and fast forward over and over to watch. All hard—cut, ripped. Nothing soft but their asses and lips, maybe. No, he's beautiful. A perfect mix of hard and soft. Like the model in a painting or a statue. That's it. Like a model, but more ancient. Too perfect almost to be part of this grimy world.

I can't tell if he's tall at first. Until we climb/descend the stairs closer. I can tell now that he is. Tall, that is. And muscled, some, in his shoulders and arms, as they stretch against his long-sleeved black T-shirt. Maybe from playing guitar, painting huge canvases, bagging groceries. His hands look soft though. (No guitar, no groceries. Probably a writer.) And his face. It's framed by long, dirty-blond hair, parted in the middle, tucked over his ears. His eyes are wide and blue and deceptively gentle. His nose is all straight lines ending in rounded angles like on a classical sculpture. As I said, he's beautiful like an ancient model. His skin is smooth, a hint of blush, like he would be apple-cheeked when he gets drunk. And his full pink lips are the softest feature of all. They're almost artificial, plastic in their color and unblemished fullness—like the wax lips you got at Halloween—but perfectly rounded. In the picture I will take, they are parted, but only a bit, for breath to escape. For moans. And for the cigarette he always keeps at the end of his arm, swinging back and forth, the burning end of a metronome, until it slides its way back into his wet pink hole like a fat beer can of a dick taking an ass that's been fucked by every man in the room in some classic porno.

I'm stumbling down each stair, never breaking eye contact, gripping the railing with one hand and fingering my camera with the other. I feel the image of him flowing from my eyes, through my nerves. I feel the particles break up, pulse out my finger into the camera to develop. I can see myself downloading these pictures in twenty minutes, if I'm lucky, and daring what I've never had the balls before to do. I'm going to put the printout of his perfect face at its most perfect moment on my pillow. Then I'm going to crouch on all fours in front of it. And finger my hole. Get it wet with spit. Stretch it while I pull on my dick and push the finger in deeper.

I imagine the hurt. The burning. I've never been fucked before. Mostly because I've been afraid. Not ready. I've been waiting for the right boy with the right dick to come along. He has. I keep pulling and pushing…

Until this dickhead on the stair behind me shoves me into the wall to get by. I wave him on with one finger and look over. The One is gone.

Thirty-five minutes later (what do I expect at rush hour), I'm in my apartment, sitting naked before him, and he is staring straight back at me. He's even more beautiful when he's angry. Or aroused. I can't tell. This has never happened to me before.

I come so many times before I fall asleep—sweating and panting and sticky and happy—that I'm sore for the rest of the week.

E. 11th & Ave. "A"

I keep my favorites pictures on the ceiling over my bed. At first, to cover up the peeling plaster. Now, to help me sleep. To help me dream. Sometimes I like to go a week without taking my camera with me, without coming, without touching my dick except to take it out to piss. Then I lie down and look up and imagine them all in one big circle jerk. I've hit the wall behind my head several times doing just that.

I put a photo of The One in the center of all of them: white boys with freckled faces and red hair who look like they're just off the bus; real blonds from California and fakes from everywhere else; brown boys and Black boys: Puerto Ricans, Cubans, Dominicans, banjee boys and gastas and brothas; Vietnamese, Thai, Chinese, just arrived and 4th generation New Yorkers; some a mix of races, a mutt of nations; all of them either bike messengers, suits, dealers, DJs, actors, writers, boys in the band, hookers or the ones who want you to believe you should pay; each with a story I've given them to get me off.

They surround The One. I stare and watch for them to take notice of him. They're in their usual enormous huddle, each one with his hand wrapped around his own hard cock. Then, he's standing in the middle of the circle. They don't swarm him. They must know he's mine. But they do turn and start making out with each other, grabbing this dick or that ass, falling into groups of three or four or fifteen. There's so much fucking and sucking going on it looks like when a painter takes his palette and twists his brush around and the colors with them. And that leaves him, standing, pulling a hand, then just a finger to his lips, those lips, and sucking it. His back arches and his other hand grips his dick and begins to pull. Almost as if he's lifting his whole slender body by his dick. He takes the wet finger and slides it behind his back and into his butt. It has to be that when he's making such a face. He pushes and pulls. I do the same. Until we come (first him, then me) and I hit my lips and chin and chest. I run my tongue over every inch of skin on my face it can reach. I convince myself that each drop of cum I swallow is his.

8th Street–NYU (subway entrance)

I'm hooked. Okay, I'm fucking obsessed. Mad. I search all over the East Village, NOHO, and LES. The Lower East Side. And The Village and Chelsea and, well, you get the idea. I come here. Same spot. Same time. Same stairs. I never see him.

I see plenty of other guys. Each picture is hotter than the next. Each one closer to the very second the seed shoots out like a volley from a canon. Or like the circus acrobat in the tight white satin suit blown out of its mouth and across the gasping crowd to the waiting net. Corny, huh? Like I said, words and I don't work so well together. I get too flowery. Too girly for my own good, my old man used to say. Still would if I ever went back. Whatever. If I had some pictures on me, I'd show you.

Anyway, none of them are him. And then about three months ago, I'm here again. I go down the steps. Nothing. I toss my token and go through the turnstile and wait on the platform. He's nowhere. It's my train and I shove my way to the doors with the rest of the crowd. I stop dead. It's him. On the other side of the doors. I want to jump or wave or shout or something. The doors open. He wades through the oncoming tide of people and when he's an inch from me, he turns and forms those lips into a smile. These are for you, he says, handing me a small brown envelope. I grab it before this suit walks through it and then shoulders and briefcases and backpacks jostle us away from each other. Now we're on opposite sides of the doors. He waves. I want to cry or blow him a kiss. Something totally over the top. Instead, I smile feebly. I feel like all I've had to eat or drink today has been coffee. I'm shaking. Not enough to notice. (Hell, I could have had a seizure right then and nobody would've noticed.)

Twenty minutes later, I'm fiddling to close the locks on my door while I unbutton and yank all my clothes off. I tear open an end of the envelope and am on my back on my bed with a very wet finger up my ass before I spill whatever is inside all over my chest. It's too big an envelope for just a letter. It has to be photos. It is.

It's me. My face. My perfect face. I've never seen what I look like when I'm coming. My dick now is twitching to stand higher and higher. The next picture is me again, coming. I don't know how I know it's that very instant but I do. I look away from myself and he's there—in the photo—with me. Biting my ear. About to come himself. I close my eyes and press my finger in as far as it can go. I let the hot, sharp pulsing subside and then rock it side to side. And back and forth. I open my eyes again and fumble for the next photo. It's us. Both of our faces twisting towards the blinding flash, eyes clenched, each face an exquisite grimace, as if the bulb—his bulb—is bursting inside me. Our faces are slick with sweat. His long hair is wet and matted to the sides of his face. Like he swam his way inside me. Like he stroked his long, muscled arms and kicked his strong but slender legs through rivers and seas of air to get to me. To get inside me.

I see him. I feel him. And I blow hard. No hands near my dick. Cum flies over my head. And then again onto my chest and the fronts and backs of the photos lying across it. And then one last time onto my stomach.

But the photo I hold in my hand is untouched. Perfect in every way.

And when I finally think to flip it over, there is his name and number.

W. 42nd & 8th Ave.

Did I call him? Of course. Did we fuck? Still are. Made some videos even that put the pictures to shame. He's my boyfriend. But we have an arrangement, BenJ E. and me. I can look at other guys—they can be naked, stroking their dicks, shooting even—just as long as I'm shooting through the lens of a camera. It's kind of old-fashioned—this arrangement and the camera I use now—but it works. No fights. No fears. Best of all, no guilt. And sometimes he watches me watching them watching…us, I guess. My camera lens or me or me and my camera lens or me and my camera lens and BenJ E. All three of us. And I like to work naked. I make BenJ E. strip down too. I want whoever I'm shooting to feel cool with it. And to know how much I love what I'm doing. How much I appreciate them for letting me see them totally exposed. In the raw. Real.

So, what do you say? Can I take your picture? Or do I have to stick my finger in my pocket and rub?

THE BEST DAY
by Michael Rhodes

In the late seventies my ex-wife, Penny, and I lived in Evansville, Kentucky. I was working as a mechanic and she was waitressing in town. We'd only gotten married a few years earlier. She wanted to have babies right away, but I wanted to wait. I told her we weren't stable enough financially yet. Anyways, we were young. I was 24, she was 19. We had a lot of growing up to do.

We had a little house in town. Had good neighbors on the block, including a nice couple, Bill and Edna, that lived right next door. They were a little older than us—Bill was maybe 30, and Edna a few years younger. We used to hang out with them a lot. Sometimes we'd have them over for barbecues, or the other way around. They had two girls, Virginia and Kelly. Penny really loved those girls.

Bill worked as a miner, and he was always trying to get me to do the same. Said I'd make good money and we could work together. I thought hard about it, mainly 'cause I think I would have liked working with Bill. But I liked the sunshine too much, and couldn't picture spending all day long where it was dark, cold, and wet.

We went to Church with them on Sundays, and lots of time when we got back Edna and Penny would take the girls into town to do shopping or something. Bill told me how much he liked his Sunday afternoons, especially when it was sunny. For him, it was next to heaven. He'd sit out there on the balcony off the second floor and just kick back.

One Sunday in June I decided to get some work done on the roof. The weather was perfect. Not a cloud in the sky, and it wasn't too hot either. We'd had some leaks the prior winter. I'd done some quick repairs to get us through, but I knew I needed to nail down some more loose planks before they blew off in the next big storm.

I had some lunch with Penny first, then she headed downtown with Edna and the girls. I gathered up my tools and took them out onto the roof. I remember how nice it felt that day to slip off my shirt in the sun. I usually wore a shirt at work, but my arms ended up getting all tan and the rest of my chest and back stayed pale. Had a smooth, pretty nice-looking chest. I don't know, guess I just thought it probably all looked nicer one color.

I stepped up onto the roof and started my inspection. I made sure to walk carefully, with light steps, in case any of the shingles was in really bad shape. The front looked decent except for just a couple of loose ones, so I got to work with my hammer and nails. I heard the back screen door open at Bill & Edna's, and knew Bill was heading out for his afternoon siesta. I reminded myself to try and hammer quiet so I didn't disturb him.

When I was done, I continued my inspection, making my way to the back of the house. I happened to look over at Bill's balcony. The view was partially obscured, but I was a little surprised to see Bill's feet sticking out over the edge of a towel. Didn't have no shoes or socks on, which was I guess a little funny to me only 'cause I'd never seen Bill without one or the other on.

I was afraid he might be napping, so I took a couple more steps forward to see if I could peek over the edge, just to see if he was asleep. Each step I took, though, got my heart beating a little faster. I didn't see any pants on him. Or shorts. I took another step and suddenly realized Bill was naked. I could see the black patch of hair between his legs. His cock was resting on top of his balls, which looked really huge even though I was quite a bit aways.

I don't know what got into me that day, but I was kind of curious to see him like this. It wasn't the kind of thing I imagined Bill doing, laying out in the nude like that. Not that he had anything to be ashamed of. Bill had a really good body, strong chest and washboard stomach. He was lucky, I guess, 'cause of the work that he did and the fact that he wasn't a big eater. It just wasn't the type of thing, though, that I ever pictured him doing. Back then, in that town, it wasn't the type of thing that you could picture *anyone* doing.

I bent down and tried inching forward, real quiet. I made sure I was out of his range of view in case he lifted his head and looked up. It was then that I saw his hand reach down and come to rest on his thigh.

I could feel something happening down in my own pants, and didn't know what all that was about. My heart started to beat a little faster. I found myself kind of wishing that something else might happen. I just stayed hunkered down like that for a few minutes, just kind of watching, to see if he was maybe gonna do something else.

Something did happen. I could see that his cock was starting to stretch out a bit. His fingers were starting to rub between his balls and his thigh. I noticed my mouth was open watching all this, and I told myself to keep it closed. All of a sudden his hand started moving up over his balls and his cock. He grabbed it, and slowly started stroking up and down.

For whatever reason, this was getting me hard too. Probably 'cause seeing something like this—well, it just wasn't the kind of thing that you imagined. Was Bill doing this all those other Sunday afternoons that Edna and the girls were away?

Then Bill did something a little strange. He took his other hand and stuck his fingers down around his balls. Then he lifted his hand back up to where his head was, even though I couldn't see it. I wondered why. First I thought it was just an itch or something. But then he did it again. And a third time. Jesus Christ, I thought. Bill was smelling his balls.

Every time he lifted his hand up, I could see he was stroking himself a little faster. It was crazy—people in this town just didn't do stuff like this. Or that was what I thought. I certainly never did stuff like that. Man, all I did was jump on top of Penny and in a few minutes it was all over. That was all I'd ever done. Sure I'd done myself before, always had since I was a kid, but that was also always over in a minute or two, tops. Bill must have been doing this for at least five minutes.

But there was more to come. I saw him lean forward over his dick. I was scared when he did this, 'cause I knew if he turned around he would see me. But I was too fascinated not to keep watching. He spread his legs out further and leaned forward. I saw the muscles on the back of his neck kind of straining. Like he was trying to bend all the way forward, down to... down to his dick.

I felt my mouth drop open again, but this time I didn't bother trying to close it. Bill kept doing this for a few minutes, straining. Then he seemed to relax a little bit and lean back. I got even more nervous, thinking he might look back now. I thought of how, if I saw him start to turn around, I'd just pretend to be looking over a piece of wood.

But he didn't look back. Instead, he spread his legs even further and leaned forward again. His right hand was gripping his dick, and I could tell he was trying to stretch it out to his mouth at the same time that he was lowering his head down. His dick was really long. I remember thinking to myself, if anyone could do what he's trying to do, it'd be him 'cause he's got a dick real long like that.

Through the crook of his arm I saw his tongue reaching out of his mouth. It was so close to his dick—almost touching it. I could feel my own dick leaking like a faucet inside my pants. Then, with one quick, concentrated effort, he leaned forward again and licked his dick.

Even from as far away as I was, I could hear a little moan carry up from the balcony. His tongue retreated about an inch or so. It was like his whole body was frozen except for his dick, which was quivering a little. I held my breath and just found myself staring at his cock.

Then all of a sudden I saw something shoot out of his dick. It hit him right below his nose and I saw his head pop back a bit. Then another shot seemed to spray his whole face. His tongue was darting out all over the place while he made his hand move up and down real fast over the shaft. Another shot came out, this time going directly into his mouth. He made a strange noise and leaned forward again, covering the head of his cock with his lips. He kept making little motions with his hand, and his lips were all puckered around his dickhead, like he was sucking at a baby bottle.

My dick felt so excited right then, I thought that if I moved and it so much as rubbed a little against my pants, it'd pop off by itself and probably send me rolling down right off the roof. I watched Bill suck on his dick for a few seconds more. Then he slowly lifted his head up and leaned his body back to its original position. His cock was still completely hard. I saw it twitch a few times against his stomach.

My legs were killing me. Slowly I stood up, feeling the muscles stretching themselves out agonizingly. Then I walked slowly, quietly back to the other side of the roof, stepping through the bedroom window and back into the house.

I'd never done anything like this before, but I swear, I dropped my pants right then and there and grabbed my cock. I was rubbing it real hard and fast when I looked down at it. I looked at it the way I saw Bill look at his. I even leaned forward a little.

I could see the head of my cock real close. It looked different to me than I'd ever seen it before. Maybe it was 'cause I didn't normally spend a lot of time looking at it. But right then, at that moment, I don't know how to explain it, I just wanted to be close to it. I leaned all the way down, til my head was just a little below where my dick was. I kept stroking it. Then I opened up my mouth and stuck out my tongue.

Soon as I did that, I could feel an orgasm coming. I stopped my hand from pumping, trying to make this last a little longer like Bill had, but it was too late. I erupted with more cum than I ever thought I could have in me. My dick has sort of a downward bent, so the first stream missed me completely, landing with a loud splurting sound on the wood floor. Then I lifted it up high and two more gushers came out and sprayed my face. Some of it dripped down my face and onto my lips. I thought of Bill sucking down his own cum, and I decided to lick it off my lips. That was the first time I'd ever tasted my own cum. First time I'd ever thought of it. It tasted a little funny, but good.

Anyways, afterwards I went in the bathroom, grabbed a towel and cleaned everything up. I couldn't believe what I'd just done. Couldn't believe what Bill had just done.

I was worried about the next time I'd see Bill. Wasn't sure how I'd react. It was during the week, and I ran into him bringing some trash cans down to the curb. He smiled and waved. I waved back. I remember thinking how strange it was that people could be so one thing one minute and something completely different the next. I didn't say anything to him that day. I just went right in the house.

I kind of avoided him during the week. I don't know why. 'Cause at the same time I was avoiding him, I was also counting down the days until Sunday. At night I'd get hard thinking about what I'd seen that day. I couldn't even think of touching Penny. I told myself that my mind was just spinning too fast at the moment that was all. Just had to get all this out of my system.

Sunday finally rolled around, and the truth is I was hornier than a dog by that point. I hadn't touched myself all week, and all I'd been thinking about was last Sunday. I had to practically push Penny out the door to do her afternoon deal with Edna.

I waited inside the house for about ten minutes, but then I couldn't stand it any more. I had to get out on the roof. I took a hammer and nails with me so I could look like I was doing something again. It felt like my dick was about to jump outta my pants. But when I got to the other side of the roof, Bill wasn't there. I felt real disappointed. I hung out there for maybe 15 minutes, but no sign of him. It was getting really hot up there, so finally I gave up and went inside.

I walked downstairs and out the side door that led to our backyard and the side of the house bordering Bill's. I tried to casually look over into the three windows on the left side of their house, to see if I might see him. Nothing. No Bill. I knew he was in there, but what the hell was he doing?

Reluctantly, I went inside. I felt kinda depressed, I guess, it's hard to put into words. I went into the sitting room in the back. That room looked out into the backyard and had a lot of windows. Even the doors that opened up into the back had windows. The neighbors from all sides of the house, if they wanted to, could look in on me. That moment, I felt really horny, and I guess a little wild.

I don't know what got into me, but I decided to take off my shirt. It felt kind of exciting. I don't think I'd ever walked around downstairs before without a shirt on, certainly not in that room. I rubbed my chest a little and just kinda stood there. Sort of wasn't sure what to do next. Or if I should do anything.

But it felt so nice standing there like that, and I was so horny, I decided to try my pants. I was real nervous when I started popping the buttons. I stopped for a second, wondering if I could really do this. But I started imagining how I might look with my pants pushed down. Like, around my ankles. The thought of it made me super-excited. So I pushed my pants down.

I knew this was crazy. Someone could see me standing like this so easy, but I didn't care. I wondered what Bill might think if he saw me standing here like this. I looked down and saw the bulge sticking out of my briefs. My dick was in one of those tingly, semi-hard states that you sometimes get when you're super horny. Like it's so ready that it can't get too hard right away.

I wanted to see it. I wanted to see it pop out. I wanted to see my underwear drop down to the floor with my jeans, and when I pictured myself standing there like that, a grown man in his own home standing there with his pants and underwear bunched up around his ankles, I just did it. I slipped 'em down and watched my dick pop out.

I caught a whiff of my dick smell and it made me kind of shaky. Suddenly I thought again how dangerous it was to be standing here like this. Any of the neighbors could see me. So I got down on the floor and lay in the sun. Damn it felt good—to be completely naked and lying in the heat like that. I thought, no wonder Bill liked this so much. It felt so good I was scared to touch myself. Thought for sure I'd pop in a second. Then I saw a little shadow in the corner move.

My heart started beating real fast. Part of it was the shadow from the bush in back, but there was another part sticking out that looked kind of round, and the way it blended into the shadow from the hedge, looking like it was kinda hiding behind it, it looked like it was someone's head. For some reason, I just knew it was Bill. I was afraid, though, to turn around. Afraid to see him seeing me. I was also scared to touch myself. What would he think if he saw me jerking off like this out in the open? I told myself, *you seen him do the same thing.* But it didn't matter. I was too afraid of what he might think.

But I was horny. I had my pants pushed down. Then I remembered Bill from last week. How I'd seen his feet first. He'd taken everything off. So I pushed my shoes off my heels and kicked off my pants and underwear. Finally, real slow, I got the edge of my sock with my big toes and pulled them off.

I was completely naked now. My dick felt so twitchy and tingly inside. I lifted myself up onto my forearms. In those days, I had a pretty good body, but it's not like I really noticed it. We only had the bathroom mirror in the house, and it was too small to look at yourself up and down. I don't know... I just never spent a lot of time checking myself out. But today was different. I found myself looking at my body the way that Bill might look at it. I started looking at my chest and stomach, and it felt kind of good to realize that I didn't have an ounce of fat on me. My stomach was smooth, not a single bulge or pad of fat, and I had a good build. I looked at the muscles on my arms, forced out a little bit because of the way they were bent. I even flexed 'em.

I looked at my naked legs and feet. Seeing myself like that, I just couldn't believe I was all nude like that. All nude on the floor.

Then I looked down at my dick. It was still mainly soft, lying forward over my balls. I noticed how light my dick hair looked in the light—almost blonde. I also saw how big my balls were, with the skin relaxing and growing in the heat of the sun. Looking at my dick made it feel super tingly again. I saw the shadow move slightly, reminding me that Bill was watching. Then my dick twitched.

It was growing out. My dick was getting hard. I didn't know what to do. Should I just reach down and grab my underwear, cover up? I felt too paralyzed to do anything. I also felt too horny. My dick was getting harder, and someone was watching, and it felt like there was nothing I could do. I swallowed hard and felt my heart start to beat real fast.

It was getting harder, but the head was stuck against my thigh. I had a pretty long one, probably about 7 or 8 inches, and so the middle part of it started to bulge up in a big arc. Christ, I felt so horny. I thought of reaching down to free it, but I just couldn't do it. But it was getting so big and hard. I was afraid.

Then all of a sudden the head popped free and the whole thing flopped back. I heard the slap of my dick hitting the skin below my stomach, then it popped up. Since my dick doesn't stick straight up, so when I'm lying back it's kind of sticking up in the air a little bit. That was what my dick was doing at that moment. Sticking hard and sort of up. I had to close my eyes for a sec 'cause I just felt so exposed and helpless.

When I opened them up again I saw my dick still hard. I tried to will it to get soft. What was Bill thinking watching this? But it wouldn't get soft. It seemed to be harder than it had ever been my whole life. I didn't know what to do. I felt like I couldn't imagine what could possibly be more embarrassing, but then I saw it.

My dick was starting to drip.

Fuck. That was all I could think. Why hadn't I thought of this? When I get super horny, my dick leaks all over the place. And now, very quickly, I saw pre-cum starting to bead up on the lips. I closed my eyes and tried to force myself to think of something else. But then I had to open my eyes again and see what was happening, and when I did I saw a slow-moving trail of pre-cum moving down the crown of my cock.

It was so disgusting. Bill not only saw me all naked with an erection like this, but now he was watching a big river of pre-cum oozing down the back of my dick. I was sure he was completely revolted by this.

But the shadow wasn't moving. He was still watching. If he was disgusted, why hadn't he moved already? Why hadn't he just turned around and gone back in the house? Maybe he liked watching other guys' dicks leak pre-cum. He seemed to like seeing stuff come out of his own. Heck, he even ate it. Maybe he wanted to watch stuff come out of my dick.

It was when I thought of this that I felt this wild, super-tingly sensation building in my dick. I can't even tell you what it felt like. It was too incredible. My whole life I'd either jacked off with my hand or come inside my wife, with her gripping my cock with her cunt and pulling the cum right out of me. But I felt something wild and sexy and incredible building up inside of me, and it was just amazing.

I looked at my dick, in a way I never had my whole life, and saw how beautiful it was. How much I wished I could get close enough to it to lick that pre-cum up and taste it. How much I wanted to take the whole cockhead in my mouth, swirl my tongue around it, and suck down some of my juice. And if I could reach that far, I imagined sucking the whole thing down my throat. I was thinking not only how good that would feel on my dick. I was thinking how good it would feel in my mouth.

I imagined Bill watching me suck my own cock. Would he think it was sexy? Would he open the door to this room from the outside, bend down next to me, and watch me take my own dick in my mouth? Would he get his face so close to my mouth that I would feel the heat of it on my skin? I pictured him moving down, staring at my dick like I was staring at it. I thought maybe his nose would wrinkle a little when he smelled my dick smell. Would I be ashamed of how my crotch stank?

I thought to myself, *maybe Bill wants to see my dick cum.* It made my dick jump up. I repeated the thought. I think Bill wants to see my dick cum. My dick jumped up again. Bill was watching my dick jump. He was watching my dick leak and jump up and down. He was standing there waiting for it to start cumming. My dick was horny. It was jumping. It wanted to cum. I thought, it wants to start squirting cum. And when I said that word, I don't know what happened to me, it was like the wildest, sexiest word I'd ever heard. It made my whole body feel so quivery and trembly inside. I almost didn't say the words to myself. But I had to.

Bill wants my dick to squirt.

I felt something building up inside, all by itself, and God I just wanted to reach down and touch it, reach down and jack it off. But I couldn't. I was frozen except for my jumpy, juice-dripping joint, and all I could do was repeat the words in my head.

Bill wants my dick to squirt.

I stared at my dick; I drank up every square centimeter of smooth or wrinkly dick-flesh, and told myself again.

Bill wants my dick to squirt.

I wanted it to squirt. I looked at my dick, and I told it silently, in my head: *Please squirt. Please squirt, dick.*

It jumped and tingled, and my body was shaking inside, and I kept telling it. *Please squirt. Please squirt.*

Squirt, dick. Squirt.

Please squirt me.

Please. Please. Squirt on me.

Please squirt.

Please squirt.

Squirt cum.

I said it out loud. "I want my dick to squirt." The sound of it was so wild and awesome and sexy, and I felt this huge rolling sensation rolling through my body. I said it again, even louder.

"Please squirt on me, dick."

My voice sounded higher. Jesus, I was panting like a dog. My heart was pounding.

I leaned forward, just staring at it. I talked to it again.

"Please squirt cum." Fuck, my voice sounded like a little girl's. But I didn't care. I kept saying it, over and over. "Please squirt, dick. Please squirt. Please make cum. Please make cum for me. Please… make squirty… cum for me!"

That was it. I felt this awesome wave of feeling through every part of my body, and suddenly my dick just began lifting up and out of the lips came this long, giant stream of cum. It was like I was pissing a river, but it was all cum. It started out on my belly and my dick kept lifting and then the stream started running up my chest, all the way up to just below my chin.

My mouth dropped open and I remember letting out a soft kind of moan as I caught a whiff of the smell. I looked down at my cock and suddenly it shot out a burst of cum and hit me dead in my mouth. I remember moaning louder as it kept erupting in pulsing bursts, spraying my chest and my chin. I was fucking drenched in cum. And even as my orgasm started to fade, my dick kept jumping up and forcing out more little squirts of cum below my belly, until it finally started to soften and left my cockhead jerking around in a puddle of cum.

I was so embarrassed. The shadow moved just a little. I closed my eyes.

I sat there for several long moments. I had to know. I had to know whether he'd seen this. Maybe I could explain it to him. Maybe he might understand. I had to move sooner or later. I couldn't just lie here like this. Maybe he'd seen me seeing his shadow. Maybe he was frozen there too. I had to talk to him, explain this, tell him he could go on back to the house, it'd be our little secret. Had to tell him. I opened my eyes and turned my head.

He was gone.

I remembered feeling a little sad at that. I turned my head back and closed my eyes, feeling the cum on me getting thinner and beginning to run down my cheeks. I opened my eyes and saw the shadow again. He was back.

I took my fingers and used them to scoop up some of the cum puddle on my belly. I thought of Bill watching me do this. I decided to just go for it. So I scooped up more and more cum off my stomach, then used my hand to catch some of the stuff dripping down my face, and when I had a bunch of cream all over my fingers I brought it to my mouth. I stuck out my tongue and licked it up just for Bill's amusement. I saw the shadow moving a little. He was probably jerking himself off.

I stroked my softening cock for him a little, just for a few minutes, to give him time to get off. Then, with the sun and the sex making me drowsy, I drifted off to sleep a little bit.

When I woke up, I could tell from where the sun was that it was mid-afternoon. I ran upstairs and cleaned up, knowing Penny would be back any minute.

The next time I saw Bill he acted like nothing had happened. But I knew he knew. And remembering that day always gets me horny, even all these years later, long after I saw Bill for the last time and Penny and I moved away from Kentucky and then split up and everything changed, I still remember it like it was yesterday. I've had a lot of great sex since then, you know, but that day, I don't know—I don't know if that could ever be topped. I'll tell you something that probably sounds real crazy. That day— sometimes I think it was the best day of my whole life.

JUST LOOKING
by Michael Huxley

I was working at home recently, quick-reading newly submitted manuscripts, grading each one according to my "5-point scale"—2.5, 3.7, 0.5 (my god, this guy calls himself a writer...?), 3.0, and etc.

I had just finished an excellent short story and was marking the top margin with a red-inked 4.8 when the phone, lying next to me on the bed, rang. It was my lover, Paul.

"Hey Babe, what's going on?" he inquired.

"I just finished reading a dynamite story from a new writer."

"Oh yeah? You give him a 5.0?"

With bored braggadocio I quipped, "You know I reserve that grade exclusively for my own work."

"Did you get all worked up, reading it?"

"As per usual..." I replied, clutching my hard-on through the workout shorts I'd failed to change out of upon returning from the gym earlier.

"You do anything about it?"

"No, but I *want* to."

"Good, hold that thought," he said. "I'm fuckin' horny as hell, saw the butchest motherfucker walkin' down the street just now, *whoa*: shirtless, torso to die for, long hair, tattoos, and what an ass... What a babe!"

"Sounds nice," I responded, ripping my Velcro fly asunder. "You... coming home for lunch?"

"I'm on my way. I want dessert first."

"No problem, I'm preparing it now." Hanging up, anticipating dessert, hauling my cock and balls through the Velcro partition, I milked my precum and savored it. *Yum...* I got up, gathered my paperwork into a pile and placed it on the dresser before stepping out of my shorts. My dick bobbing before me, I quickly snagged a porno film from our collection— *"Biker Pigs from Hell," perfect!*—slammed it into the VCR and, turning it on, reclaimed my place on the bed. Oh yeah, there he was: a naked Bo Garrett, shot from behind, fucking the shit out of some sleazeball lying on his back, whose legs Mr. Garrett was holding high in the air.

The butchest motherfucker... torso to die for, long hair, tattoos, and what an ass! And how he was moving it! *You go for it, Bo. Dig it, man. Yeah.*

Luxuriantly if cautiously, I played with my wet erection, but *man* did I feel like shooting a big one. *Get your ass home, Paul...* I thought, resisting the urge to just go for it. After maybe ten minutes, Bo and his bottom-buddy disengaged and managed to walk to the Harley chopper in the background, where they fucked some more and finally shot their loads, jerking themselves off, snarling and cursing like the Pigs they were depicting. *Holy shit*, I thought, *I wanna do that*. Masochistically, I rewound the money shot and watched it again—and then again—before rewinding the film back to the beginning of the fucking scene. I hit "play," and settled into doing just that when I heard Paul's truck pull in.

The bedroom door was open, the doorframe suddenly filled with my lover who, grimy from his morning's house renovation and witness to my hedonic hand-play, said: *"Jesus*, Babe, look at you… Y'havin' a good time? Fuck yeah, you are! Mmm… 'Biker Pigs', huh?" He stepped closer to the bed, where he stripped naked in a flash. A gorgeous man if I do say so myself, the love of my life's wonderful dick was already hard, transecting his fist. Remaining standing, he began to watch the film, stroking himself, commenting: "Y'gotta admire the way that man fucks…"

"Babe…" I implored, drawing myself up a bit. "C'mere. Let's make out, suck dicks a little. Please…"

Giving sudden voice to concern, Paul said: "Oh, don't stop what you're doing; you look so beautiful! I don't wanna make love, Michael. I wanna get off watchin' the film, watchin' *you* watch it. Let's have a good wank, Babe. That okay with you?"

Nonplussed for about a half second, I readily complied, more than content to watch Bo Garrett's hot ass churning, his big dick slipping in and out of the other guy's slick anal grip. It was a stunning, extended fuck scene, nicely edited and shot mostly from mid-range. Both actors were obviously enjoying themselves immensely, as were Paul and I, participating as both voyeurs and exhibitionists. Oscillating my visual focus between the sizzling television screen and Paul jerking off, I gave myself completely over to pleasuring myself stereoscopically, every precummy hand stroke, rapturous.

Once again disengaged, Bo and his playmate were facing one another on the Harley, jerking off, talking dirty, getting close to orgasm. The other guy shoots off first, his face a twisted mask, as copious spurts bolt from his piss-slit in thick, white increments, spattering the bike's seat. Bo follows suit a few moments later, matching his co-star's discharge shot for shot and then some. I noted for the umpteenth time the way Garrett's upper lip curls, sneers involuntarily, right before he lets loose with his first, dense man-blast of cum. Paul, watching the scene intently, obviously on the brink himself, moved to my side of the bed, which afforded a closer study of his writhing, fist-fucking, *shouting* detonation of ecstasy. Watching him slam his wad so forcefully ushered my own crescendo at once, which spawned similarly self-induced arcs of mind-bending pleasure. *Ascending, ascending, YEAH…*

***

What man could ever forget the first time he brought himself to sexual climax? By the age of twelve, I'd been playing with my dick for as many years before that momentous occasion as I could remember. But, enjoyable as those hands of solitaire were, they never resulted in either "getting the white stuff," or the "super-good feeling" rumored to accompany that elusive phenomenon. Perhaps, suggested the more cocky representatives of the schoolyard grapevine, I was still too young. *But then again*, I counter-thought, *perhaps not.*

Suspecting that I just wasn't jacking off long enough, I stripped naked in my bedroom, home alone one evening. I sat on the edge of my bed, feet on the floor, my silky hard-on jutting straight up from my lap, and began moving the deliciously sensitive skin up and down my aching boner. I took my time, glancing at a magazine, whose cover featured a good-looking, U.S. Army "grunt" in Viet Nam. I remember the photo vividly: the G.I. was stripped to the sweaty waistband of his camouflage fatigue pants, wore a grimy bandana on his head, and was in bad need of a shave. His dog tags bivouacked in a nestle of dark chest hair, he was lighting a cigarette, cupping the match...

Time passed pleasurably enough, but nothing out of the ordinary was happening just yet. Determined, I quickened my pace somewhat, unconsciously allowing the P.F.C. to lure me into a rhythm of hand-to-boner-involvement I had heretofore never experienced. I certainly didn't understand it at the time, but felt myself becoming more involved with the image of the soldier, more caught up in the moment, as my enjoyment increased proportionately. It was taking forever, it seemed. But *what* was? What was the "it" I expected to happen? Whatever, I just kept that sweet skin a-movin' up and down my unsuspecting boner, having a grand ole time, just *looking...*

After a healthy, meat-beating while, I swallowed hard and thought to myself, *Man, this is starting to feel pretty damn good, in a different kind of way.* I persevered, breathing faster and sweating a little. My heart was racing. *Damn*, I thought, fixating on the magazine cover, *this guy looks so cool...* My cock continued to feel better and better; I was fucking loving it! Suddenly I felt an intense wave of pleasure from deep within my cock. Thinking, *oh, this is startin' t'feel REALLY good*, the wave subsided, but hot on its heels another, more potent one overtook it. Followed by another and another, and *another*, each wave proved more intense than the one preceding it. I didn't think I could tolerate the pleasure growing any stronger, any *sharper*, but neither could I stop jerking off or exclaiming the word "Oh!" despite my joyous consternation. All at once my penis was gripped in an unrelenting frenzy of ecstasy. Unaware of why, I dropped the magazine, stood up, bent my knees a little, thrust my cock in the air, and let my first load fly sky high, screaming: "OH, *SHIT*..."

I had no idea anything could feel so... "good" seems an inadequate word, but there you have it.

I was shocked by how quickly the mood went away, but it returned with a vengeance later that evening while lying in bed, thinking about what had transpired earlier. I jerked off again, with the same excellent result only much *much* quicker in the messing of my sheets. From that day forward, I became hooked something fierce to getting myself off, so much so that I began feeling guilty about how many times a day I felt compelled to do it.

For no logical reason, I had an impossible time picturing myself as a grown man jerking off, yet I couldn't fathom ever being able to stop. Hard as I tried, I could not keep my hands off my pud, indulging compulsively in orgasmic escape with my military hero and, got forbid, while looking at myself in the mirror! I was continuously getting hard, oftentimes at the most inconvenient moments—staring at the crucifix during Mass, in the locker room before and after P.E., on a field trip with my classmates to the state correctional facility—and I knew of only one way to make those boners go away. Dashing to the nearest restroom, hands in my pockets, I increasingly viewed myself as a crazed sex junkie, and resolved to end the cycle of guilt by confessing to my family's parish priest.

It took all the courage I possessed to utter the sin of masturbation in that confessional, whispering it shamefully through the screen.

"Say three Hail Marys, three Our Fathers, and never do it again" was the priest's fairly indifferent-sounding penance-prescription. It seemed I'd gotten off lucky! But would I ever get off again?

The prayers were easy enough to accomplish, and I actually lasted (get this, now) *six weeks* with the second half of my penance, but inevitably one afternoon, beyond desperate for an orgasm, I caved in. Standing before the bathroom mirror, wanking frantically, I blew a load of such magnificent intensity into the sink that I fell to my knees, where—resisting the urge to rend my shirt and gnash my teeth—I flatly refused to beg God's forgiveness.

No, I resolved, I would never, *ever* confess the "sin" of masturbation again. Instead, I left the Catholic Church at fifteen, never to return to it, or any other organized system of (what I have come to view as) moral indoctrination, or mind control. In essence I concocted my own religion, set myself up as god, and elevated masturbation in status from sin to sacrament. Thus was my first major battle with self-loathing won. Dropping countless loads along the path to self-discovery, there have proven plenty more skirmishes, of course—far more intense waves of conflict (that Viet Nam grunt was definitely not a *PlayBOY* centerfold), but many, many more sacraments to hold sacred as well—Just Looking being but one.

I CAN SEE FOR MILES
by Marshall Moore

Amazing, what you can find in thrift shops. The ones in Berkeley and San Francisco can be disappointing, as thrift stores go, because the prices are high and everyone even halfway hip shops there. The ones down in Hayward have provided some of my best finds. I pick up half of my clothes and two thirds of the shit in my apartment in places like this. People who live that deep in the suburbs demonstrate yet again their resounding lack of style and taste by getting rid of the good stuff (*Martha, what's a Prada? Why did Billy send us these things when he was on vacation in Italy? He should have sent us pasta instead. I know what that is. But I'm not wearing this shirt out of the house.*)

"Check this out," Colin said. He's the one who unearthed the thing first.

My first reaction when he showed me the overhead projector was mild surprise. Schools don't part with audio-visual equipment easily. Not even the semi-well-funded ones within commuting distance of Silicon Valley.

"I doubt it works," I said. "It can't possibly."

"Plug it in," said the clerk, eavesdropping.

Colin and I exchanged our *What an asshole* look. I hoisted the overhead out of its bin and handed it over. The clerk, a swarthy bearded man in a turban, surveyed us both for a second before undoing the rubber band around the power cord and stooping to find an electrical outlet. I turned away to avoid seeing a terrible case of plumber's crack. A bright rhomboid of light shone on the wall behind him.

"Too cool," Colin said. He looked like was about to dance a little jig or jump up in the air to kick his heels together. Colin is a seven-year-old hiding in a thirtyish body. Despite his age and the three years he's lived in the States, he still has the plummy voice of a British schoolboy. "You want it?"

"What the hell am I going to do with an overhead projector?" I asked him.

"You're an intelligent lad, Jacob. You'll think of something."

"Why don't you buy it?"

"There's no room in my flat. If I buy one more gadget my roommate will call the building inspector and have the place condemned."

"Good reason. What the hell—I'll do something with it."

We forked over cash for our purchases—some clothes, a few books, a small bookcase for the apartment I had just moved into—and left. Colin was driving today—fine with me, let him deal with the constipated traffic on I-880. Once the bottleneck eased up, he punched the accelerator and swerved into the fast lane, his Audi accelerating effortlessly up to 85mph.

"Maniac," I told him, turning down his loud hip-hop to make sure he'd hear me.

"No, it's just that we'd need another hour to get to Ikea at the rate we were going. I'd like to get back to the city before dinnertime. The Bay Bridge'll be a bitch."

"It's always a bitch."

Colin turned up Dr. Dre instead of replying.

I just bought an overhead projector, I thought. *How stupid is that?* That's how it started.

***

Three weeks earlier, I had moved into a one-bedroom apartment in a mid-rise elevator building in lower Pacific Heights. Descriptions like that amuse the part of my mind that's still anchored in eastern North Carolina, where the only buildings over six stories are some dormitories and the medical school tower over in Greenville, a college town 45 minutes east of my hometown, Wilson. The descriptions contain more information that may be obvious to the uninitiated. For example:

In San Francisco, one-bedroom apartments are a scarce and therefore expensive commodity. Your name can languish on a waiting list for months, and depending on the neighborhood, you can expect your monthly rent to be at least $2000. It's insane. If your credit isn't immaculate, your job prospects gleaming, and your trust fund well-managed, forget it. That I can afford a place correctly suggests I've done well for myself.

Saying I live in a mid-rise elevator building cracks me up because the part of me I call the secret hick still grooves on the idea of any residential structure too tall for stairs to be a comfortable means of getting to my apartment. I'm on the sixth floor and have a pretty good view of the Financial District high-rises. On clear days I can see a sliver of the East Bay between some of them. I grew up in a three-bedroom ranch house in a subdivision named Windermere Estates, and my parents had a station wagon the size of a hearse. Now I live in Babylon by the Bay in a still-mostly-unfurnished apartment with a decent view, and I drive an old T-top Porsche 911.

And a view. But I'm getting to that.

Saying I live in lower Pacific Heights gives folks from out of town the idea my neighborhood is somewhat swankier than it is. I could also say I live in Japantown or the Western Addition, but Pacific Heights sounds better. I aspire; therefore, I am.

Now for my favorite part: the view. Not the high-rise office towers, not the fog as it drifts in off the Pacific, swallowing a block at a time. Yes, I can see all that. On a clear day, I can see for miles. But I want to talk about the view of the apartment directly across the street and one floor down. This guy lives there. My bedroom faces his. After sunset I found I could sit in my apartment with the lights down, and if I looked at the right time, he would get home from work—I thought he might be an attorney—and change clothes. And do other things. It was beyond belief. Not the kind of thing you'd see in Wilson, North Carolina. Never in a million years, and I loved it. Love it. I wouldn't say I got obsessed with him, but hell, you take your perks where you find them. Either he didn't realize he could be seen, or he didn't give a damn.

I thought, *Maybe he's an exhibitionist.*
Hell, who am I kidding? I fucking know he is.
I spy with my little eye.
And with my binoculars, I magnify.

Hot doesn't even come close to describing this guy, but other adjectives do. *Chinese*, for example. I walked across the street my first week in the apartment and checked the names on the door buzzer panel. The building itself is a bit odd: only four units per floor, and the other surnames listed (Jones, Mkele, Suydam) suggested non-Asian ethnicities. *T. Xu* was printed on the card in the slot I deduced was his.

His hair, in a ponytail by day, hung down to his shoulders, perfect obsidian black.

Wide shoulders, a sculpted body, narrow hips...

Cheekbones to die for. The kind of face meant to be photographed. I'd love to know where he works out, to get a body like that.

Handsome uncircumcised dick. Big. Anyone who says Asians aren't hung hasn't slept with enough of them. I would watch him jack off with the lights on. Did he suspect I was across the street with my binoculars in one hand and my own cock in the other, keeping time with him? Sometimes we would come at the same time. Sometimes the towels we used to clean up with were the same color.

I fucking love San Francisco.

***

By now you're getting the idea I'm not the kind of guy content to do nothing but watch. Don't get me wrong, Mr. Xu put on a hell of a show. Nothing demure about him. This one guy I pegged as his boyfriend—a white guy, red hair, nice build—either came over a couple of times a week, or lived there. I couldn't tell. Whatever their arrangement was, I watched them rut like barnyard animals.

One night I sat there with a glass of wine and tortured myself with the visuals as long as I could, binoculars in one trembling hand, the other wrapped around the glass to keep from beating off. T. Xu and the red-haired boy shed their clothes like they hadn't seen each other in months, like one of them was just back from the war. Black blurs of tattoos on T. Xu's smooth skin, glint of light reflecting off a nipple ring. The white guy had a pierced navel. Down on the floor, 69ing, T. Xu's foreskin visible from here, sliding up and down as his boyfriend alternately stroked his cock and sucked it, sometimes doing both at the same time. Jesus wept.

Both mouths crept lower: the rim-job version of 69.

Crawling across the floor like two dogs sniffing each other the first time they meet, the boyfriend ate T. Xu's ass, face buried between those perfect tan globes. T. Xu's face contorted, a mix of raw pleasure, with a stripe of amusement in the mix, as if he was getting off on the goofiness of what they were doing as much as the sensation itself.

I drained my glass and forced myself to walk to the kitchen for a refill. If I touched my own cock—if I even stared at it long enough—it would blow. The weight of my gaze felt like a mouth. I couldn't look at myself. I couldn't touch myself. Yet. I wanted to prolong this.

When I returned, they were fucking. I got over my pang of disappointment that I didn't see the preliminaries—T. Xu putting on the rubber, greasing his boyfriend's ass, plunging. That first thrust. The wince on the white boy's face as T. Xu's cock slid home.

Timing is everything. I sipped wine, trembled, took out my dick when I saw their rhythm increase. An internal voice said *Thank God* when I had my hand wrapped around myself.

Slowly, slowly…

As T. Xu's mouth opened and his eyes shut, and his body convulsed, flooding his lover with come, I sprayed my own load across my window.

T. Xu looked out at the night as if he knew he'd just given a performance. I set down my binoculars and offered unspoken thanks. Something passed between us. I couldn't name it, but it was there. It was.

***

Back to the present. I lit a cigarette and studied the overhead projector on my bedroom floor as the sun sank toward the horizon. The crane-like shadow cast by the neck of the overhead projector lengthened, the air itself seeming to deepen in hue like denim fading backwards. With only three pieces of furniture (bed, nightstand, chest of drawers) in my room, I felt a sense of space, of possibilities waiting to be revealed. No clutter. No baggage. Smoke curled in the air overhead, silvery but tending more toward white in the dimming sunlight.

The streetlamps switched on.

The walls of T. Xu's bedroom were painted cream, the trim and moulding a dramatic pink. T. Xu's furniture was black lacquered stuff his grandmother might have brought over from Shanghai. In the solemnly-attired Financial District, T. Xu dressed dramatically, black and anthracite and stark white at times, and from the way he carried himself, he knew how good he looked. I'll confess to seeing him on the street one day and following him back to his building. Hell, while I'm at it, I'll also confess to arranging sightings, just to see him order a sandwich in a deli or eat dim sum at this terrific place in the Rincon Center I wouldn't have found on my own. I watched him eat and felt envy for the food that he put in his mouth. I wanted it to be my come he was swallowing.

I had an idea as I looked into his room the night I brought the projector home. Two pictures I had seen on his walls convinced me the thought coalescing in my head might work. I didn't recognize the photographer—couldn't get a close enough look, even with my binoculars, because the angle was all wrong—but T. Xu had at least two black-and-white nudes. I could see them from about the navel down: both were men, muscles bulging, cocks like fire hoses, Hercules and Patroclus.

T. Xu has a taste for visuals.

I almost became an electrical engineer. Halfway through undergrad school (NC State), I decided to switch to computer science. Still have a knack for circuitry and wiring. You can have my soldering iron when you pry it out of my cold, dead fingers.

My idea: I could modify the overhead projector.

He dug visuals? I could supply visuals. He had provided me with enough of them, I thought it was only fair.

***

If you wanted technical details you'd be reading *Popular Mechanics*. It's enough to say I needed a stronger bulb (halogen instead of incandescent), a couple of extra mirrors, some wires, blah blah blah, and naughty pictures to project into his bedroom.

I went to work every day with an extra spring in my step until I had the overhead projector finished. The train ride down the Peninsula to work seemed quicker. I'd stare off into space imagining what I'd download off the Net and print on transparencies to beam through her window in the middle of the night.

It never occurred to me that he might object. I mean—he's a gay guy. What gay man with blood in his veins is going to object to unexpected offerings of pornography in the middle of the night, when he's lying there with a midnight boner, trying to decide whether he's awake enough for a wank?

It took me about a week of tinkering and testing until I had got the range and resolution right.

My first test took place just after midnight. We live on a fairly quiet street, so there wasn't much concern about distracting a driver and causing a wreck if he or she looked up at the wrong time. I live in a corner unit, and across the street from my living room is a retirement home for Japanese people. The building is painted off-white. It was the perfect canvas. I calculated the distance to be about the same as that between T. Xu's bedroom and mine. There was no moment of introspection before I took the fresh transparency out of the new Epson printer I'd picked up (new, not used) for this project, no contemplative staring at the marble-statue manscape I'd downloaded from one of the porno sites I'd found. No last-minute soul-searching. Of course I was going to do this. Hell, I hadn't been this turned on since I was thirteen and walking around with a permanent hard-on, whacking off every time I had the chance.

I hope I don't give some random retired Japanese lady a heart attack, I thought, flipping the switch.

Beautiful. A cock like an elephant's trunk unfurled on the white façade of the retirement home, out of focus at first but coming sharper as I fiddled with the knobs I'd recently lubricated. Pubes resolved into view. I felt very proud of myself, and somewhat terrified at the same time.

Heart racing, I stared one more second to confirm for myself that I was, in fact, gazing out the window at a gigantic dick, and that the dick was, in fact, easily recognizable as such. Then I shut off the overhead.

"Christ, I need a beer."

I needed something else, too. Once the shock began to subside, I noticed that restless, almost itchy sensation—almost external, the way the urge to get off comes at me sometimes. I shut my eyes and saw an enormous penis swimming in the black-red space behind my vision. Was there a towel nearby? Unlikely. What the hell, I needed to wash a load of laundry. I stretched out on the sofa and unzipped, took myself out, picturing T. Xu's hand around his own cock when I projected image after image onto his bedroom walls. I knew what the sweat on the palm of his hand would feel like, and I knew how it would taste if I were to lick it—pungent, salty. He fingered his asshole for me, in my mind, sliding a finger inside while his other hand worked his dick. When I came the sensation ripped through me like a shotgun blast, leaving me out of breath the way it did when I was a teenager and could still count the number of orgasms I'd had on the fingers of the same hand I used on myself. Come spurted across my T-shirt. I took it off and used it to wipe up, then went to the kitchen for that beer.

If I wanted this to work I had to keep track of the border between novelty and nuisance. Interrupting his sleep with dazzling images of nakedness and copulation wouldn't get me anywhere if it turned him into a furious, sleep-starved bastard and he called the cops. Out of necessity, the San Francisco police have a sense of humor. I didn't want to find out how far it extended. Nor did I want to find out how a criminal record would affect my career potential. If I waited until a few minutes after he turned out the lights, and kept the image only long enough for him to notice it before switching off the overhead, I felt sure this project of mine wouldn't be too intrusive.

Don't get me wrong: I knew I was walking on thin ice with this thing.

The first night, a Tuesday, I hurried home from dinner with Colin, his girlfriend, and his girlfriend's ex-girlfriend to be ready when T. Xu went to bed. They noticed I was distracted, and I gave them an excuse about too much work and too little time to finish all of it. Silicon Valley people always swallow that one. In any case, I believed they were going to have a threesome later, so they couldn't have been too sorry to see me go.

At home, I had downloaded and retouched several images already.

The cock and balls I'd beamed onto the wall of the retirement home across the street, elephant-like in proportion to the guy they belonged to;

A black-and-white shot of a naked skate-punk guy with the kind of body I figured (guessed, hoped) T. Xu would dig, lean and muscular, not over-developed;

A man meditating in the lotus position, a red gerbera daisy between his teeth and a tremendous erect cock jutting up from between his legs;

A male couple having sex, all curves and skin and flesh, both with long black hair—intriguingly difficult to discern where one guy ended and the other began.

There was no particular order to these. They just appealed to me. The photographs all had a bold quality, but were tasteful at the same time, artistic. My criterion for selecting an image to beam across the street was simple: would I object to seeing it appear for a few seconds on my own bedroom wall in the middle of the night, initial shock notwithstanding?

In the bedroom, I slid the first transparency across the glass window of the projector. My hands shook. I focused the image on the outer wall next to T. Xu's window, took a deep breath, and moved the beam of light to send the same anatomy into the bedroom.

I counted out loud: *One, two, three…*

Then I switched off the overhead.

In the dark of my bedroom, I crouched beneath the windowsill, heart racing like a greyhound. I peered out to see if anything would happen. Dim light in the previously-dark room: he had turned a lamp on. I saw his outline in the window briefly. Gloriously nude. What a chest. Developed but not too much. No hair whatsoever. Cock visible, but detail and proportion impossible to discern. No matter, I already knew what it looked like, had already committed it to memory. He disappeared, then reappeared in his window wearing a robe. Could he see me? I froze. He seemed to be looking right at me. After a few seconds of this, he closed the curtains.

I didn't sleep a wink that night.

***

Called in sick the next day. Promised my boss I'd work from home. You can get away with that in Silicon Valley.

***

Wednesday night: the naked skater boy appeared on T. Xu's bedroom wall. The same thing happened. He switched on his lamp, put on his robe (I guess he had stowed it by his bed this time), and checked outside the window. Could he tell where the image had originated? Was he grooving on this, or was I pissing him off? There was no way of knowing, but my gut told me it was the former. Probably.

This time, I didn't have quite the adrenaline-terror rush. Testosterone took over; I needed a towel five minutes after I switched off the overhead. My cock almost burst through the front of my jeans. In my imagination, T. Xu wrapped his legs around my shoulders as I slid my cock inside of him, meeting little resistance at the point of entry, which I'd have already explored with my tongue and a finger or two. But it was the look I imagined crossing his face, his look of mind-blown pleasure, that sent me over the edge. He said my name. We blew like mortar fire and lay still, drenched in sweat, panting.

***

If T. Xu objected, he did nothing to interfere with the pictures I sent. He simply had to close the curtains, but he didn't. After a few nights he quit turning on the light after I switched off the projector. Questions proliferated: Was he used to this? Did he give a shit? Was he grooving on it as much as I was, lying in bed doing the things I hoped he was doing, even half as turned on as I was? Had I lost my fucking mind?

Colin noticed my haggard, lack-of-sleep attitude at work right away.

"What's his name?" he asked me, following me down the hall. "You're getting laid, aren't you? Come on, 'fess up, nobody walks around with that grin on their face those bags under their eyes if they're not getting any."

"You're a sick man, Colin. I think you need professional help."

"Bite my ass, you warped bastard. I know something's up, and sooner or later you're going to tell me what it is."

"OK, fine, you're right, something is up, and sooner or later I'm going to tell you all about it. But not today."

"Soon, then?"
"Soon."

***

I created more transparencies from Internet sites there seemed to be no end of and beamed pictures across the street for a week before the obvious thing struck me: if I was doing this because I ultimately wanted to meet him, he might as well know what I looked like.

It was time to buy a digital camera and pose for my own pictures.

The thing I haven't addressed until now is what I look like, and whether an attractive man would give me the time of day. In theory, what was stopping me from just approaching T. Xu on the street, introducing myself, asking if he'd like to join me for a coffee after work sometime. This had crossed my mind, but to be honest, I am incompetent when it comes to approaching men. My tongue ties itself in a knot and I get this heavy queasy feeling in my guts. It just doesn't work.

There's no sane reason for this. While I wouldn't say my existence is going to give the Matt Damons and Ben Afflecks of the world anything to worry about, I'm a good-looking guy. Photogenic, even. I have friends who flinch when they see pictures of themselves, but shots of me always turn out looking pretty good. Ethnically I'm kind of a mutt, Baltic on my mother's side and Mediterranean on my father's. The result is olive skin, dark brown hair, light blue eyes. I could have done a whole lot worse. And I work out four times a week. I'm pretty well-built, to tell the truth, stomach flat, muscles all present and accounted for. Below the waist I got lucky but I've never gone so far as to take a measuring tape to it. Sleep with enough guys and you figure out where you stand before long. It's long and thick, more than a mouthful. If I fucked you with it, you'd remember me fondly the next day. I'm not egotistical about the way I look but I know I get noticed. This is San Francisco. Both women and men turn their heads.

Doesn't mean I have the talent for approaching people, though. I don't. Men I'm attracted to are like the citizens of countries I've visited, where I don't speak the language and can't decode the alphabet. Like being stranded in Burma or Armenia and not knowing how to ask for the restroom. What am I supposed to do, other than flail and look desperate? Maybe if I had become a different kind of engineer I'd know how to bridge the distance without taking approximately nine thousand pictures of myself in varying states of undress and sitting up all of one Saturday night trying to figure out which one(s) to beam through T. Xu's window.

T-shirt and jeans. Black T-shirt, white T-shirt, couple of logo T-shirts to see how they'd look.

Brooks Brothers suit with white shirt and subtle, tasteful anthracite tie with a pattern of little wishbone things he wouldn't be able to see.

Jeans, no shirt.

No jeans, no shirt, just boxers.

Boxers?

That was about as sexy as a goddamn gunny sack. I took them off and looked down at myself. *Jacob, you are fucking nuts. But at least you're fucking nuts with a pretty good-sized dick.*

I shot pictures of myself anyway.

Put boxer briefs on. That's better. There's something sexy about having Calvin Klein's name circling your waist on a band of elastic, especially when your abs are visible, your package bulges, and you haven't got so much body hair you look like someone stapled a carpet to your chest. I'll admit I can see why people get into this look.

Stretched out on the bed looking as smutty as possible, my hand in my underwear gripping myself.

Standing on my head against the living room wall, nude, dick hanging down toward my navel. Don't ask where I got that idea, and why I didn't break my neck trying it out.

Finally I narrowed the field down to four, and that Sunday night I beamed the first one into T. Xu's bedroom: me in jeans with no T-shirt.

Somehow this was the scariest part. Kind of like I was asking him out on a date and scared shitless he'd say "No."

The light came on again this time, but he never came to the window to look outside.

He couldn't know it was me he was looking at, and not some nameless stud I'd downloaded out of cyberspace.

Monday night: me in the suit, but with a twist. I'd opened the fly and pulled my dick out. Little bit of a non sequitur, there, the business attire and the penis. Very Mapplethorpe.

The light stayed dark.

Fuck.

Tuesday night: me, nude, standing in the doorway separating my bedroom and my living room. I liked this shot, because it looked less contrived than the other ones.

Wednesday night, the same shot, but written in magic marker across my chest on the slide: MEET?

The lights flipped on and stayed on this time.

I could see his outline against the window.

Then he closed the curtains.

Thursday was rough. Colin looked at me funny all day, and offered to call 911 when he caught me staring out into space.

"Go home," he told me. "Beat the traffic. And tell this bloke you're losing sleep over I'll beat the shit out of him if he doesn't—I don't know, stop whatever he's doing so you don't look like you gave too much blood at the Red Cross."

Thursday night: a different nude shot, me again, sitting Indian-style on the floor of my apartment. I'LL STOP IF YOU WANT, I wrote on the transparency. I sat on the edge of my bed after I switched off the overhead, smoking one cigarette after another.

The phone rang, and I jumped off the bed and shouted in surprise and shock.

"Hello?"

Static and a dull background roar told me somebody was calling from downstairs.

"Is this the guy with the overhead projector?" asked a man's voice.

A wave of panic broke over me, and I said nothing.

"You are, aren't you? You don't have to answer, because I've known since the second night who you were."

Oh Jesus. I heard an Asian accent. It was him.

"I'm downstairs. You want me to come up, don't you?"

Without saying a word, I pressed the 9 on my number pad to buzz him up.

When the knock came, I opened the door without looking through the peephole first, and when I saw the man standing there—a *white* man with red hair and green eyes, the ostensible boyfriend of T. Xu—standing there I staggered back as if I'd been gut-punched.

"Can I help you?" I finally asked.

He stepped inside without invitation and closed the door behind himself.

"Who the fuck are you?"

"Thomas's roommate," he said, extending his hand. "My name's Anthony, and it's really nice to meet you. At last."

Anthony looked like the stereotypical boy next door, more or less, but with that buffed look and the updated duck's-ass haircut half of the gay guys in the Castro seem to have. Not bad looking at all. He wasn't Thomas but I wouldn't have pushed him out of bed. Was I wrong about this, though? My panic escalated. I'd been thinking he was like Thomas's boyfriend or something, and he was here to kick my ass, or at least try...

Thomas?

I had never known what the T stood for.

"OK, here's the deal," he said. "I'm going to cut to the chase because I know you want to know what the hell I'm doing here after he called from downstairs. Thomas is just starting to come out, OK? This is a little too intense for him. We switched bedrooms a few days into your video projection project because he dug the shit you were projecting onto his walls but dug being able to get to sleep on time even more. So I'm the one you've been serenading for the last week or so, if you want to call it that."

My legs wanted to drop out from underneath me. I started to stammer an apology but Anthony held up a hand to stop me before I could utter a word.

"You probably don't need me to tell you that what you've done isn't legal," he went on.

I shook my head "No." Like a masturbating Catholic teenager I made a thousand guilt-crazed promises to God in my head just then.

"That had crossed my mind," I managed to say.

"So you can probably appreciate the precarious position you've put yourself in," Anthony said.

I nodded.

"And you probably would appreciate a chance to convince me not to press charges, or file suit, or whatever," he continued. "Because I will, if you give me reason. It's what I do for a living, and I'm really good at it."

I didn't nod this time, but I felt my eyes widen.

"I guess the question becomes, just how much do you want to avoid having to tell a few of San Francisco's finest what you've been up to for the last few weeks?"

"I have money," I said.

Anthony shook his head "No." "Wasn't quite what I had in mind," he told me, grinning like the devil. "Why don't we have a seat on the sofa. You can pour us something to drink, and we'll see what we can agree on. I know you're an intelligent guy, Jacob. You know a good deal when you're being offered one."

I poured Glenlivet over ice for us both, drained my own glass, refilled it, returned to the living room, sat at the opposite end of the sofa as if I expected him to lunge at me.

"This is extortion," I told him.

"I'm an attorney," he replied, unzipping his jeans. "I'm familiar with the concept. But you probably don't have anything to worry about. If you have any sense, you'll get to know me pretty well. I can keep my word if you're willing to live up to your end of the deal."

Anthony took out his cock and looked at me without saying a word.

I set down my drink and moved carefully across the sofa. I had no choice, really. I took him in my mouth and told myself I liked it. After a second or two, I got lost in the taste of him and didn't need further convincing. He had a big one, and had just taken a shower from the smell. Soap is not the best aphrodisiac, as it turns out. Blackmail is better.

As I sucked him off, Anthony explained his terms, and gave me until ten o'clock the following night to consider, although I had made up my mind before he left my apartment. Hell, I had made up my mind before he blew a load across my face. He forced me to kneel before him to receive it.

I think he knew I'd accepted his terms, too. I accepted his come willingly enough. Licked some off my fingers, just because.

What the hell, I thought when the door closed behind him, *even if I change my mind and decide I'm not into it, and it's just for two weeks, the same length of time I was projecting those pictures across the street. I suppose at some point I must have wondered what it would be like to be some other guy's fuck toy—Yes, Sir, whatever you want, Sir, absolutely, I'd love to lick your ass again—and it can't be much worse than getting arrested. Who knows? Maybe I'll like it.*

I licked his salt off my lips and went to the kitchen to refill my glass of Glenlivet.

HOME TO STAY
by Rick Jackson

You might think it would be fun living in an open barracks bay with 95 other young men, all in their prime and oozing hard, sweaty sexuality. You'd be wrong, though. It's hell. I know because I enlisted thinking that being around lean Marine bodies 24 hours a day would be like one long Chippendale's show.

I was right there. One of the first elements of basic training is to break down individual hang-ups. Marines must ask permission to piss or shit—and then do it with others lined up, watching them as they wait for their turns at the porcelain. Guys lounge around the barracks bay in shorts or less, hard muscles popping out in rippling knots from their thick necks down to their meaty calves.

It says something about the cruelty of fate that the biggest tease of the bunch ended up in the rack right across from mine. The guy made the average Calvin Klein model look like the dog's lunch. During those first three weeks of boot camp, I would lie in my rack, exhausted from the day's drills and marches and PT, desperate for sleep, only to have young Brad MacGregor stretched out naked as a glutton's prayer not four feet away.

The barracks were always dark after Taps, but moonlight had a nasty habit of streaming through a window to glisten across his hard recruit body, usually draped across the loins only by the corner of a sheet like a Michelangelo marble. The easy rise and fall of his broad, hairless pecs nearly drove me crazy—but they were nothing compared with the early-morning woodies that made his sheet stand tall and tasty.

Some nights I spent more time in the head spanking off than I did in my rack, but I was sure nothing short of a lobotomy could banish the waking and sleeping dreams of MacGregor's taut Marine body that made my life such a nightmare. I was wrong. Just when I was sure my lack of sleep and frazzled nerves were going to get me washed out of boot camp in disgrace, some passing god must have taken pity on me.

I woke up about 0330 to find MacGregor's rack empty and my bladder full enough to rupture. As I shambled into the pisser to drain, the back of my mind registered the noise of a shower running. I'd seen Mac showering before, of course—I showered with him every chance I got. For obvious reasons, though, I could never really *watch* him shower. Admire the steamy water streaming down his muscled torso, watch him flex and twist in animal pleasure as the gushing torrent licked the soap from his naked flesh, or take careful note of the tight joy of his powerful glutes grinding against the lucky hand that soaped his shithole. That night I finally had a chance to stand outside the shower and watch his reflection in a well-placed mirror to see all I had been missing.

As I stood there in the darkness, looking into the brightly-lit shower, I saw more than any randy young voyeur deserves in a cosmic cycle of lifetimes. For the first few seconds I was too taken with his perfect beauty to notice what he was doing, but the way he was going at it soon left little doubt. His right hand was frothing soap, stroking rabidly along something half the size of M. Eiffel's erection and infinitely more appealing. Mac's head was back, eyes shut and mouth agape as he worked, oblivious to anything but answering the ancient call of man's fiercest need.

The water boiled off the back of his head like a steamy nimbus, splashing down onto his shoulders and cascading in frantic ripples down towards the firm ass he had planted against the tile. His tits were stiff with pleasure and his belly and hips answered every cue to fuck hard up into the tight Marine fist that was then the essence of his destiny. For a few seconds, his beaver-brown eyes opened and looked out past the blond lashes that helped make my dreams such torment. I worried for a passing moment of sanity that he might catch me watching him, but I was well hidden by the darkness and my own timidity and his eyes were focused far beyond any mortal realm.

How long did I stand watching him work, agonized more by my own limitations than by the unattainable perfection of his body? Time had ceased to function except in answer to the pounding of his fist and the heaving of his chest. All I know is that when I found my balls at last, my dick felt ready to split along the seams and I saw the world as though for the first time. In a very real sense in that instant, when my priggish fears dropped away and the lush landscape of certainty opened up before me, I became a man. I could have stayed there in the dark, hiding like a boy. I could have spanked one load after another until even Onan would have shuddered in envy. I could have, but I didn't. I'd watched the action long enough. Sooner or later, the time comes when a real man needs to stride boldly from the shadows and take what he needs.

That night, finally, I left the darkness and padded into the shower to help my warrior brother complete his mission. I ignored the risk to my military career. I ignored the sodden shorts that soon disappeared anyway. I even ignored what Mac might think when I reached out and took his thick dick away from him. Just then, I didn't care about anything but busting the nut of my young life.

Mac pretended to be shocked and offended for a moment, but, looking back, I think he must have wanted me as much as I needed him. He certainly didn't run screaming naked into the night. Instead of outraged virtue, those big brown eyes smoldered momentarily with the heat of the ages and then slipped silently shut as his hips picked up their rhythm again, fucking this time up into my soapy paw. The sizzle of the shower almost drowned out the low moans of pleasure that echoed every thrust and taunted me to whip him harder.

He must have worked my shorts off. I was too busy to notice until he hefted my poor overworked balls and took me firmly in hand to return the favor. He was awkward at first because of the unfamiliar angle, but soon learned his craft and set seriously to work. The feel of his powerful hands jacking me off seemed suddenly to snap me out of a magical spell and dropped me into an even more enraptured reality. This reality was of stiff dicks and hard muscle and tight ass that replaced all the steamy zephyrs and idealized forms of my romantic enchantment.

I kept my hand on station for him to fuck, but leaned forward to show each of his tits in turn what the dangerous edge of a man's teeth could do. Mac's helpless body convulsed in building rapture as my mouth moved north to lap the musk from his pits and then up towards his ears for a tongue-fuck he could write home about. His jack-hand spazzed, but I didn't care. I was more interested in licking and touching and possessing every inch of his perfect young body than I was in having him spank me off. If there was one thing I'd had enough of in the last month, it was hand jobs.

When my lips finally met Mac's, I think he was startled for a moment, but maybe it was the way I'd finally let his dick slap down against my belly as my hands reached around to grab his full-flaring Marine butt. His hips didn't miss a stroke as he switched to fucking upwards hard against my belly, but his ass was soon the center of my affection. His powerful Corps-built glutes ground against my palms, filling them to overflowing as I wriggled my fingers deep down into his hairless crack in search of the secret wonder I knew lay hidden there.

I had to compete with the gushing stream of steamy water, but the rigid rules of fluid dynamics were nothing compared to my determination to show Mac's tight recruit shithole how good one Marine can feel. By the time my fuckfingers found their target and sliced across his tender, parboiled asshole, I had spread his glutes wide and almost lifted him off his feet. His body ground and writhed against mine as our lips locked tight until the pressure of the moment and the unfamiliar feel of a man's hands up his ass exploded his heavy balls into a storm of flying sperm. His load blew up between our bellies and seemed suddenly to envelop us in a swirling cyclone of creamy white Corps-cum.

Mac's head slammed back so hard against the tile that he'd have knocked himself senseless if we hadn't already gotten him that way. He jerked and twisted and bucked and heaved against me, spewing and spurting like the honoree at an exorcism until even his massive Marine body passed its limits and collapsed into my arm, a helpless hulk of his former glory. Above the sizzle of the water, all I could hear were his gasps for air and his punctuated mantra: Oh, God—Oh, God—Oh, God—Oh, God—Oh, God—Oh, God…"

I knew that if we were both to see the face of the infinite, there was no time like the present. In one fluid motion, I pulled my fingers out of his ass, dropped his body face-first against the tiled wall, rubbered up, and shoved my desperate nine inches of Marine recruit training against his shithole to start my Marine career with a *semper fi* flourish.

Mac was born a virgin and had stayed that way until I found his ass that night in the shower. The poor gorgeous bastard had no clue what to expect, but he knew soul-deep and gut-sure that he needed to be fucked more than he needed anything else in his military life. I'd had my fingers up his ass, but they did no more than tickle his fancy. My baton-sized dick was about to do the same thing boot camp does on a different scale: break him down absolutely and then rebuild a new, improved Marine on the ruins of his former self.

Looking back on the pain a needledick named David caused me the first time I was boned, I can only imagine what my swollen Marine member must have done to Mac's nervous system.
He somehow managed to keep from screaming out and waking everyone in southern California, but his body held nothing else back.

Muscle knotted on muscle as his hands clawed helplessly at the tile and his guts plunged irretrievably down my dick. By the time my pubes were shredding what little was left of his shithole, his liver was already scratching away at my swollen knob, teasing me with the possibility of dislocating his pancreas if he were a bad Marine. Nine inches of slick jarhead guts waved and rippled along as many inches of swollen Marine dick in an instinctive timeless tango that knew both violent conquest and transcendent surrender.

My hands on his pecs pulled him closer to me, harder down my dick. His hands echoed my need, reaching back to grab my butt and force my cock even farther up into his helpless body, begging me to fuck him hard and fast and deep enough that we would both know he could take anything Nature had to throw against him.

By then, I needed more than to bust a nut. I even needed more than to posses Mac's hard Marine body. I needed him. I needed to prove myself and accept his surrender. I needed to be his brother, to share his strafing fire and take him into my foxhole. In a subtle, unspoken way no one outside the military can possibly understand, I needed to seal our Marine bond by fusing our flesh and flushing part of me far enough up into his core that it would remain there until his final hour.

Bonding and warrior nobility aside, on a baser level I also needed to fuck his ass until my heads came off—and Mac needed it even more. His hands had stopped clawing at the wall by then, but, as he braced his forearms against the tile and clenched his jaw and whimpered with each brutally reaming fuckthrust up into his vitals, I saw his body surrender as his soul had done. In the magic of a man's most sublime moment, his powerful warrior body began confusing pain and pleasure, reaping rapture where only agony had been sown. Then his whimpers died away and a low, almost subsonic groan of ecstasy took their place—a sound that grew and matured with every slicing stroke of my plow along his firm, fertile furrow.

Our soapy, jism-covered bodies slammed helplessly together and fucked Mac forward into the wall until we were both lucky just to be standing. My mortal mistake was taking my teeth from his neck and leaning back to watch my dick drill up through his powerful mounds of Marine man-muscle and slide into his asshole. I've always liked seeing my work up close and personal, but that night Mac was too much of a good thing to endure. The instant my brain realized what my dick had known—that the Marine body wrapped around my reaming unit was studly, perfect, boy-next-door Mac, I lost my load quicker than a Texas dope smuggler caught in a speed trap.

My whole universe exploded up Mac's once-tight ass and kept on exploding until my nuts ached with over-achievement and I was half drowned by the boiling water we'd somehow stumbled into. We ended up on the deck, a slick and sublime mess of arms and legs and still-stiff dicks that knew neither of us was finished for the night. By dawn, we limped back to our racks and, for once I was able to sleep—for all of about four minutes before the lights went on and a new Marine day began.

I haven't gotten any more sleep the last several weeks than I got before, but even our drill instructor has noticed how my outlook on life is much improved. Several other recruits in our company have joined our late-night workouts lately, but Mac and I always come back where we belong in the end. We always will.

THE BOY NEXT DOOR
by Kyle Stone

He was lying naked, sprawled out on a towel on the enclosed roof of the garage. No one could see from the street or even from the lower floors of the neighboring houses. Only from up here, through the dusty cobwebs of the old attic window was the angle just right. And who ever came up here? By the looks of the place, it must have been a long time between visitors.

I knelt in front of the dirt-streaked window and stared, filling my eyes with his image. Now I saw he wasn't quite naked but wore an old Speedo faded to almost the exact color of his lightly tanned skin. Somehow that thin barrier between me and his cock aroused me. Rather then disappointment, I felt the heat of desire so sudden and fierce it took my breath away. I rested my forehead on the window, drawing him in; that golden skin glistening with suntan oil, the long legs, one knee drawn up, the swell of his cock, the slight hollow of his stomach, the faint line of fair hair crawling up from under his scant swimsuit flaring out to his nipples. I could almost taste those cinnamon tits, the fine fair hair that swirled around them. One arm was thrown over his face so that all I could see was the sun-streaked hair, longer then usual, and the sparkle of a diamond in his ear. I moaned, a soft sound, stifled almost at once as I unzipped my jeans and my hand snaked inside my underwear to grasp my hot swelling flesh. My breath panted back at me against the window, smelling of coffee and dust. I was coming fast. I slid my knees wider apart and threw back my head as my body started to shake with my orgasm.

"Zak? Where are you?" Kevin's voice barely penetrated as I collapsed on the dusty floor, my hand and jockeys sticky with come. I could hear him on the second floor, looking into one room after another. Would he think of the attic? I glanced out the round window. The boy was gone.

I had come to this house to see if Kevin and I could start again. It had been my idea, but now I wondered why. Was it this rambling old house he had just inherited that I coveted? Or did I want him? Kevin Conners, tall, broad-shouldered, dark eyes like bitter chocolate and a body he kept toned but was completely comfortable with? Why had we broken up in the first place?

My head was pounding. Sex and memories, heat and dust. I sat cross-legged on the floor, looking around the attic trying to remember why I had come up here. The space was jammed with cardboard boxes, old chairs in various stages of despair, and a large spotted mirror half covered with a yellowed sheet. When I saw the two guitar cases propped against the wall, I remembered.

Below me, Kevin rattled down the back stairs. I picked up the guitars and padded down to the second floor, dropped the instruments in my room and slipped into the bathroom for a quick shower.

Almost at once I heard Kevin at the door. "There you are! I was looking all over!"

He sounded relieved and I could see his face, the lines of worry smoothing away as he talked, his hands, those big hands I loved to feel on my body, spread wide as he prattled on. Was I being fair to him?

The shower still running, I stepped over to the door and opened it. "Get in here," I said.

His mouth was still open, caught in mid sentence. He stared at me. I watched him in the mirror, taking in my body, reddened from the hot water, the hair on my chest swirled this way and that, my hair plastered to my head. My cock was half-erect. His eyes stopped there and he began to throw off his shirt and pants, peeled off his jockeys and socks. For once, he wasn't talking.

"You always know how to get a guy hot," he said, following me into the tub and grabbing my ass with his huge hands. My cock reached for him. He sank to his knees, the water cascading over his head as he took me in his mouth and drank deeply, like a man dying of thirst. I threw my head back and closed my eyes, seeing the boy on the roof, his slender body stretched out in the sun, taut with longing, thrumming with desire. I grabbed Kevin's hair and arched my back, thrusting deeper into his throat. He pulled away as I came, and I sank to my knees and covered his mouth with mine, tasting a faint trace of my own juices. I wondered what the boy next door's mouth tasted like, what his face looked like. Kevin squealed as I bit his lip hard, and I tasted a sweet, metallic suggestion of blood. He pulled away. His eyes were wide and sparkling. He was panting. A tiny bubble of blood blossomed on his lip, burst, trickled down his chin. He wiped his fingers across his mouth, leaving a red smudge. I reached back and turned off the water. For a moment the bathroom echoed with our panting. I looked down and realized Kevin had come. When I bit him?

"Fuck," said Kevin, sinking back on his heels. "I'd almost forgotten."

I laughed. I had been away a long time.

"So you're staying for my party?" He looked so eager, his eyes shining, his hair dripping around his face. He wanted this so badly. Did he think a party could decide our future?

"Sure," I said. "I wouldn't miss it for the world."

He hugged me. Kissed me once. Twice, lingering this time, his tongue gently probing. I tasted blood. Soap. I slid my fingers down his back, down his crack, burying themselves between the tight globes of his ass. He wiggled away.

"Ah come on. You know you want this," I teased.

"I know. I do, but not now, okay, Zak?" He stood up and climbed awkwardly out of the tub. His cock was already stiffening. He grabbed a towel, seeming embarrassed by how much he wanted me. "It's getting late," he said. "I have to pick up a few things at the market. You'll be here?"

"You want me to wait in the tub?"

He threw a towel at me. "You know what I mean."

Yes. I knew what he meant. Trust. That was it. He felt he couldn't trust me anymore. What I would do. When I would go. He was uncertain about why I had come back. So was I.

I got out of the tub, watched him go down the hall to his bedroom. He turned and waved, just before disappearing. As I dried myself off, my own ambivalence burned inside, making me uneasy. Kevin was a kind, generous man, ready to forgive and forget. He had a good body. He loved me. He wanted nothing more then to make me happy. Why was I still thinking about the boy on the roof?

***

I spent the rest of the afternoon repairing and restringing the old guitars. One of them had a beautiful tone and I suspected might be quite valuable. Just another example of Kevin's generosity, giving me things before he had any idea of their value. Why did I find that annoying?

By eight that night, the house was humming with party activity. The caterers had arrived, bringing their staff of servers and all the hustle and bustle of the Oscars. I began to wonder if my modest wardrobe was up to this standard. I might have known Kevin would pull out all the stops. Was this party for me? For him? A way to push me somehow into staying? My head was beginning to ache with all the questions.

When I came downstairs an hour later, dressed in a new black tee-shirt, black jeans and my silver and turquoise belt buckle, the first floor was transformed. Candles burned everywhere, music drifted from the expensive speaker system and wonderful smells of spiced meat and apples and chilli wafted through the high-ceilinged rooms. The place was already filling up. Before I knew it, Kevin was at my side, beaming, his hand resting proprietarily on my back. I looked around at the half-remembered faces, people I had never really known. A few new faces were there, too. Sergei, Jim, Bob, Juan. They all blurred and slipped from my memory as fast as I heard them.

Except one—Christopher.

His vivid blue eyes looked right into mine. The look was startling, sending a tingle all through me. He was blond, tall and willowy, graceful as a dancer. It was the glint of the diamond earring that clicked it all into place.

"The boy next door," I murmured.

"Well, not exactly," Kevin said. "Chris is staying across the street with his aunts."

We shook hands. Did he hold on a little too long? Did I?

The French doors were wide open and outside the evening had turned hot and humid. Rain spat suddenly, sending a few people running with shrieks of laughter to the shelter of the living room. Lightning forked across the sky. So much for a long walk to get rid of all this sexual tension, I thought. Chris was smiling. Did he read my mind? It occurred to me that being a real host who could disappear to get people drinks was not a bad way to go with these events.

A party has its own rhythm, ebbing and flowing, the noise level rising as more alcohol is consumed. Gradually the crowd seemed to be absorbed by the old house. At one point I checked upstairs and found two young things entwined in the shadows outside the bedroom Kevin was using as a storeroom. They paid no attention to me. I opened the door of my own bedroom and saw two more embracing against the wall. The one against the wall had shoved down the other's trousers far enough to show me the hard swell of the top of his dark ass. I wondered if concern for their wardrobe was all that kept them off the floor. At least they weren't on my bed, I thought, not that I had been there much myself lately.

Sensing my presence, they pulled apart and adjusted their clothing. "Excuse. I did not know this is your room," one of them mumbled. Sergei. Who had come with an older guy with a Boston accent. Aha. I wondered now expensive he was. I wondered what had made me so cynical. Before I could say anything else, they were both out of the room, sliding out of my sight with practiced ease. I didn't want him, anyway.

The storm had passed as quickly as it had appeared. As I flung open the window, the humid air seeped in, bringing the sigh of the garden, the hum of insects, the drip of water from the drainpipe in the corner. I watched the moon, an uneven three quarters of a circle, slide in and out of the ragged clouds as the noise from the party slowly dwindled to a faint rumble of conversation. Now I could hear the calls of departure coming from the front door, car doors slamming, engines revving into action. I should be there with Kevin. I was just deciding to join him when I caught sight of Chris down in the garden, his golden head plainly visible in the moonlight. He was crossing by the path along the swimming pool to the small change cabin at the other end of the garden. When he got there, he opened the door and stood inside for a moment, as if waiting. I could see him through the little diamond paned window, as he took off his clothes. Was he going swimming? Or meeting someone?

Without stopping to think, I went out into the corridor and down the enclosed back stairs to the kitchen. Two of the caterers were packing up glasses. They paid no attention as I slid out the back door into the garden.

Candlelight spilled out onto the patio and the uncertain moonlight cast deeper shadows around the cabin and the shrubbery that surrounded it. I stood for a moment in the throbbing heat of the summer night and felt more alive then I had for a long time. The cabin door was closed now but the windows were open. A candle flame flickered inside, casting tall shadows in the wall behind. Two men, circling each other like boxers, their arms on each others shoulders.

I took off my shoes and socks. I reached back inside and switched off the light that illuminated the pool. I didn't want them to be distracted.

I needn't have worried. By the time I made my way across the patio and up the path to the cabin, they were oblivious of everything but each other. I stood in the bushes, my bare feet squishing in the damp earth, my black denims already wet from the foliage and clinging to my legs. The dankness and the heat, the golden interior of the cabin and the two men inside, unaware of my presence sent currents like electricity snapping through me, making my heart beat faster, my breath shorten into shallow pants. From here I had a good view through the open window. Chris's blond hair was already plastered to his well-shaped head. His shoulders were sweating in the golden candlelight. But I still couldn't see the other guy, except that he was dark, shorter then Chris and with well developed upper arms. For one piercingly painful moment, I thought it was Kevin. Then, with a sudden move, Chris flung open the door, not caring who saw him in oppressive heat of that small space. I saw Sergei's face.

The stocky dark man was on all fours, and Chris was trying to hold his sweat-slicked ass in place as his engorged cock slid into the crack in his ass. I felt my own cock jerk and pulled my jeans open, trying to release it. My hands felt clumsy, shaking with lust, as I shoved my jeans down into the muddy ground and kicked them into the wet shrubbery. The damp air pressed against my bare legs, my throbbing cock. I clenched my teeth, willing myself not to utter a sound as I felt my orgasm start to build. I took my hands away from my cock, watched it, hard, pale and straining against the heavy air, begging for release. Not yet. Not yet.

Inside the cabin, Sergei was whimpering and groaning, bucking against Chris's thrusts, pushing back, raising the blond man almost off his feet as he urged him deeper, deeper into his hole. The thin wooden walls were vibrating as Chris's ass hit the wall behind him. The candle flame shuddered and leapt uncertainly.

"Keep it down!" Chris whispered. "Shhh."

Sergei made some kind of strangled cry and dropped his head, swinging it from side to side like an exhausted animal. Chris was riding him hard, now, and the whole cabin rocked with their lust. I sank to the muddy ground, rubbing my aching cock against the stalk of dripping foliage, panting into the damp air, my eyes fastened on the two golden sweating figures in the cabin.

Chris began to grunt, louder and louder until at last he shouted— his voice hoarse and triumphant as he collapsed into Sergei.

I was shaking, my hands loose around my own jerking cock as hot strings of cum hit the broad leafed plants in front of me. I sank back on my heels, trembling. And then I felt it.

A hand, touching my bare ass. I froze.

"Hey, hey." Kevin was whispering behind me. One hand cupping my ass cheek firmly. One hand snaking over my shoulder, playing with my nipple. He was naked. I could feel his cock pressing against my back, his breath stirring the hair at the back of my neck. The candle in the cabin was snuffed out and I leaned against Kevin, letting the night take me, not caring about the others. I was dimly aware of them slipping away, while Kevin eased me back onto the muddy ground and climbed on top of me.

"Having a good time?" he asked. "Enjoy the show?"

I looked up at him. In the moonlight, in the dampness of the dripping garden, he looked like a different person, wild and unpredictable as an ancient Greek sprite.

I ran my hands over his chest, lingering on the nipples. "How did you know I was out here?" I asked softly, feeling the muscle under his warm skin as my hands strayed.

"Because they were out here," he said.

"And you know that because..."

"Because I paid them."

"What? You mean Sergei, right? You paid him as a gift for Chris?"

"Why should I give a damn about Chris?" he said, his urgent cock pressing against my balls. "It was a present for you."

"You mean...You paid them *both*?"

"Shut up and put your legs on my shoulders."

I did. My head in the mud, my ass grinding into the crushed leaves and wet stalks of zinnias and marigolds and petunias, I gave myself to Kevin at last, completely, as I had never done before. The sharp scent of the crushed flowers washed over me, confusing my senses. I felt Kevin everywhere, in the air, pressing down on me, inside me, mixing with the heady perfumes that pounded through my blood. And when it was over, I followed him into the swimming pool without question. We both knew I would be staying. I didn't have to say a word.

SANDY HOOK UNSPOOLING
by Leo Cardini

At this hour of the morning it's unusual to meet another beach-goer strolling along the shore. He's still so far off all I can tell in our gradual approach is that he's tall, well-proportioned and as completely naked as I am.

My left hand brushes against the moist tip of my dickhead. Every nerve ending it grazes sparks with pleasure. This is becoming a habit; I see a man who turns me on and there go my fingertips skating across my dickhead. As a result, whenever I'm here at Sandy Hook, well within the signs a mile apart that read "Beyond This Point You May Encounter Nude Sunbathers" and "Entering Clothed Area" my dickhead's used to constant attention, which it likes. See, you can tell by the way its head perks up and stretches forward, like a frisky dog running ahead of his master to sniff a stranger.

The anticipation heightens my senses. I become acutely aware of the mellow, early morning August sun. The persistent crash and clamor of the incoming tide, the cold, wet sand beneath my feet, and, of course, the constant reposition of my cock and balls buffeted back and forth against my thighs as I stroll along this stretch of beach where nudity's sanctioned. It's federal property, and there are no federal laws against nudity.

Manhattan gleams like Oz in the distance some five miles north across the Atlantic. Like most regulars at Sandy Hook, what I still see most conspicuously even after nearly a year is the absence of the World Trade Center. I actually witnessed the tragedy here at Sandy Hook. There I was, on a glorious September morning, chatting with Jay, another regular, when he stares over my shoulder and then interrupts with, "You're not going to believe this, Leo, but I think there's a fire in the World Trade Center."

But that's another story.[1] The present drama is this approaching man. His deeply-tanned, muscular body gleams with the effects of his morning exercise. He walks tall, chest out, arms swinging by his sides, as if seduced by the sweet physicality of promenading naked along the shore, his robust stride as steady as the rhythm of a jackoff hand set on medium. He has thick, wavy black hair combed back and a ruggedly handsome face, with dark eyes, the deep sunsquint lines of an outdoors man, and a strong jaw line.

---

[1] Leo Cardini's non-fictional account of that fateful day in his sexual history, "Paradise Lost", will soon appear in the STARbooks anthology, *Wet Nightmares, Wet Dreams*, edited by Michael Huxley.

My eyes travel downward. The beautiful spread of black hair that fans out over his chest narrows to a dark trail crossing over the rockhard terrain of his abs, spreading out like an oasis around his tight innie of a navel and finally plunging down into his lush black bush. Below hangs a magnificent piece of meat that swings heavily back and forth as he approaches; dark and thick with a major blue vein traveling a ragged course along the topside.

When he's just a few yards away from me, he smiles. It's a broad, inviting smile inching up slightly higher into his left cheek than the right, giving him a rakish look. He's so downright manly, I could melt.

I smile back, and as I do, he unashamedly lowers his eyes to my dick.

As his eyes shift from mine to my meat, my mind shifts from the present to a moment in the past in Brockton, Massachusetts. I was still in high school, and my father and I were showering after a swim in the communal men's shower room at the Montello Public Pool. He was always in superb physical shape, having been a boxer before he married my mom, who made him give it up.

On this particular afternoon, I'd glanced over at him, as I did every time I thought I could get away with it to capture some fresh image of his body for my nightly jackoff sessions in bed. While soaping up his armpits he turned his gaze in my direction, lowering it until his eyes rested on my meat. And then he actually let it linger there. My very own father was staring at my dick!

I felt the warmth of his gaze along my shaft. It was an honest-to-god physical sensation uniting my dick with my dad's consciousness. The intimacy of the connection was more intense than anything I'd ever felt before.

What was he thinking as he stared at my dick? There were so many possibilities that stormed my imagination, possibilities I later sorted out and examined one by one, many times over, in the privacy of my bedroom, hard and naked under the sheets.

Maybe he was thinking about something totally unrelated to the moment, like bills to be paid or yard work to be done. Yeah, it's possible. And it was most likely the case. But *maybe*—and I like this so much more—just *maybe* he was checking out the size of my meat, proud to see that like father, like son, for surely my dad knew he was, as they say, hung like a horse.

Maybe he was thinking about what I did with it. Did he conjure up the image of me stroking my meat, using the same repertoire of cockstrokes he himself had developed? Did he see me in bed fucking a girl? Or did he have any idea at all his son was more interested in other studs, admiring the image of my topman status when I fucked a buddy, beaming inside and proudly thinking, "That's my son!"

And maybe, could it be possible, he was interested in me for himself? This is taboo territory way beyond the no trespassing signs in my mind; not that I don't sneak in there now and then when I have the guts for it. But here it is. I'm just going to blurt it out. Sexually, I'd have been willing to do anything for my dad. I'd have licked his nuts and sucked his cock, I'd have eaten out his ass, I've have let him shove my face down on his dick to swallow his load, and I'd have let him fuck me up the ass with all his strength.

All these possibilities brought to mind by the feel of my father's gaze burning into my meat.

I knew what was coming next. My father had his routine. After he soaped up his pits, he reached down into his crotch, grabbing his dickhead with an overhand grip and stretching out his meat before attacking it with his bar of soap. It was just a habit, meaning so little to him, but so much to me when I'd mentally replay it in slow motion afterwards when no one was around.

But on this particular afternoon his eyes were still on my meat as he stretched out his. And before releasing it, he looked up at me to say something. Our eyes met and the intimacy of the connection—my eyes connecting with his, connecting with his thoughts, connecting with his cock—hit me like a thunderbolt. He opened his mouth to say something and then we both heard the approach of another man.

Shit! It was this lean, Latin-looking stud I'd seen around the pool with giggly girls flirting with him. If my father wasn't there, I'd be checking out if he could be had.

Whatever my father was going to say to me, he didn't. He just moved on to soaping up his crotch and rinsing it off, giving his equipment the same tough, no-nonsense treatment he always gave it.

Maybe the moment had passed for *him*. But that stare, the thoughts it might have prompted, the words he might have spoken, and the acts that might have followed, well, every time a man looks at my meat, part of me goes back to that moment as a springboard for fresh adventures.

"Nice meat." I hear my father say. But it's not my father's voice and I'm pulled back into the present with this stud who now raises his admiring gaze to my eyes.

"Thanks," is all I reply.

We've both stopped, barely a yard apart, silent, as if uncertain of what to say next.

"Leo," I say extending my hand.

"Lou," he replies, taking it. Our names are so similar. He has large hands and an almost too-firm grip.

I can never come up with small talk when I need it most, so I cut to the chase.

"I've got a couple of windbreakers set up over there," I say, tugging on my dick with one hand while pointing up at them with the other.

They're some thirty yards or so away, at the foot of the dunes. "Wanna join me?"

He smiles and I feel the warmth of his eyes as they travel up and down my body, taking in all of me. He makes no effort to conceal the pleasure in what he sees, which gives me such a thrill my half-hard cock flexes forward, arresting his gaze as it begins to stiffen.

"Definitely" he finally says, eyes back to mine. I imagine I see the fading reflection of my dick in his eyes as his memory stores it away. "On my way back, ok? I want to work up a good sweat and then take a dip before I join you."

"Sure," I say, resisting the urge to offer to clean the sweat off his body with my tongue.

"Later, then," he says with a nod. And with that, he continues along with his broad stride, heading towards the "Entering Clothed Area" sign.

That men like Lou can postpone sex—which I can never do—makes them all the manlier in my eyes, and all the more desirable. I like that I'm part of a larger scenario for Lou: work up a sweat, dip in the ocean, drop by Leo's for sex.

As he walks away, I stare after him, weighing the advantages and disadvantages of a pre-sex swim. When you write enough erotica, you actually do pause to think about such things. It's one of the fringe benefits. On one hand, I think, though I like the taste of salty balls, I'd much rather work on ones coated with a thin layer of sweat, licking the man clean with my hyperactive tongue. But on the other hand, there's nothing more annoying than rimming a man with sand in his crack.

I trek across the beach. I don't know what it is about this section of the shore, but as you approach the dunes, the ocean sounds suddenly distant and it turns eerily quiet. It's like you've stepped into a SciFi world gone porn. A world of infinite desert sparsely populated with hot, naked men with time on their hands, where foot travel over the burning sand is the only mode of transportation. An exception are the rangers, the scourge of the beach, who roar out of nowhere on their motor vehicles to swoop down on you, catching you in the act and leading you off to jail.

I look up at the forbidden dunes with their thin vegetation and decaying "no trespassing" signs. There was a time before my time when you could roam them for sex and get it on right there, but they became so well-known a cruising area they were placed off-limits as a "conservation measure."

I love the serenity and the seclusion of the area. My nearest neighbor must be a hundred yards away. The thing is, you can only settle here from mid-August to the end of the season, after the fucking piping plovers have bred and raised their young. They're an endangered species. By then, most of the regulars are entrenched in their routine of settling down on the first quarter-mile of beach. Besides it's closest to the parking lot, which is still a good ten or fifteen minute walk.

Like most beaches, there's a straight, then a mixed, and finally a gay section, which is of course where I've been hanging out, in the thick of things, surrounded by naked men sunning with spreadapart legs.

But back to the present moment. My "camp" is two brightly-striped, three-paneled cloth windbreakers, each secured by four wooden poles driven into the ground with a rubber mallet. They enclose a space large enough for a beach blanket and my well-known purple beach bag.

I spread another large towel, a bold favorite of mine, in front of the windbreakers. That's where I like to sunbathe. When someone cruises by that I'm interested in, I can invite him inside my windbreakers.

I lay down inside under the sun with my legs spread open. I reach for my half-hard dick and lazily slow-stroke it into a full erection, anticipating Lou's visit. I close my eyes to enjoy the sweet rise and fall of my balls as I stroke. They might be on the large side, but they're very sensitive; so sensitive it feels like the sun's decided to take advantage of me, lapping my nuts with its warm rays.

It's possible, I think, that Lou's "on my way back, ok?" really meant "no thanks." But I don't want to consider that possibility. No, I'll dwell instead on the way he stared at my meat. Oh yeah. I feel it again, the heat of his gaze scanning the topside of my dickshaft.

I'll be honest with you: I love men looking at me, and I love being wanted for my body. But what turns me on most of all is when a man looks at my meat and I know he's thinking about it.

I've a tight, lean body I work out hard to maintain, I'm reasonably good-looking, with thick black hair, dark eyes and high cheekbones, and I know I have a winning smile. Well, I like it when men call me hot, handsome or friendly-looking, but what I like most of all is when a man says something like, "You've got a *beautiful* dick," which usually happens after the man's been in my crotch for a while licking, sucking and looking.

A lot of men like to lick and suck; not all men like to look. When a man looks at my meat, I in turn look into his mind. I want to see what he's thinking. I want to see how he sees me through the filters of his dreams and desires.

So many men have called my dick "beautiful," which always struck me as such an odd adjective for something that's the essence of masculinity, that one day I looked at my hard-on in the mirror. I checked it out in profile with my hips thrust forward. It stood up rock hard, and what with its slight upcurve, kissed my navel. Then I checked it out again, this time facing the mirror. And, yeah, I saw what men mean. It *is* beautiful! It's big, dark, smooth-shafted and thick, with a riot of thin blue veins, and an over-sized, mushroom-shaped dickhead that flushes crimson through my tan when I'm really aroused. Below, my two medium-large nuts rest comfortably in a smooth-shaven ball sack with a good hang to it.

Ah, the way Lou stared at it. I open my eyes, prop myself up on one elbow and look down the stretch of my smoothshaven chest and tight abs to my dick. I tug on my nuts to force it straight up so I can see the topside, where Lou's eyes had traveled, re-experiencing the sensation, wondering what he'd think if he could see it now that it's hard.

Okay, so I'm admiring my own dick, imagining it through the eyes of another man. So what? If you want to be honest about it, you've done the same yourself many times, haven't you? In fact, why don't you pull it out right now, if you haven't done so already, and look at it. Yeah, check out your meat to see it the way other men see it. Does your dickhead swell at the thought of it? Does your cockstroke hand resist when you try to let go? Does your free hand reach up to tweak a nipple, or down to give your nuts a good tug, or around to slide a finger up your hole? Yeah, I thought so.

Well, now you know how I feel when men look at me and I see the lust in their eyes. And also, now you know why I write this stuff. I love turning men on. In fact, I'm thinking about you this very moment, wondering what's going on in your crotch.

Is Lou looking in his mind's eye at what I'm staring at now? Does it make his cockshaft thicken and his dickhead flex, like mine's doing?

Then it happens, the way it always happens whenever I'm horny at Sandy Hook and the sun's beating down on me, bleaching my brains. My mind "unspools." Threads of facts and threads of fantasies spin free, taking over my imagination, weaving scenarios and binding me up in them.

As you've already noticed, today's theme seems to be my father. In my mind, he and Lou merge into one man. I actually envision their two bodies fusing into one. The image is so sweet and satisfying, I feel it deep in my nuts as the sun continues to lap at them, and soon I'm back in the showers at the swimming pool with my dad, and he's staring at my crotch.

"Nice meat, son."

"Thanks," I say, caught off-guard, thrilled, but unsure how to respond.

I look at him. He's still looking at my cock, but now he's busy soaping up his crotch. I think of the cause and effect: he looks at my cock, he has thoughts I don't know about, and then he spends a little more time than usual soaping up his cock and his balls. I feel myself stiffening. I don't know what I want to do more; hide it or show it off.

"Yeah," he muses out loud for me to hear, "like father, like son."

He grabs his dick, yanks it up out of the way, and attacks his balls and below with the soap.

Oh, to be that bar of soap, that poor, manhandled bar of soap!

"That's going to make a lot of girls happy..."

He's still staring at me, and no way can I disguise my hard-on that's sticking out at three o'clock and rising.

And then—fuck!—this Latino hunk I'd seen around the pool walks in.

My father looks over at him, and then at me with, "…or guys."

The stud's holding his towel in front of his crotch, instead of wearing it, like most men here do. He checks out our presence, tears away his towel and steps into the shower room by the nozzle next to mine. He has a thick rubbery dick responsive to his every movement that never stops flopping around.

He glances down at mine, looks up at me, smiles, and then busies himself with his shower.

"If you haven't figured it out yet, son," my dad continues, under his breath, "there's hardly a man in the world who hasn't been sucked off some time or another by another man."

My dick leaps up at this indirect admission that my dad's been sucked off by another guy.

And then he leans into my ear and whispers, "*He's* a cocksucker, you know."

I look into his eyes, speechless.

"You can always tell by the way they look at your dick."

Does that mean my father knows about *me*?

"Damn! My shampoo."

Before I can say "use mine," he's tiptoeing dripping wet out to his locker.

Is my father fixing me up for a blowjob? I'm liking the kinky direction this unspooling's taking.

I turn to see the stud's staring at my dick again, which is now unmistakably hard. He's stroking his own meat, which turns out to be a real whopper, and he gets down on his knees in front of me.

My dad's more or less said it's okay for me to get my dick sucked by another dude. Yeah, but he didn't necessarily mean he'd want to be there to watch.

Would my dad want to watch me get sucked off?

The thought unspools like a thousand voices wrapping themselves around me.

Time slows down as the stud stares at my meat, contemplating it. No sane person in his situation would take so much time, but then cocksuckers aren't sane people. They're above sanity.

Maybe, I think, he and my dad planned this. Which brings me back to: *Would my dad want to watch me get sucked off?*

Slowly, he leans into my crotch, wrapping his lips around my dickhead and closing his eyes as he gives my piss hole a few swipes.

I audibly gasp.

He slides his mouth down to the base. His lips are stretched wide and his nose is buried in my bush. He works his way up and down my dick with long, measured suckstrokes. He hardly gags, just the occasional spasm, which can happen to the best of us, and I'm transported up into cocksuck heaven.

- 172 -

"Go ahead. Don't stop for me."

I'd closed my eyes and didn't realize my father had come back, until he spoke.

Yes! My dad *would* want to watch me get sucked off. He's even standing guard at the entrance to the showers.

The dude contracts his throat muscles around my dickhead and I moan loudly, looking into my father's eyes to see him staring at my crotch. I want to be his eyes and I want to know what he's thinking as he sees me getting sucked off.

"Nice," is all he says, though, grabbing hold of his dick and stroking it.

But it's not my father's voice. And the sound of the shower is really the rustle of dune grass as the wind sweeps through it. The sweet mouth of the Latin-looking cocksucker returns to its original form as my own left hand, and I open my eyes to see Lou standing there watching me.

"Just do what you're doing," he says, pulling on his semi-hard dick. He has the same habit my father had of stretching it out across his thigh and holding it there briefly.

I close my eyes again and stroke my cock slowly in showoff fashion, thinking about Lou, thinking about my father, the two of them connected by the same stare, the same interest in watching me work on my meat.

A cloud passes over the sun. Surprised on such a sunny day, I open my eyes just enough to see it's actually Lou, who's moved around to the front of my windbreakers to watch me up through my spreadapart legs.

I feel his gaze on my nuts, sweetening the sensation of their slow rise and fall. I lower my lids and I imagine his eyes hiking up the neat seam of my ball sack, scrambling over my cockgripping fingers and sliding up my dickhead to my pre-cummy piss hole.

The suns returns and I glimpse Lou watching me from another angle. His dick's fully hard now, and he's slowstroking it at the same speed I'm using on mine. I imagine myself through Lou's eyes, capturing mental images of myself from all sides.

Then the glow of the sun against my eyelids disappears again and I look up to see that Lou's stepped noiselessly into my windbreakers and he's standing above me with his hands on his hips and his feet planted on either side of my chest. His big balls hang suspended above me, clinging to the base of the shaded underside of his thick shaft as it stretches out over my face. His piss hole stares down at me, oozing out a shiny strand of pre-cum, and I wonder what tales it would tell if it could talk.

I rise slowly, propping myself up with the heels of my hands behind me.

My tongue reaches his dangling strand of pre-cum, anchoring it, a ladder to Lou's piss hole. But I realize this union of tongue, pre-cum and dickhead takes place above the concealment of the windbreakers. If a ranger sees us, there's no way we could convince him that we were just chatting.

Lou must've tuned into my apprehensions. He scans the beach left to right. Even the play of his straining neck muscles drives me wild. Then he lowers himself onto the blanket, ass on heels with his legs wide apart, and I kneel in front of him. From this position we can see beyond the windbreakers with only our heads showing.

He takes my shaft in his hand and looks me in the eyes.

"You must make a lot of men very happy with this," he says with a wicked smile, giving it a squeeze.

The pressure of his warm, firm hand around my dick sets my mind a-spooling once again, blending the past and present, the real and the unreal, into one heady mix.

I look into Lou's eyes to see my father admiring my cock. In this scenario I decide my dad's straight by preference, but bi as far as experience goes because he's had the occasional blowjob by men as muscled and masculine as he is. It's just something locker room buddies do to help each other out. And he knows he's got a queerboy for a son, which doesn't bother him, really, because, as anyone can see, his son's a stud. No sir, no limp-wristed sissy boy here. *His* boy's all man.

"I sure try."

"Do you shove it down their throats when they need it bad?"

"If that's the way they want it, yes."

"I'd sure like to see that. And what about *you*? Are you a good cocksucker?"

"One of the best," I boast. Well, it's the truth. "But I don't get to do it enough."

"Oh?"

He squeezes my dick to show his interest.

"Yeah. You see, every time I go down on a man, sooner or later he pulls me off, looks at mine, and says something like 'You've got a beautiful dick.' Then he goes down on me. I guess I have a talent for meeting good cocksuckers."

"That must be damn frustrating."

"It is. I could show *you* what a good cocksucker I am, if you want."

"Well, I'd sure appreciate that. As you can see," he continues, dragging my eyes with his to his thick shaft, "I need a blowjob in the *worst* way."

"Anything for a buddy in need."

I crouch low between his legs until my eyes and his piss hole stare dead-on at each other. I lower my lids and slide out my tongue until the moist tip of it meets the moist tip of his dickhead. When they connect, it's like my tongue sends a current through his cock. It leaps up into the air before settling down on my tongue.

I look up at him. Oh yeah, he's looking down at me. I flick my tongue across his piss hole again and again, and together we watch his cock's acrobatics.

The only time I ever saw my father's cock was with furtive glances when we were naked around each other, which was usually in some locker room. We did a lot together before he died the year I went away to college. I always wanted the opportunity just to stare at it at leisure, examining details like I was admiring a favorite work of art in a museum.

"You don't mind if I just look a little, do you?"

One look at the wide smile that spreads across Lou's face and you know he likes the idea of *that*.

"You can look at it all you want," he says drawing out the words as if they felt good in his mouth.

He repositions himself, sitting back on his hands and butt with knees slightly bent and legs stretched wide open. He's made his body completely available to me.

The sun must be about eleven o'clock high now. Under its brutally piercing gaze there are no shadows, no hidden territory, no secrets between Lou's legs. Everything's out, the presentation's raw and bold.

I prop myself up on my elbows between his legs to gaze at him. Oh, he too has such a beautiful piece of meat—so thick, so tanned, so veiny.

Below, his two large nuts hang heavy in his straining sack. The image of Atlas bearing the world on his shoulders flashes into my mind. The writer in me unspools a man punished by the gods, transformed into a ball sack, forced into the service of an over-endowed, big-balled Greek hero during his many adventures fighting misshapen men and mythical monsters with savage dicks that'd rip you apart if shoved up your ass.

I stow away the thought and continue my examination below his sack, gazing at the hard, swollen territory. His hole's out of sight, but as if he could read my mind, he leans back on his forearms, lifts his legs and it comes into view. It's a beautiful sight and I dive into his asscrack, licking the entire, salty, sand-free length of it again and again with the flat of my tongue. I can tell he likes it by the way he lifts his legs further opening up his crack wider. I probe the tight pucker of his hole with the tip of my tongue and he groans.

I could spend the rest of eternity in his asscrack, but eventually he lowers his legs again. With the map of his meat in my mind, I close my eyes and plant the flat of my tongue below his nuts, eliciting a drawn-out moan. I take my time, slowing licking up his nuts again and again until they're good and wet. Though they're big, I do manage both of them into my mouth to give them a good tonguing, but it's like his tightening sack's battling me for possession, and when I finally give up, his spit-soaked ball-bearer gleams in the sun.

I tongue my way up to his shaft. Each lick a little higher than the one before it until I can tell I'm crossing the wide smooth territory of his clean cut, and up into the narrow corridor below his piss hole, meeting the downward flow of his pre-cum. I continue licking, knowing at any time I want I can wrap my lips around his cockhead, and luxuriating in all the time at my disposal, time to spend lost in the world of this man; to lick, to worship, to suck, to stare.

"Want to join us?"

I open my eyes. We're being watched. I recognize the dude. We've exchanged nods as we passed each other by the shore. But we were always with friends, so nothing happened, though our eyes did spark with interest.

He's a tight-muscled Hispanic with a gym-sculpted body and a deep, all-over tan, maybe five foot ten. He has a lean face with dark, intense eyes. His black hair's short, his bush is trimmed down to a quarter-inch, and the rest of his smooth, glistening body's completely shaved. He reminds me of a greyhound; keen, sleek, toned. His huge half-hard Latino dick's dark, smooth-shafted and uncut, with a pronounced downcurve. Behind it, his nuts cluster snug in their thick-skinned, furrowed ball sack.

He doesn't smile, but his eyes simmer with desire, so I wave him in to join us.

As he does, Lou takes my hard cock and gives it a shake, arresting Greyhound's attention. I unspool myself into Greyhound's eyes looking at my own dick. He likes its size, its thickness, its pre-cummy dickhead.

"His dick needs servicing," Lou says to him.

I unspool further, into Greyhound's mind. He hears Lou's words; they mingle with the sight of my meat, and the monstrous cockhunger inside takes possession of him once more.

He drops to his knees, and with no preliminaries leans over and deepthroats my dick. He takes it down to the base, gags briefly as his throat adjusts to my size, and then slides up and down my dick with such suction it feels swollen far beyond its usual dimensions.

He sucks me slowly, deeply, never breaking his rhythm as the three of us readjust. Lou kneels with open legs behind me, his dick hard against the small of my back as he wraps his arms around my chest and rests his chin on my right shoulder to watch. Our faces are so close sometimes his cheek rests against mine. Out of the corner of my eyes I watch Lou watching the blowjob I'm getting. He has a half-smile on his face and a thoughtful expression.

Much sooner than I'd like, I feel the beginnings of an orgasm sweet and thick as honey deep inside my balls, so I take Greyhound's head in my hands to pull him off my dick.

He refuses to let go and tries to shake his head free of my hands.

Lou knee steps around to my side and pulls him off my dick.

Greyhound's eyes blaze. He lunges for my meat, but Lou pushes him away from it and slaps him hard on the cheek. Greyhound looks at him with a sex-crazed expression and then looks at my throbbing, spit-shiny dick with a tortured expression on his face like he needed it bad. He looks back at Lou with pleading eyes.

"Rangers," Lou cautions.

Yes, there they are, still at a distance, patrolling the beach in their jeep. The three of us sit, innocent as can be, forearms wrapped around our knees as we look out at the ocean. Although we don't watch the jeep directly, we're always aware of exactly where it is.

"Wanna fuck him?" Lou asks me.

I turn into an unspooling thread of desire.

"Wanna fuck him?" my Dad asks me.

Me and my dad at Sandy Hook. My dad knows I liked getting sucked off by men. He even watched once in the showers at the Montello pool. He said it happens all the time. Neither one of us has ever said anything that acknowledges I'm gay, but I know he knows.

"Sure, I want to fuck him. He's a hot man."

That's a pretty clear admission I'm gay, isn't it?

The rangers pass by about fifteen feet in front of us.

"He wants to fuck you up the ass," he says to Greyhound.

As the jeep makes its way along the shore, Greyhound turns towards him and nods yes.

"It's not too big for you, is it?" Lou says to cocktease him.

Greyhound nods no. He has one arm under his bent legs to stroke his rigid downcurver kissing my beach blanket with pre-cummy piss lips.

I suspect there isn't a dad in the world that hasn't at some time or another checked out the size of his son's meat. I don't mean he necessarily lusts after it, but I'm sure every dad who discovers his son has a big dick, takes a certain pride in it. Most dads envision their sons fucking a girl. What does a dad see when he imagines his son fucking another man?

Once the rangers are safely past, Greyhound kneels over onto his forearms with his wide open asscrack staring up at us, the sun shining directly down into it.

Together Lou and I examine his smooth-shaven butt hole that clenches repeatedly to lure us in. Could I ever as a boy scout earn a badge in buttfucking spools off my mind?

"Maybe we could *both* fuck him," Lou suggests, sliding in his fuckfinger.

Greyhound growls deep in his throat.

"I mean, one at a time," he adds.

Like father and son at a whorehouse, I think.

"Do you have any lube?" Lou asks.

I reach into my beach bag where I keep a stash of supplies—poppers, condoms, a fresh cumcloth and such—and pull out a small bottle of KY. Lou's taken the opportunity to rearrange Greyhound on his back, kneeling open-legged behind him to pull up his legs, providing his abs as a cushion for Greyhound's head. Greyhound's blessedly flexible and Lou presses his ankles against his shoulders. This is very important, and I'm relieved. Legs waving in the air attract the attention of the rangers.

As Lou looks on, I lube up Greyhound's hole. He closes his eyes and his mouth falls opens as he grabs hold of his meat and slowstrokes it. His face is the picture of bliss and I wonder if, while I unspool a fantasy about my dad watching me fuck another dude, he might be in the middle of his own unspool, running along mine like a parallel universe.

I lube up my dick too and the KY combines with Lou's gaze so my cock's extra-slick and super-sensitive.

It's easy sliding into Greyhound, he takes it like a first-class bottom and I watch my thick shaft burrow itself inside him. When I'm all the way in and my bush hides the union of cock and hole, I look up to see Lou watching. He catches my gaze and gives me a wink.

"Look at him," Lou says, admiring Greyhound's body. He looks like concentrated lust squeezed into a tight, lean body glistening with a thin sheen of sweat. His thick downcurver looks several sizes too large for his body—he can hardly get his cockstroking hand around it. His skin's fully retracted, his drooling dickhead joins the audience, and his large, egg-shaped nuts are so snug in his tight ballsack that looks like wet leather dried taut by the sun they hardly move as he strokes himself.

"Ok, fuck him, Lou orders me.

"Ok son, fuck him," I hear my father say.

I begin pistoning in and out and the moment becomes perfect. My dick feels enormous in its urgent state, like Greyhound's torso is simply a sheathe to give me pleasure. The sun beats down on us, some repositioning takes place, and Greyhound's head is now on the blanket, face up with Lou's nuts in his mouth, licking them. Lou's shaft sticks straight up, hard, moist, inviting as he scans the beach for returning rangers.

I close my eyes. My mind unspools wildly, prompted by the sweet feeling between my legs. I thrust hard and deep into Greyhound, again and again, secure in the thought my dad's standing guard.

As I feel the cum galloping up my dickshaft I see myself through my father's eyes as a man. A man fucking another man, but still a man, and he's proud on some primitive level that his son has a cock and knows how to use it.

"Ohhhhhh" I moan as I ram my cock up Greyhound's ass, shooting what seems like an endless supply of cum. I don't care about rangers anymore. My head flings back, then forward, I ride the bronco and tame him as he shoots his own load of white, shiny cum pooling all over his chest, yelling out, muffled by his mouthful of Lou's nuts.

I look at Lou. He's looking back at me. I look down at his throbbing dick.

"Yeah, suck it."

"Yeah, suck it, son."

"You know you want to."

"You know you want to."

Yes I do, badly. I close my eyes and fling myself into a land of taboos, and fall onto Greyhound to suck my dad's hard piece of manmeat. Taking it deep, not even gagging, proud to show off that this same son who can fuck ass with such force can also suck dick like a man. His breathing becomes loud and ragged, I open my eyes to look up at him, and I see his face contorted with the ecstasy of the moment and he finally breaks out into a roar as hot cum spurts out down my throat.

When we finally come to rest and disentangle, Greyhound rises, wiping the sweat off his brow and the cum off his chest with a small towel I offer him.

"Well, I guess my work here is done," he says half to himself and I wonder what the course of his unspooling is that it should lead to such a statement.

These are the first words he's said to us. And the last. He nods at each of us and leaves.

Lou says to me, "You should've seen yourself."

I will. Many times in the future, through Lou's eyes. Through Greyhound's eyes. Through my father's eyes.

SIZE 12s AND LONGING
by Simon Sheppard

Sunday Morning

The boots are so much like his father's boots.

The tenants in the building next door have moved out. The window across the airshaft, where a hideous chintz curtain has hung for months, now is bare; he can see into a corner of his new neighbor's room. Almost nothing to see: bare walls, a scarred wood floor. On that floor, a pair of scuffed work boots.

The boots are so much like his father's boots.

Sunday Night

Lying sleepless in bed, he remembers how he'd felt as a small boy when his father came home from his construction jobs. His father's powerful hands unlacing, pulling off his sturdy boots. The smell, strong, male, that rose from the still-warm leather. The indescribable feelings he'd had when his father, stripped down to his underwear, let his son use his belly as a pillow while they lay on the floor in front of the TV. His father's warmth, the closeness of his crotch.

In bed, he rubs his spit-wet hands across his swollen dick until he comes.

Monday Morning

The boots are still there early the next morning. There are no other clues to who has moved into the room. Trembling slightly, he goes next door, leaving a pair of heavy gray woolen socks on his unknown neighbor's doorstep. He rings the bell and hurries back to his window, his heart pounding, his mouth dry.

Moments later, he sees his first glimpse of the man next door. Hairy, naked calves and feet are clearly visible against the bare wood floor. But strain as he might, the angle makes it impossible to see any more. The man next door is pulling one of the socks on, slowly, caressing his foot as he does so. Then the second. He takes a boot in his powerful hands and pulls it on over the gray wool sock, tightening the laces and tying them firmly. The second boot, and then the man is gone.

The day passes slowly for him. His mind is lost in images of the stranger's muscular forearms, covered with coarse black hair, so like his father's. He wants to run his hands down the sinewy arms, down to the man's strong hands, hands that have touched the manboots. He longs to caress those boots, kiss them, to nuzzle his face against them, be gripped by the warmth, the strength, the power.

Monday Night

When he gets home, there is a brown paper sack at his door. Once inside his apartment, he opens the sack and finds the pair of wool socks, still moist with sweat. He places them to his face and inhales deeply—a strong, exciting smell, just slightly tinged with the tang of ammonia. He strips down, rubs the socks over his torso, down his belly, over his pulsating dick. "Daddy," he murmurs. "Daddy."

Tuesday Morning

He awakes before dawn, goes next door and leaves a neatly wrapped pair of white briefs, the brand his father used to wear, hanging from the doorknob. He rings the bell, rushes back to his vantage point, and waits. The neighbor's light is on. The boots are still there, but there's no sign of the man.

He waits at his neighbor's window, stroking his crotch until he thinks he'll explode. Nothing, no sign. The light goes off.

Disappointed, he returns to his bedroom, pulls out his cock, makes himself come. In the split second of peak excitement before he shoots, his father's face appears to him, so clearly it makes him gasp. As the warm, viscous cum trickles down his belly, he can feel his father's immense arms wrapping themselves around him, around his boyself.

Tuesday Night

There's a knock at the door. He gets up, pulling a sheet around his naked body. No one is there, just the same neatly wrapped package he'd left that morning. He opens it. The briefs have been worn. They smell sweetly of crotch-sweat. There's a piss-stain at the crotch. And they're stiffened, the stiffness of dried cum. He returns to bed, gently lays the briefs on his pillow, sleeps all night with his face against them, dreaming of his father, the strange, seductive memories of discipline and love.

Wednesday Morning

When he opens the door, the boots are on his doorstep. Tucked into one of them is a note that reads, "Take good care of these. I'll want them back."

He brings the boots inside, strokes them, buries his nose in them. His dick is so hard it nearly hurts. He lowers his jeans, takes the left boot and ties the shoelace around the base of his hard dick, letting the shoe swing freely between his thighs. He opens the other boot wide, buries his face in it, inhaling deeply. He can't stop himself; he ejaculates in big, spasming spurts. When he looks down, the scuffed leather of the daddyboot hanging from his cock is gleaming wet with his cum.

Wednesday Night

When he gets home, he strips down, takes as hot a shower as he can stand, and then carefully, reverently puts on the briefs, socks, and boots. He looks at himself in the mirror, running his hand under the elastic waistband, grasping his hardening dick. He goes out to the window on the airshaft. The room across the way is dark. He stands there for what might be hours, stroking himself. Across the way, there's a dimly perceptible movement. It's his daddy, his bootmaster, his unknown lover. He's been watching. The sudden shaft of a flashlight's beam illuminates the stranger's feet. Then, just as suddenly, the light goes out. The window across from him is empty.

Thursday Morning

He gets up with a hard-on, thinking of the man next door. He puts on the briefs, a pair of tattered shorts, the wool socks, the too-large boots. He shuffles out to the airshaft, stands staring into the window. Nothing. Bare walls. Bare floor. He waits a half-hour, an hour. Nothing.

Thursday Night

Still no sign of the man next door.
All day he has felt an aching, a longing. The feelings he felt when he and his father went swimming at the public pool, when they changed into swimsuits in the locker room, when he saw his father naked, saw his father's immense and beautiful cock. How would it feel to touch that man-dick, caress it, worship it? The remembered smell of chlorine fills his nostrils. He pulls down the bedcovers, carefully lays out the briefs midway down the bed, places the socks and boots where his father's invisible feet would be. He curls up on the floor at the foot of the bed, drifts off to a night of dreams, warm and powerful, always just out of reach.

Friday Morning

There's a note slipped under his door. It reads, "Tonight." Just that. He leaves the boots, socks, and briefs in a bundle at his daddy's door.

Friday Night

It's been hard, very hard, to make it through the day. When he gets home, he showers, dresses, goes next door. The apartment is unlocked.

It's dark inside. He shuts the door behind himself, gets down on his knees with his head lowered, his eyes fixed on the floor. The light goes on. "I've been waiting for you, boy." The voice of a man who is older, bigger, stronger than him.

Daddy walks forward. He can see Daddy's boots, only Daddy's boots. He lowers his face to the floor, caressing the worn leather with his cheek. Daddy bends over, lays his strong, masculine hands on his shoulders, his neck, gently strokes his hair. They are powerful hands that could administer pain or give protection. They are his Father's hands. He can barely breathe. "Daddy," he whispers. "Daddy, I need you so much."

He uses his teeth to untie Daddy's bootlaces. Daddy steps out of his boots. He inhales deeply, the ripe smell of Daddy's feet. His hands clasped behind his back, he uses his mouth to peel off the moist gray wool socks. Daddy's feet are before him. He kisses them, licks them, worships their power.

"Put your hands on my dick, boy." He can hardly believe the privilege he's been given. He runs his trembling hands up the hairy legs, up to the stiffened briefs from which he frees Daddy's stiff flesh. Still gazing at Daddy's feet, his head against Daddy's naked thighs, he strokes the big dick until, with a grunt torn from his manthroat, Daddy shoots his spunk all over his boy's back.

He keeps his eyes cast down as Daddy reaches under his arms, draws him up, up to his hairy chest, up to his beating heart, a place of ultimate safety and warmth. Then Daddy loosens his embrace, steps backward. The light goes out. He turns, walks out of Daddy's apartment, closes the door behind himself. He hears the click of the lock.

He has not seen Daddy's face.

Saturday Morning

He awakes to the sound of a moving van in the street below. Two young women are moving into the apartment across the airshaft. Even before he's gone next door to ask, he knows what their answer will be—no one has been in the apartment, they think, since an elderly Romanian couple moved out the week before.

Saturday Night

When he returns home that evening, the window across the airshaft has been hung with a beige Venetian blind. It isn't till his key is in the lock that he sees them: the scuffed work boots are sitting on his doormat. Tenderly, he picks them up, carries them inside. He strokes the angle of the worn heels, sniffs the now-fading scent. Daddy has gone, but he still has Daddy's boots. He clutches them to his chest. The twilight deepens.

BUSTED
by M. Christian

"Fucking faggots." His narrow brass nametag, polished to a glimmering shine so perfect that Cisco could see his face in it, read Mansfield. Sergeant Mansfield of the Tucson PD.

Tucson, Cisco thought as the spit-polished Mansfield led them back through the station, is an awful place to get busted. Still, he had to admit, it was a freaky kind of turn-on to have real cop handcuffs on his wrists and be at the mercy of such a hard-core butch specimen as Sergeant Mansfield.

Even the cells were like some kind of queer porn-film stage set: two rows of three empty cells. Drains in the floor. Bare bulbs set harsh caged fixtures, hung high in a steel-beam ceiling. Steel-frame bunks and steel toilets. The place stank of booze, piss, fear, and anger. Cisco ached he was so hard.

He looked quickly over at Larry, who was marching along beside him—hands also cuffed behind his lean back, Mansfield's right hand on his shoulder. As if feeling Steven's eyes, Larry returned the look with a sly smile. They'd been together for a while—a trick that had turned into a three month cross-country debauchery—and he knew that sweet little grin: tonight in their cement and steel cell ... well, it was going to be special.

"Goddamn fucking faggots," Mansfield rumbled again in his bass tones as he pushed them both, hard towards an empty cell at the end of the block.

Stumbling in, Larry turned and flopped down on the cot, letting his legs sprawl apart. The day had been hot, and had gotten hotter as the sun had climbed. They'd started with jeans and had quickly changed into muscle T's and shorts, so when Larry fell, and his legs spread, there was his dick—hard and glistening with a tiny pearl of pre-come—pointing straight up at the gleaming, stone faced Sergeant Mansfield.

"Fucking goddamn faggots!" Mansfield bellowed, like thunder from on high as he slammed the cell door. As if in perfect accompaniment to the heavy bass of his voice, the steel crash of the door closing echoed for a long time in the concrete room.

Mansfield glared at them, huffing and snorting like a shorn buffalo. Watching strong, narrow eyes, Cisco bent own and wrapped his hand around Larry's exposed cock, using his thumb to smear the fat head with slick pre-come.

"Goddamn," Mansfield said, lower in tone, eyes wider.

Kneeling on the merciless concrete floor, Cisco kissed the glistening head, tasting salt and bitter excitement. Already hard and throbbing in his own denim shorts, Cisco felt his cock eagerly beat in time with his hammering heart. A kiss is never enough, and with a grunting "goddamn" from Mansfield on the other side of the bars, Cisco slowly opened his mouth and slowly swallowed Larry's thick cock.

Cisco sucked him, sucked him good and long—pumping his head up and down on Larry's iron-hard dick. He swallowed and swallowed till he could feel the bulbous head slide up and down, in and out of his throat.

Then he stopped. He stopped before Larry could shoot his load. "Hello, fucker," Cisco said, turning to look up at his boyfriend, slowly stroking Larry's thick dick. "Hello, faggot," Larry answered, reaching down to grab Cisco's own pulsing, rock-hard dick.

"You know, officer," Cisco said, head now turned to look at the dark shape of Sergeant Mansfield of the Tucson police department, "I don't think we were ever strip searched." So he stood, and taking the bottom of the T-shirt, quickly pulled if off over his head.

Cisco was proud of his body, and of the attention it got him. So he stood there in the cell and showed it off. The lighting wasn't perfect, the atmosphere was definitely rough trade, but Cisco was still damned fine: sharp definition, rippled stomach, divine abs, thick nipples.

He stood there for a moment, just basking in the lust coming from Larry, and the heavy breathing rolling from Sergeant Mansfield.

The shorts came next: khaki dropping to his shoes. With practiced grace, he kicked them off, sending them flapping to hit the bars. He stood there, naked and hard, staring at the gun barrel eyes of the cop. Still standing, still staring, Larry lifted his thin, fine hand and wrapped it around his still-slick dick and slowly started to jerk himself off.

Back and forth, never blinking, never taking his eyes off Mansfield, he stroked his dick. Sure, Larry had a good body. It was tight and strong, but it was his dick that really stopped conversations. Long, strong and straight, it took a long couple of seconds for his hand to go all the way from his base to the rosy-red, thick head—and those where good, damn good, seconds.

As Larry stroked himself, slowly jerking off, Cisco—too turned on for words, got down and crawled slowly from the side of the bunk and behind him. There, he looked up, taking a nice long moment to savor the tightness of his boyfriend's hard ass. After a beat, though, his cock was too insistent to just let him look up at Larry's tight ass—so, squatting behind him, he started to slowly, worshipfully, caress him.

More than ideal—if there could be such a thing: solid, strong, tight, with just the right amount of scratchy hair. Cisco's hands worked him, kneaded his firm cheeks, gently parting them as he sought his pink asshole.

Still jerking off, eyes still latched onto Sergeant Mansfield—who stood, a hands breath, away from the bars—Larry let his face slip into a wry smile and slowly, meticulously spread his legs.

That was all that Cisco needed. First, one finger, then two ... three ... four: kneeling behind Larry's glorious ass, Cisco steadily, persistently, pushed his fingers into his asshole. Four, four, four—with everything except his thumb, he rocked his hand in and out of his tight, strong hole. He fucked him, just that way, for what seemed like hours.

Kneeling down between his perfect ass cheeks, Cisco shoved his hand in and out—but always short of his entire fist. He knew Larry, knew how that would drive him wild—and Cisco was bound and determined to make him wait as long as possible.

"Fuck" Sergeant Mansfield mumbled, under his breath, almost not even spoken at all. From where Larry stood, the cop was a dark form, a kind of leather and polished brass statue standing just beyond the bars. But he was watching—very intently he was watching.

Larry loved an audience. So he started to jerk off in earnest as Cisco half-fucked him up the ass. "Oh, yeah," he said, an actor on stage to the audience: "Oh, yeah! Do it, fuck my asshole. Fuck it good and hard. I want to feel it—want to feel it all the way up inside me. Fuck me, Cisco, fuck my asshole!"

Mansfield bust, exploded in a sweaty fury: nightstick drawn, it mashed across the bars with a discordant crash of sound. "Fuckers!" he screamed, spittle flying through the air. "FUCKERS!"

Too much force, too little control, the nightstick got caught, flipped down and through the spaces between the steel bars. It landed with a heavy lumber chime on the cement floor.

Without moving from where he was half-fucking Larry, Cisco bent down and retrieved it, neatly spinning it around till its polished wooden tip was in front of his lips.

Mansfield froze at the sight, his fury vanishing in wide-eyed fascination.

Cisco licked it slowly moving his mouth and tongue around the polished tip. His own cock pulsing with a ferocious hunger as he imagined it being Larry's cock in his mouth, filling him with his salty cream. Maybe even with Sergeant Mansfield's cock up his ass as a special treat.

It was a steamy ballet, a smutty tableau, an orchestra of cocks and ass. Larry standing proud and very hard, legs spread, and hand wrapped around his magnificent dick; Cisco between his legs, hand up his ass, Mansfield's nightstick in his mouth, sucking it like he was trying to make it come down his throat.

Finally, it was too much—like something heated to the point of ignition, the ballet, the tableau, the orchestra exploded into quick action. Cisco folded his hand, neat and perfectly, and shoved his whole fat hand up Cisco's so-hungry ass—feeding the sweet orifice his fingers, wrist, and whole arm. Larry moaned, a subterranean sound of primeval glory as his cock quaked, strained and finally jetted a long, creamy burst of cum out, clear across the cell. His cum landed with a perfect splat on the boot of Sergeant Mansfield of the Tucson police department.

For a moment, nothing happened. Larry, Cisco, and the big cop froze where they were. Seconds stretched. Then Mansfield growled, like a slow avalanche, and reached down to his ring of keys on his belt. "Fucking faggots," he said—and for a moment Larry and Cisco felt a warm swell of terror at his anger—but then added: "Let me show you how it's done."

Later, *much* later, exhausted and spent, Larry sprawled on the cot, Mansfield snoring like a grizzly—Cisco changed his mind: Tucson was the best place to get busted.

NUDE PARTY
by Jay Starre

Once or twice a year the Vancouver Nudist Society throws a party. As a porn writer I do a lot of things for "research." At least, I tell my friends that. I had heard about these parties and decided I'd better go. Just to see if some of the things rumored about them were true. Maybe I would find a hot story there.

At the door I checked my clothing, retaining only a key chain I fastened to my wrist. No stranger to being naked around other men, it was still a sexual thrill to strip in the alcove while music blared from beyond and a hundred nude men waited.

I strode into the melee buck-naked. I was comfortable with my body, which if not perfect is at least tall and well-muscled. There were some hotties, and I spotted one outstanding example almost immediately. On the short side, which I like, and built with symmetrical perfection, he had close-cropped blond hair and a long fat dick. Once I laid eyes on him I followed him from a discreet distance, fascinated by his sexy allure.

He threaded his way through the other men, all eyes seeming to follow. He did not meet any of the looks, but not out of arrogance, as might be expected. It was the opposite. He actually seemed shy. I liked that. Maybe there would be more than a story here. Maybe there would be someone I could fall in lust with.

As I imagined my hands exploring his taut limbs, and very fetching ass, he led me toward the far end of the room. Then to my dismay, he disappeared into a doorway that gaped pitch-black emptiness. It was a back room, unlit. I had heard about that too. I sighed, and determined I'd look around and wait him out. I was not big on unlit back rooms. I had sampled their pleasures once or twice, for research of course. I'm not really a slut. But I prefer to see what I'm doing, and who I'm doing it to.

I feasted on the view while I waited. Hairy men mingled with smoothly shaved boy-toys. Big chunky asses and taut dimpled butts paraded past. Cocks in all shapes and sizes, cut with their purple heads showing, and uncut with their disguising hoods, flopped and waved from all directions. I was half-hard most of the time. There were massive chests I longed to suckle on, and bulging biceps I would have loved to wrap my hands around.

I was pretty worked up by the time my blond buzz-cut emerged from the dark room. He brushed past me without seeming to notice me. I smelled sex. I glanced down at his crotch, and his cock was jutting out from his waist, fat and glistening. It had been sucked off, or was coated with lube. He had obviously been doing something in there. I was a little disappointed, being hypocritically judgmental of his activities. Or maybe I was just jealous.

I followed the tight curve of his sexy ass, again from a discreet distance. It was still fairly early and I didn't really think he would be leaving soon. And if he did, it was still a blast to check out the crowd. Naked flesh bumped me as I would my way through the increasingly busy room. Music was so loud a conversation was practically impossible. I saw a few people I knew, although they were just acquaintances, and I did not bother to speak to them.

I was intent on blond buzz-cut. I was just thinking of approaching him when he disappeared into the crowd. I muscled my way past men into the far corner of the big room in the direction I had seen him head. Someone's hand ran over my bare ass. I shivered at the touch, my cock twitching and growing stiffer. I was getting hornier by the moment.

Finally, there he was, leaning against a wall with his feet planted wide apart, his compact body poised for action. And it was action he was creating. He was stroking his slick cock, the fat meat rising right up to a full hard-on as I approached. Before I reached him, half a dozen other naked dudes surrounded him.

I moved in behind one of them, his shoulders just low enough to offer me a perfect view of the unfolding scene. Buzz was jerking off while the group watched. He was staring at the crowd, a half-smile of dreamy lust on his small lips. I imagined my mouth on those bowed lips, and my cock rose up stiff and drooling.

That's when I noticed the others were beginning to jerk off too. All of them. And like some kind of yoked sexual beast, all six of them moved closer at once. They were only a few feet from him as he continued flogging his fat meat. I followed in close and watched, not jerking off but just watching.

Blond buzz-cut was loving it. His eyes shone, half-shut. He was whacking his cock with faster and faster strokes. One of his hands had been running over his own torso, pinching his nipples and rubbing his flat stomach. He was completely hairless, or at least appeared to be in the dim light. His skin gleamed with a sheen of sweat. Hard muscle rippled under the pale flesh. His fingers stroked that flesh, while we all watched with utter fascination. He had an audience, and he played them.

As he jerked his cock, his other hand went lower, cupping his hairless ballsack. The shaved crotch made his cock and balls seem fuller and fatter. He thrust his hips forward toward us and I shivered at the sight. Then his fingers moved down under his balls, and he spread his legs wider apart. He squatted slightly, and I knew what he was doing. He was playing with his own asshole.

With the loud music, there was no need to speak, and no one was. It was all done wordlessly. Buzz jerked off in front of us, flaunting his beautiful body in the raunchiest way possible. He even pulled his fingers from his ass and spit on then, then shoved them back down under his balls. When he began to wriggle his ass over those fingers, I knew I'd blow my wad if I even touched my cock.

I realized this was maybe his thing—getting watched, drooled over and jerked off on. I am comfortable being naked in front of a group, but having sex in front of a crowd is entirely another matter. Apparently this guy had no such inhibitions. And along with the other men, I was his captive audience. I loved watching him play with himself. I loved the way his arm tensed as it whipped over his juicy cock. I got off on the way his hand dug around under his balls, poking at his parted crack while he humped his own fingers lewdly. He seemed to have lost any inhibitions. It was awesome.

That's when the first man shot his load on buzz-cut. The naked dude farthest on the right, lurched forward that last foot or two and blew his nut. A rocketing stream of jizz splattered our performer's arm and stomach. I was both horrified and electrified. That beautiful body was being sprayed like a dog with sticky cum.

"Cum on me," he grunted out, just barely louder than the music.

That was the signal others were waiting for. Another stepped forward and thrust his hips in the air. Yanking rapid-fire on his cock, he sprayed a thick load on buzz cut's thigh. I shivered as his smile grew wider. His hand was flying over his own cock, and his fingers were working way up into his ass from under his balls.

Another dude moved in to spray his load. This one leaned right against buzz-cut and rubbed his cock along buzz cut's side as he pumped an oozing wad out. The jizz dribbled down buzz cut's smooth stomach.

I could smell jizz along with the funk of sexual sweat. It was grossly kinky, and so at odds with the physical perfection of our performer. He could seemingly have any man he wanted. But he wanted this. My cock was aching, but I didn't want to just spray him like the others.

But I did watch, with utter fascination. Three more men jerked themselves to orgasm while buzz-cut continued whacking off and fingering his ass. Cum ran over his chest, stomach, and thighs. His smile grew tense, his body arched and he finally joining the others. His fat cock erupted while his fingers poked up his asshole.

I glanced sideways. All eyes were on him. I looked back. His eyes were on me. I stood rooted to the spot, aware of my lurching cock and ache for release. Should I follow the others' example and step forward to jerk off over the beautiful exhibitionist?

"Condoms?" a voice rudely shouted at my shoulder.

I turned to see one of the waiters, naked as the rest of us. He was grinning wickedly. In his raised hand he held a platter. I had noticed him before, and smirked at the tray of condoms. Now I grabbed one off the platter without a word and turned back to buzz-cut.

What did I have in mind? It had suddenly come to me. I knew what I craved more than anything at the moment. To replace those fingers up his ass with my aching cock.

I shoved past the man in front of me. Buzz-cut was watching me, his chest heaving as his cock dribbled out the last of a copious load. Would he reject me? I would find out.

I moved in to stand in front of him, our bodies just barely touching. He was not moving, although his hands were still on his cock and up under his ass. Then he grinned, a real smile.

"Do you want to fuck me? Right here in front of everyone?"

His voice was surprisingly soft, for his shameless words. I could smell him. Cum. Seat. Sex stench. I had done a lot of kinky, slutty things, and enjoyed them all at the time, only slightly embarrassed afterwards. But this was a first. I didn't really want to perform in front of anyone, but I wanted to fuck him so badly I didn't care about anyone else or what anyone else thought.

I rolled the condom over my cock, rubbing it against his stomach as I did. I hadn't touched him yet, except with the head of my cock. Now I finally reached out and grasped his shoulders. They were as solid as I had anticipated. Deltoids bunched. He continued smiling as I turned him in my hands. He obliged, facing the wall and spreading his legs. He leaned forward, one hand still snaking up into his asscrack from in front. The he squatted slightly. He was offering himself. It was so fucking sexy.

"Fuck his ass, man!" I heard someone call from behind us.

For a moment I was acutely aware of being watched, but then I had that beautiful body in front of me. I looked down to see he had two fingers on his asshole, digging into it. Raunchy and hot! I rubbed my cock up into that deep crack, amazed at how smooth the flesh was. Shaved smooth as satin. Then I reached around him and ran my hands over his taut torso. Sticky, wet cum coated his skin. I shivered.

My cock rubbed up and down his crack, gaining lube from his sweaty flesh. His fingers slid from his asshole, and my cockhead poked at the abandoned orifice. It was all squishy and slick. He had lubed it already! How fucking hot was that? He had lubed up his ass and come naked to this crowd of men. He wanted it, and he wanted everyone to see him get it.

The pulse of the music urged me on. So did the catcalls from behind. My cockhead rubbed the slippery lips of his asshole, distended and swollen. He had obviously opened it up already with his own fingers. He squatted and shoved backwards, actually capturing my cock with his own buttlips. Then he just relaxed. My cock slid into heated ass. Quivering flesh wrapped it lovingly. Buzz-cut hardly moved, his body had grown slack and loose. The tension must have dissipated with his orgasm. Now he just sucked me inside him with a slow, languorous slurp.

I held my hips against his ass and let my cock slide into him inch by inch. He was bottomless. One long moment later I was buried to the balls. Shuddering with intense passion, I leaned into him, stroking his sweaty cum-coated sides and feeling my cock pulse deep in his hot bowels.

I could have remained like that forever. He seemed content too. He leaned into the wall and remained motionless, all except his spasming asshole. It caressed my buried cock with little convulsions. Heat held me inside him.

Then he began to move. Slowly at first, he pumped his hips over my cock. Small movements of his hips began to massage my boner. I held stock-still reveling in the sensation. And I sensed his satisfaction. He could feel the length of my hard pole up his ass. He was working it so that his asshole felt good. He was rubbing his own butthole with my cock.

I let him. I leaned into him and held my cock motionless. There was only his asshole and my cock.

But there was more. Music thumped around us, and other men had replaced those who had already blown their loads. I sensed more cocks jerking off behind us. They were going to spray us with their cum. Suddenly I was buzz-cut, an exhibitionist and a voyeur all in one. I had wondered what it felt like for buzz as all eyes watched him. Now I knew, at least for me. I gave in to it, spreading my own legs and arching my back, showing off my own ass. I was fucking and not ashamed of it. I was almost arrogant in it.

I ran my hands all over his tight body as he fucked himself over my cock. His actions grew faster. He suddenly seemed hungry for my cock. He bucked over it. I succumbed and began to fuck back. We slammed into each other. My cock was on fire with the friction of his spasming asshole.

Then warm jizz hit my back. It drooled down onto my naked ass. That was too much. I rammed deep and shot. At the same time I heard my own deep moan and pulled out of buzz-cut's ass. I tore off the condom over my cock and jammed it against his writhing butt. I shot my load all over a heaving cheek.

I inhaled cum it seemed. Another load was spraying my ass just as I was draining over buzz cut's cheeks. I think a third load sprayed me too before I stumbled backwards and faced the crowd.

There were faces I recognized, grinning. I managed to grin back, embarrassment the last thing on my mind. I was simply drained. I had wallowed in buzz-cut's uninhibited sexuality. I needed air.

I cleaned up in the bathroom and then wandered back into the crowd. It was busier than ever. And there was sex going on just about everywhere. Although I was satisfied, I still had a lingering craving for buzz. I wanted to look at him again. Had he really been as awesome as I remembered?

But I couldn't find him. I don't think he left. I think he disappeared into the dark room and remained there for whatever hungers he still had unsatisfied. I could have waited him out, but I realized it was not to be that night.

I went home instead. I had a lot to think about. And remember.

A VIEW FROM THE DECK
by Lewis Frederick

My new apartment was nothing like the upscale loft I had shared with my partner, Stephen, before he caught me there with a trick and invited me to leave. The new place did have one advantage though—four drop-dead gorgeous straight guys lived right next door and the view from my second-story deck was nothing short of spectacular.

Situated in a large complex inhabited mainly by young singles, my flat had the anonymous, antiseptic quality common to many modern apartments. Its monotony was broken only by the occasional weekend block party or late-night lovers' marathon overheard through thin plasterboard walls. The chief thing to recommend it was the scenery.

Four twenty-something young men shared the place adjoining mine. Each one of these guys was better looking than the next. I never could make up my mind who made me the hottest, but spent a lot of time on my deck trying to decide the matter over my first cup of coffee or an evening cocktail.

Always an early riser, I would take my morning paper out to the deck and listen to them begin to rustle about. They made quite a show, just waking up and getting ready to go to work, or school, or wherever it was they went during the day. I have always loved the sounds men in groups make beginning their day; the snorting and yawning as they stretch; the mumbled curses when somebody rumples somebody else's hair; the inevitable butt-slapping and towel-snapping that ensues whenever bodies intertwine in that uniquely male ballet that occurs only around sinks and showers.

Just like the shameless voyeur that I am, I would observe the little litanies of their lives, eavesdropping on their wake-up routines and after-hours arguments about who forgot to pay the light bill or who drank the last beer. I savored small, stolen glimpses of them, rushing in and out of their unit, late for work or a date, smoothing tousled hair and straightening ties. Occasionally, one of them might saunter out onto their own deck, wearing only gym shorts, talking to some girlfriend on a cell phone, with the sweat from an interrupted work-out dripping from his taut torso and collecting in the curled hair around his navel. He might glance up to see me watching him like a spider, then throw me a quick wave before ducking back into his apartment. More often, he might flash me that angry straight male boundary signal that says, "What the hell are *you* looking at?"

I guess the torture of living next-door to a handful of straight boys was my fair punishment for messing around behind Stephen's back. I have always had a roving eye, but Stephen knew that long before we ever settled in together. It was part of the package that was me, which isn't such a bad package after all, I must say.

I may be pushing middle-age, but have had the luck to mature gracefully, staying muscled and tanned, easing gently into the kind of salt-and-pepper good looks that draw flattering comparisons to Harrison Ford. I inherited just enough money to get away with dabbling in different careers without ever having to work too hard at any of them. Most of my friends described me as a real catch.

Thing is, there was just this little problem with fidelity and me. I couldn't be faithful to Stephen or anyone else I'd ever lived with, no matter how hard I tried. So here I was, living in a young singles' complex, wondering what might come next in my life. Then, in answer to that question, came the "Summer of the Straight Guys;" and I'm here to testify: straight guys do the damnedest things.

It all started the night my handsome neighbors threw a big mixer. I didn't mind the noise because the activity next door provided so much entertainment. Sitting on my deck, nursing a long string of cocktails, I watched the attractive couples mingle. My neighbors obviously worked or studied in some multicultural setting like the nearby state university, or one of the many international corporations in the area. Beautiful young people of every race, color and nationality chattered in amiable queues and diverse dialects over drinks and finger food. I have never seen so many gorgeous men in one place in my life.

Pairs drifted out onto their deck now and then, arms linked in intricate, intimate body language, the aura of imminent sexual encounters hanging palpable in the evening breeze, like the scent of some exotic flower. The subliminal libidinal tension in the air mounted throughout the evening. Couples began sneaking kisses in side rooms, sliding hot hands down each other's backs and murmuring urgent messages in each other's ears that provoked seductive smiles or outright laughter in return. Pairs began making out on the crowded sofa and easy chairs in the main room, or drifting off across the complex grounds for outdoor recreation, who knew where.

Only one of the neighbor boys seemed apart from these pursuits, though not through any apparent choice of his own. Time after time, I watched the tall, gangly blond with the impossibly big hands end up alone again on the deck after awkward dialogues with a string of vacuous girls. Over the chatter of the crowd inside, I couldn't be sure what his problem was, but it appeared to me he kept making the fatal mistake of trying to engage in intelligent conversation with a series of young women who clearly weren't capable of it. One by one, they drifted in and out of his space on the deck, swirling cocktail glasses in jeweled hands, tossing their shining heads in pretty, petulant gestures that seemed lost on the serious young man as he asked them sensible questions about their work or studies.

Then I got another glimpse into what might be the source of his dating dilemma.

One of his roommates burst out on the deck, bringing him a beer and ribbing him for being a wallflower. "What's the matter with you, Chad?" he chided. "I keep sending beautiful babes out here to bag you and they keep coming back inside empty-handed!"

Chad shrugged and smiled a crooked smile. "Guess I just don't have your touch, Mark," he sighed.

"Well there's nothing to it," Mark said. "You just gotta *go for it!* I'm sending out another batch now and I expect you to *nail* one of these chicks, you hear me?" Mark turned to go back into the apartment, and in the glance Chad through after him, I knew there was something more to this story. In the tall blond's deep-set blue eyes I thought I recognized sadness, even longing.

I knew that look all too well. The boy is in love with his roommate, I realized.

As if he had read my mind, Chad threw a sudden startled look at me across the space between our decks, then continued to scrutinize me as if wondering what to do next. Startled myself by the intensity of his gaze, I countered with my best Harrison Ford smile.

"Busted," I said, raising my glass in a mock toast. "You caught me red-handed. I'm an eavesdropper, it's true. But I never repeat a word. Honest."

Chad continued to bore a hole in me with those violet eyes for what seemed like forever. Then he finally managed a smile in return.

"Mark means well," he sighed. "He just doesn't get my taste in women."

"Which is ... *what?*" I ventured.

He shot me another guarded glance before answering. "Selective ... very selective," he said slowly.

Despite Mark's promise to send more babes out to Chad, no further women came out to dangle their charms as the big blond and I eased into exploratory banter. Probably from months of spying, I felt I knew this young man far better than I actually did. I also knew he couldn't possibly feel the same way, having never given me a second glance. But as we moved into more familiar conversation, I saw him drop his guard and soon relax the tense, fighter stance in his shoulders. Leaning over the rail of his deck, he chatted in an amiable way, tossing his head now and then to remove the long, golden shock of hair that kept falling across his high forehead.

"Looks like you're very selective indeed," I chuckled. "All alone over there in the midst of a crowd."

He glanced over his shoulder at the throng milling about the apartment. "I know," he said with a wry look. "Not exactly my best night, is it?"

"Seems you're just not much of a party animal," I offered.

"Definitely not," he agreed with another rueful look.

I felt a familiar stir in my loins as he grew pensive again. "What *do* you like, then?" I asked, shifting my weight in my chaise lounge to hide the bulge beginning to show in my crotch.

"Not this scene," he said, tossing his head back toward his apartment and sending the golden shock of hair flying again. "As a matter of fact, I'm just about out of here."

"Where to?" I asked, emboldened somehow beyond explanation. This was, after all, a straight guy. Wasn't it?

He gave me a direct look that took my breath for a second. "I'm not sure," he said in a level tone. "Got any suggestions?"

My mind raced. *Oh, my God, do I ever!* I thought. Still, I managed to sound casual in response. "I was just about to take a stroll—if you're game."

He answered without a second's hesitation. "See you downstairs."

Exactly one minute later we were shaking hands on the sidewalk below our apartments. He had a rough, catcher's mitt of a hand that encircled mine so thoroughly my fingers completely disappeared in his clasp. I became aware once I was standing in front of him just how truly tall and lanky he was, like a big Labrador puppy just beginning to find a true sense of his mounting size and strength. He had a man's weathered face, though, ruggedly handsome, and already etched with deep laugh lines and crow's feet despite his relative youth. We exchanged names and pleasantries for a bit, while I took in the sheer bulk of him, as patient and calm as a draft horse, and equally free of artifice.

"Where to, then?" he asked.

"I don't know. Let's just ... saunter," I suggested. We fell into step beside each other, and looking down at the sidewalk, I noticed that his feet were huge too. What was the old urban myth? Something about "Big feet, big dick?"

He had a fine mind, I soon found out, though that was the least of his attractions for me, now anyway. He talked easily about his graduate studies in Anthropology and his plans for a career studying indigenous peoples across the world. He had an insatiable interest, he said, for anything different or unusual in the human species. Somehow, we found ourselves talking about third and fourth-gender peoples among Native American tribes, including the legendary male "Two Spirits" who cross-dressed and had same-sex relations with fellow tribesmen as part of their culture's spiritual practices. I had read something of these people, sometimes called *berdaches*, but it was he who first introduced the subject of them tonight.

I found myself reflecting on his choice of topic as a curious one for a first conversation with me. What was he getting at, I wondered, as we continued strolling across the expansive apartment complex grounds for a long, long time, chatting and chortling amongst ourselves like two old friends. He was an avid conversationalist, and I found myself asking him countless questions, just to hear the quick answers he formulated, and to savor the deep, resonant timbre of his strong bass voice.

Finally we found ourselves at the now-locked gates of the wood privacy fence around the closed swimming pool. He leaned against the prominent padlock and heaved a great sigh.

"Too bad," he said. "I could really go for a dip just now."

I threw him a challenging grin. "You're tall enough to step over these gates if you wanted to."

He grinned back and pondered aloud. "Think I could?"

"I'll bet you something really good that you can." I said. With that, he jacked one gargantuan leg as high as his head and threw it over the gate. Almost effortlessly, he leveraged himself over the gate and landed on the other side like a pole-vaulter.

"Your turn," he said, reaching a long arm over the top to give me a hand up. I grabbed onto the giant paw dangling in front of me and struggled to pull myself up. He may have been string-bean thin but he was strong as well. The muscles and raised blue veins of his arm bulged sensuously as he pulled me up and over the gate. I landed next to him on the opposite side, stumbling a bit as I hit the ground. He grabbed my shoulders to steady me and I looked up into those impossibly deep blue eyes. We were both breathing heavily just then, partly from our exertion and partly from something else.

"So what do I win?" he asked softly, the breath from his parted lips falling sweet and musky on my face. *Damn,* I thought, *straight men! There's just no figuring them out.*

And with that I dropped to my knees and pressed my open mouth into his crotch. He let out a sharp breath and I heard him whisper "*Yes!*" The thickening length snaking down his pants leg told me "yes" in another language. Reaching up to feel it, I began to entertain some fears about what I had gotten myself into. The boy had to be hiding a pet python in there. I felt for the end of it a long while and finally located the bulbous knob, throbbing hot and damp beneath my fingers even through the fabric of his khakis.

Checking out the setting, I reassured myself we were hidden from all view by the tall privacy fence. That was the last bit of encouragement I needed. With frenzied, fumbling fingers I unzipped his pants and pulled them down around his knees. There lay the most magnificent cock I had ever encountered, drooping heavily from its own sheer weight and mass, the tip already beginning to weep a trail of silvery precum down the length of his sinewy thigh. To fit it all into my mouth seemed out of the question; I just licked my way around the base and shaft, lapping hungrily at the warm satin, burying my nose appreciatively in the moist, golden brown bush of coarse pubic hair surrounding it. Two equally impressive ball-bearings dangled in the low-hanging sack beneath it. One by one, I took them in my mouth too, letting them roll against my tongue and teeth gently, enjoying the smell of his crimped sack mixed with my own saliva. All the while, he moaned softly but continuously, repeating the whispered, prayerful words, *"Yes, yes, yes, yes!"*

Eventually I could delay the inevitable gagging session no longer. Steeling myself with a deep breath, I took the pulsing pink head of his cock into my mouth and tasted the salty promise of his precum. The width of his broad flange filled my mouth from side to side and I worked my lips slowly down the blue shaft. Inch by inch, I swallowed more and more of him, stifling my gag reflex until I had most of him down my throat. Grabbing his firm ass cheeks in each hand, I pulled him with one final, hard thrust all the way into me, burying my nose at last in his bush. He put a hand on either side of my head, cradling me in his grip, and let out a long sigh.

"Nobody's ever done that to me," he whispered in awe. "This is a first." He began undulating his hips gently, causing the long ball sack below my chin to slap softly against my jaw-line. "Don't stop," he pleaded urgently. "Whatever you do, please don't stop."

I had no intention of stopping. This was the happiest I had been in a very long time. I just kept working my throat around his cock and swallowing precum to my heart's content. Meanwhile Chad moaned and sighed and whispered sweet nonsense syllables in that special non-verbal language that's never been captured in writing but has been spoken since the dawn of time by all men getting a good blow-job.

Unfortunately, ecstasy can't last forever and a slight twitch at the base of my friend's long shaft signaled the big event was near. Anticipating what lay ahead, I debated what I wanted to do most with it—swallow it, rub it all over my face, or let him shoot it on the ground, then roll in it like a happy puppy. Chad took the decision out of my hands with yet another pleasant surprise. This guy was full of them, I realized.

"Not yet," he whispered urgently. "I want us to come at the same time." And with that he jerked me to my feet and knelt down on the ground in front of me, all in one swift, fluid motion. There he wriggled the pre-cum soaked shorts I was wearing to my ankles and took my own swollen tool deep into his mouth with a contented sigh, proceeding to give me the best head I had ever received from anyone, gay or straight. He worked at my thick member so adroitly in fact that I soon found my knees wobbling and had to lie down on the rough concrete beneath us. Chad never lost his stride, but once I was settled supine on the ground, worked that fat snake of his back into my smacking lips.

"Now," he murmured softly around my own dick in his mouth. "Now ... now ... *Now!*"

With that he erupted, and I don't use the word lightly or figuratively. I had never swallowed, licked, choked on and totally savored so much jism in my life as I did that night with Chad. The guy just kept coming and coming, like some bunny selling batteries. The pulsing current that filled my mouth tasted sweet and fruity—almost like some fine dessert wine. Most guys' cum has a little bitterness or brine to it, but not Chad's. I just lay there for a bit, letting the last traces of it marinate my tongue, relishing the heavy aftertaste of it. But I couldn't lay dormant for long.

True to his wishes that we come together, feeling him shoot so much triggered one of the finest orgasms I'd ever had as well. Even as a young man, I never made as much man-milk as Chad had just given me, but I shot more that night than I had in a long time. He rose to the occasion in noble fashion, especially for a supposedly straight guy. I fully expected him to pull away and spit when I first unleashed my load onto his hot tongue, but he surprised me again. Rather than pulling back, he burrowed his face deeper into my pubes, taking every inch of my rod and every drop of my semen into his hungry mouth. As I shot spurt after spurt of burning cum deep into his gullet, I heard him chuckle in a contented way and felt his breath warm my crotch as he continued to indulge in long sighs.

Eventually, we had to disengage from each other just to catch a deep breath that didn't have a dick in the middle of it. We rolled over on our sides, propped ourselves up on our elbows and just looked at each other, grinning.

"That was *amazing*," he finally said with an appreciative smile.

"Yes, it was," I agreed. "Where did you learn to do all that?"

He flushed a little at that and I felt bad for embarrassing him. "Self taught," he said. "Really. Though I will admit I've dreamed about it a long time and imagined what I would do."

"But probably not with your older neighbor, huh?" I asked, remembering the yearning glance he had thrown after his roommate Mark. He blushed ever deeper at my question but once more met my eyes with his usual candor.

"No, definitely not with my older neighbor," he admitted. "I had somebody else much closer to my age in mind." He looked away and took a long breath, as if considering something with great caution. Then he looked back at me for a long time and finally took the plunge.

"But that somebody else is suddenly the last thing on my mind," he continued. "In fact, I doubt I'll ever think about that somebody else again. I think I just met someone who's a lot more interesting."

He faltered a bit on the last words and looked down at his big hands. "That is, if this other someone is interested in me."

Normally, in my sorry, sordid past, this would have been my big cue to run like hell. But something about this incredibly big, callow, tender young man tugged at my jaded heartstrings. If nothing else, I had to admire his courage. In one fell swoop, the guy had just had his first man-to-man sexual experience, admitted to being in love with his roommate, and gone out on a major limb with me. You don't meet someone with that kind of guts every day now—especially not in the crazy gay world I'd navigated so glibly most of my meaningless little life.

I took a long breath of my own before I looked him back in the eye with every bit of courage and candor I could muster. "That other somebody is very interested," I said in the most level tone I could manage. My teeth that were actually chattering with a lifetime accumulation of carefully cultivated commitment fears.

He smiled his huge grin and leapt to his feet. "Then I guess we better get out of here before the security guard finds us." He reached down that giant hand again and offered me a boost.

"Not on your life," I declined, climbing nimbly to my feet on my own. "I may have a few years on you, youngster, but you'll never need to carry me."

We took our sweet time strolling back to our adjoining apartments, mainly just basking in the afterglow of good sex, chatting occasionally about little things in that special way new lovers have of making everything seem magical. Once back at our places, we found the party had cooled considerably. The lights were out in the boys' apartment, and only the flicker of candlelight on bedroom walls reached down to us on the sidewalk.

"Looks like you might be locked out," I suggested with a sly smile.

He made a face of mock gravity. "Uh-oh. Where am I going to sleep then?"

"I know a place," I replied. "But it's kinda old and worn out. There's been a lot of traffic in this place."

He turned to me and dropped the tongue-in-cheek tone. "I don't care," he said, taking my face in his hands, making my head feel tiny suddenly. "I'm willing to risk it with you if you're willing to risk it with me."

I had a hard time stopping myself from whooping and cavorting at that point. Instead, I just took his hands from my face and tried in vain to contain them in mine.

"Then it looks like we better go home," I said, and together we went into what would soon become "our place."

***

That was years ago now, and Chad continues to surprise me daily in one wonderful way or another. He finished his graduate degrees and soon went on to become a renowned expert on cross-gender native peoples across the globe. I gladly quit my last insignificant little business venture to became his research assistant, and have traveled the planet with him ever since, studying beside him and living in wattle huts with cross-dressing shamans, everywhere from Indonesia to Idaho.

Chad has continued to be full of surprises all right. The first surprise was that he had a lot more to offer than that monster inside his pants. But the biggest surprise has been his ability to bring out the best in me. From the first time we were together, I've never looked at another man;

well, not seriously, anyway—not in the relentless, cruising way that I always used to.

Despite being several years younger than me, Chad has taught something nobody else could: when you've found the best there is, why go looking for something more?

BLUE
by Greg Wharton

I moved to Chicago several months ago for a job with a design firm and rented this great apartment close to Foster Beach. I bought a cat that I named Cat. Everything was going well, but I was lonely. And horny. I was having what you might call a slump, a dry spell. That was until this last week when I started seeing Blue.

I'm a creature of habit. I roll, well, actually crawl, out of bed at 6:45 every morning after slamming the snooze on my alarm several times. I grab my glasses off the bedside table and stumble to the kitchen barefoot in my boxers where I attack the difficult task of feeding Cat. I'm not what you would call a morning person.

I light my first cigarette and fight with the espresso machine until it cooperates and produces my first caffeine of the day. I then light another cigarette and head into the bathroom to put in my eyes. I proceed with the exciting tasks of relieving myself, and shaving. About halfway through the shower, I usually wake up.

The first morning I saw Blue I was only halfway through my first cigarette when I happened to look out my kitchen window and noticed him walking through his kitchen. The window faces the back of another apartment, presumably the same as mine. I hadn't ever seen anyone in the apartment before as the blinds had always been closed and it startled me.

I watched him as he stopped at his counter and poured himself some coffee. He was wearing only bright blue briefs, and he had a roaring hard-on. Forgetting my half-smoked fag in the ashtray, and my now-cooling espresso, I focused my surprisingly awake eyes on the show. Guess he didn't notice me because I hadn't turned on my lights yet. Cool.

The man turned around and leaned back against the counter. His hair was black, or maybe dark brown, and was shorn short military style. He rubbed his cock through his briefs. He was tall, but had a nice trim body. Just the way I like them: long and slim. His large hands rubbed back and forth across his bulge. Even with the twenty-some feet and two windows between us, I could make out every detail of his cock.

I rubbed my own now very hard cock, and decided I had to go with this great luck while I had it and shed my boxers. Never one to be brave and actually do it public or at a club, I figured "What the fuck" since I was in my own kitchen. Though not as long as his, my cock is thick. I immediately started stroking it with both hands as I leaned back against my counter and watched him do the same.

He pulled his briefs down slowly, his nicely veined cock sprung to freedom with a snap and slapped up against his belly. He took it in his right hand and stroked it while his left hand explored his chest, finding a nipple and pinching himself. I closed my eyes for a moment and tried to remember what a cock tasted like.

He stopped stroking just long enough to taste his coffee, and his long cock stood at attention, curving up into the air. He then went back to his hard-on with added zeal. He cupped his hairy balls with his left hand and jerked his length with his right. He spread his legs wider and lifted his head so that it seemed as if he was looking straight into my eyes, then erupted his load. He shot out into the air, landing what looked to me about five feet away. He pumped again, and shot another load just as far.

This was unbelievable. I was watching my own private sex show! In my kitchen at 7:00 in the morning! I fucked my fist on my cock as hard as I could and screamed out as I too shot halfway across the kitchen, almost catching Cat still doing her "I'm hungry, damn it" dance.

I closed my eyes as I jerked on my cock a few more times. When I opened them, he was gone. I fed Cat, poured my now cold espresso into a cup, wiped my mess up with a paper towel, and lit another cigarette. What just happened? I went into the bathroom, feeling happier than I had since I had moved here, and got ready for work. What a way to start the day!

***

That night when I returned home after a bitch of a long day, my mystery neighbor's blinds were again closed. I spent the entire evening peeking my head around the corner to see if he had lifted them. I finally went to bed and jerked off, imagining what I would do with a cock like his, and wondering if I had only dreamt this morning's adventure.

***

I awoke as usual the next morning and stumbled into the kitchen as I had every other morning for the last several months, only this time I had someone waiting for me. Yikes, I forgot!

Blue was already there with hard-on in hand, staring right at me. His blue briefs were pulled down around his hips. This time I knew he could see me. He was looking right at me with a nasty smile on his lips and his cock was at full attention. I froze. He must have known I was watching yesterday!

I flipped on the lights and tentatively slipped my boxers off slowly. We locked eyes and slowly started a mutual jerk-off in rhythm with each other. We came at the same time, ejaculating straight towards the other's kitchen.

***

My mornings the rest of the week changed. I would wake up earlier and go to the bathroom first to make sure I didn't have bed hair or anything crusty and dried on my face. I would put in my eyes and then run fully awake into my kitchen. Despite her whining, I would ignore feeding Cat her breakfast until I was done with Blue.

He arrived each morning in his same blue briefs, but our activity got more intricate.

Yesterday, he came in as usual and we had our foreplay of rubbing cocks through underwear. He pulled his briefs off and took his long cock in hand. I followed suit. He turned his face to his left and raised his arm. He made an exaggerated smelling motion. This was hot, very hot, and I imagined my face buried in his armpit. I closed my eyes and tried to smell it.

Blue then hopped up on the counter that faced the window. He spread his legs, and I got the full view of his hairy balls hanging low and his length of cock standing straight up in the air above them. As all our encounters had been in unison, I quickly lifted myself onto the counter and assumed the same position.

He spread his legs wider resting one leg on the other counter by his sink. He slumped down a little with his back against the cupboards so his ass hung over the edge and reached under with his left hand. With two fingers, he spread his cheeks right at the pucker. I was so excited my cock almost erupted right then and there. I wished I were there to put my mouth to it, to taste his ass. I wanted to lick it, to stick my tongue in his hole and chow down.

I followed suit, but lifted both legs into the air and used both hands to spread my ass as far as it would go. He started pumping his long cock with strong fast strokes as he watched. I continued to hold my ass open for his viewing pleasure, with my legs straight up into the air, not even thinking about the fact I could easily fall off the counter. My cock was leaking and my balls ached. I needed to shoot soon. I let go with my left hand and rubbed my fingers up the shaft collecting my spilled juice and wiped them on my tongue. With a huge grin, I leaned my head back and imagined it was him on my tongue.

He stuck his middle finger in his mouth and sucked on it. He then placed it back under his ass and inserted it completely up his hole with one motion. His head jerked down for a moment. I could see that his cock was having small spasms and leaking as well.

With little grace and a few seconds of anxiety, I maneuvered myself so that I kneeled on the kitchen counter with my back to him. I licked two fingers, then reached under and stuck them both up my ass.

- 206 -

When they were in as far as the position would allow I started a slow fuck of my own, grinding onto my fingers as I would if they were his cock. I looked over my shoulder and coyly watched him watch me.

He continued to fuck his ass with his long finger and his cock looked as if it would burst, then lifted both his legs up into the air and inserted a second long finger. This was all he needed. His cock erupted and he leaned into it. He was almost able to put it in his mouth! He shot again and again all over his face, each time opening his mouth and sticking out his tongue.

I pulled my fingers from my ass, turned back around, and sat back down watching him in amazement. Though I knew I couldn't reach it, I dipped my head to receive my own offering and was rewarded with a strong mouthful of hot sperm as it erupted from my cock. I beat it with purpose. My cock seemed to shoot its contents in slow motion up into my open lips and outstretched tongue.

***

It's 6:45. I'm in my kitchen ready for Blue. I've brushed my teeth and inserted my eyes. I've even fed Cat already. I'm wide awake, and ready. Boy, am I ready!

Blue hasn't appeared yet. I'm smoking and feeling far too anxious. It's okay I rationalize. A guy can't have this much luck every day. Maybe he overslept. Maybe he met someone else and is still in bed. No, he'll show. I'll just start without him. I pull off my boxers and angrily fuck my cock in frustration. I stop when my doorbell rings.

My doorbell?

I run to the door and my heart stops when I look out the peephole. It's Blue. He's wearing jeans, no shirt or shoes. I fumble with the locks and nearly knock myself in the head as I open the door. I stand there naked and look face-to-face for the first time with the man I have had sex with every morning this last week. He smiles.

I'm speechless. He reaches out and wraps his long fingers around my rock hard cock. "Morning. Make me some coffee?"

I pull him into my apartment. Well, I back up and my cock pulls him into the apartment. "I'm a, well..." I stammer, as he immediately kneels in front of me. He wraps both his hands around my fat cock. "Oh..." Oh my god. "Oh my..."

I lean over him and close the door, as I feel his mouth make contact.

The slump is over. My dry spell has ended.

ON BOURBON STREET
by Max Reynolds

"Suck it, baby, suck it!"

Dash couldn't believe he had heard himself saying that, yelling it in the crowd at Mardi Gras, grabbing his crotch in one hand, a drink in the other. His dick had been suddenly rock-hard in his hand and it had surprised him. Some girls had flashed their tits at him and Terry and they had responded as 19-year-olds AWOL from college on a manufactured spring break would, with the most overtly crass sexuality they could muster, grabbing their dicks and jerking them in the direction of the drunken girls.

Terry had been from New Orleans. He had tossed the girls beads with the deft expertise that comes from a lifetime of practice. One of the girls had mooned Terry then, had run the beads down the crack of her ass and then tossed them back to Terry. The boys had yelled "Ooo la la" but Dash had felt his cock go limp again.

Nearly twenty years ago but he remembered it so vividly, that night in the streets of the French Quarter thronged thick and deep with all manner of people—college girls gone wild like the pack that had flashed them, guys drunker than they were looking for some heavy action, drag queens in feathers and sequins, near-naked prostitutes in six-inch heels and scattered among them all a few families with kids. It was wild, just wild.

The Boston-born Dash had never been south of the Mason-Dixon line before that trip with Terry, his best friend from college. Terry had explained that he always was home for Mardi Gras. "Only time I ever missed it was the year they called it off 'cause the police went on strike," he boasted. "Damn shame, too, since I was finally old enough to get laid."

Terry. Terrance Gerard Breaux III, scion of an elite Garden District lawyer with an interest in politics and a well-heeled debutante who managed to keep her looks despite a serious afternoon drinking problem. Terry and Dash had met freshman year at Fordham. Two Catholic boys with a penchant for tennis and trouble.

"What the hell kind of a name is Dash?" Terry had asked him when they met on the courts at school one chilly late afternoon in early spring. "You a sprinter?"

Dash could have been. He was long and lean like a runner, his thighs strong and well-shaped, his arms just built up enough from the slam serve that had landed him in amateur tournaments since he was twelve. He had the sultry good looks of his Irish parents: shiny black hair with a wave that crested over his high forehead, creamy skin that looked like it had been poured over him and eyes as clear blue as any Caribbean water. Dash looked like an athlete.

"No. I'm the last of the litter," he had explained. "It wasn't that they ran out of names at kid number seven, I just was born post-McCarthy to a couple of socialists. I'm named for one of their heroes—Dashiel Hammett. Except I'm Dashiel McDevlin."

Terry had laughed loud and long, then, as he grabbed Dash's hand and shook it hard, like they were sealing a business deal instead of meeting for the first time to play singles. "My name sucks, too, Dash. Sounds just as faggy as yours. Come on and let me beat those pants right off you." They had played three sets and Terry, with a lithe grace Dash had rarely seen on the courts and a keen eye for a missed opportunity had aced every one. They'd gone out for drinks and a few weeks later were angling to change roommates. Terry was the best friend he'd never quite had in high school. Terry was the smart, smart-assed, too-good-looking, pseudo-jock who excelled at everything from the political science he was majoring in to scoring with women using his poor-Catholic-boy-too-guilty-to-get-laid line that wooed them every time. Dash had had neither the desire nor the stamina to compete with Terry anywhere but the classroom and the courts, but that night on Bourbon Street he had decided to match him drink for drink and trouble for trouble.

Dash stepped out onto the balcony overlooking Bourbon Street, pressed his palms to the railing and leaned over to gaze at the scene below. He breathed in the steaminess of the night, tugged at his tie, pulling it from his shirt and dropped it onto the balcony railing. Dash unbuttoned the first three buttons of the stark white shirt that always seemed *de rigueur* for the sort of business meeting that he had been to earlier and ran his hands over the top of his chest and back along his neck. He wanted a drink and a walk through the French Quarter. He wanted to hear some jazz at the Old Absinthe House and stick his card up on the wall as he had wanted to do that night with Terry except he was too young to have a card then. *God, it was hot.* Hard to believe it was barely spring, the air seemed as full and thick and laden with scent as late summer. Hard to believe it was almost twenty years since he had last been here, he and Terry stumbling through the streets below him, being initiated into the annual Mardi Gras pilgrimage that was Terry's birthright. An ache overtook him. He needed that drink. Now. He turned back into toward his room, his tie still hanging on the railing and headed out into the night.

They had been reeling drunk by dark. Terry had led him from one bar to the next. No one was carding, no one was the least bit interested in how old they were or how much trouble they were willing to get into as long as it didn't involve guns or knives or too much punching. Which was why when Terry had led him into the small corridor lobby of an unmarked building on Bourbon Street with pictures out front that swam before his eyes like Al Hirt and Chris Connelly and the Preservation Hall Band had done earlier, Dash had assumed they were headed into yet another sleazy little bar with bad music and more teasing women than you could shake your dick at.

But it wasn't a bar or even a club like the little jazz-and-strip joint they had gone into when Dash was still sober enough to be certain of where he was and what he was doing. Now he was just staggering along behind Terry and hoping his friend remembered how to get them home to his parents' house before they passed out in the street.

Mirrors lined the walls of the lobby of the strange little L-shaped place they were in and the light glowed amber from somewhere above them. Dash could see shapes hovering near doors that opened off the back of the lobby. The red carpet was swirled with gold and the pattern made Dash feel like he was swimming. Music piped around them; a sexy, disco beat. Yet unlike all the places they had been that afternoon and night, this one seemed almost empty. Once they closed the door on Bourbon Street it seemed eerily quiet except for the gentle thrum of the music and the distant sound of voices. Dash felt his cock harden as it had earlier in the street when Terry had grabbed at him and the girls had flashed him. He turned away slightly to mask the bulge in his jeans. How could he be this drunk and this hard all at once?

Terry gave Dash a little shove on the shoulder and pushed him forward toward a narrow hallway where the doors were. "What do you feel like seeing?"

"Seeing?" Dash hadn't understood the question and suddenly felt he had drunk way too much. He set his drink down on a standing ashtray and walked toward a drinking fountain in the shadowy recesses of the room and took a long drink, trying to rinse some of the alcohol from his system or at least his mouth. This place was different from the others and he was suddenly wary, acutely attuned to his dick throbbing with the sensual music that seemed to surround and stroke them.

"Porn, Dash, porn," Terry had half-laughed, half-whispered the words to him and made a gesture like jerking off. So they were in a porn theatre. The little doors off the back were, Dash figured, entrance to the movies. He felt a little queasy. He had never been in a porno house before. Was this his Catholic guilt rising up as it had so inopportunely in the past?

"Hey man, it's your party, you choose." Dash sounded too jocular even to himself, but Terry was wasted and didn't notice. He slung his arm around Dash and took a swig from the drink he still held, pulling him close enough to Dash that he could feel the heat of Terry's face against his, the slight fuzzing of five-o'clock-shadow grazing his cheek. Dash's pants felt tight, his thighs too hot. Somehow this little sojourn was a mistake, he could feel it, but he didn't know why, still Terry was propelling him forward into the dark and he felt powerless to resist. He wished he hadn't put his drink down, now.

The doors seemed too small for entry. Short and low. The boys had to hunch over to go through into the dark, dank little room that smelled of aftershave and spunk. There were three hard leather-like chairs flush against the wall and barely three feet in front of them was a small screen like the kind they had had in junior high for those educational films that were twenty years out of date. Dash dropped into one of the chairs and stretched his legs as far as the space would allow. Suddenly he felt a wave of sexual heat crest over him. He wanted to stand up, his back to Terry and jerk off fast and hard until he came all over the floor. His hand drifted to his dick pulsing in his pants. He had rarely felt such a need to come and come fast as he did now. Would that be what they did here? Watch the movies and jerk off together, laughing and jostling each other like he and his buddies had done in high school, flipping through magazines stolen from his older brothers or someone else's, imagining their dicks tucked tight into some girl's pussy or ass.

He had always wanted ass, always wanted to take a girl from behind, never looking at her face. Catholic guilt or Catholic perversion, he wasn't sure. Some girls had gone for it in high school. It seemed to turn them on and there was no risk of getting pregnant. He'd liked the tightness of it, the power he felt when he thrust into them, grabbing their soft cheeks in both hands. He never came so hard any other way.

He wanted that now, Dash thought, to plunge his dick into a soft, willing ass. He could come right now from the thought. He could feel the wet spot on his jeans, the pre-ejaculate dampening the denim near the zipper. He slowly eased it down a little, reaching his fingers in and squeezing the head of his cock just enough to take his own breath away. *God, he was so ready.*

Terry stood by a small metal box near the door looking intently at the film choices. He tossed some quarters in the slot and sauntered over to the seat next to Dash and slipped into it.

"We're going to watch a bunch of stuff," drawled Terry in that strange Southern-Brooklynese accent that was New Orleans born-and-bred. "I want to do some kink, okay? It's Mardi Gras, man, and we are going to bust out for the night. You ready to whack with me?"

Dash had shivered a bit in the damp room then, had felt the hairs on his arms bristle a little and had unconsciously rolled down the sleeves of his shirt. Terry was nudging him the way he always did, like everything in life was some kind of dare, like the first day they met to this minute. Terry, always the leader, always the risk-taker, never, like the scholarship-burdened Dash, worried about getting kicked out of school or getting into trouble so deep only a lawyer like Terry's own father could get him out.

Dash felt that trouble brewing now but for once he didn't care. They were ten states away from school and he was just drunk enough to let himself enjoy whatever came next. "Like I said, Terry, it's your party. I'm game. It's my first Mardi Gras, after all, and tomorrow we've got to go to Mass, so the penance is going to come soon enough."

He sunk back in his seat as the screen flickered to life, grainy and white, illuminating him and Terry in the harsh glow so unlike the soft amber light of the lobby. Terry leaned into him, his muscular body pressing against him at shoulder, hip and thigh. Dash heard Terry's zipper buzz down and glanced sideways as he pulled his thick dick out of his pants.

On the screen a black man was taking off his clothes as two white women dressed in nothing but garter belts, stockings and shoes, watched, their breasts large and shaped with an unreal roundness. The man's cock was like the stereotypes Dash had always heard about in Roxbury where he grew up. He'd never seen a black dick before, hadn't had many black friends before Fordham. This guy was hung like the proverbial horse and the sight of his long, dark prick gave Dash a wave of pleasure that ran straight through his own cock.

"When you grow up in the South," Terry was saying to him as he languidly stroked his dick in front of Dash, "you get a craving for miscegenation. It's my fervent desire to play with as many black girls as I can get my hands on. And then have the photos delivered to my parents at dinner, of course, preferably with guests all around. There is nothing more forbidden than crossing the color line, my friend. At least not here, anyway."

Dash recoiled a bit from Terry's words. The racism, he thought, was unmistakable and he felt implicated by saying nothing. Yet the man on the screen enticed him with the big black dick he plunged into first one, then the other white girl, slamming harder and harder until he was about to come, then pulling the long shaft out and stroking it hard up over the head until it began to spurt all over the ass of one of the women.

The image made him forget his politics, forget integrity, forget everything but his own throbbing dick and a sudden unknown desire to press it up against that black man's ass and watch it slip, starkly white, in between those chocolatey cheeks.

He was close to coming now, so close he had to push his cock away for a minute, press his finger to the tip hard to pinch back the flood he was almost ready for. Dash liked to tease himself when he jerked off, liked to stroke his balls faster and harder without touching his dick until his cock would sway before him, rock-hard and red with desire and need. He liked to stand against a wall, his legs splayed out, his balls tight, his cock like a stick in his hand and stroke, stroke, stroke until he was just about to come and then stop and turn his face to the wall, pressing his thighs against it, feeling his dick slide against the cool tile or smooth plaster. The image in his head was always the same: cool, silky ass cheeks pressed up toward him, fingers pulling the globes apart, the hole quivering and ready for him to enter, his dick in one hand, his fingers exploring the sweet opening with the other. Sometimes he wanted to press his mouth there and sometimes he had done so, running his tongue over the tiny throbbing rim. He wanted to do that now, taste that big, strong man on the screen, lick his ass and flick his tongue at those dark balls.

Dash jerked up in his seat, the fantasy and what it meant catching him off-guard. *Faggot.* The word he had heard tossed about the streets of Roxbury, the word he himself had pelted at one or another classmate or the foppish librarian who lived one block over from his parent's house, came unbidden to his mind. *Not* a faggot, he thought. It's Mardi Gras and I'm kinking it up with my best friend in a porno house on Bourbon Street and one day I'll be telling my sons this story and we'll all have a big, bawdy laugh over it.

He could feel it then, Terry's hand on his thigh and the word nearly came out of his mouth but was stopped by the intensity of his cock pulsing and pushing at his hand, his pants, anything. Fuck this, he was ready.

The screen had shifted to a different scene. Two men stood in a locker room talking about some game, towels wrapped loosely around their waists. One man was blonde, tanned and strongly built, his legs long and rippled with muscle like his arms. The other was the color of coffee with two creams, lithe and sinewy, with the body of a swimmer, just slightly taller than the other man.

It took only seconds for the towels to slip and fall as the men jousted in fake argument over the game they had just played. When the towels were gone the men stood naked in front of each other, dicks hard, swinging in the air, aching for touch.

Terry's hand was gripping Dash's thigh now, gripping it hard, his eyes riveted to the screen as the men wrestled each other and then each took the other's dick in his hand and began to stroke methodically, grunting as if pressing weights.

"I want that," Terry half-breathed, half-whispered and Dash wasn't sure he had actually heard the words. Until Terry repeated them as the men began to come onto each other's thighs, crying out with the force of their orgasms. The screen went blank and Terry turned in the creamy light and looked at Dash with those amber eyes that were like an animal's, not a person's. "I want that. Let's do that. It's Lent tomorrow—we can give it up then."

The joke lingered in the air. The room had warmed from their bodies. Dash felt a mixture of fear and excitement. For months he had done nothing but press himself against one wall or another, in the dorm, at the gym, in the bathroom. He wanted to press his cock into flesh.

The screen had come alive again, this time with a group of men in a steam room. The men were black, brown and white, once again dressed only in towels, each positioned differently around a small sauna bed of hot rocks. One man, Italian perhaps, or Latino, walked toward the rocks and splashed them with water. Dash knew now his towel would slip and the same trajectory would follow.

This time the towel *didn't* slip but was pulled from the man by another, who whipped it back against the Latino's tanned ass.

Dash stood up and turned to face Terry. His cock stood out from his body as if he were about to piss. He moved between Terry's spread legs and watched as Terry stroked his own balls inside his pants.

"Let's do this," Dash said, his voice low and gruff, the voice of sex and desire and deep, aching need.

"Tell me what." Terry breathed the words rather than spoke them. He had seemed to go limp in his seat, not unlike the way some of the girls Dash had been with would slither down in their chairs as he proposed what he wanted to them.

"Stand up." At six feet even, Dash had two, maybe three inches on Terry's compact frame. Terry stood, thick cock swinging at an almost ninety-degree angle from his body, it was that stiff, that ready for what was going to happen.

"Turn around. Please." Dash felt that rush of power he had felt in the past as his cock had readied itself to pass between the cheeks of this or that girl, pulse behind the tiny sphincter. "I'm going to slide my cock in you, okay? I'm going to open you up and slide into you and you are going to feel it in your balls and in your dick and it's going to make you come harder than you've ever come in your life. Okay?"

The words had rushed out in a whispered torrent. Forceful, but quiet. Dash wanted this now, wanted it the way he had wanted that black man's ass, that black man's cock. Terry wasn't his best friend any longer. He was a man whose towel had slipped in the locker room to reveal a round, tanned ass ready for his long, slender cock.

He reached into his back pocket and pulled out a condom. He'd always used them with the girls. He liked the way they gripped his cock and held him as he pushed inside. The tip was wet as he rolled it over his dick. Terry was standing against the screen now, scenes of men sucking each other's cocks flashing over his torso. He took Dash's dick in his hand and just held it for a minute as if weighing it, checking a pulse, making sure everything was in order.

"It's not as thick as mine," he said but didn't let go. Dash was aching with desire now, aching to feel his dick between those hot cheeks, aching, aching to thrust and squeeze and push and probe and reach around and fondle and then explode. He pushed against Terry, the wet tip of his cock pressing into Terry's stomach.

Terry walked over to the chairs and bent over, pulling down his pants and offering his ass. Dash had his cock in his hand now and closed his eyes for a minute, feeling faint with booze and the ache in his balls. It seemed like the two of them had been there for hours, dicks hard and throbbing and yet neither of them coming. He knew it had only been ten, maybe twenty minutes but he could feel the tightness in his thighs, the ache deep in his groin.

"Careful, okay?" The slight edge of fear in Terry's voice made him stop. He leaned into Terry, pushed against his ass, rubbing his cock against the hard buttocks that had chased him all over the tennis courts with a speed that had never failed to mesmerize him.

He wet his fingers and played along the rim of Terry's ass, feeling the soft hairs that he knew were blond, even though he couldn't see them in this light. He heard Terry gasp, felt the slight jerking motion as Terry stroked himself. He pushed the tip of his cock tentatively against Terry's quivering asshole and felt his friend shudder. Then he pushed in, slow at first, to release the sphincter, then a little deeper.

"God it's so good," the words came in a gasp from Terry and he pushed his ass back onto Dash's long dick. Dash bent over him, chest flush against Terry's back, hands gripping Terry at the hips, thrusting, thrusting, feeling his balls slap lightly against the base of Terry's ass, feeling the pleasure washing over him in wave after wave, seeing his friend playing tennis, that black man jerking off onto the woman's ass, the Latino guy getting his dick sucked hard by another Latino. Terry's tight ass enveloped him, sucked him in, caressed his pulsing cock. He was so ready to come now, so ready, so ready.

He reached forward and took Terry's cock from his hand and began to stroke it in time to his own thrusting. Terry gripped the chair hard, telling him over and over again to "Do it, do it, fuck me, fill me up, jerk me off, make me come, make me come, please make me come. Let me feel it, let me have it."

The words took him there faster than the sweet sucking of Terry's ass on his cock. Had this been what he had wanted all along? His cock in a man's ass, his cock deep inside another man while his hand stroked his dick and balls and felt the pressure build in both of them until he thrust hard— once, twice, again and then it was over with such explosive power he thought he'd faint, his hand whacking Terry's cock so fast the sound of it filled the room until Terry cried out, "Oh yes, make me come, make me come, I'm coming so hard, don't stop, don't let go." The hot spunk spilled over Dash's hand as Terry shoved hard against his strokes. They had come within seconds of each other and the intensity had been almost unbearable.

Dash let go of Terry's still-hard cock and held his hand to the small of Terry's back as he slowly slid his dick from Terry's ass. He pulled a tissue from the box on the floor next to the chairs and rolled the condom into it, took another and wiped his hands, gave one to Terry who was pulling up his pants.

"So," Terry said, his eyes just missing Dash's. "Great films or what?"

Dash hunched over the bar and played with his drink, holding it in both hands and rolling the short high-ball glass that held two fingers of scotch back and forth. He wasn't sure why he had decided to stay over in New Orleans. He needed to get back to Boston by Thursday for the presentations and there was work to be done before that. He swiveled around on the barstool and looked out over the crowd.

He was over-dressed in his dark blue suit, even without the tie. He ran a hand through his hair, unchanged in the last twenty years except it was now attractively shot through with a few iron-gray streaks, just as his father's had been. He had kept his long, lean body as well, just as his father had. Dash watched the men dancing, watched the sidling and the bumping and the fake-fucking that was happening all across the dance floor. He felt the familiar pulsing in his groin, felt his cock go hard as two men came close to him, stomachs touching, tonguing each other's mouths as they danced backward and forward with each other, hands on each other's shoulders.

It had never left him in all these years, this desire for men's cocks, balls and asses. He and Terry had never touched each other again, had made some secret bargain to not speak about what happened, to in fact pretend it had not. They never mentioned the little theatre, or what they'd done there. They'd walked back out into the crowd and drunk some more and then wandered home to Terry's house to be met by the glare of his father as they fell through the door at dawn.

They'd never mentioned the little porno house or the way Dash had taken Terry hard and made them both come better than they'd ever come in their lives. They'd gone back to New York and continued to play tennis and get drunk and try to outstrip each other at everything. Terry had met a girl, a black girl of course, and gotten engaged the year they graduated. Dash had been best man at their wedding, had driven them to the airport for the honeymoon that would be followed by a two-year Peace Corps stint in Burundi and a distance that allowed them both to lose touch.

Now Dash was back in New Orleans and the memories would not stop coming and he knew before the night was out he would be back in the little theatre he had passed three times now between the meeting and dinner and this bar and with him would be one of the men who danced before him now. With him would be the muscled young dancer with the short corked dreadlocks in the blue t-shirt and loose khakis who had already danced past him several times, each time his hand playing over his cock. Dash would be in the theatre, bathed in the flickering images of men sucking each other's cocks, stroking each other's dicks, bending each other over and fucking, fucking, fucking like he couldn't wait to do now. Dash would go and sit and watch the bad, grainy super-8s and unzip his pants and watch as the boy took his dick in his mouth. Dash would stand against the wall and play with his own cock until it was as hard as it had been that night with Terry and then bend the boy over, fondling his dick and balls and toying with the rippled flesh of his dark, hairless asshole.

These days he carried all he needed: little tubes of lube, condoms and packets of handiwipes for after. He knew exactly what he liked, he'd known since high school. His appetites had grown but never varied in all these years. He put his drink back on the bar and tossed a twenty next to it. He ambled over to the young black dancer and touched him lightly on the arm. They walked out of the bar and onto Bourbon Street. The night was deep and hot and as Dash looked out over the little grid of streets he could see the theatre at the end of the block. He whispered into the ear of his companion, rested his hand lightly on the young man's ass and they walked, silent, toward the theatre, their cocks stiffening with the promise of the night and their own limitless desires.

THE CONTRIBUTORS

Jim Buck is, among other things, a writer, thespian, amateur astronomer, absinthe drinker, and professional dilettante. Jim's journalistic endeavors have been published in *Unzipped, All Man, Eclipse,* and elsewhere. His erotic fiction appears in *Skinflicks* (Companion Press), *Afterwords: Real Sex from Gay Men's Diaries* (Alyson Books), the forthcoming *Boyfriends From Hell* (Green Candy Press), and on numerous websites. He lives in New Orleans with his partner, three dogs, and a cat, and he's never been happier.

Leo Cardini is the author of the best-selling *Mineshaft Nights*. His erotica has appeared in numerous magazines. "All my writing is autobiographical," he reports. "Every other word of it is absolutely true." Further information on Leo can be found in better men's rooms stalls everywhere.

M. Christian's work can be seen in *The Best American Erotica, Best Gay Erotica, Best Lesbian Erotica, Best Fetish Erotica,* and over 150 other books, magazines, and websites. He's the editor of over 12 anthologies, including *The Burning Pen, Love Under Foot* (with Greg Wharton), *Best S/M Erotica, Bad Boys* (with Paul J. Willis), and many others. He's the author of three collections, including *Dirty Words* (gay erotica) and *Speaking Parts* (lesbian erotica). For more info, check out www.mchristian.com.

Lewis Frederick is a freelance writer from Louisville, Kentucky who lives with his life partner on a small farm in southern Indiana. He also teaches at a small, private university and has a private practice as a psychotherapist specializing in work with gay men in Louisville. Having published extensively in professional journals, he made his STARbooks' debut in *Boys on the Prowl* (Mar. 2000) and has since contributed to *Huge 2, Taboo, Saints and Sinners,* and now, *View to a Thrill.*

Greg Herren's first novel, *Murder in the Rue Dauphine,* is a Lambda Literary Award finalist for Gay Mystery. His second novel, *Bourbon Street Blues,* was recently released by Kensington. Former editor of the Lambda Book Report, his reviews, articles and interviews have been published in many publications, and his short fiction has appeared in many anthologies including *Rebel Yell 2, M2M,* and *Harrington Gay Fiction Quarterly.*

William Holden lives in the heart of gay Atlanta with his partner of 6 years. He has recently left the corporate world and is pursuing his graduate studies in Library and Information Sciences, while volunteering at the National Archives. He contributes the start of his writing to his partner

Mark who encouraged him to take the ultimate leap of faith. He has also been published in the Alyson books anthologies *Sex Buddies*, *Slow Grind*, and *Hard Drive*.

Since **Michael Huxley** made his STARbooks' debut in *Fever!* (Summer, 2000), the author has contributed significantly to the STARbooks anthologies *Seduced 2*, *Wild and Willing*, *Fantasies Made Flesh*, *Saints and Sinners,* and now *View to a Thrill*. A published poet—most recently in the poetry journal, *Priapus,* (autumn, 2002, New Directions Press, Paris)—and former contributor to Denver Colorado's groundbreaking *Out Front*, his work will soon appear in the poetry collection, *Van Gogh's Ear* (French Connection Press, Paris/New York). Having accepted the position of Editorial Director at STARbooks Press in April, 2002, Huxley now finds himself dying for the sins of porn writers on a full-time basis. Michael Huxley resides in Sarasota, Florida with his long-time lover, Paul. Please feel free to contact The Editor at mikeh@starbookspress.com.

Randall Kent Ivey's fiction and non-fiction have appeared in journals and magazines throughout the country and on the Internet. He published a collection of non-erotica called *The Shape of a Man: A Novella and Five Stories* in the spring of 2002. His story "My Antonio" appears in the anthology *Sex Buddies* by Alyson Books (2003).

A popular author of gay erotica with an oftentimes military flavor, **Rick Jackson** is the *nom de guerre* of a frequent contributor to STARbooks Press. His book *Shipmates* was published by Prowler Press in London. Because he spends most of his time sailing about with the Navy in these Don't-Ask-Don't-Tell times, security demands that his true identity be kept classified—from all but the very juiciest sailors and Marines. Before beginning his very satisfying career afloat, Rick earned BAs in History and German, an MA in English, played hard in the Peace Corps, and plumbed the depths of hot, hard men across the globe. Although his frequent deployments keep him very, very busy with his fellow warriors, he sometimes is able to receive email at RickJacksn@aol.com. Mr. Jackson lives in Hawaii.

Bart Magma enjoys proving that old age and treachery will always overcome youth and beauty. He has been previously published in *Tough Guys* (Black Books) and now that he's been encouraged, you'll probably never get rid of him.

Marshall Moore is the author of *The Concrete Sky*, recently published by the Southern Tier Editions imprint of the Haworth Press. His short fiction and book reviews have appeared in various places, some of which you've probably heard of. A North Carolina native, he now lives with his partner in

Portland, Oregon. For more information, please visit his website: www.marshallmoore.net.

Ian Philips is a flaming Sodomite and gentleman Sadist. He is also Managing Editor for the Damron Company's best-selling LGBTIQ travel guide series, Mother Emeritus of AttaGirl Press, and Editor at Extra Large for Suspect Thoughts Press. His literate filth has strutted the paper and ink boards at a variety of venues including *Best Gay Erotica, Best Transgender Erotica, The Best of the Best Meat Erotica*, and *The Mammoth Book of Best New Erotica 2*. His first collection of erotic fiction, *See Dick Deconstruct: Literotica for the Satirically Bent*, won the first-ever Lambda Literary Award in the category of Erotica. His second collection, *Satyriasis: Literotica2*, will appear in fall 2003 from Suspect Thoughts Press. He resides in modest infamy in San Francisco—where else?—with author Greg Wharton. To read his fiction, surf on over to www.ianphilips.com.

Felice Picano's first book was a finalist for the PEN/Hemingway Award. Since then he has published over twenty volumes of fiction, poetry, memoirs, etc. Considered a founder of modern gay literature along with the six other members of the Violet Quill Club, Picano also founded two publishing companies: the SeaHorse Press and Gay Presses of New York. He's been a regular writer for the *San Francisco Examiner, The Lesbian Gay Review*, and *Lambda Book Report*. Among his many award-winning books, are the novels, *Like People in History, The Book of Lies*, and *Onyx*. Picano books due out in 2003 are *The New Joy of Gay Sex, Third Edition*, 2003,with Charles Silverstein (HarperCollins) and Haworth Press reprints in a uniform edition of Picano's memoir-trilogy, *Ambidextrous, Men Who Loved Me*, and *A House on the Ocean, A House on the Bay*. A longtime resident of New York, he currently lives in Los Angeles.

Max Reynolds is the pseudonym of an award-winning journalist and *bon vivant* from Philadelphia. These are Reynolds' first pieces of published erotica, but certainly not the last.

Michael Rhodes lives on the West Coast, where he works in the public sector and writes for pleasure whenever the demands of daily life can be temporarily held at bay. He has published in business trade magazines, the erotic anthologies *Sex Buddies* (Alyson books) and *View to a Thrill* (STARbooks). He has a fascination with "dark, spiritual and perverse" themes and is finishing up a novel centered on the same.

Simon Sheppard is the author of *Hotter Than Hell and Other Stories* and the forthcoming non-fiction book *Kinkorama*, as well as co-editor, with M. Christian, of *Rough Stuff* and *Roughed Up*. His next short fiction collection,

In Deep, will be published by Alyson Books in 2003, and his work also appears in over 75 other book, including several editions of *The Best American Erotica* and all but one of *Best Gay Erotica*. He loiters beefily at www.simonsheppard.com.

Jay Starre writes gay erotica from his computer in Vancouver, BC. Well-known in that city as first runner-up in the Mr. BC Leather 2002 contest, his stories can be found in the local gay bookstore in such anthologies as *Buttmen 1 and 2, Full Body Contact* and *Best of Friction*.

Kyle Stone's name first appeared as the author of the scorching SM/SF erotic adventure novel *The Initiation of PB 500* in 1993 (reissued in 2001). This was soon followed by a sequel, *The Citadel*, and three more novels. Stone's short stories have appeared in many gay magazines and anthologies. The latest are collected in *MENagerie* (2000).

Tom G Tongue: Tom (and his tongue) reside in Atlanta. Despite a short diversion in the Northeastern US, Tom is Georgia born-and-raised. He's been an erotica fanatic since he encountered his first dirty paperback, many years ago. He began writing tales for the Nifty Archive a few years ago, and, through encouragement of readers there, submitted his work to several publishers, Paul Willis, and *A View to a Thrill* being one. Tom wants to thank his friends for their support.

Greg Wharton is the publisher of Suspect Thoughts Press, and an editor of two web magazines, *SuspectThoughts.com* and *VelvetMafia.com*. He is also the editor of the anthologies *The Best of the Best Meat Erotica, Law of Desire: Tales of Gay Male Lust and Obsession* (with Ian Philips), *The Love That Dare Not Speak Its Name: Essays on Queer Sexuality and Desire, Love Under Foot: An Erotic Celebration of Feet* (with M. Christian), and *Of the Flesh: Dangerous New Fiction*. A collection of Wharton's own short fiction will be released in 2003. He lives in San Francisco where he is hard at work on a novel.

Born and raised an Okie, **Mark Wildyr** graduated Texas Christian University in Ft. Worth, Texas. Following service in the US Army, he pursued a career in banking, finance, and administration, recently turning to freelance writing to explore his interest in multicultural interaction as well as personal and sexual growth. He has contributed numerous short stories to anthologies published by STARbooks Press, Alyson Publications, and Companion Press. He resides in Albuquerque, New Mexico, the setting of many of his stories.

ABOUT THE EDITOR

Paul J. Willis has written reviews and articles for several magazines and newspapers including *Unzipped Monthly*, *Foreword*, *Philadelphia Gay News*, *The Gulf Coast Arts Review*, and *The Times-Picayune*. This is his first anthology for STARbooks, and he is also the editor of Sex Buddies (Alyson Books) and co-editor with M. Christian for the erotic collection *Bad Boys* (Alyson Books). He currently works as the program coordinator for the Tennessee Williams/New Orleans Literary Festival. And in May of 2003, Willis organized the first annual "Saints and Sinners" alternative literary festival, a new outreach program for the NO/AIDS Task Force. Information on this event can be found at www.sasfest.com. Paul resides in New Orleans with his partner, Greg Herren.

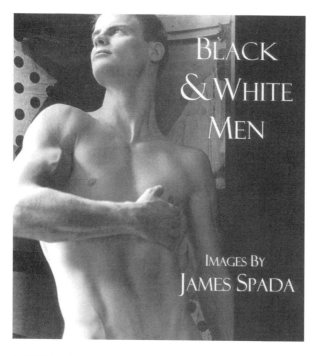